Palo Alto City Library

The individual borrower is responsible for all library material borrowed on his or her card.

Charges as determined by the CITY OF PALO ALTO will be assessed for each overdue item.

Damaged or non-returned property will be billed to the individual borrower by the CITY OF PALO ALTO.

P.O. Box 10250, Palo Alto, CA 94303

NANJING 1937

A Love Story

Weatherhead Books on Asia

Weatherhead Books on Asia
Columbia University

LITERATURE
David Der-wei Wang, Editor

Ye Zhaoyan, *Nanjing 1937: A Love Story*, translated by Michael Berry
Makoto Oda, *The Breaking Jewel*, translated by Donald Keene

HISTORY, SOCIETY, AND CULTURE
Carol Gluck, Editor

NANJING 1937

A Love Story

Ye Zhaoyan

Translated with an Introduction by Michael Berry

Columbia University Press   New York

COLUMBIA UNIVERSITY PRESS
Publishers Since 1893
New York   Chichester, West Sussex

Yijiusanqi nian de aiqing copyright © 1996 by Ye Zhaoyan
Translation copyright © 2002 Michael Berry

Library of Congress Cataloging-in-Publication Data
Ye, Zhaoyan, 1957–
    [Yi jiu san qi nian de ai qing. English]
    Nanjing 1937 : a love story / Ye Zhaoyan ; translated
with an introduction by Michael Berry.
        p.   cm. — (Weatherhead books on Asia)
    ISBN 0–231–12754–5
    1. Ye, Zhaoyan, 1957–Translations into English.
I. Berry, Michael. II. Title. III. Series.
PL2924.C533 Y513 2002
895.1'352—dc21   2002024156

CONTENTS

Notes and Acknowledgments   vii

Translator's Introduction   1

Nanjing 1937: A Love Story   9

Author's Afterword   341

Glossary of Historical Figures   345

NOTES AND ACKNOWLEDGMENTS

All Chinese names have been romanized in accordance with the pinyin system. Exceptions to this rule have been made for historical figures known in the West by alternate or nonstandard systems of romanization, such as Chiang Kai-shek (Jiang Jieshi) and Sun Yat-sen (Sun Zhongshan), and western-educated figures who preferred anglicized abbreviations, such as T. V. Soong (Song Ziwen) and H. H. K'ung (Kong Xiangxi).

As a work of historical fiction, the novel features appearances by and references to several dozen military, political, and cultural figures who were prominent in Republican China. For the convenience of the western reader, a comprehensive Glossary of Historical Figures has been appended at the end of this volume. This translation was based on the 1996 Jiangsu wenyi edition of the novel. Some minor textual changes were made with the author's permission.

Thanks go first to Ye Zhaoyan for his support of this translation. I am also indebted to the outside reviewers solicited by Columbia University Press, especially Professor Yunzhong Shu of Queens College, who provided extensive comments and insightful suggestions; and to Wen-yi Chang, who read the manuscript in its entirety against the original. Special thanks also go to Leslie Kriesel, whose literary and editorial sensibilities helped the true voice of this novel shine through. Thanks to Emily Mahon for the beautiful jacket design. I would also like to extend my heartfelt thanks to my family, Chenke Zhou, Joshua Tanzer, my classmates and colleagues at Columbia University, and Professors John Balcom, Howard Goldblatt, Tomi Suzuki, and Xudong Zhang. Finally, I would like to thank Jennifer Crewe at Columbia University Press and especially Professor David Der-wei Wang. It is thanks to their interest and support of this novel that Ye Zhaoyan's vision may be shared with a new group of readers.

M.B.

NANJING 1937

A Love Story

TRANSLATOR'S INTRODUCTION

The year 1937 is but a cloud of mist passing before my eyes. My gaze
is caught lingering on this particular era of the past, but, as a writer,
I find myself unable to truly understand that history that historians
call history. I see only shattered pieces, broken fragments, and a hand-
ful of melancholic stories destined to come to naught, all quietly play-
ing out upon the grand stage of history.

—Ye Zhaoyan[1]

Since his appearance on the literary scene in the early 1980s,[2]
Ye Zhaoyan (b. 1957) has established himself as one of contemporary
China's most creative, daring, and imaginative practitioners of literary
art. A prolific writer, he has created a body of work difficult to catego-
rize due to his chameleonlike versatility and tireless experimentation
with different literary forms and genres. From the tradition of *The Schol-*
ars (c. 1750) to the legacy of Qian Zhongshu; from May Fourth to Mandarin Ducks; from roman à clef to postmodernist collage; and from

hard-boiled detective fiction to the avant-garde, Ye's literary field of vision seems to know no boundaries. The addictive storylines and the stunning visuality of Ye's work have won the Nanjing-based writer a loyal readership in Chinese-speaking communities and led to foreign translations and film adaptations.[3] At the same time, Ye Zhaoyan has been actively involved in a larger project of rewriting and reimagining the Mandarin Duck and Butterfly tradition, a popular romantic literary genre that flourished in Republican China.[4] Ye's fascination with this page in (literary) history is perhaps best demonstrated by his masterpiece *Evening Moor on the Qinhuai*,[5] a collection of historical novellas set in Republican-era Nanjing.

One key to Ye Zhaoyan's attachment to preliberation China is the literary family from which he hails. His father, Ye Zhicheng (1926–1992), was a noted writer, as was his grandfather, Ye Shengtao (1894–1988), also an influential educator and editor and the author of the 1928 classic *Ni Huanzhi*,[6] one of the first full-length modern vernacular novels.[7] Ye Zhaoyan is one of the few contemporary Chinese writers to hold a graduate degree in Chinese literature; he earned his M.A. from Nanjing University in 1986, writing his thesis on one of the crowning achievements of preliberation literature, Qian Zhongshu's *Fortress Besieged*.[8] After graduation, Ye worked as an editor for the Jiangsu Arts and Literature Publishing House. In 1991, he left the publishing world to pursue writing full time; he has since produced an astounding twenty-seven books, including a seven-volume set of collected works.

First published in 1996, *Nanjing 1937: A Love Story* is perhaps Ye Zhaoyan's most ambitious project to date. Individually embodying the genre-crossing complexity that characterizes his body of work, the novel also captures Ye's nostalgic passion for rewriting missing pages from Republican China's past. *Nanjing 1937* is the tale of a man seemingly incapable of love who falls for the most unlikely woman during the most inconceivable of times. Ding Wenyu, the only son of a powerful Shanghai banker, is smitten with a young married woman, Ren Yuchan, and is sent abroad by his father as a cure for his lovesickness. Some seventeen years later, Ding returns to China only to fall even harder for Yuchan's younger sister, Yuyuan—on her wedding day. Progressing at an unhurried pace, *Nanjing 1937* traces the development of this unlikely love story, subtly juxtaposing Ding's romantic advancements with the military advancements of the Japanese army, to which the city would fall in December 1937.

This connection between love and war is not only made through Ye's meticulously crafted narrative structure but also enhanced by his clever use of language. Militaristic terminology describing Ding's pursuit of Yuyuan, as well as other romantic subplots in the text, permeates the novel:

> He [Ding Wenyu] continuously sought out different types of women, and once he *achieved his target*, he would immediately *initiate his next campaign*. He was like a *general* who endured a *hundred battles, charging forward* amid a sea of women, time after time facing setbacks, time after time losing face for all to see. Even though he usually came off as *the glorious victor in his battles*, his soul had already long been covered with scars. (32)

> Running from the *battlefield defeated* made it look as if she [Yuyuan] were guilty of some wrongdoing. (114)

> She [Qu Manli] began her little talk as if she were *launching an attack*. (266)

> Ding Wenyu decided to *strengthen his romantic offensive* on Yuyuan. (307) (MY ITALICS)

Such passages reinforce the link between the novel's two seemingly contradictory and mutually exclusive narrative lines, which are signaled even in the book's title, *Nanjing 1937: A Love Story*.[9] In a time and place inextricably connected with horrific images of violence and war, on the eve of what historians would later deem the "Rape of Nanjing," how could there be room for love or romance?

One answer to this question lies in the pages of Chinese literary history and the tradition of fictional romance set in times of national calamity. *Nanjing 1937* inevitably invites comparisons to earlier works in the Chinese literary tradition, from the Qing drama *The Peach Blossom Fan* (1699) to Eileen Chang's modern classic, "Love in a Fallen City" (1943), both of which have left their marks on Ye's novel.[10] But the true intertextual skeleton key can be found in Qian Zhongshu's

3

classic *Fortress Besieged* (1946). The similarities between the two novels are stunning—from the temporal framework of 1937 and the protagonists' respective educational and career backgrounds as dilettante foreign students who return to China to become college professors, to their detached aloofness toward the times in which they live. Indeed, it would not be a stretch to read *Nanjing 1937* as a contemporary rejoinder to Qian Zhongshu's landmark novel.

For the title of his novel, Qian Zhongshu borrowed Trollope's conception of the fortress besieged. In Qian's hands, the phrase quickly became a brilliantly understated allegory for the contradictions in our everyday lives; the saying can perhaps be no better articulated than by Qian's wife, writer Yang Jiang:

> Those trapped in a fortress besieged long to escape,
> Those outside want to charge in.
> Such is one's marriage, and one's career,
> Such is the way of most human desires.[11]

Exactly half a century later, in 1996, Ye Zhaoyan echoes this philosophy in his novel *Nanjing 1937*, where characters seem to be eternally trapped in a fortress of desires and discontent. Ye Zhaoyan's brilliance, however, lies in the fact that he does not merely rearticulate Qian's allegory but develops it in an ironically tragic way. As the Japanese army descends on the capital and the curtain of history falls, the fortress (or, rather, city) besieged is lifted from the allegorical to the literal level and the reader realizes that Ye Zhaoyan has constructed a true "fortress beseiged."

Ye Zhaoyan's literary and historical vision is complex and marked by a penchant for the unexpected. Indeed, the strategies of representation employed by the author could not be more different from those of previous works of historical fiction set against the Rape of Nanjing, such as A Long's *Nanjing* (1939)[12] or Zhou Erfu's *The Fall of Nanjing* (1987). The massacre that commenced on December 13 seems to have permanently stained the spatial-temporal coordinate of Nanjing in 1937 with images of rape and murder, even though during the previous eleven and a half months of that year the city saw virtually unprecedented prosperity. Though the indelible December tragedy constantly lurks just beyond the horizon of his novel, Ye Zhaoyan's repeated descriptions of the grandeur of the budding capital—its booming real estate market, rapid development, flourishing economy, and political dynamism—all remind us of its lost splendor, bearing testament to a side of Nanjing's past often obscured by the shadow of calamity.

Popular culture of the day also plays a key role in *Nanjing 1937*, from descriptions of the popular music and stage performances to depictions of the latest gossip and fashions. The meticulous attention paid to everything from cultural pastimes like mahjong to cultural icons like Mei Yanfang points to a deconstruction of the grand and sublime discourses that have dominated so many historical and even literary representations of the era. Ye's Nanjing is a world where notions of popular culture are (re)inscribed onto, and sometimes in place of, more traditional historical narratives. Monumental figures like Zhou Enlai and Deng Xiaoping are relegated to minor characters who appear fleetingly on the streets of Paris. Chinese fighter pilots are remembered not for their heroic deeds in the air but for their superstitious bedside manners. Even the Rape of Nanjing, the purported subject of the novel, is subverted. However, Ye's inability to depict the massacre at year's end should not be seen as an failure to face the vicissitudes of a blood-stained past but rather as a passionate attempt to remember what was lost.

That is not to say that Ye Zhaoyan does not leave us with questions to ponder. For although he shies away from graphic illustrations of the Rape of Nanjing, he does not exercise the same restraint when depicting acts of violence committed by Chinese characters against their compatriots. What does it mean when the most vicious and cold-blooded acts portrayed in a novel set in 1937 Nanjing are not committed by the Japanese (or even against the Japanese) but are, rather, indigenous acts of Chinese violence? Ye's understated criticism points back, however subtly, to a Lu Xunian critique of the Chinese national character. Ye Zhaoyan, however, is not one for moralizing, and *Nanjing 1937*'s complex combination of satire and sentimentality may very well leave many readers poised between loving and loathing his characters.

Returning to our earlier question, as the city falls, how can we reconcile this "love story" born of the ashes of war? Then again, perhaps we would be better off asking whether Ding Wenyu's driving passion is love at all—or merely a twisted obsession.[13] In the world of Ye Zhaoyan's 1937 Nanjing, there is, indeed, a fine line between love and obsession, satire and sentimentality, comedy and tragedy, splendor and decadence, history and allegory. These thematic coordinates intersect and blur, creating a sophisticated and stirring fictional pastische. The year 1937 saw not only the fall of the ancient capital of Nanjing but also the pinnacle of its development; in his novel, Ye Zhaoyan captures both. And although the novel comes to an end on December 13, 1937, the day the massacre begins, the reader knows all too well how the story ends. Ye Zhaoyan, admittedly, may not understand "that history that historians call history," but in the end, what he leaves us with is precisely the melancholic power and unbearable weight of History.

NOTES

1. Ye Zhaoyan, "Preface" (*Xie zai qianmian*) in *Yijiusanqi nian de aiqing* (Nanjing: Jiangsu wenyi, 1996), 5.

2. Ye Zhaoyan's first published short stories appeared in 1980, but he did not begin to gain wide recognition until the publication of his 1988 work, *Tale of the Date Tree* (*Zaoshu de gushi*).

3. One case in point is Ye's 1994 novel, *Flower Shadows* (*Hua Ying*), which was adapted by Fifth Generation director Chen Kaige (along with Wang Anyi, who co-wrote the screenplay) for his 1995 motion picture, *Temptress Moon* (*Fengyue*). The following year the novel was translated into French under the title *La Jeune Maîtresse* (Paris: Philippe Picquier, 1996). Film rights for *Nanjing 1937: A Love Story* have been purchased by actor/director Jiang Wen.

4. Tragic romances are just one fictional strain that falls under the umbrella of Mandarin Duck fiction; others include scandal fiction, detective stories, and chivalrous martial arts tales. For more on Mandarin Duck and Butterfly literature, see Perry Link's influential study, *Mandarin Ducks and Butterflies: Popular Fiction in Early Twentieth-Century Chinese Cities* (Berkeley: University of California Press, 1981).

5. The four award-winning novellas that make up *Evening Moor on the Qinhuai* (*Ye bo Qinhuai*) were serialized in three PRC literary journals between 1987 and 1990 before being collected in a single volume in 1991.

6. *Ni Huanzhi* was translated by A. C. Barnes as *Schoolmaster Ni Huan-chih* (Peking: Foreign Languages Press, 1958).

7. The Ye family can now claim four generations of published writers. In 2001, Ye Zhaoyan's seventeen-year-old daughter published her first book, a collection of essays on America.

8. *Fortress Besieged* (*Wei cheng*) was first serialized in *Literary Renaissance* and appeared in book form in 1947. The work is generally considered the last great literary masterpiece of the preliberation era. It is a satiric novel that traces the romantic and professional misadventures of Fang Hongjian, who after several years of foreign study abroad returns to China, bogus degree in hand, to teach at a provincial university. An English edition translated by Jeanne Kelly and Nathan K. Mao appeared in 1979 (Bloomington: Indiana University Press).

9. A more literal translation of the book's title, *Yijiusanqi nian de aiqing*, would read "The Romance of 1937."

10. Even the subplot involving Ding Wenyu's rickshaw puller Monk's involvement with an overbearing older woman will remind readers of the protagonist of Lao She's *Rickshaw* or, to an even greater degree, of Ding Erhe from Zhang Henshui's *Deep in the Night* (*Shen ye chen*).

11. Quoted in Zhang Wenjiang, *Yingzao babita de zhizhe: Qian Zhongshu zhuan* (Shanghai: Shanghai Arts and Literature Publishing House, 1993), 57.

12. Although completed in 1939, A Long's novel was only published posthumously in 1987, under the revised title *Nanjing Blood Sacrifice* (*Nanjing xueji*).

13. A parallel to Ding Wenyu's obsession can be found in his rickshaw puller and sometime companion, Monk. The twisted love triangle in which Monk finds himself caught constitutes the most significant subplot of the novel and represents a darker alternative outcome to obsessive love. The obsessions that drive both Ding and Monk are fundamentally the same—Ding's fanatical letter writing represents the manifestation of a "cultured obsession," while Monk's social and educational background leaves him with no alternative but to express his obsession through violence.

Chapter One

I

January 1, 1937 was a Friday. It was a clear, cool day; the northern cold front had just passed and the temperature had begun to warm up a bit. Although the Nationalist government had already declared the lunar calendar obsolete, the atmosphere among the people during the western New Year celebration fell short of the anticipated excitement. All over the country, conferences were being held for New Year's Day. From the central government all the way down, auditoriums were packed with high-sounding stately meetings. It seemed as if anyone who didn't attend a conference wasn't really celebrating the new year. The year 1937 arrived amid a wave of strong anti-Japanese sentiment. The Xi'an Incident* and its peaceful resolution not long before had raised Chiang Kai-shek's

*An episode that occurred in December 1936 when a former warlord, General Zhang Xueliang, kidnapped Chiang Kai-shek in an effort to force Chiang to take a more anti-Japanese stance and join with the CCP in a second united Chinese front against Japan.

prestige to an unprecedented level. Nationwide, there were magnificent fireworks displays in celebration of the Republic of China's auspicious turn for the better. Initially, the most widespread fear among the people had been that the Xi'an Incident would incite a large-scale civil war. They were also worried that for the Japanese, who had long set their sights on Chinese soil, the Incident would provide the perfect opportunity to strike in a time of weakness. Amid the grand rejoicing of the soldiers and citizens of China, Chiang Kai-shek safely returned to the capital, Nanjing. With his promise never again to bow down to the power of Japan, the long-anticipated initial stages of a democratic and unified anti-Japanese campaign had finally begun. The desperation in the hearts of the Chinese people seemed to have been replaced with a newfound hope.

On New Year's Day 1937 there was a virtual flood of government bigwigs in Nanjing who, after rushing to a never-ending series of meetings, came down with colds. Attending conferences became a heavy burden for those party and government VIPs. But there were at least three that couldn't be missed. First was paying homage at Sun Yat-sen's mausoleum. This was also the most utterly exhausting. Each year on the first day of the new year, one had to respectfully take part in this ritual. Of the visitors who climbed the steps to the mausoleum, there wasn't a soul who didn't come down panting for air and reeking with sweat. After that, one had to rush to the Central Party Headquarters on Hunan Road to hear Yu Youren deliver his New Year's speech. Finally, one had to go to the Nationalist Government Building to listen to Chairman Lin Sen's address. Every word uttered would be printed in the newspapers the next day, but attending these three events in person observed a kind of official decorum and indicated an individual's status in the government hierarchy—and this was something no one was willing to give up. Rushing back and forth, many of the people in attendance ended up with the chills and broke out into a series of feverish sweats. Those older gentlemen a bit on the frail side were sneezing before Lin Sen's address was even finished.

Ding Wenyu also caught a cold on New Year's Day, but it certainly had nothing to do with attending conferences or speeches. Except for a single wedding ceremony, he didn't go anywhere. He had long since thrown all those large red invitations with golden trim into the wastepaper basket. Although Ding Wenyu had already earned quite a name for himself, what really set him apart was his peculiar character. What other people went out of their way for he was always slow to take to heart. It was as if he couldn't even understand what there was worth celebrating on New Year's Day. We know that he caught a cold because he recorded this tidbit in his diary. Ding Wenyu habitually recorded his whereabouts and personal experiences in his diary; on New Year's Day, he surprisingly added the following passage:

> Today is a special day. I have a terrible cold and a runny nose, which toward the evening has grown especially acute. It is a good thing that the day wasn't a complete waste, because during an annoying wedding banquet, I ran into the beautiful Miss B. Instantly, my heart was thrown into disarray by this exquisite young girl. Here I describe her as a lovely and attractive girl, but actually today was her wedding day. As I write these words, it is very possible that she is already no longer a girl at all. Ah, why must women marry such vulgar creatures as men? I have no extravagant or ulterior motive; I desire only to be her eternal friend. This shall be the greatest happiness of my life. I shall do my utmost to carry this out.

It was the first day of 1937 when Ding Wenyu, already a middle-aged married man, in the strong cursive writing of his diary, first conveyed his fanatical feelings of love at first sight for Yuyuan. Because his diary was written only for himself, not to mention the fact that it was written in English, his wording and phrasing came across as a bit brazen. From simply looking at that day's diary entry, one would never guess that any kind of noteworthy story would unfold between him and Ren Yuyuan—the woman referred to as Miss B. Since it was written for his eyes only, inordinate comments about bold and beautiful women repeatedly appeared in Ding Wenyu's diary.

In actuality, only a fraction of his nearly one-thousand-word journal entry that day was devoted to Yuyuan and his cold. Most of the entry recorded vile remarks about another woman, a certain Miss Chen. For Ding Wenyu, the first day of 1937 was an abnormally difficult day. He had stayed up all night playing mah-jongg with Miss Chen at the Morning Cloud House near the Temple of Confucius. This was indeed a bitter task; Ding Wenyu truly despised the game that has been hailed as the quintessence of Chinese culture. Just one month before, he had made the acquaintance of this already passé pop singer, a single woman with a passable appearance. Besides singing, Miss Chen's biggest source of entertainment was playing mah-jongg. If Ding Wenyu wanted to get close to her, his only means would be to accompany her at the mah-jongg table. The night before, Ding Wenyu had lost miserably. By the time the sun rose and he saw Miss Chen home to rest, his eyelids were fighting to stay open. He had been yawning all night, his sole desire being to rush home and get some sleep. Yet the moment he lay down in bed, all he could do was toss and turn, unable to sleep.

The schools were closed for vacation, and children with nothing better to do set off firecrackers left over from the celebration of Chiang Kai-shek's return from Xi'an—right under the window of Ding Wenyu's faculty apartment. As if they were intentionally trying to antagonize Ding Wenyu, the children used an extremely economical method when lighting the firecrackers—separating long strings of them into single units so they could light them one at a time. Curled up beneath his comforter, Ding Wenyu had just slipped into a groggy slumber when he was awakened by the explosive sound. He was about to lose his temper but figured that there was no reason for him to act rashly with the kids. And so, between the periodic blasts, he would capriciously think of Miss Chen. She seemed a prize prey that could be taken at any moment. As far as winning the hearts of women went, Ding Wenyu considered himself an expert. Getting Miss Chen into bed was but a matter of time. With much difficulty, he finally got some sleep. It was already past noon and the annoying kids outside were gone when Ding Wenyu awoke, suddenly remembering an afternoon wedding ceremony that he was supposed to attend.

Monk, the rickshaw puller, had arrived early and set his three-wheeled rickshaw down near the university gate. He basked in the sun napping as he waited for Ding Wenyu to arrive. These days Monk's rickshaw had practically become Ding Wenyu's private chariot. Ding Wenyu was already quite late and there was still no sign of him. The longer he waited, the hungrier Monk got. Finally he rushed to the small stall across the street and bought four large pork buns to fill himself up. The plentiful warmth of the sun shone down, and Monk's face looked carefree and content. At the campus gate, the university intercom system was relaying a recording of Government Chairman Lin Sen's radio address from the Central New Year's Day Celebration Meeting. The topic of his speech

was self-reliance, and the quality of the recording was pitiful, as screeches of electronic feedback periodically came through the speakers. Male
and female university students emerged through the campus gates in
dribs and drabs. One student wearing a long blue cloth gown and pulling
a female student by the hand approached Monk and requested his serv-
ices in a thick Manchurian accent. Monk had already passed up several
customers that morning. He opened his eyes, lazily sized up this young
couple, and then quickly closed his eyes again.

The university student said, "What's wrong with you? Are you going
to take us or not? Say something!" Monk was a reckless fellow with a
leisurely attitude who paid no heed to others. One look at him in his un-
buttoned semi-new cotton jacket and you knew he was someone who
took his sweet time. He was not an easy fellow to deal with. Monk intentionally didn't make a sound, continuing to rest his eyes. The student
repeated his question, but Monk simply went on ignoring him. The university student's temper started to burn. He scolded Monk while his girl-
friend standing beside him chimed in. The student indignantly snorted:
"What the hell is going on these days? You're nothing but a lousy rickshaw puller! So what's with the stinking attitude?"

When Ding Wenyu arrived at the campus gate, that pair of young students were still harassing Monk. Monk was indeed bored, so he took advantage of the argument to help pass the time. He paid no heed to the
guy, spending all of his energy arguing with the girl, holding on to her
every word and not letting go. That girl was a student in the department
of foreign languages. She wasn't especially good at arguing, and as soon
as she became anxious she'd stutter; once she started stammering she became increasingly nervous. Suddenly she caught sight of Ding Wenyu,
who had already walked up beside her. She hastily shut her trap and
grabbed hold of her boyfriend's sleeve, signaling him to stop arguing. No
matter how you look at it, carrying on with an incoherent rickshaw puller
in front of a professor is out of character for two university students. Not
complying, the guy wanted to continue his battle of the tongues. His girl-
friend, seeing that her efforts were to no avail, began to turn red. It was
a good thing that Ding Wenyu wasn't paying attention to what happened. He looked a bit ridiculous, wearing a red nightcap, a trim western suit, a large red tie, and an oversized gray wool overcoat, and carrying a cane in his right hand. He looked like he was still half-asleep.

When Monk tilted his head and caught sight of Ding Wenyu, he made as if nothing had happened. Smiling, Monk greeted him: "Mr. Ding, did you get enough rest?"

Ding Wenyu muttered an irrelevant answer and climbed into the rickshaw. The male university student glared angrily at him, but Ding didn't sense a thing. Turning around, he stared in the direction of the girl student. Her face turned even redder and she looked away. Finally she couldn't help it and burst out with a snicker. The female student had once taken his class. Ding Wenyu always had a somewhat indecent look in his eyes. There wasn't a single girl in the school who didn't know about him. He was the star professor of the department of foreign languages, and all the girls enjoyed his classes. The jokes about him were too numerous to mention—and most of them had to do with his interest in female students. Whenever Ding Wenyu's gaze fell upon a pretty student, his eyes shimmered without even the slightest hint of shame. Once, after walking into the classroom, Ding Wenyu suddenly refused to teach. The reason? Too few girls, so he wasn't in the mood. As soon as girls from the department of foreign languages mentioned Ding Wenyu in the dormitory, they would instantly cover their mouths to hold in the laughter.

As the rickshaw passed The House for Reciting Classics, Ding Wenyu dug his gold watch out of his jacket pocket, looked at the time, and asked Monk if he could speed it up. Monk, who was obviously already quite close with Ding Wenyu, turned his head, displaying a set of snow-white teeth, and uttered laughingly, "Don't tell me that Mr. Ding has his days when he is in a rush. Everyone says that you're not even afraid to be late for class!" Ding felt he had a point, so he calmed down, made himself more comfortable, and let Monk slow down. Since the Nationalist government had established its capital in Nanjing, the streets of the city had changed quite a bit. Sun Yat-sen Avenue stretched out from the heart of the city with one road after another linked together. All over they were breaking ground on new construction projects, and new stores were opening almost every day. No wonder people who had departed Nanjing just a few years ago said that they could barely recognize the place when they returned. A rickshaw-puller friend of Monk's approached and said something to Monk. Naturally it was some dirty joke, after which the two of them snickered and jokingly cursed each other.

Monk's mouth didn't get a moment of rest the whole trip. The glaring sunlight was brilliant, and the rickshaw happened to be headed south. The radiance of the sun made it difficult for Ding Wenyu to open his eyes, so he simply shut them. He couldn't help but open his mouth and let out an enormous yawn. The exaggerated yawning sound caused Monk to turn around. Monk knew that Ding Wenyu still hadn't gotten enough sleep. That morning at dawn it had been he who rushed to the Morning Cloud House at the Temple of Confucius to pick up Ding Wenyu after his morning tea and take him back to campus. At the time, they had agreed that Ding would ride Monk's rickshaw again at noon. Ding Wenyu had grown accustomed to Monk's rickshaw, and Monk disliked running up and down the street looking for business. He liked customers like Ding Wenyu—liberal with money and pleasant to chat with on the road.

II

When Ding Wenyu arrived at the Officers' Moral Endeavor Association compound, Yuyuan and Yu Kerun's wedding was already approaching its end. In the Nanjing of 1937, the OMEA compound was an almost mystical place. It was located on East Sun Yat-sen Road; if you were on the eastern side of the Central Hospital and continued straight over the Sun Yat-sen Bridge, you'd run into it in no time. Usually it was only the handful of personages with some degree of status who showed their faces there. Designed by a well-known architect, the compound was the paradigm synthesis of Chinese and western architectural styles. It was composed of several complementary palace-style halls; from the outside its upturned eaves looked typically Chinese, but the internal structure was completely western. In Nanjing in 1937, getting through the door at the OMEA compound was decisive in determining who you were. The fashionable topic of conversation among Nanjing citizens was the never-ending gossip about government and party big shots, which is not all that different from what we see today in Beijing. As if he were a famous movie star, Chiang Kai-shek could twitch and it would instantly become the talk of the town. For example, gossip articles such as YU YOUREN INJURED FOOT, VICE-COMMITTEE CHAIRMAN FENG COMES DOWN

INOR AILMENT, or YESTERDAY WELL-KNOWN FIGURE ENTERED
L FOR HERNIA OPERATION repeatedly appeared on the front pages
newspapers. People carried on endlessly about those political
.........es. Even long after Nanjing fell, this habit stubbornly held on.

It was rare that anyone rode up to the OMEA compound in a rickshaw; the majority of visitors came in automobiles. The unique quality of the compound was that all of the employees wore military uniforms, from the doorman to the attendants in the compound dining hall. It was almost impossible for someone without background to get in—the doorman would often admit people only after close scrutiny of their clothing and manners; usually it only took one glance to pick out someone with influence. Naturally, there was the occasional exception—for example, the senior statesman Wu Zhihui. Wu never rode in automobiles, nor did he take rickshaws; though advanced in years, he simply walked to the compound on his own two feet. There are many jokes about Wu Zhihui. In 1938 during a cocktail party in Wuhan—by then Nanjing had already fallen and the Japanese forces were closing in on Wuhan—Wu Zhihui, holding a glass of wine, approached Wang Jingwei and dropped to his knees with a loud thud. Wu pleaded: "Mr. Wang, the country is already in dire straits. You must take a stand and clean up this terrible situation." All of the high-level leaders at the party stood there stupefied, and even Wang Jingwei was clueless as to how to react. Finally, with a painful look on his face, Wang also knelt and pleaded: "Elder Wu, please, if you have something to say, let's stand up and talk!" Wu Zhihui was unwilling to get up, so Wang Jingwei was forced to kneel with him. Once they got down on their knees, they were there for quite some time. The people at the party didn't know whether to laugh or cry. It wouldn't be right for them to pick the kneeling men up, yet they couldn't just leave them like that. In the end, affairs of state became a trifling matter. Wu Zhihui was a veteran member of the Revolutionary Alliance, but he was also an odd character who liked to flaunt his seniority. When mixing with the upper classes of society, he frequently grabbed attention for his unorthodox behavior. On one occasion, the doorman at the OMEA compound came a hair's breadth away from losing his meal ticket on account of Wu Zhihui's strange manners: he stopped Wu Zhihui at the door as if driving away a beggar. In the end, even Chiang Kai-shek lost his temper over the incident.

At the entrance to the compound, Ding Wenyu didn't run into any kind of difficulty. Apparently the doorman, still remembering the Wu Zhihui incident, took him for some big shot like Wu. Those who would dare strut past the compound gates were by no means common citizens; moreover, it was obvious from the way Ding Wenyu was decked out that he was *not* your average Joe. Gathered in the main hall were celebrities of all shapes and sizes. Strutting straight in with an imposing air, Ding Wenyu looked like a character in a movie. It was not his first time there. Ding walked confidently straight to the buffet table and picked up a glass of wine. The hall was heated, and a waiter approached Ding, politely requesting that he remove his coat. The waiter was also prepared to take Ding's cane and red nightcap to the coatroom. Only after the waiter's approach did Ding Wenyu realize just how uncultured he must have appeared by rushing straight to the buffet. Although his mannerisms were a bit ridiculous, Ding never lost his gentlemanlike demeanor. Carrying a cane around with him was a fashionable habit he had picked up while studying in Europe. He handed his cane to the waiter but refused to remove the nightcap from his head. Wearing a nightcap was Ding Wenyu's trademark. Sometimes he would wear a sharp western suit, at other times a long mandarin jacket, but only on the hottest summer days would he remove his red woolen nightcap.

After Ding Wenyu's eye-catching appearance at the tail end of the wedding reception, everyone who knew him nodded in succession. Both the bride's and the groom's families were quite close to Ding Wenyu. The groom's elder brother Yu Kexia was a friend of Ding's from his days as a foreign student in Germany. At that time the Yu family's economic situation was not very good, and Yu Kexia would often fret over where his next meal was coming from. It was during this time that Ding Wenyu became his "parental provider." Whenever Yu was in bad straits, he would seek out Ding's help—he knew that Ding Wenyu's father was a wealthy boss in the banking industry. There was even a period when Yu Kexia told everyone he bumped into that Ding and he were blood brothers, often citing an infamous event that occurred while they were vacationing in France. One night during their vacation, Ding brought a blonde prostitute back to their hotel, and that night the three of them slept in the same room. There was nothing better than this particularly unusual relationship to illustrate their close friendship. Naturally, each time this story was told, a footnote had to be added. Yu Kexia was a man who kept his body pure as a pearl. His ulterior motive for telling this tale was to express his lofty ideals. For only someone with phenomenal willpower could on a long, lonely night in a foreign land remain unmoved by the moans of carnal pleasure beside him.

At the time of the wedding, Yu Kexia was the vice-director of the Provincial Education Office, and there was a rumor that the presidency of a certain national university had already been reserved for him. During 1937 in the capital of Nanjing, the treasured seat of university president was a prerequisite for a post as a high-level cadre in the Ministry of Education. It was his younger brother's wedding day, so of course Yu Kexia solemnly played the role of host, presiding over the wedding with full airs. He looked like a windup toy duck swaggering all around, spreading inside information about his imminent promotion. He was hoping that people would express their opinion on whether he should stoop to take the job. Even though he consistently maintained that he never had his eye on the position and repeatedly expressed how difficult the job was, to be undertaken only by someone willing to sacrifice himself for his work, in actuality, it was Yu Kexia himself who invented these rumors and let them out—he released them like a flock of pigeons. When Ding Wenyu appeared before him, Yu Kexia, who had been in a state of happiness, jumped as if he had been electrocuted. Smiling ear to ear, Yu rushed over to Ding Wenyu and admonished him for arriving so late.

"You never got rid of those bad habits you picked up in Europe!" After this line of Chinese, Yu Kexia instantly added a flurry of German. This kind of artificial act was unquestionably intended to remind those around them that he had once studied in Europe. It was too bad that his German was never truly fluent; it was, however, good enough to pull the wool over the eyes of everyone that night. Ignoring the puzzled look on Ding Wenyu's face, Yu Kexia continued to milk his shoddy German for all it was worth. When Ding Wenyu finally responded with a line of German, Yu Kexia was virtually tongue-tied. Laughing, he switched back to Chinese and teased Ding: "So what kind of trouble have you been getting yourself into these days?"

Yu Kexia's voice was especially loud, and almost all eyes in the hall instantly fell on Ding Wenyu. Yu Kexia's question left Ding somewhat at a loss as to how to respond. Not far from the main hall, a dance was being held. Ding Wenyu scanned the area and, not seeing any stunning beauties, lacked the inspiration to continue his perfunctory conversation with Yu. He turned and headed for the dance hall. Yu Kexia chased after to prevent Ding from escaping. Grabbing hold of him, he asked Ding to pay his respects to Yuyuan's father, Old Ren Bojin. Since he was indeed attending a wedding, Ding couldn't completely escape these kinds of formalities. Having been dragged before Ren Bojin, he reluctantly expressed his best wishes to the old man. Old Ren Bojin was a senior figure in the military and had been a classmate of Ding's cousin Ding Gongqia at the Japanese Military Academy. The relationship between the Ding and Ren clans spanned several generations. Ren Bojin and Ding Wenyu's father were especially close, but Ding Wenyu did not have much of an impression of the elder military statesman. What little he did have wasn't very good. Twenty years earlier, a barely seventeen-year-old Ding Wenyu had absurdly pursued Ren Bojin's eldest daughter, Yuchan. Yuchan was Old Ren Bojin's daughter by his deceased first wife—she was a full twenty-four years older than her youngest sister Yuyuan, the bride that day. This love story, which ended in naught, didn't destroy the solid relationship between the Ren and Ding families, but it did make things a bit awkward.

It was obvious that Ren Bojin was not terribly fond of Ding Wenyu. One look at Ding's indecent mannerisms was enough to make Old Ren frown. Ding Wenyu stiffened up and sat down with Old Ren for a while but didn't really have anything to say; he just respectfully answered all of Lady Miyako's questions. Miyako wasn't as stiff as her husband and didn't want to make Ding Wenyu feel uncomfortable. She not only had no ill feeling toward Ding, but, seeing him so uncomfortable, was even led, out of the goodness of her heart, to make some conversation with the poor fellow. Although Ding Wenyu was almost forty years old, in front of Old Ren Bojin he became an inexperienced child all over again.

III

At the wedding ceremony that night, the biggest embarrassment Ding Wenyu caused stemmed from the way he wantonly stared at the bride Yuyuan. Everyone felt that his actions were quite inappropriate.

That red woolen nightcap was already enough to make him look like a ridiculous clown. Moreover, the guests had long since caught wind of the various rumors about his absurd behavior. And so, when he lustily stared at Yuyuan, there were more than a few people who couldn't help but laugh. Ding Wenyu, however, wasn't afraid of making a fool of himself. The place was in an uproar, with groups of people chatting and laughing. Like a mischievous child trying to hide from a strict teacher, Ding Wenyu took advantage of the chaos to slip away from Old Ren Bojin. Because he had not slept well the night before, Ding drank glass after glass of wine to drive away his exhaustion. By the time he entered the dance hall the music was just ending. People were walking off the dance floor and the pit musicians had just set down their instruments, preparing to take a rest before their next set. Ding Wenyu downed the glass of wine in his hand and upon turning around—saw Yuyuan. When he first laid eyes on Yuyuan he only caught sight of her profile. He had only intended to drop a casual glance; never did he imagine that his eyes would freeze on her like that. Holding the empty glass in his hand, he stood like a wooden column, completely captivated.

Then from God knows where appeared a rather rash young man with a dirty white scarf around his neck who sped down toward the music pit. He pushed aside a resting musician and climbed up onto his chair; then, waving his fist in the air, he began delivering a lecture. The patrons of the dance hall were quite surprised. Those outside also noticed that something strange was going on and rushed over to see what all the excitement was about. The young lecturer was obviously a student, but because he was a bit too excited, his speech was not terribly successful. For the people of Nanjing in 1937, speeches were already a commonplace— "resist Japan and save our dying nation" was a lecture topic already known to everyone. As if he were reciting from a textbook, the young man enumerated the various instances of Japanese invasion and provocation against China from the Sino-Japanese War of 1894–1895 on up. Tears rolled down his cheeks as he spoke, and when he came to a pause everyone responded with thunderous applause.

There were a few other young people there who had the appearance of students peddling that day's newspaper. It was a small, privately run paper, and on the front page there was nothing but a single colossal exclamation point. Only on the second page was there a boldface headline stating that since the Mukden Incident,* five years and three months had passed, during which four Manchurian provinces had already fallen into Japanese hands. Because all of Ding Wenyu's attention was focused on Yuyuan, he didn't have the slightest reaction when a female student waved a newspaper in front of his face. Because most of the people attending the wedding were pillars of upper-class society, they were all generous when it came to helping people out with money and had no qualms about buying a copy of that small, crude, unevenly printed newspaper. The stubborn student interpreted Ding Wenyu's blank stare as an intentional refusal to purchase the paper and wouldn't leave him alone. It was as if she wanted to test just how shameless this unpatriotic chap was.

The young lecturer announced that he wasn't against everyone having a good time, he just hoped that amid their pleasure they would not forget the Chinese soil that had already fallen into the hands of the Japanese. Our imminent national calamity must be our priority, and to forget our national humiliation is a contemptible action, he declared. Since the Mukden Incident, people had grown accustomed to various organized marches, people shouting slogans, and an array of fund-raising campaigns. The selling of the newspaper in itself had a kind of fund-raising quality, as each of the students had a small strawboard box hanging from their neck. Written in a forceful hand on each donation box were the words: COME TOGETHER IN A TIME OF NATIONAL CALAMITY / DONATE IN THE NAME OF NATIONALISM. To barge into the OMEA compound like that, those students must have had some connections. It was obvious that they were the children of some bigwigs. Nanjing was the capital city and it had all kinds of princes and missies whose parents were in the upper government ranks. There were rich dandies who lived for the day, eating, drinking, gambling, and whoring their way through their befuddled and decadent lives. There were also earnest youths who were sincerely patriotic and worked for the "resist Japan and save our dying nation" campaign, ready at any time to rush to the battlefield and courageously fight the enemy. Someone had already recognized the girl in the student uniform as the daughter of a certain special committee member of the

---

*A conflict that broke out between Japanese and Chinese troops on September 18, 1931. The Mukden Incident, also known as the Manchurian Incident, occurred just outside modern-day Shenyang and became the pretext for the Japanese to mobilize its troops and occupy Manchuria.

Nationalist Government Construction Committee. The post of special committee member was a exceptional appointment. Among those on the committee were T. V. Soong, H. H. K'ung, Examination President Dai Chuanxian, and the former mayor of the Nanjing municipality, Liu Jiwen, all renowned during their time.

Ding Wenyu remained unmoved. His hesitation to donate a little money, under these conditions, attracted even more attention. His eyes were like nails, staring deep and unwavering at the bride Yuyuan. Even when Yuyuan had turned around and become conscious of Ding's ill-intentioned gaze, he still rudely stared without the slightest flutter.

Several people noticed Ding Wenyu's lack of propriety; one person almost got up to tell him about it but was afraid he would embarrass Ding if he said anything. Under the harassment of his gaze, Yuyuan couldn't help but blush. She was embarrassed to look directly at him but couldn't help feeling curious—more than once she pretended to look at some other area of the hall just to steal a quick glance at Ding Wenyu. Finally, Ding Wenyu snapped out of his trance. Removing his wallet from his jacket pocket, he pulled out a bill and ran after that female student, who had already left him in great disappointment. Under the watchful eyes of the crowd, Ding diligently stuffed the bill into the paper box attached to the girl's torso.

The young lad delivering the lecture waved his fist again and called for the band to play "March of the Volunteer Army." Because this song was banned from being performed in most public venues, the conductor was unsure whether to carry out this order. Then Ding Wenyu began to applaud, seeming unquestionably in support of the song being performed. Following Ding's lead, all the young people in the hall joined in with cheers and applause. By this point, the orchestra had virtually no choice but to play the song. In Nanjing in 1937, because of diplomatic considerations, all openly anti-Japanese lyrics were banned; however, this ban had the opposite effect. In reality, songs in the vain of "resist Japan and save our dying nation" could not only be heard everywhere but during this specific period, they also became the most popular form of entertainment. At any given time you could hear people in the streets and alleyways humming these songs. It didn't matter if it was a old man with snowy hair or a child first learning how to speak, whether they sang with perfect melody or completely out of tune; one thing was for sure—everyone was singing those songs. When the solemn and stirring melody of "March of the Volunteer Army" struck up at the wedding of Yuyuan and Yu Kerun, there was not a soul in attendance left unmoved. As the tune approached the halfway point, several people began to quietly hum along, ultimately joining in heartfelt song. War between China and Japan would not formally erupt until July 7, 1937, but the vast majority of Chinese with high morale had long been spiritually prepared for battle.

While everyone was wrapped up in song, Ding Wenyu continued stealing furtive glances at the bride Yuyuan. This wasn't actually the first time he had laid eyes on her; it was simply that in the past she hadn't left any particular impression on him. Old Ren Bojin had six precious daughters but was never able to father a son. This would have been a major issue for any traditional Chinese patriarch, but Old Ren didn't seem to be too concerned. However, as a career military man and an elder figure in military circles, Old Ren did seem to somewhat regret not having a son to carry on his unfinished work. Most of the sons-in-law he selected served in the military. Yuyuan, his youngest and most adored daughter, threw herself into military work immediately after her middle-school graduation to become a soldier. At the wedding that day, Yuyuan in her brand-new army uniform came as a breath of fresh air to everyone in attendance. People had already grown tired of brides with heavy make-up wearing long white gowns, and the pleasant simplicity of Yuyuan's unadorned uniform won everyone over. Ding Wenyu had never imagined that a beautiful girl could look so extraordinary in a military uniform. Yuyuan's gorgeous face and slender body were enhanced to a level of the utmost beauty.

"The bride is truly stunning," a female student uttered with admiration. Her hand clasped the small paper box that hung around her neck, rocking the clanking money inside in sync with the melody. At the wedding that day, there indeed couldn't have been any other woman more spectacular than Yuyuan.

After singing "March of the Volunteer Army," the young people still hadn't gotten enough and quickly followed up with a rendition of "Anthem of the Great Road," another song composed by Nie Er. Because it was the theme song of a popular film, it was quite the rage for a time, known to virtually every household in Nanjing. Already in the early 1930s, going to motion pictures had become an extremely fashionable pastime; anything that had any connection with films was an immediate attention-grabber. After that, they sang the melancholy "On the Songhua River," followed by "Fighting Back to My Hometown," another song ordered banned from all public events. More than once, its passionate lyrics had been cited by the Japanese as proof that the Chinese government encouraged anti-Japanese sentiment.

Yuyuan, who was obviously no singer, stood not far from Ding Wenyu slightly humming along, afraid that she would embarrass herself if she sang off-key. Ding Wenyu saw her lips moving but couldn't hear her voice. By this point, what Yuyuan was singing and whether or not she could even carry a tune were already of infinitesimal importance to Ding Wenyu. He hoped she would go on singing like that for all eternity—that way he could forever feast his eyes on Yuyuan's beauty.

By comparison, Yu Kerun, who was also wearing his military uniform, appeared somewhat inferior to his new bride. Yu Kerun was a recognized airplane pilot and a prominent drillmaster at the Aviation Academy. His most outstanding flight in recent memory had been on October 29 of the preceding year, when he took part in Chiang Kai-shek's birthday celebration. He led students from the Aviation Academy as they flew in a hedge-hopping exercise over the reviewing stand while changing their formation. Their performance won a citation from Chiang Kai-shek, whose lecture, delivered in his characteristic thick Ningbo, left quite an impression on the lively students of the Aviation Academy. From then on, during their tense training sessions they would often imitate Chiang's pronunciation in an affected manner, not forgetting to put new words in the Generalissimo's mouth. Afterward they would all joke among themselves. That day at the wedding, Yu Kerun didn't look too much like a groom; it was a shame that although his spanking-new uniform fit him snugly, it looked a bit out of place given the present circumstances. Yuyuan's military outfit, on the other hand, brought out her prominence even more—while smug young male officers decked out in uniforms could be seen crawling all over the streets of Nanjing, female soldiers remained relatively rare creatures.

As far as Ding Wenyu was concerned, the newlyweds resembled neither bride nor groom. The impression Yuyuan gave was of a fairy maiden descending to the mortal world, whereas Yu Kerun resembled some high official's adjutant or bodyguard. At places like the OMEA compound it was all too common to see young officers in their sharp uniforms like Yu Kerun. They would always be following close behind those government VIPs, trying to come off as high honchos because of who they were with. These young graduates of the Military Academy were the cream of the crop, the future pillars of the Central Military.

Yu Kexia grinned as he introduced his younger brother to Ding Wenyu. Out of politeness Ding wanted to shake his hand, but Yu Kerun suddenly stood at attention and saluted Ding. As Yu raised his right hand to his forehead, his leather shoes lightly snapped together, scaring the living daylights out of Ding Wenyu.

"This is one of the bad habits he picked up at the Military Academy," Yu Kexia laughingly explained. "If he doesn't stand at attention and salute, it's as if he is not a real soldier."

Attempting to cover up his own embarrassment, Ding Wenyu returned a salute to Yu Kerun. He had learned this move from American movies. It was a bit exaggerated, but more than that, it was simply ridiculous.

Yu Kexia waved his hand, signaling Yu Kerun to go off and mingle somewhere else. "Besides thinking about knocking heads with the Japanese, young people today don't know what serious matters to take up." Yu Kexia grumbled. He felt that the wedding that day was a bit spoiled and couldn't help but complain a bit. "All young people know how to do is make noise. 'Resist Japan, resist Japan!' If simply mouthing high-minded slogans and singing songs could scare away the Japanese army and recover our four lost provinces in Manchuria, China would have reached salvation long ago! What is the use of an angry mouth against a superpower like Japan? If these youngsters keep on making trouble like this, I don't know how we are going to succeed in resisting the Japanese. Who knows, maybe we really will end up with a subjugated nation and party." Yu Kexia, who rattled on endlessly expressing his opinions, hoped that Ding Wenyu would get his point and realize the fact that his views actually represented those of most insightful party leaders. "I'm going to be frank with you. Not long ago I met with the Minister of the Board of Military Affairs, General He Yingqin. We had a broad discussion about both domestic and foreign issues, and what do you know? General He and myself had the same opinions. There is also Mr. Hu Shi; do you know what Hu Shi had to say?"

"Hu Shi, that guy is an expert in bullshitting." Ding Wenyu sarcastically responded. He didn't have the slightest interest in Yu Kexia's topic of conversation; his comment was just a way of releasing his frustration. Hu Shi was a cultural celebrity, but not all intellectuals were fond of him. From the Mukden Incident until the eve of the war, Hu Shi consistently looked the other way when it came to Japan's aggression, echoing the government's policy of nonresistance. Because of this, he won the general scorn of the people. During that particular gathering, Ding Wenyu could not care less about whether or not China should resist Japan. The eager look in his eyes as he searched Yuyuan's alluring image had already surpassed what one normally refers to as lust.

Just as that flock of students who had barged in were leaving, the wedding ceremony, which was already beginning to wind down, reached another lull. Amid the gradually building strains of music, people danced to a final number. It was a long tango, and without the slightest thought, Ding Wenyu grabbed the chunky, rich woman standing beside him and dragged her out to the dance floor. The rich woman was a bit confused, because it was rare that anyone would invite a hefty lady like herself to dance. Her husband, who was busy launching consecutive attacks on a number of other women, was unwilling even out of politeness to dance a number with his own wife. Her anger at being continually ignored had long been brewing when she mistook Ding Wenyu's crude advance as evidence of her charm.

"How come you waited until now to finally ask me?" she asked. The rich woman wore heavy make-up and had thin black eyebrows, which looked like they were painted on. She gazed intently at Ding Wenyu's woolen nightcap and in a delicate voice that didn't seem to fit her appearance whispered, "My husband says that you are a very famous professor."

"Famous professor? I'm sure what your husband meant was that I am just a famous playboy," he answered. Feeling like he was pushing a mountain, Ding Wenyu tried to prod the rich lady over toward Yuyuan. And then, Ding and Yuyuan's eyes finally met—it was just for a fleeting moment, then Yuyuan quickly shifted her gaze. Because they were such a terrible match, Ding Wenyu and the rich woman's dance was a disaster. They stepped on each other's toes, and time and time again, the rich woman even felt that Ding was intentionally rubbing against her breasts. Her waist was so thick that for Ding Wenyu to place his hands on her hips he would have no choice but to press right up against her. It was a good thing that Ding Wenyu quickly figured out how to get close to

Yuyuan: since it was so difficult to lead "the mountain" forward, all he had to do was stand with his back to Yuyuan and let the fat lady push him closer to his target. The rich woman's enthusiasm exceeded what Ding had anticipated. She felt he was a bit aggressive, but on the other hand, she secretly hoped Ding would attempt to take some liberties with her. Perhaps it was simply because she was angry at her husband; then again, perhaps after all those years of loneliness she couldn't help but press her meat as tightly against Ding Wenyu as she could.

IV

After the dance was over, Ding Wenyu sharply pushed the chunky, rich lady aside and, with a couple of giant steps, rushed to Yuyuan's side. Then with the utmost sincerity, Ding Wenyu expressed to Yuyuan his desire to have the next dance. His request led everyone around to break out in hysterical sniggers. Yuyuan covered her mouth and turned red with laughter. It was obvious to everyone that the dancing was already over. The musicians had put away their music and the conductor had already placed his baton down on his music stand to gracefully run his fingers through his long, flowing hair. One after another, people swarmed out, taking their coats from the doorman as they got to the door. The distraught look on Ding Wenyu's face left an even more comical impression on everyone present. Ding reluctantly gazed at the backs of the newlyweds as they prepared to depart, and a feeling of jealousy welled up in his heart.

Yuyuan bade farewell to her parents and the other guests who were leaving the wedding ceremony. It was obvious that she felt this Ding Wenyu was quite an interesting character—even though all he seemed to do was make a fool of himself at the wedding, Yuyuan wasn't at all annoyed. Ding Wenyu had long before left a waggish impression on her, this bookworm who twenty years ago had pursued her oldest sister and made himself the secret object of laughter and ridicule among Yuyuan's family. Her oldest sister Yuchan was far off in America and couldn't attend the wedding; who knows what would have gone through *her* mind had she been able to witness Ding Wenyu's behavior. With perfect poise, Yuyuan walked over to Ding Wenyu and extended her hand. She was perhaps the only one in her family who had never pulled his leg.

When congratulating the newlyweds, virtually all of the guests had offered the same polite greetings. Yuyuan couldn't imagine what Ding would say, but after she offered her hand and saw that he had absolutely no reaction, she started to feel uncomfortable. He stood there gaping and dumbstruck with a faint smile on his face, staring blankly at her. She hesitated for a moment, wondering if she should pull back, when Ding Wenyu suddenly grabbed hold of the exquisitely fair hand before him. Ding held her hand firmly with both hands, unwilling to let go. The more she tried to pull her hand back, the tighter Ding held on.

"How could a girl as beautiful as you just run off and get married so rashly?" Ding Wenyu asked, shocking everyone around who heard him.

"Mr. Ding," Yuyuan responded, "you are such a kidder."

Ding Wenyu answered with a serious tone: "Now why would I kid you?"

The expression on Yuyuan's face slightly changed and she forcefully tried to pull her hand back. Seizing the opportunity and not in the least considering the implications of his words, Ding Wenyu switched to Japanese and boldly continued, "If I had laid eyes on you earlier, the groom today very well might have been me, am I right?" Because Yuyuan's mother, Lady Miyako, was Japanese and her father, Old Ren, was a graduate of the Japanese Military Academy, their whole family could speak fluent Japanese. Yuyuan understood every word Ding said. She pulled her hand away with a powerful tug that almost knocked him down. For a middle-aged married man, Ding had clearly gone too far—one must choose the proper time and person when flirting. Yuyuan's face once again turned red, but this time it was from anger. In the end, however, she was a girl with manners, so she simply pretended she didn't understand what he said, turned away, and made small talk with some other guests.

The Rens came over to bid farewell to their daughter once again. Miyako hugged Yuyuan and whispered good luck in quickly bearing her husband a baby boy. Miyako, who had been wracked by guilt all her life for not bearing a son, hoped that fate would not lead her daughter down the same disastrous road. Yuyuan was her youngest daughter, and her husband's most precious treasure. Thinking of Yuyuan finally getting married, Lady Miyako couldn't help but shed tears of sadness. She had already lived several decades in China, far surpassing her time spent in Japan, the country of her birth. Since marrying a Chinese husband, Lady Miyako had become an all-out Chinese wife. In 1937, Miyako began to sense the Chinese people's universal hatred of Japan because of its invasion of China. Whether it was her own beloved husband or the six daughters she herself had raised, they all advocated war with Japan. When she married Ren Bojin, Ren's two daughters by his first wife, Madame Li, were three and not quite one, but Miyako treated them as if they were her own flesh and blood. The entire family overlooked the fact that she was Japanese, and even Miyako herself practically forgot about her native country. She never wore a kimono, and she even forgot how to cook Japanese food. Her husband and daughters were everything to her, and she didn't want to do anything that would make them unhappy.

Her mother's tears also moved Yuyuan, and her eyes immediately turned red. She was too embarrassed to cry so she turned away, put her head on her father's shoulder, and mischievously rubbed her face against his jacket. Old Ren could feel his own tears beginning to brew and said laughingly, "Stop this laughing one minute, crying the next. If you truly miss your mother and your old man, come back to visit often and we'll know you mean it."

Until the moment she climbed into the jeep driven by Yu Kerun, the smile on her face was extremely forced. Everyone thought she was unwilling to leave her parents, but actually all she was thinking about was how angry she was at Ding Wenyu. Of course you have to leave your parents when you marry; there was no way Yuyuan was going to get too upset over that. What was annoying her was Ding Wenyu's unreasonable behavior; he had no right to say such ridiculous things. Ding's lack of decorum made her feel as if she had been made fun of. He really was just as frivolous, shameless, brazen, and indifferent to becoming a laughingstock as the rumors made him out to be.

With consummate poor timing, the military jeep died immediately after the engine started. Yu Kerun had no choice but to hop down and, under the eyes of all present, lift the hood and adjust the fuel line. Brand-new jeeps like this one often had annoying breakdowns. As the groom tried to fix the problem, Yuyuan, who was sitting in the jeep waiting, had the uneasy feeling of being the target of everyone's attention. It's always a mess when things don't end when they are supposed to end. The well-wishers around had already said all their good-byes, so all they could do was stand there, waving repeatedly and making small talk to pass the time.

Yuyuan tried her best not to turn and look at Ding Wenyu, but finally, feeling she had been wronged, she couldn't help herself. She turned her head and saw an extremely dejected Ding Wenyu standing near the swinging door, hanging his head and staring into space like a defeated cock. By then he had already put on his gray wool overcoat and was holding his purely decorative cane. Yuyuan felt extremely uncomfortable about those types of men who carried around "culture canes," which had been the rage in Europe, yet for some reason she felt that it was quite appropriate for a strange clown like Ding Wenyu to carry one. Ding Wenyu's appearance of loneliness helped soothe Yuyuan's anger; it also sparked in her a sense of pity for him. Although he had gone a bit too far, Yuyuan herself by no means let him off easy.

With a belly full of emotion, Ding Wenyu climbed into Monk's rickshaw just before Yu Kerun restarted the jeep. The sun had yet to disappear behind the mountain, but it had already lost its might. Monk, whose face was so frozen that it was turning blue, used an electrical cord to tighten the short cotton jacket around his waist and pulled Ding Wenyu away. A crestfallen and dejected Ding Wenyu did not bid farewell to a single soul. He was also slow to make conversation with Monk. He felt that the way Monk detachedly concentrated on pulling the rickshaw perfectly matched his own mood at that moment. The army jeep driven by Yu Kerun turned at Pearl Road and caught up to the rickshaw. Yuyuan noticed Ding Wenyu tightly wrapped in his woolen overcoat, curled up in the rickshaw. His eyes were tightly shut, and it looked as if he was shivering. His hands still clasped that cane. Suddenly Ding Wenyu's eyes seemed to open and Yuyuan quickly looked away.

Chapter Two

I

When Ding Wenyu first inconceivably fell for Yuyuan, many people believed he was simply suffering from the same rabid insanity that had driven him to blindly pursue her eldest sister Yuchan some twenty years earlier. Everyone felt that the whole thing was a bit ludicrous and that after a good laugh it would all pass. If he weren't always causing an uproar, Ding Wenyu wouldn't be Ding Wenyu. His second fall into the quicksand of love seemed like nothing more than an idiot pulling yet another idiotic stunt. In the beginning, even Ding Wenyu himself felt that his out-of-bounds infatuation was simply a continuation of his unconsummated love from his seventeenth year—a rekindling of the dying embers of his flame of passion. In the pages of his diary, he repeatedly examined his conscience, questioned himself, provided his own answers, and ultimately reached a conclusion: although the women he loved were half-sisters, and although they were both married, these two tempests of love had not the slightest connection.

Ding Wenyu's love for Yuchan and her sister Yuyuan was equally fanatical, and both drove him to the brink of insanity; however, the fundamental point of departure for each case was obviously quite distinct. The Ding Wenyu of twenty years ago was a horse of another color; since the starting point was different, the result must necessarily be different as well. Seventeen-year-old Ding Wenyu was a teenager with scant life experience; he was extremely childish and had absolutely no knowledge of women. Yuchan was his first love and it was a story right out of a fairy tale, a romantic ode being played out. The Ding Wenyu of twenty years later was an old hand when it came to women. He was a playboy, a master at seeking pleasure. Ding was notorious for the number of women he had tasted, more than he could even recall. The word "love" by this time in his life had already lost all practical meaning. He continuously sought out different types of women, and once he achieved his conquest, he would immediately initiate his next campaign. He was like a general who had endured a hundred battles, charging forward amid a sea of women, time after time facing setbacks, time after time losing face for all to see. Even though he usually came off as the glorious victor, his soul had long ago been covered with scars. While old wounds turn to scars, new wounds continue to bleed. When it all began, no one took Ding Wenyu's love for Yuyuan seriously; everyone simply thought that he had fallen for yet another new woman.

The pure and honest Ding Wenyu of twenty years before had long since vanished into thin air. Back then, he'd been a teenager in the prime of his youth. Having just returned from Japan with his father, Ding was preparing to study at Southeast University. At the time it was quite unusual for a university student to be so young. He had pathetic grades in Chinese and mathematics and looked like a big kid. Ding Wenyu's father aimed to enable his son, who already had a firm grip on two foreign languages, to absorb some Chinese culture at a pure Chinese-style university. Ding Wenyu had stayed with his father in Japan for five years, during which time Japanese had practically become Ding's mother tongue. Ding's father also specially hired a home instructor for his son. The tutor was a foreign student from Germany who was responsible for teaching Ding German and English. When he returned home at the age of seventeen, the first thing that young Ding Wenyu displayed to the masses was his genius in the area of foreign languages. He could already speak fluent Japanese and German. One time during a stopover in Beiping, his father took him to the home of the Minister of War, Duan Qirui. As it happened, there was also a visitor from Germany present. Duan Qirui had studied military tactics in Germany and in his stubborn mind, the well-trained German army was the most powerful armed force in the world. As Duan explained the rules of the Chinese chess game *go*, he from time to time showed off his not particularly adept German.

Ding Wenyu's fluid interchange with the German guest immediately led Duan Qirui to feel that this was a child destined to study at the Tactical Academy in Germany. Since ancient times, young people have always been the stock from which heroes are made, Duan Qirui exclaimed with emotion. Chinese students studying military affairs in Germany have wasted too much precious time getting past the language barrier—he had a keen understanding of this. However, if someone with a background like Ding Wenyu's were to study military tactics, he without doubt would have a boundless future. The Northern Warlord government simply had too few outstanding military men.

Ding Wenyu's father, however, had no choice but to politely decline Director Duan's kind recommendation. He himself wished Ding Wenyu would become an investor, ultimately following in the footsteps of his father, a Shanghai banking mogul. Everything the Ding family had had been built up during the Westernization Movement. Ding's grandfather had attained the title of *jinshi*, the highest degree of the imperial examination system, but his ranking among other Qing officials was not very high. At one point he served as assistant to Viceroy Zhang Zhidong of the Jiangxi and Jiangnan regions; later he achieved great things in the business world. The Ding family clan was immense, as were its business endeavors. The other branches of the family were all blessed with numerous children. Ding Wenyu's grandfather had not only left inexhaustible wealth to his children and grandchildren, he had also laid out the most perfect plan to protect this family fortune. There was no lack of talented individuals among Ding Wenyu's father's generation. Those who went into government became high officials. Those who inherited family businesses went on to open textile factories, reeling mills, and flour mills. Some of them went on to become compradors, in which case they worked directly for foreigners. By Ding Wenyu's generation, the field was wide open. For example, his cousin Ding Gongqia had studied military affairs in Japan and was an elder member of the Revolutionary Alliance. After the establishment of the Republic, he started moving around the upper echelons of the military. It was actually because of him that Ding Wenyu first came into contact with Yuchan. Ding Wenyu had another cousin who was one of the founding members of the Chinese Communist Party; then the cards changed hands and he turned his back on the CCP to become a Central Committee member of the Nationalist Party. Ding had yet another cousin who even went so far as to become a leader of the secret anti-Qing organization, the Hongmen Society, for whom he openly recruited members around the Tianjin concessions.

One could say that Ding Wenyu's father's business was like the sun at high noon. During the warlord period he had been the president of the Shanghai branch of the Bank of China, and for a long time he had held an important post at the Ministry of Finance. His sole regret was that his treasured son Wenyu was the only one of his children to survive. His wife gave birth to several children afterward, but none of them made it to adulthood. Ding Wenyu's father had high hopes for his son and paid a pretty penny educating him, but because he spoiled Ding Wenyu too much, in the end Ding failed to live up to his expectations. The higher the hope, the harder one falls when let down. Even after Ding Wenyu had reached adulthood, a day still had not gone by that his old man didn't worry about him. As if Ding Wenyu intentionally wanted to oppose his old man, he constantly did whatever would make his father most upset.

Many thought that his unbelievable pursuit of Yuchan at the age of seventeen was the earliest signal that Ding Wenyu was destined to become a playboy. This was but his first time in the world of women, and already, with no looking back, he was heading straight for disaster. As soon as news got out, Ding Wenyu's father struck like lightning; then, after his temper had quelled a bit, he decided to immediately discontinue the studies of his unreasonable son. Ding's father had his cousin Ding Gongqia accompany him back to Shanghai for a period of self-examination as if he were a criminal. Because there was a direct train line from Shanghai to Nanjing, Ding Wenyu's father had no choice but to hire someone to keep an eye on him. This was to prevent Ding Wenyu from slipping off like a thief back to Nanjing and continuing to accost the pure and innocent Yuchan.

That instance of frenzied and unbridled love almost destroyed Ding Wenyu. Everything quickly progressed almost to the point of no return. Ding Wenyu wasn't eating or drinking and had repeatedly threatened suicide, saying he had decided to sacrifice himself for the woman he loved. His father had taken the strictest measures in guarding him, but Ding Wenyu still managed to gather a hefty sum of money and buy off his guardian. That gave him the chance to board a night train and, just as dawn approached, Ding Wenyu secretly slipped back into Nanjing. He stood for what seemed like forever in the alley across from Yuchan's home. Like a specter, hiding behind an electric pole, Ding insanely awaited the appearance of Yuchan. He held his post there from dawn all the way until the sun disappeared behind the Purple Mountain. In the evening he found a dirty hotel near the Temple of Confucius to stay at. It was a dry autumn night. A fat prostitute cautiously knocked on his hotel room door and slipped in. Noticing that his lips were chapped, she told him that according to Chinese medicine he had too much internal heat and asked him if he needed a woman to help him get rid of some of that excess steam. This being the first time Ding Wenyu had found himself in this type of situation, he was so terrified that he cowered, shivering, and mumbled incoherently, not knowing what to say.

Before being driven away, the fat prostitute consoled him in the most benevolent manner. Gazing at Ding Wenyu's pale face, she left him with some earnest advice: "Listen here, young fellow, there's no need to be afraid. The more you're afraid, the more it proves how bad you really need it."

II

Ding Wenyu first fell in love with Yuyuan's eldest sister Yuchan because of a pair of adorable children. The first of these was Yuyuan, who was a mere six months old, and the second was Yuchan's three-year-old son Tianxi. At the time, Yuchan was relaxing under the shade of a tree watching the two children. Yuyuan was asleep in her rattan cradle, while her three-year-old nephew was on the lush green lawn chasing after a rubber ball. The ball rolled over to the edge of Ding Wenyu's foot and he mischievously stepped on it, keeping it from the grasp of Tianxi.

Tianxi didn't cry, but with all his might he struggled to push Ding Wenyu's foot away—his little face turned bright red with frustration.

It was during this ludicrous scene that Yuchan laid eyes on her maniac pursuer, Ding Wenyu. Ding carried on his game until Tianxi finally lost his temper. He grabbed Ding Wenyu's calf and took a ferocious bite. Ding was in so much pain that he let out a blaring howl. Little Tianxi took advantage of the opportunity to retrieve his ball and, having attained full-scale victory, made his getaway. Yuchan, who was over in the shade reading a book, couldn't help but laugh. She had already silently taken notice of Ding Wenyu's arrival and the fact that his face was red all the way down to his neck.

"Are you the young fellow who just returned from Japan and can't speak anything but Japanese?" Yuchan asked, speaking as if she were addressing a child.

Ding Wenyu was dumbfounded. He did not reply; instead he just stared foolishly at Yuchan.

Yuchan continued, "Hey, can you speak Chinese or not?"

Ding Wenyu flashed Yuchan a childish grin; what an absurd question, of course he understood Chinese. Yuchan didn't really suspect him of not speaking Chinese, she just wanted to find something to tease him about. So this was how everything unwittingly began—neither Ding Wenyu nor Yuchan ever anticipated what would develop. In the beginning everything was quite normal; Yuchan chatted and joked with Ding Wenyu like a big sister would. Out of curiosity, she continuously raised a bunch of questions and Ding truthfully answered each and every one. Since returning home from Japan, he had felt an air of estrangement everywhere he went, but the care Yuchan showed gave him a feeling of extreme closeness. During meals Yuchan had specially arranged for him to sit beside her and, just as if she were taking care of a little brother, she put food on his plate and trotted out what few facts she knew about him to share with everyone at the table. At the dinner table, Ding Wenyu came across as having terrible manners; under the eyes of everyone present, he moved his favorite dish, the sautéed shelled shrimp, right in front of his bowl for himself to feast on.

His cousin Ding Gongqia, who had taken him to the Ren family compound, couldn't help but lecture Ding Wenyu as if he were scolding a child. Although they were first cousins, the twenty-odd-year age gap between them meant that they were of two separate generations. The atmosphere during the meal was extremely upbeat. After scolding his cousin, Ding Gongqia took advantage of the opportunity to tell a few jokes about him. Ding Wenyu was a child who had been spoiled rotten; there was no shortage of material to poke fun at. At the time, Ding Gongqia had a position in the Ministry of Military Affairs of the Northern Warlord government, an idle post that provided a title but no power. The purpose of this visit to his old classmate from his days in Japan was to introduce the Rens to his cousin Ding Wenyu—that way when he came to study in Nanjing he would have a place to go during vacations. Ding Gongqia was also carrying out the orders of the Ministry of Military Affairs, inquiring as to whether or not Ren Bojin had any interest in the position of president of the Baoding Military Academy. Ren Bojin had once received distinction for actions in battle while working with General Cai E in suppressing Yuan Shikai. General Cai E and Ren Bojin had been classmates at the Japanese Military Academy; Cai E was a year above Ren, but they held the same views on the need to construct a modern army for national defense.

It was during that meal that Ding Wenyu first heard Ren Bojin's prediction that China and Japan were bound to clash. As Ren Bojin sipped his southern rice wine, he admitted that Japan had indeed given much aid to China during the past few years. For example, they had provided the breeding ground for the Anti-Qing Alliance and fostered many talented individuals with modern skills; however, the enmity that had developed since the Sino-Japanese War of 1894–1895 was simply too deep. "Moreover," he said, "Japan's ambition is to dominate all of Asia. If they want to attain their goal, they will have no choice but to conquer China first. If China does not quickly develop an army for national defense, the outcome will be unthinkable."

"If in the future war should break out between China and Japan, the decisive battle must take place along the Long-Hai line,"* Ren Bojin added, his analysis carrying a prophetic element. "Ever since ancient times, the area around Xuzhou and Huaihai has been a battlefield. If,

---

*The geographic area that follows the Long-Hai rail line, which runs between the cities of Lianyungang and Lanzhou, passing through Jiangsu, Anhui, Henan, Shaanxi, and Gansu Provinces.

when the time comes, our military cannot defeat the Japanese army there, then we will be forced to move west and wage a protracted war in order to wear them down. Japan is a tiny land mass whose resources cannot sustain a drawn-out conflict."

Twenty years later, Ren Bojin's views were proven completely correct. Ding Gongqia asked Ren Bojin to compare the military strength of China and Japan, encouraging him to speak freely and say whatever was on his mind. With fervor, Ren Bojin expressed all the opinions he had bottled up thus far. Coming to a close, Ren heaved a sigh and exclaimed: "If we were to compare military strength at the time of the Sino-Japanese War, then China attaining victory over Japan wouldn't be completely out of the question. But if we compare the military power of today, then I'm afraid things don't look very promising."

Ding Gongqia asked, "So what you mean, my good brother Bojin, is that a Chinese victory is an impossibility and that we are way out of our league?"

"Now I wouldn't put it like that," Ren Bojin responded. "Comparing military strength is one thing, the will of the people is another. Since the Sino-Japanese War, China has had to pay indemnities, has had its land taken away, and has been forced to cede Formosa. How were the Chinese people able to swallow this? It takes courage for a man to fight for his country, and the sheer number of volunteers alone shows the weight of the people's support for our cause. This is where we have a bit of an advantage. It is a shame that after years of continual fighting among the warlords, the only thing they know how to do is squabble over territory. Meanwhile, Japan's craving to destroy us fails to die. Year after year they build up their military, and besides increasing the power of the army, they are sparing no effort in developing their navy. Because of this, the coming War of Resistance will change from a land assault into three-dimensional warfare on land, air, and sea. When the time comes, Lord only knows just how much of a disadvantage we will be at!"

Ding Wenyu, who had already eaten his fill, stood up and was preparing to do something else when Ding Gongqia held his arm to stop him. Ding Gongqia felt that although his cousin was a mere seventeen-year-old boy, he still had a responsibility to show some interest in the future and fate of his country. Even if he didn't have the least bit of interest, he should still, even if solely out of politeness, listen to Ren Bojin's penetrating analysis.

"When we were studying at the Military Academy, I was constantly thinking that it would be up to our generation to shoulder the responsibility of founding a national defense power capable of protecting our country. In the end, however, if we didn't end up idle at home or washing dirty laundry for the warlords, we simply became warlords ourselves!" Ren Bojin stated that he had no interest in taking the position of president of the Baoding Military Academy. He knew that the Northern Warlord government was fickle and could change at any moment, so if he went he would be a mere puppet with no real power or influence.

Twenty years later, the Second Sino-Japanese War would fully break out; Ding Wenyu, thinking back to Ren Bojin's words at the dinner table that night, couldn't help admiring the uncanny accuracy of his predictions. In Ding Wenyu's mind, Ren Bojin was eternally an elegant Confucian general in civilian clothes, having absolutely nothing in common with those philistine soldiers and officers whom one often came across in the streets. Never in his life did Ding Wenyu feel any genuine interest in the affairs of country and state. As Ding Gongqia and Ren Bojin continued with their armchair strategizing, Ding Wenyu stopped Yuchan and wouldn't let her get up. Since he had to sit there and listen to this pointless chatter, he had the right to request that Yuchan share in his torture. After a while he finally leaned over and whispered in Yuchan's ear that they should find a way to get out of there. Once again Yuchan could not help but giggle. Her laugh had an indescribable softness, which left a rather green Ding Wenyu with a feeling of extreme intimacy. From beside her earlobe, he smelled a particularly feminine fragrance. Once this scent made its way into his nose, he lost control of his senses and came a hair away from planting a kiss right on Yuchan's neck.

The meal had already reached its tail end and aside from Yuchan and Ding Wenyu, only Ding Gongqia and Ren Bojin were left at the table. Ding Wenyu suddenly took the liberty of patting Yuchan on the behind. This scared the wits out of Yuchan, but she noticed that her father was still speaking and Ding Gongqia kept nodding his head—they obviously hadn't the smallest clue as to what had just occurred. Ding Wenyu pressed his hand against her ass and wouldn't remove it. Yuchan didn't really take this childish gesture to heart; she simply extended her hand and lightly pinched Ding Wenyu's leg, warning him not to go overboard. Yuchan was by no means a frivolous woman, and then-seventeen-year-old Ding

Wenyu didn't even know what it meant to flirt. At the time he was enraptured by the poems of Byron and Schiller and occasionally read some depressing Japanese romance novels. One thing he never imagined was that his first love would occur so unexpectedly—it was as if a spark suddenly met fuel and violently ignited. But just as seventeen-year-old Ding Wenyu was preparing to fall in love with a woman, he found himself walking right into a battlefield.

III

In the ensuing days, Ding Wenyu became completely ensnared in love. Long before he set foot in the Ren household, he had heard Ding Gongqia and his father discussing Yuchan. Ding Gongqia had once wanted to bring the Ding and Ren families together in marriage; he wanted his oldest son to marry Yuchan, but Ding Wenyu's uncle had his own plans for his grandson's marriage arrangements. Because of this, Ding Gongqia felt that he had let his old friend down somewhat. Yuchan's later marriage seemed far from happy—she married an officer from Sichuan who within five years had already taken two concubines. Young Ding Wenyu's first love was born of his duty-bound feeling that Yuchan should be rescued from her unfortunate marriage.

During their days as guests at the Ren household, it was arranged that Ding Gongqia and his cousin would stay in the guest room in the eastern wing. Ding Gongqia and Ren Bojin had endless things to catch up about, leaving Ding Wenyu to spend the majority of his time on the lawn chatting with Yuchan. He childishly played with little Tianxi and with the utmost seriousness consoled Yuyuan who, in her rattan cradle, had just awakened in tears. Yuyuan's wet nurse was always asking for vacation time so she could slip away, with the result that the responsibility of taking care of Yuyuan fell on Yuchan's shoulders. When he thought about the fact that six-month-old Yuyuan was actually Yuchan's kid sister, Ding Wenyu couldn't help but feel it was quite hilarious. He watched Yuchan holding Yuyuan in her arms as three-year-old Tianxi played mischievously beside them. He said that at first he thought that Yuchan was the mother of both children.

Yuchan said that she herself often had that same misconception. She told Ding Wenyu that ever since *he* had shown up, she at times even felt that she had three children! She told him that although he was just a few years younger than she and could have been her little brother, he acted more like the big brother little Tianxi never had! All Yuchan was trying to do by exaggerating their age difference was add a layer of protection to their intimacy. Under the pretense of her seniority, Yuchan mistakenly believed that the all-around care and closeness she expressed was completely without fault, which meant of course that Ding Wenyu's bold flirting was also not necessarily too impertinent. Just as Ding Wenyu hadn't the slightest experience when it came to women, so Yuchan had not the faintest understanding of the complicated nature of men. During the era in which she lived, a man's taking a concubine was a symbol of his professional success. Although deep down Yuchan didn't like it, she was never allowed to express her dissatisfaction. Her husband was perfectly justified in his visits to brothels—he could even take his dirty case of gonorrhea back home as a trophy of battle and share it with his wife—however, his wife wasn't allowed to reveal even an ounce of discontent.

Who could have thought that things would evolve so quickly? Perhaps it was due to the hot weather. People become light-headed with the sudden onset of a heat wave and fail to take the consequences of their actions into consideration. After lunch, when everyone was taking their afternoon naps and Yuchan had finally lulled the uneasy sleeper Tianxi into dreamland, she made a futile effort at coaxing Yuyuan to sleep. As if the barely six-month-old Yuyuan sensed that something was going to happen, she opened her eyes wide and hung on, resisting sleep. Yuchan sat hopelessly beside the cradle, gently rocking it. Ding Wenyu was pacing back and forth beside them, as if reciting an incantation in hope that Yuyuan would hurry up and close her eyes. Then, completely inadvertently, he caught a fleeting glimpse of Yuchan's full breasts under her open collar. At exactly that moment, Yuchan raised her head as if she sensed Ding Wenyu's eyes on her. Ding Wenyu felt extremely embarrassed, and in order to hide his abashment he, without even being taught, resorted to a boldly awkward yet effective move. From across the cradle he abruptly grabbed Yuchan's face and began to kiss his way from between her eyebrows down to her mouth.

Without question, Yuchan was scared silly: for the longest time she had not the slightest reaction. When Ding Wenyu's lips finally reached Yuchan's mouth, he sucked hard as if he were slurping up some kind of fluid—it made a terribly strange sound. Only when Yuyuan suddenly cried from her cradle did Yuchan finally snap out of her trance. She forcefully pulled his hands off her and pushed him back.

"Who could imagine that someone as young as you could be so disgusting?" Yuchan said, her face turning red. She continued to rock the cradle as she spoke with indignation.

Although Ding Wenyu was at a loss as to how to respond, he didn't at all regret his actions.

Yuchan added, "Dear heavens! You're but a child!"

Ding Wenyu resolutely responded, "No, I'm *not* a child." In order to emphasize the power of his words, he made an extremely important addition to his statement. "You may not believe me, but I have already decided that I am going to marry you. I've already started to plan everything." He didn't know what he should say after that, but he knew that if he wanted to cover up his embarrassment and awkwardness, his sole option would be to slip away like a child after making trouble before Yuchan chased him away. Knowing the right time to retreat is just as important as knowing the right time to attack—and Ding Wenyu indeed played this move quite beautifully.

During dinner that night, Lady Miyako was the first to discover that something was wrong. She realized that Yuchan wasn't sitting beside Ding Wenyu as she usually did, and during the course of the entire meal neither of them uttered a single word. They didn't sit there in their own little world laughing and gossiping as before, nor did Ding Wenyu unscrupulously help himself to serving after serving of the dishes he liked. Yuchan no longer took care of him like a kid brother. The two of them didn't even dare to make eye contact. Ding Gongqia and Ren Bojin continued their broad discussion, comparing military strength among the various warlords and predicting the impending tangled warfare and its outcome. Two weeks earlier in Beiping, the pigtailed general Zhang Xun had given his support to restoring the abdicated Manchu emperor, Aisin-Gioro Pu Yi—a preposterous farce that lasted just twelve days before becoming a ridiculous page in history. On the other hand, on the seventeenth of that month, Sun Yat-sen had gone from Shanghai to Guangzhou aboard the naval warship *Sea Trea-sure*. There, under the protection of the southwest warlords Tang Jiyao and Lu Rongting, he took the position of "grand marshal" of a new constitutional government. Ren Bojin was very fond of Sun Yat-sen's political stances, but he deeply regretted the fact that Sun was without any truly outstanding military personnel and lacked an army that would stay loyal to him.

"Sun Yat-sen relies too heavily on the military power of others, and sooner or later the day will come when he will pay a heavy price for this." Ren Bojin had seemingly already predicted the outcome of the following year, when Sun Yat-sen would be driven out of power. The very same warlords who had lent support in raising him to power would force him to resign his position. "He should realize that while he is using others, others are actually using him as well."

After Yuchan left the table, Ding Wenyu immediately set down his chopsticks and followed her like a pale ghost. It was already completely dark out, and Yuchan realized the seriousness of the situation. With deliberate intentions to escape entanglement with Ding Wenyu, she made the firm decision not to give him even the slightest opportunity to be alone with her. Ding Wenyu followed behind her, but just as he was about to say something, Yuchan instantly got up to go somewhere else. She rushed into her third sister Yujiao's room and went together with Yujiao into the bathroom and sat with her on the bamboo mat in the courtyard to cool off. Thick-skinned and brazen, Ding Wenyu tried to enter into their conversation, but Yuchan sternly replied: "This is girl talk; it is not appropriate that you stay and listen."

Not until the middle of the night did Ding Wenyu get an opportunity to say everything that he had to say. Taking no heed of the consequences, he rushed to the open window of Yuchan's bedroom and rapped on the glass. When he was certain that Yuchan knew what he was doing and could verify that she was listening, he whispered in the most childish of manners: "You are the only one for me!"

At first Yuchan hadn't planned on responding to him, but she was afraid that if she didn't say anything Ding Wenyu might stand there outside the window all night like an idiot. Now that things had progressed to this level, Ding Wenyu was capable of anything. The whole situation was already out of line, and the Ren compound was crowded with chatterbox busybodies—on a humid, sleepless night like that, heaven only knew if anyone was eavesdropping. Yuchan hesitated for quite some time before she finally came out with a clear-headed response: "Cut the nonsense. Right now the best thing for you to do is to leave here as soon as possible."

Satisfied with her response, Ding Wenyu returned to his room and went to sleep. That night he slept like a baby. In his dream he discovered he had already transformed into a true man through and through; he had become father of a slew of children, a family tyrant who could order Yuchan around as he wished. The next day he slept quite late, but the first thing he did upon waking was decide that he must take another step in conveying his inner feelings to Yuchan. In order not to leave her with the misconception that he was just playing around, Ding Wenyu decided that he would restate his resolution to marry her. But in the end his avowal came to naught; Yuchan had absolutely no interest in listening. Just as he began, Yuchan rudely cut him off. In fact this type of avowal was completely unnecessary. Perhaps saying that he wanted to avow himself to Yuchan wouldn't be as accurate as saying he wanted to avow himself to *himself*. And saying that he wanted to prove to Yuchan that he indeed loved her would not be as accurate as saying that he wanted to prove to *himself* that he truly loved her.

In actuality, Ding Wenyu's intense love for Yuchan became uncontrollably "intense" only after meeting with rejection. Yuchan had the impression that Ding Wenyu was nothing more than an excessive version of *The Dream of the Red Chamber*'s Jia Baoyu, falling head over heels for any girl who looked halfway decent. Although she felt that Ding was just playing a game with her, in reality the only one playing a game was Yuchan. Deep down there isn't a single woman who would dislike a man taking interest in her, whether a white-haired old man or a boy without whiskers. Yuchan did not hesitate to reject Ding Wenyu, stubbornly resisting his forward attacks. Under Ding Wenyu's overbearing offense, she became even more resolute, leaving even less room to stretch the rules. There was no way that she would let the pranks of a little child go to her head and bring her reputation down to the dirt.

In the end, Ding Gongqia apologetically took Ding Wenyu away. Originally his intention had been to find some close friends to look after Ding Wenyu while he studied at Southeast University. This farcical affair, however, made it so that Ding Gongqia didn't have the face to visit the Ren compound for a long time thereafter. Actually there was no need for him to be apologetic, because there wasn't a single person in the Ren house who disliked Ding Wenyu. All along, they simply felt he was a headstrong child and joked about his ridiculous actions. No one except Yuchan could have imagined just how far Ding Wenyu would go. And even supposing that Yuchan couldn't really make heads or tails of Ding's actions, she had already been scared enough by him—ever since the jokes started getting out, she never again had the courage to be caught alone with Ding Wenyu.

One after another, Ding Wenyu wrote a series of nauseating letters to Yuchan; as soon as these came into her hands, she tore them up right there in front of the deliverer. However, on account of Yuchan's stubbornness, Ding Wenyu became even more insane. He not only believed that Yuchan's behavior illustrated that she was a woman with moral integrity but also thought that this was her way of testing his love. Only after love has passed through a trial by fire, withstanding the hardships of the frost and wind, does it truly become sweet. Never has love easily attained been true love. Like a small bird escaped from its cage, Ding Wenyu flew back to Nanjing on the night train. The next day, when one of the Rens' servants reported seeing Ding Wenyu hiding behind the electric pole across the street, the entire Ren household was thrown into disarray. The first decision Yuchan made was that this incident must be concealed from her father. Three days later, Ding Wenyu was still waiting across the street, and Yuchan was forced to make a second cruelhearted decision. She had one of the servants inform Ding Wenyu, who had now fallen into absolute agony, that if he did not immediately return to his father's side in Shanghai, the Ren family would contact the police and have them take Ding back.

Like a wanted man, Ding Wenyu desperately took to his heels, returning to the filthy hotel room where he had stayed on his first night. And when that fat prostitute, whom he had earlier driven away in the midst of panic, once again entered his room, he miserably covered his face and broke down in tears. The fat prostitute said, "Child, what's making you so sad? Did one of your parents die or something?"

Ding Wenyu wanted to tell that fat prostitute to get the hell out, but his weeping was too strong and he couldn't utter a single word.

45

The fat prostitute continued: "What's there to be so upset about? If you want to talk about sadness, look at me. I'm someone who is truly miserable."

Ding Wenyu raised his head and gazed at the chunky hooker through his tears. Her face had a thick layer of rouge and her red lipstick was applied unevenly. She had two buck teeth and an empty look in her eyes. Knowing with one look that he was an inexperienced little rooster, she winked at him and said in an affected manner:

"We both want different things—one of us wants love, one of us wants money. Child, what I've got here is love, and a young master like you doesn't look like he's short on money. Just listen to me and I'll guarantee that you'll feel so good that for the rest of your life you won't know what sadness is!"

IV

On Ding Wenyu's first night with a woman, he felt nothing *but* sadness—not an ounce of pleasure. The chunky prostitute was after the money in Ding Wenyu's pocket, but Ding Wenyu wasn't after anything; he simply didn't know how to stop her. As far as Ding Wenyu was concerned, this surprise attack would forever be a most horrid memory. As if she were slitting a chicken's throat and slicing open its stomach, the fat hooker forcefully tore open the buttons on Ding's school uniform and pulled his shirt open to each side. She then pulled off his leather belt. As if skinning a frog, she skillfully slid down his pants—all the way to his ankles. Before Ding Wenyu was even prepared, the fat prostitute was already straddled on top of him.

Every bone in Ding Wenyu's body was sore after rubbing against that hard plank bed. What the hooker displayed was far from the consummate technique and perfect skill that she had boasted of. Actually the two of them were simply consummating a deal that neither was particularly eager to fulfill; their movements were crude, dull, and without even the slightest hint of passion. Ding Wenyu felt like he could barely breathe. By the time he could finally heave a deep breath, everything had already come to a pitiful close. It ended as it began—actually it was over *before* it even began. The hefty hooker did not, however, just take his money and instantly hit the road; completely out of sympathy, she said that she would be willing to stay. For absolutely no extra charge she would agree to help Ding get through the remaining hours of that long, seemingly endless night. But this time Ding Wenyu seemed to finally strengthen up and took a stand. Without the slightest hesitation, Ding asked her to leave immediately. He also told her to close the door behind her because he didn't even want to get out of bed. Until sunrise he lay in that same position. As soon as dawn arrived, he turned over, got out of bed, and without even taking his luggage, grabbed a rickshaw and went directly to the train station.

All at once, seventeen-year-old Ding Wenyu had grown up. After he got back to Shanghai, his frowning father had a serious man-to-man talk with Ding Wenyu, who was still in a trancelike state. His father realized that Shanghai and Nanjing were too close, and his best option would be to have his son fly far and high, off to a distant land. During their talk, he asked him whether or not he would be willing to study abroad in Europe. Ding Wenyu's father thought that his son, tortured and blinded by love, would flatly refuse. He had already thought out all kinds of strategies to force him to go. However, to his surprise, Ding Wenyu not only agreed to go but eagerly asked his father how soon he could leave.

"Approximately how long does the ship take to get there? I hope I don't get seasick this time," Ding Wenyu said nonchalantly. It was as if his sole worry about leaving China was whether or not he would vomit all over the steamer like a drunken idiot.

Many years later, Ding Wenyu's father would deeply regret driving his son out of the country, but at the time he felt this was the best cure for his lovesickness. Ding Wenyu decided to go to France to study. His surprised father asked him why he didn't want to go to Germany or England. Ding's father felt that since his son already had an impressive command of German and his English wasn't bad, he should probably go to England, where he would be able to improve his English. Ding Wenyu, however, told his father that the reason he wanted to go to France was to study a completely new language. Only something entirely new could have been sufficient to occupy Ding Wenyu enough to pull him out of the quagmire of love. In the arena of foreign languages, there was no question that Ding Wenyu was a genius. Years later, the languages he had mastered would prove to be a constant marvel to all those who were acquainted with him. Even in his wildest dreams, his father never would have imagined that his son would spend twelve years in Europe and another five in America. Seventeen years later, when Ding returned to China, he was proficient in virtually every European language. That was because for seventeen years, besides continually studying foreign tongues like a talking parrot, Ding Wenyu didn't do anything at all respectable.

During his years abroad, Ding Wenyu broke free of all fetters and became an all-out playboy. In fact, in the short month before he went abroad, Ding Wenyu had already virtually erased all traces of Yuchan from his memory and seduced the French tutor his father had hired. His young female French teacher, Marceline, was the wife of an employee at a foreign firm in Shanghai; she was fervent, stunning, and didn't take well to rules. Ding Wenyu's father's intention in hiring her was to provide his son with a rudimentary understanding of the French language before he went to France. In the end, however, Ding Wenyu not only showed an outstanding aptitude at learning French, he also learned something about French women.

One week after the October Revolution broke out in Russia, Ding Wenyu boarded a ship and set out for France. On board the vessel, people from various countries heatedly discussed the potential outcome of the revolution. Ding Wenyu caught sight of a beautiful, young, single French girl who looked just like Marceline. She must have been about the same age as Marceline, and from behind you could easily mistake them for the same person. Although in an extremely short time he had had sexual experiences with two unusual women, two mature women from different countries at that, Ding Wenyu was at heart still a shy kid—he had yet to get to the point where he could shamelessly flirt with women of all shapes, sizes, and colors. What he thought about most was still love—he wanted to love someone, just as he longed to be truly loved. In his heart, love was still an almost holy word that could not be trampled. He firmly believed that he would be able to die for a woman he genuinely loved.

While Ding Wenyu was aboard the steamer, he momentarily thought back to Yuchan and felt a kind of unspeakable perplexity about all the things he had done. The long sea journey was extremely dull. The occasional sound of the steam whistle blowing was the only sign that the boat was still moving. One evening, as the boat crawled directly toward the setting sun, in the ocean dyed a deep red, the French girl who resembled Marceline walked over toward Ding and greeted him in pidgin English. Ding Wenyu was caught by surprise, and a string of strange thoughts passed through his mind. He smiled and nodded at the French girl, and suddenly realized that there was no way he could ever die for Yuchan. That was not because he held his own life to be particularly important; it was due rather to the sudden new inspiration brought on by the beautiful sea and this stunning French girl. Everything had just begun, his ocean of life was boundless, and he suddenly realized that he could forget Yuchan without even the slightest regret.

The French girl's name was exactly the same as that of Louis the Sixteenth's queen, sent to the guillotine during the French Revolution. Ding Wenyu never understood why she should have a name like that. During their long, floating journey on the sea, Ding Wenyu and the French girl became quite close. He even simplified her name, Marie Antoinette, by combining the first and last syllables, "Ma-te"—it sounded just like the popular Chinese curse word "Ma-de," or "Your mother!" At first their common language was English, which both could speak haltingly, but Ding Wenyu soon requested that Ma-te use French as much as possible. Each time Ma-te said a word, Ding Wenyu learned a word. At first, this primitive method of learning made her feel very uncomfortable, but she quickly grew accustomed to it.

Ding Wenyu's extraordinary talent for grasping languages deeply surprised Ma-te. Perhaps it was on account of his foundation in German and English that his progress in French was so rapid. It was obvious that Ma-te was quite taken with his studious spirit—she taught him tirelessly, and they spoke English less and less frequently. Occasionally Ding Wenyu would completely misunderstand something that she said, but these mistakes were in themselves also extremely entertaining. While on the deck, effusive Ma-te often clapped her hands and bawled with laughter at something Ding had said, causing everyone to turn and stare at them.

One day a Chinese businessman on the same ship discreetly grabbed hold of Ding Wenyu to express his admiration of Ding's romantic exploits. He modestly asked Ding to teach him the secret to his success and asked what method Ding used to win her heart. The look on Ding Wenyu's face turned a bit ugly; although the Chinese businessman didn't have any ill intentions in asking these questions, his words were indeed a kind of insult. The Chinese businessman seemed to look at the lively and vivacious Ma-te as nothing better than one of those western prostitutes in the Shanghai concession areas who made their living selling their flesh. Getting an inch and going for the mile, the businessman even asked Ding about the probability of *his* getting into bed with Ma-te—he even brazenly expressed his willingness to cut Ding an introduction fee. Beside himself with anger, Ding Wenyu spit in the Chinese businessman's face. The other foreigners on the ship couldn't figure out what conflict had arisen between these two Chinese; they all glared at them with a look of disdain. Because of his close relationship with Ma-te, more than a few of the lonely men on board the ship harbored an indescribable hostility toward Ding Wenyu.

While he was in France, Ma-te became Ding Wenyu's closest friend of the opposite sex. Difficult as it may have been for others to believe, they always maintained a purely platonic friendship. For a long time, it seemed as if there were but a thin piece of paper between them and with one puncture the floodgates would naturally pour open. Examining his conscience later, Ding Wenyu would realize that of all the females he knew after Yuchan and before Yuyuan, Ma-te was the sole woman that he could ever have been capable of loving. The reason he never punctured that piece of thin paper was not that he didn't love her, and even less that he didn't want to—on the contrary, he loved her too much, he wanted her too much. Sometimes not tearing that thin piece of paper can be the most beautiful thing in the world. Once you puncture it, all of the things that were once so gorgeous and enchanting disappear like the wind. Before Ma-te married another man, Ding Wenyu often wandered the streets and alleys of Paris with her, the two friends strolling freely without destination. Their walks not only enabled Ding Wenyu to become familiar with Paris, they also lured him into a romance with that city imbued with the spirit of freedom. For many years, Ding Wenyu's relationship with Ma-te was especially peculiar: the intimacy of their friendship grew, but still they never once crossed the line between friendship and romance. Later Ding Wenyu also became great friends with Ma-te's husband, Mirabeau—the two of them kept no secrets from each other. Moreover, Ma-te's first son gave Ding Wenyu the nickname *"le lapin chinois,"* or "Chinese Rabbit," because the first present he gave the child was a furry little rabbit. After Ma-te gave birth, Ding would never visit them empty-handed; he would always bring flowers for Mate, a bottle of wine for Mirabeau, or some kind of toy for their children. Their children loved the toys Ding brought so much that they never put them down.

During his stay in Europe, Paris was the center of Ding Wenyu's activities. He traversed virtually every inch of Europe's mainland, studying languages like mad at every top European university. In order to quickly master each language, he expanded his realm of study from the classroom to the entire society. Roaming all around like a vagrant, he learned the real, living language of the people at the seaports and train stations, in the hotels, and at the whorehouses. Because his method of study was so effective, he never took to heart the importance of a western university diploma or degree. He spent a full seventeen years abroad, during which he registered for classes at several famous universities in Europe and America, but not a single school was able to entice him enough to settle down, finish his studies, and get a degree. For a rich kid like Ding Wenyu, there was absolutely no need for a western diploma to adorn his appearance.

Ding Wenyu made the acquaintance of a wide range of world-famous cultural personages during his time abroad. Many of these people had yet to make any kind of name for themselves. He crossed paths with America's Ernest Hemingway, Russia's Vladimir Nabokov, and Argentina's Jorge Luis Borges, and on different occasions, Ding Wenyu had chatted with these three writers from different countries who would later become famous. The interesting thing was that these three men of completely different literary styles were all born the same year—they were just one year older than Ding Wenyu, and just like him, they were all foreigners in Paris, this city of freedom. Ding Wenyu even paid a visit to the poet Erza Pound, the representative figure of the avant-garde literary movement of the twenties who had a very deep interest in China and even translated selected Tang poems and *The Analects*. That day, Pound was in high spirits, speaking endlessly with Ding about another outstanding poet, Yeats. Because Pound had served as Yeats's secretary, he would often have to recite Yeats's poems in public forums. Pound told Ding Wenyu how on one occasion he had tried to prevent Yeats from printing a play; but instead of beating around the bush, he told Yeats flat out that the play was pure rubbish. Stubborn as a nail, Yeats still published his play, but he added a preface at the beginning saying, "Erza Pound said this is rubbish." Ding Wenyu was left with a wonderful impression of Pound. Another figure who left a deep impression upon him was Jean-Paul Sartre, who was then still a student at L'Ecole normale supérieure. During a student theater production, Sartre played the role of the dislikable principal Lanson. His acting was terrible, but the lines he recited were brilliant. Someone told Ding Wenyu that the lines were written by Sartre himself; they said that this guy was a brilliant student with an extremely keen interest in philosophy.

For a period of time, Pablo Picasso's studio was on the street next to the one where Ding lived. Moreover, when another outstanding painter, Amedeo Modigliani, died of tuberculosis and his model/lover drowned herself in misery, Ding Wenyu personally witnessed the scene when they pulled her body out of the river. The body, guarded by police, attracted a crowd of spectators who made all kinds of frivolous comments about the woman. Ding Wenyu couldn't see what was so captivating and beautiful about that dead model, nor could he understand what was so wonderful about the works of this Modigliani character, who would later be heralded as a genius—the only thing that shook him was this model's obstinate decision. To sacrifice oneself for love is a choice of almost indescribable wonder. What Ding Wenyu couldn't figure out was, given that this man was loved so deeply by another, what would it have been like if the tables had been turned? If that model had met with some misfortune, what would Modigliani have done?

Whenever the stiff academic atmosphere at Oxford, Cambridge, Berlin, or Leipzig brought Ding Wenyu to the point of suffocation, he would sneak back to Paris to breath the fresh air of freedom. Paris in the twenties and thirties was a paradise for artists, and Ding Wenyu ran into many Chinese who had come there to study art. At a small inn on the bank of the Seine River, he had, on more than one occasion, taken Xu Beihong and his wife to dinner. He also treated Zhang Daofan, who would later become one of the most important Nationalist officials, and Chen Yi, later the field marshal for the Chinese Communist Party, to coffee. The majority of Chinese foreign students in Europe were quite poor, and generous Ding Wenyu became the one on whom these starving students often relied to fill their bellies. Amid their happy laughter and chatter, they would drag Ding into a small inn like he was a wanted man; then, as if they were beating down a local tyrant and dividing his land, they spent every last franc in Ding's pocket. Those students without anything to wear would even go so far as to take the clothes right off his back and then, without hesitation, leave their own pawn tickets with Ding to redeem. Without exception, all of the Chinese students in Europe at the time had some dealings with pawnbrokers—a Chinese foreign student who didn't have to borrow money to get by wasn't a true foreign student. Study under adversity created a group of rare talents. Some of those people, who at the time couldn't have been more inconspicuous, took like fish to water upon going home to China. One after another they all distinguished themselves in the political arena and embarked on glorious official careers.

One day Ding Wenyu went along with a few artsy types to visit the studio of a French painter who was just starting to get a little notice. They wanted to see just how this painter approached his work. But that artist didn't paint a thing; full of zest, he simply watched as his models paced back and forth. The two naked, blonde girls walked around that narrow space unconstrained, while the painter remained still and watched them; then he would suddenly clap his hands to indicate that he wanted the models to hold their positions. With his eyes wide open, he would stare nervously at them, his gaze not wavering from the bodies of the two models. Then after a while he would wave his hands for the models to continue walking. The interesting thing was that this artist allowed people to watch him observing his models but firmly refused to let them watch him work after he picked up his brush.

"The crux of the issue is first getting a picture in your mind." As he was on the street leaving the studio, Ding Wenyu couldn't help but think back to the words the painter had just uttered. Years later, this sentence would still resonate in Ding's mind.

Paris in early summer was easily enough to cheer someone up; beautiful French girls waited for the trolley as Ding and his friends stood by the station trying to decide where to go for dinner. It was then that a couple of Chinese students suddenly appeared, quickly approaching the station. They exchanged greetings with Ding Wenyu and his artist friends, some of whom knew each other. Among that group of Chinese students who rushed by, the handsome young fellow with bright piercing eyes was Zhou Enlai; the short young man beside him who kept looking all around was

Deng Xiaoping. Ding Wenyu did not have a deep impression of these students who would later become two of the most famous and important figures in the history of the Chinese Communist Party. In his diary he just took note of their names, but he never again mentioned them.

V

Only in the summer of 1934 when Ding Wenyu once again set foot in the Shanghai seaport did he finally realize that it had been seventeen years since he had been home. Adding the five years he had been in Japan, the days of his life spent in his motherland didn't even come close to his time spent abroad. A crowd of people from Shanghai surrounded him, twitting and jabbering away in Shanghai dialect. As far as Ding Wenyu was concerned, China had once again become a strange place. Ding Wenyu couldn't understand Shanghainese, nor did he have any plans to learn it—even though with his special talent at learning languages and lingos, picking up this dialect would be a snap. It seemed as if everyone was trying to be the first one off the ship as they all pushed toward the exit. Ding Wenyu stood on the deck in hesitation, unsure if he should follow the crowd out. Suddenly he caught sight of his father, who had aged so much that Ding barely recognized him. His father had brought Ding Wenyu's fiancée to the port to welcome him—this was the welcome home gift Ding's father had prepared for him.

Nothing could have been more ridiculous than Ding Wenyu's marriage. While he was abroad, marriage never once crossed his mind. He never felt he was short on women; they were simply too plentiful a commodity, and he had long grown accustomed to having relations with women from all different countries. Ding Wenyu never bragged about how many women he had slept with—he already had enough bad and eccentric habits in this department. To use the word "decadent" to describe Ding Wenyu would be quite appropriate; he adored the new and despised the old and had interest in women of every skin color and nationality. Whenever he traveled in Europe he would go all out in his search for local prostitutes and, like lightning, he would become familiar with the slang and double-talk used between the whores and their johns. Ding Wenyu was also an expert at picking up unscrupulous women on vacation. With one look, he could pick out which woman might be his next prey, and then score a quick victory—his arrow was rarely shot in vain. Ding Wenyu had a deep understanding of the importance of timing: he would never waste time, and he was even less likely to carelessly go in for the kill at a rash moment.

Ding Wenyu took full advantage of his time flirting with women to improve his foreign-language proficiency and correct inaccurately pronounced words. For him, picking up women was like killing two birds with one stone. No matter how secretive he tried to be, news of his lewd actions still broadly circulated among the other Chinese students, and there was no way to keep this information from reaching his father's ears. Because of his son's wild behavior, this banking tycoon was at his wit's end. He had attempted to force his son home by cutting his funding, but fearing that Ding Wenyu would starve to death on the streets of some foreign country, he quickly changed his mind. Never in his life was Ding Wenyu short on cash—it was without question that with no money, a rich kid like him would run into trouble. All Ding Wenyu's father had was this one precious son, so no matter what his son might do, he still did not dare take such a big risk. After Ding Wenyu passed his thirtieth birthday, his father began to fret over his marriage. He searched everywhere for prospects and never stopped sending his overseas son photos of potential mates. As for those glossy, near-identical head shots taken by the photography studio, Ding Wenyu usually simply threw them away without a second glance. That's because Ding could not imagine how a useless person like him could ever start a family, raise kids, and be tied down by a woman he didn't even know—it would be the death of him!

The force that impelled Ding Wenyu to return to China was his father's serious illness. After his father became ill, he wrote a sincere letter lamenting that before he got to the terminal stage, he wanted to inform his distant son Ding Wenyu of his condition. "By the time this letter gets to you," wrote Mr. Ding to his son, "it is very possible that I will no longer be with you." He wasn't that concerned about seeing his son before he died—it didn't matter. There wasn't enough time anyway; back then airplanes still couldn't fly overseas, so by the time Ding Wenyu received the letter and took a ship home, everything would already be over. Ding Wenyu's father told his son that during the worst period of his illness, his sole regret was that his headstrong son was unable to understand the pressing desire of a critically ill man to have a grandson to hold. His son had grown up and his wings were stiff, so he didn't want to force him to do anything that he did not want to; nor did he want to insist that his son carry on his career in banking. As an enlightened old man, Ding Wenyu's father only wished that his son could have a respectable marriage and a grandson to bring this old man comfort. He was already old and there were many things in the world that he could not care less about; he just hoped that he could live to see the continuation of his line of the family tree.

For the very first time, Ding's father's letter gave rise to intense thoughts of home in his wandering son. Ding Wenyu discovered that tears were streaming down his face as he read the letter. He thought back to that photo his father had sent him one year before, in which his father looked as if he were forcing himself to lift up his spirit. He had indeed grown old, and his eyes no longer sparkled like they used to. The longing for home within Ding's heart could no longer be suppressed and changed into a kind of indescribable sorrow. "I should really get the fuck home!" After he uttered this rather vulgar outburst, he buried his head in his arms and began to bawl his heart out. The next day he rushed down to the cable office and had an express telegram sent to his father. In the telegram he told his father that he was not only going to buy a ticket for the next steamer home but also would marry the woman of his father's choosing. One week before Ding Wenyu arrived back in Shanghai, virtually all of the Shanghai newspapers as well as the two main papers in the capital of Nanjing were running eye-catching announcements: after completing his studies abroad, Ding Wenyu was to return home and marry the daughter of the "Steel King," Hao Ruyong—a pair of one-inch-square photos of the bride and groom even showed up conspicuously on the front pages of these newspapers.

Ding Wenyu's marriage caused quite a sensation, but it wasn't Ding Wenyu who stole the limelight at the wedding banquet—it was Ding's father. The ceremony was held at a luxurious high-class hotel. Because Ding Wenyu's mother had passed away while he was abroad, his father had already taken three concubines. It was plain to see that Ding Wenyu's antics had, for a time, led his father to lose all hope in his son—and so the old man wanted to give one last throw at producing himself another heir. During that momentous wedding banquet, none of his concubines displayed the slightest willingness to yield. Each was gorgeously dressed and beautifully made up, and each greeted guests as if she were the mistress of the house. It was impossible for any of the guests not to gossip about this trio, and naturally the topic of conversation eventually made its way back to Ding Wenyu's father. There were those who envied the old man for being surrounded by beauties like that, and then there were those who sighed as they exclaimed: "Too much love potion is bad for one's health. Keeping those three satisfied must not be an easy task!" Although Ding Wenyu's father was radiant with smiles and glowing with happiness, it was without question that he was nearly at the end of his rope. Though he had barely drunk any alcohol, as the ceremony was coming to a close, he was already walking in circles like a senile old man and stammering when he spoke.

Ding Wenyu wasn't short of experience making small talk with women he had never met, but before his bride Peitao, it was as if his hands were bound and his feet were tied—for the first time he was at a complete loss as to what to do. The bride was a straight-laced woman, different from those loose women who make a living selling their flesh— and Ding Wenyu was beside himself as to how he should deal with her. That year Peitao was twenty-three years old, and in light of the tendency to "marry early" during the 1930s, at her age she was no spring chicken. Already on her not-so-terribly-striking face, you could see that she was a beauty past her prime. But just as Ding Wenyu felt dissatisfied with her from day one, Peitao also felt that Ding Wenyu was a far cry from her knight in shining armor. From their first night in the bridal chamber, both parties were left with a nightmarish impression. An inexperienced virgin like Peitao simply left an old hand like Ding Wenyu at a complete loss. Failure after failure left both parties irritated. When morning came, baggy-eyed Ding Wenyu dragged himself out of bed; he looked so bad that anyone who laid eyes on him was astonished. That day he had several perfunctory engagements—he had to accompany his father to call on a few big shots, pay a visit to his father's bank to see the employees, and attend the opening ceremony of a new trading company. At bedtime, Ding Wenyu was dead on his feet and didn't utter a single word; he simply collapsed on the bed and was out like a light. Ding was snoring loudly, and in the middle of the night he awoke to discover that Peitao had turned on the light and was glaring at him with a most unfriendly gaze.

"Did you get enough sleep?" Peitao coldly asked him. Then, even more detached and bitter, she continued, "You've had your sleep, now it's *my* turn to get some shuteye!"

Ding Wenyu knew that for the remainder of the night neither Peitao nor he got any real sleep. No matter how Ding Wenyu tried to humor her, Peitao didn't say a word to him for three days straight. Never had Ding come across such a haughty and spoiled little missy as she. Her attitude during their honeymoon wasn't much better. Ding Wenyu didn't know what he had done to offend her. In public she displayed excellent manners but as soon as she and Ding were alone, her face immediately clouded over. It was as if she was eternally looking down upon Ding Wenyu; no matter what she said, it always came out sour and sharp-tongued. Even making love was no exception; she simply lay there as if fulfilling some kind of obligation. She received him without the slightest reaction, as if she were asleep.

"From now on when you do that thing, I'm sorry but would you please turn off the light?" One time, just as things were coming to a close and Ding Wenyu was still panting, Peitao with a perfectly straight face rudely complained, "You can still do it with the light off!"

The second their honeymoon was over, Peitao found an excuse to go back and stay at her parents' home. At the same time, with a belly full of anger and resentment, Ding Wenyu even more inconceivably began to look up prostitutes and fool around. When Ding Wenyu's father asked again of his plans for the future, Ding gave a terse response. He was preparing to arrange for his wife to live in the Shanghai concession area while he went to the capital of Nanjing to look for work. Although he still had not settled on what kind of job he would do, one thing was certain—he would not remain in Shanghai. He did not dare tell his father he did not like Peitao, so he only said that he did not like Shanghai as a city. Ding Wenyu's father was in full agreement with his son's plans. For a student returning from abroad, the capital was naturally *the* place to show off one's talents. As a father, he had the utmost faith in his son's future. He was confident that many people would be more than happy to help Ding Wenyu get a job. As soon as Ding Wenyu's honeymoon was over, his father took a trip with him to Nanjing, where they passed among the upper echelons of society, showing themselves off at a variety of public gatherings.

During an open-air concert for party big shots, Ding Wenyu was able to demonstrate his remarkable foreign language skills. The concert was held at the outdoor theater at the foot of Dr. Sun Yat-sen's mausoleum. As far as the people of Nanjing were concerned, the outdoor theater, which was composed of 12 fan-shaped areas that could accommodate an audience of 3,000, was the most attractive part of the Sun Yat-sen mausoleum scenic area. The famous architects Guan Songseng and Yang Tingbao had designed it, skillfully utilizing the shape of the low-lying land to make the entire theater resemble a large, emerald folding fan with the most beautiful acoustics. The theater was not just for concerts; more important was its function in providing party VIPs with an elegant place to converge. On warm, sunny spring days and golden autumn afternoons of limpid skies and faint clouds, hordes of guards stood at the road entrance as party big shots and foreign diplomats with their wives appeared one after another at the winding corridor outside the theater. This corridor was 150 meters long and 6 meters wide with reinforced concrete on either side; tall Chinese wistaria ivy brazenly wound around the walls, creating an indescribably beautiful emerald walkway. When the Chinese wisteria was in bloom, armies of honeybees flew back and forth, the fragrance of flowers was everywhere, and upper-class women passed like clouds.

So many years after their last meeting, it was there that Ding Wenyu again saw Ren Bojin and his wife, Lady Miyako. However, at such an elegant and exciting venue, Ding Wenyu didn't have time to get nostalgic. It was the first time that his bare eyes had witnessed the Generalissimo Chiang Kai-shek and Madame Chiang, Soong May-ling. He also saw an utterly gloomy Wang Jingwei and his wife, Chen Bijun. He caught sight of the Minister of the Board of Military Affairs, General He Yingqin, wearing an army uniform. He Yingqin kept leaning over to the Generalissimo's ear to whisper something. Government Chairman Lin Sen sat there with a very serious expression, and not far from him was the former warlord and vice-chair of the Military Affairs Committee, Feng Yuxiang. With his tall and broad physique, Feng Yuxiang truly stood out from the crowd. A wife of an officer from the British Embassy surprisingly discovered that Ding Wenyu's London accent was even better than that of her own husband, who had lived in London almost twenty years! Ding Wenyu not only spoke very fluently, he also gave a remarkably true-to-life imitation of the language used by London's shady lower-strata characters. All of the foreigners at the theater contended to test Ding Wenyu with their own mother tongues. His unbelievable performance left everyone with their eyes staring and mouths gaping. Ding Wenyu took turns speaking in English, French, German, Spanish, Italian, and Romanian. For the English speakers he gave a demonstration on the differences between American English and British English. For the German speakers he showed the variances between German spoken in Switzerland and Germany. That day Ding Wenyu found himself getting quite worked up in front of his exclusive little audience; he was in such good form that not even Ding himself could believe it.

At the time of his performance, Madame Chiang, Soong May-ling, was also present. Amid her praises, she indicated that Ding could start working immediately in the Ministry of Foreign Affairs, if he so desired. In response to Madame Chiang's words, Tang Youren, the executive vice-minister of the Ministry of Foreign Affairs who would be assassinated in December of the same year, made Ding a job offer on the spot. Ding Wenyu, however, immediately expressed that he had no interest in taking a bureaucratic administrative position. Those Chinese students he had met during his days in Europe had, in just the course of a few years, already managed to make something of themselves. In what seemed to be a matter of days, Ding and his old student buddies suddenly found themselves looking at one another with new eyes. Zhang Daofan, who back in Paris used to always show up on Ding's doorstep just before mealtime and borrow money but never return it, had already ascended to the level of executive vice-minister of the Ministry of Communications. Then there was Xie Qinghui, who had stayed in Paris three years, yet because he spent all his time with other Chinese, couldn't speak a word of French—he was already some kind of committee member. Times change indeed; one after another, all of those old friends of Ding's who were now the new elite came over to greet him. Just before the concert formally started, Ding Wenyu realized that he was completely surrounded by powerful and important figures—it was these people who were controlling the fate of China.

Ding Wenyu decided to become a professor in the department of foreign languages at a university. Although he did not have an official degree or diploma, no one dared question his capability. He quickly became one of the most well-known professors on campus—there were many reasons he ended up making a name for himself even though he never tried to. Students secretly discussed his almost-legendary foreign language abilities. Also circulating were all types of jokes about him, some based on fact, others sheer fiction. His classes were warmly welcomed by students because he never lectured on any true knowledge—from day one, he had declared that he didn't have an ounce of scholarship. In class he freely chatted about his bitter experiences abroad, giving interesting anecdotes from his personal experience. He was unbridled during his lectures, simply saying whatever was on his mind. He openly mocked those top-notch European universities and foully cursed his own school's hallowed "advisor system" by which every student had their own personal advisor. It was the first time these students were exposed to the slang of lower-class society, the dirty cant that was popular down at the dock, and the jargon used in the brothels. During Ding Wenyu's lectures, his classroom was constantly exploding with wave after wave of uncontrollable laughter. This joyful laughter continued even long after class was dismissed.

VI

Ding Wenyu inconceivably fell for Yuyuan at her own wedding. From day one this affair appeared utterly preposterous. People couldn't help but believe that this was a game—in the beginning even Ding Wenyu doubted his own sincerity. After all, he had long passed through the battlefield of women; it was impossible for him to fall in love at first sight with a freshly married, naïve little girl who was practically a complete stranger! He assumed that losing his head at the wedding was nothing more than a case of being unable to shake off the role he had grown accustomed to playing. For a man like Ding, whose heart had already grown a thick callus, falling in love with *any* woman was a virtual impossibility. But in the end he truly couldn't stop thinking of her, and for the next few days he used the most vulgar language to record his sentiments in his diary:

> For many days now I have been constantly thinking of that girl named B. I suspect the reason that I cannot forget her is simply because I want to sleep with her. Beautiful B, if only I could lay you down, it would be just too perfect. Why can't I forget B?

Because his family was settled in Shanghai, Ding Wenyu had no choice—he was obliged to return once every month. His father had already reserved a first-class seat for Ding for the last day of every month on the Blue Steel Express. All Ding had to do was find his way to the train station. First-class seats on the Blue Steel Express were the highest-class sleeper coaches; the facilities were exceptional—double-occupancy rooms with red velvet carpeting and a small rest room. The ticket price was also exceptional—much more than a normal first-class sleeper coach. But even with such luxurious treatment, Ding Wenyu was still not in the least bit happy. Each time he went back to Shanghai, he would have a feeling of unspeakable uneasiness. He and Peitao never seemed to see eye to eye. Even though he occasionally attempted to break down the wall between them, each time the result always went contrary to his wishes—the more he tried, the more hopeless the situation became. Peitao was always the kind of woman you could never make heads or tails of, extremely headstrong, yet she never came off as naïve. She was like a hedgehog, always viciously pricking Ding Wenyu when he least expected it and then quickly rolling up into a ball; no matter how Ding tried, he couldn't get her to open back up. Although they ate at the same table, shopped in the same stores, and slept in the same bed, both of them constantly carried around a bellyful of pent-up resentment—from start to finish they were both utterly miserable.

Just before he first came upon Yuyuan, there had been a period when Ding Wenyu's diary had grown extremely dull. All he did was mechanically record his daily actions; his dull words barely conveyed even a hint of emotion. When mentioning Peitao, he was unable to cover up the depression that this mistaken marriage had brought him. During the year after his marriage, his ridiculous acts were innumerable, and he became even more decadent than when he was living abroad. Because Peitao was always complaining of a stomachache or about her period, she constantly refused to have sex with Ding. Thus began Ding's pattern of visiting the brothels around the foreign concessions whenever he returned to Shanghai. At first he acted surreptitiously, but before long he became completely brazen and unscrupulous. In the beginning, this was simply a method of expressing his anger toward Peitao, but eventually, he completely lost control of himself and his preposterous actions just kept getting worse and worse.

During the days around the fifth anniversary of the Mukden Incident, the streets and alleys were brimming with anti-Japanese sentiment. Angry crowds marched, shouting slogans to boycott Japanese goods and demanding that the Nationalist government dispatch troops to recover the four fallen Manchurian provinces. Ding Wenyu used an extremely absurd means to express his own childish anti-Japanese feelings. He led a bunch of his idle buddies over to a brothel in the Hongkou section of the Japanese concession, where they barged in and caused quite a ruckus. They were there all day; Ding spent every last cent in his pocket and even slapped a Japanese prostitute in the face. This was the first time in his entire life he had ever hit someone; moreover, it was a woman. Although he was already drunk, as soon as he slapped her he sobered up and became conscious of how despicable he was. Like a child, he broke out in violent tears and insisted that the prostitute give him two slaps back. Through his tears he muttered that even if all Japanese were bad, there was still no way that a prostitute could be bad.

Ding Wenyu's father was shocked by his son's outrageous behavior and feared he would pick up gonorrhea or syphilis. When his father privately expressed his concerns, Ding Wenyu shamelessly told him he had an extremely easy but effective method to stop the spread of any disease. He displayed the small glass vial that he always carried. Within it was purple crystallized potassium permanganate. This was passed on to him by a German doctor who liked to visit prostitutes. Ding told his father that all you had to do was take your thing and let it sit in a .005 percent solution for two minutes after having done it, and everything would be guaranteed safe and sound.

"Don't tell me you don't feel you are disgracing yourself by doing this," his father said, sighing disappointedly.

"Anyway, it's not the first time that I have disgraced myself," Ding Wenyu said as if completely untroubled.

Ding's father ended the conversation by asking his son, "With you running about like this, how are you able to face your wife?"

Ding's father's concerns were completely without warrant. When Peitao learned of Ding Wenyu's preposterous actions, she, after a brief period of anger, felt a kind of freedom. Since he had already found a place to release his shamelessness, she no longer had to act as his piss pot. That metaphor came out accidentally during an argument, and the image made Ding

Wenyu feel so ashamed he wanted to crawl into a little hole, because those filthy words truly did not seem to come from the mouth of the well-educated daughter of the Steel King. Before this, Peitao, with her belly full of complaints, would at the most compare herself to the goose that lays the golden eggs, grabbed by his father to continue their family tree. "On what basis should I keep the family line going for the Ding family?" Peitao asked resentfully. "Why don't you just return to Nanjing and never come back?"

And so Ding Wenyu tried as best he could to remain in Nanjing and avoid trips back to Shanghai. He never liked that city and he had even less sentimental attachment to Peitao. In Nanjing he lived in an apartment building specially equipped for well-known professors and hired a not-so-bad-looking servant to take care of his errands. Even if his father cut all financial support, the hefty salary of a star university professor would still be enough for Ding to live quite extravagantly. A steady stream of jokes about him seemed to be produced. Ding Wenyu had started frequenting the Nanjing brothels eight months prior to first meeting Yuyuan. However, before he even actually began this behavior, people had started to gossip openly about his hanging around the pleasure district near the Temple of Confucius. There were simply too many rumors about Ding Wenyu. Some said he chased girl students, others said there was something going on between him and his pretty maid, and there were even those who maintained that he was having a homosexual affair with his rickshaw puller Monk! Ding Wenyu paid no attention to all these different rumors, having grown accustomed during his time studying in Europe to not taking gossip to heart.

Although the Nationalist government had sent down orders outlawing prostitution, Nanjing never truly resolved the problem. The louder the shouts to ban prostitution, the more prostitutes appeared. After a completely random incident early on, Ding Wenyu and the rickshaw puller Monk became partners of sorts. If he wanted to satisfy his desire to call on prostitutes, Ding needed a connection like Monk who knew his way around town. Owing to the New Life Movement,* prostitution in Nanjing was partially concealed. As if hiding their face behind a *pipa*, or Chinese lute, many courtesans hid themselves by posing as hotel maids,

---

*A moral campaign started by Chiang Kai-shek in 1934 to counter Communist ideology with a new movement that combined Confucianism, Christianity, nationalism, and to some extent fascism.

bar girls, private dancers, or sing-song girls. Getting close to them would be much easier if there was someone who could introduce him.

Heaven only knows how many unlicensed prostitutes made their living selling their skin in the Nanjing of 1937. The day after the Marco Polo Bridge Incident* on July 7, 1937, Japanese soldiers at the Marco Polo Bridge came to real blows with the Chinese army. That day, one of the important newspapers in the capital printed the following article on page five under the heading PROSTITUTE CLIQUE FORCIBLY SOLICITS PATRONS:

> Nanjing is a city that has outlawed prostitution. However, according to an unofficial report printed in the *Daxia Evening News*, around City Government Road an unlicensed prostitute ring has been aggressively soliciting patrons. Although illegal prostitute cliques are ultimately to blame for these instances of reckless and unruly behavior, the government authorities cannot be ignorant of the fact that unlicensed brothels have flooded the city. Perhaps doing away with prostitution remains an utter impossibility in real life, but in formality the government has no choice but to declare them illegal—thus we have the occurrence of this strange phenomenon.
>
> In this situation, we are left with two results: first, the free spread of venereal diseases causes irreparable harm to the health of our citizens. Second, those official organs with the power to arrest unlicensed prostitutes can increase their revenue by imposing fines. Then there are those even more disdainful government employees who use the opportunity to make extra income through bribes.
>
> Although we advocate outlawing prostitution, we are not necessarily against legalized prostitution. We simply feel that in carrying out policies, the government should practice what it preaches. Hanging a sheep's head in the window while selling dogmeat is the most intolerable of actions.

Nanjing in the 1930s was a flourishing city. Even in 1937 when the country had come to the brink of utter collapse and all around people were

---

*The Marco Polo Bridge Incident refers to the Japanese army's hostile takeover of the strategically situated Marco Polo Bridge on July 7, 1937. This conflict effectively marked the beginning of the War of Resistance, also known as the Second Sino-Japanese War.

shouting slogans to "resist Japan and save the dying nation," the carefree citizens still leisurely went on their jolly way—eating, drinking, and having a good old time as if nothing was wrong. The ways of the self-indulgent old-style intellectual had seemingly seeped into the lifestyle of the average Nanjing citizen. A couplet best represents the mindset of wealthy Nanjing people at the time; the entire notion of "wine and women" was contained within. The first line read, "Those who live near the Temple of Confucius tire not of delicacies and fine meats." The second line went, "Nearing the left shore of the Qinhuai River, the flowers are in bloom and the moon is full." Ding Wenyu took like a fish to water to life in a city like this, indulging in pleasure and forgetting about everything else.

Miss Chen, whose acquaintance he had made not long before, was a social butterfly who had already gone out of season. Earlier on, this Miss Chen, who was then quite the center of attention, had shacked up with the head of some government ministry; however, in just a few years' time, there was no one around willing to shell out money for her. In Nanjing during the 1930s, one popular practice was touting sing-song girls. Pampered sons of influential families, powerful military officers, government officials, and businessmen who had just made it big all started to "sponsor" female singers of their liking as a new kind of pleasurable hobby. This practice caused the status of sing-song girls to skyrocket. There was a period where those girls who sang *Dagu* or Drum Song, Beijing opera, Kunqu opera, Yangzhou opera, and Huangmei opera all started to sing the popular songs of the day!

For a time, Miss Chen also moved Ding Wenyu. But it was precisely because he had feelings for her that Ding held off rushing into bed with her; instead he wasted an incredible amount of time accompanying Miss Chen during her all-night games of mah-jongg. What truly moved Ding Wenyu was not Miss Chen's gorgeous appearance but her aura of fleeting youth. She seemingly never realized this; never did she give a second thought to her future. Ding Wenyu also used to rarely think about tomorrow. After meeting Miss Chen, however, he often pondered her eventual fate. Thick rouge already couldn't completely conceal the wrinkles around her eyes. Because she was a heavy smoker, her smile revealed a mouthful of nicotine-stained teeth; nevertheless, she went right on smoking like a chimney. During Miss Chen's days in the spotlight, you couldn't count the number of men who courted her. Back then you could have opened a small florist with the flowers given to her every day. The more flattery that came, the more popular those sing-song girls became; and the more popular they were, the more suitors they had. Besides singing, there were a few other duties that came with being a sing-song girl, such as having to attend endless dinner parties. Virtually all sing-song girls also knew at least a few slightly deceptive tricks; for example, Miss Chen was known to be able to predict the future. For a time, she even earned the esteemed nickname "Witch Chen." As her popularity started to decline, Miss Chen used fortune telling to flirt with men—this became her primary strategy.

Ding Wenyu had Miss Chen read his fortune on several different occasions, and each time she gave him a slightly different prediction. Miss Chen would always use a set of poker cards to do her fortune telling. She spread the deck out chaotically on a table and, using some method that no one else could figure out, she would suddenly pull two cards out of the messy pile. After whiffing them under her nose for some time, she would begin her prediction based on the type of card. What surprised Ding Wenyu was that even though she relied solely on her nose, Miss Chen was able to smell which card it was—without fail, it only took one whiff and she would hit the nail on the head. Miss Chen's rare talent passed many tests; a group of people once blindfolded her with a black cloth and had her identify each card by its smell, and her unbelievable performance left everyone around in complete astonishment.

"You will fall for a woman," Miss Chen once said while she was reading Ding Wenyu's fortune. She gazed at the card in her hand for a long time before finally continuing, somewhat hesitantly, "Moreover, you will go crazy for her."

"I indeed have already fallen for a woman," Ding replied with a slick smirk, "moreover, I *am* crazy for her!" When Miss Chen made her prediction, Ding Wenyu had yet to come upon Yuyuan—he simply thought Miss Chen was joking and didn't take her words to heart. He was an old hand at the game of love and quite adept when it came to flirting with Miss Chen, but she paid him no heed and continued staring unwaveringly at that poker card. Ding Wenyu laughingly uttered, "Anyone would be able to tell that I'm crazy for you."

"No, I'm not the one," Miss Chen said seriously, slowly turning her eyes to Ding. "But when you find her, you *will* truly go crazy for her."

Chapter Three

I

Yuyuan later heard Ding Wenyu speak of Miss Chen's premonition, but at first she really didn't take it to heart. It was questionable just how reliable sweet talk like that was, coming from the mouth of a playboy like Ding Wenyu. Actually, there was nothing out of the ordinary about Ding Wenyu's exaggerated remarks; Yuyuan just felt a bit frustrated because she didn't think he should say such bold things to her face. Then again, she couldn't be *that* angry—there isn't a woman in the world who doesn't like getting compliments. During her honeymoon, Yuyuan was incessantly disturbed by an array of unhappy events—it got to the point where she could barely fend for herself, let alone look out for others. She had a stubborn cold, and just as it seemed to be clearing up, it would come back even stronger. Her mother's old stomach ailment acted up again and they had no choice but to admit her to the hospital for treatment. Then, one of Yuyuan's good friends died in a tragic car accident—on her way home from Yuyuan's. The groom, Yu Kerun, kept running off—he always had a different excuse, a Military Academy class reunion, a birthday celebration for a superior from the Aviation Academy, or flying the Generalissimo from Nanjing to Ningbo. Because they were staying at Yu Kerun's elder brother's residence, the lively Yuyuan felt terribly bored all alone in that empty room when Yu Kerun wasn't in. Her days as a newlywed were not at all as interesting as she had imagined they would be.

Yuyuan and Yu Kerun had not known each other for a very long time. Her five elder sisters had all married military men, so Yuyuan had a premonition that she would also marry a man in uniform. As Old Ren Bojin's most beloved daughter, Yuyuan felt that in order to make her father happy she should marry a serviceman. She and Yu Kerun had met by chance during one of the Ministry of Military Affairs' annual New Year's Eve balls. Yuyuan was young and beautiful, Yu Kerun was handsome and spirited. The pair raised eyebrows with their elegant dancing and quickly became the object of everyone's envy and admiration—there wasn't a pair of eyes in the hall that wasn't focused on them. Actually, as the music was coming to an end, they were the only two still left on the dance floor. Even though they had only just met there, none of the other dancers could hold a candle to them. As the number ended, everyone erupted with thunderous applause and requested an encore performance.

It wasn't at all odd that Yuyuan should have such remarkable skills on the dance floor—every weekend the headquarters of her division held dances to which young and pretty female soldiers would usually be dragged along. There was never a shortage of dance fans among high-ranking Nationalist military officers, and then there were those foreign military advisers—when they took to the dance floor it became an all-night affair. However, there were very few young officers who actually knew how to dance. First off, they rarely had the opportunity to dance with a woman, and according to the standards of the New Life Movement they should endure the hard life, strengthening themselves in order to serve their country to the best of their ability. If they spent too much time at the dance hall they would be suspected of being hedonists. Moreover, young officers of lower ranks found it extremely difficult to get into the small dance hall reserved exclusively for high-ranking officers and foreign military advisers. Yu Kerun's amazing moves on the dance floor made all the other woman soldiers jealous, and they secretly asked around trying to find out just who the handsome guy in the leather pilot's jacket was. When Yuyuan told them that not even she knew, they all instantly suspected her of lying. Anyone could tell from their seamless harmony that they were an old couple; they were perfect together—each move on the dance floor seemed to have been rehearsed beforehand. No one could believe it was the first time they had danced together. They themselves could barely believe it.

During the months following the dance, Yuyuan and Yu Kerun's relationship developed at lightning speed. That thing called "fate" was at work, silently tying them together with a red, invisible silk string. Exactly one year later, they finally held their wedding ceremony at the OMEA compound. And so, smoothly, without the slightest hitch, the young and promising Yu Kerun became Yuyuan's dream groom. In the Nationalist military scheme of things, pilots stood out from the rest—to marry a pilot was the fantasy of many girls at the time, even though the Chinese air force was still quite undeveloped and didn't have any real fighting capabilities. There were constantly unfriendly rumors flying around about air force pilots. Yuyuan had ample reason to believe that it was purely out of jealousy that, one after another, her girlfriends kept giving her completely unnecessary warnings. Her friends told her that all pilots were playboys because there were simply too many women after them.

When a prostitute who had been arrested for drug use was asked by a reporter from a small paper to talk about what kind of person her dream man would be, she instantly set her mind on those pilots who soar through the blue heavens. "Just thinking about a man flying in the sky like a bird, you can't help but get so excited that you clamp your legs together," she couldn't refrain from blurting out. The reporter quite obscenely quoted the prostitute's original words, leading readers to incessantly debate the actual implications of her statement. One reader with nothing better to do even telephoned the press telling them that he felt what the prostitute meant was "spread your legs open" and not "clamp your legs together," as the reporter had written. In a diary entry from 1937, the well-known educator Zhu Kezhen wrote: "It is said that the chair of the Aviation Committee Zhou Zhirou has recently been fired, the reason being that out of two thousand planes only two hundred and fifty or so can fly. Moreover, most pilots have been infected with venereal disease. Of 200 men, only around 70 are able to clock four consecutive hours of airtime." Although that year Chinese pilots had given a remarkable performance during a Sino-Japanese air battle, with several pilots even sacrificing themselves for their country, the unscrupulous behavior of some had indeed become a topic of conversation among ordinary people. Zhu Kezhen's diary may not be 100 percent accurate, but it is enough to demonstrate the nature of the problem.

Yuyuan and Yu Kerun were both the kind of people who are somewhat overconfident about themselves. It wasn't because she had faith in her husband that Yuyuan failed to take her friends' warnings to heart, but rather because she had too much faith in herself. She had deep, unwavering confidence in her own charm. On her wedding day, upon returning to the bridal chamber, Yuyuan noticed a prominent lipstick mark on Yu Kerun's neck just below his left ear; it was obviously left by another woman because Yuyuan never wore heavy lipstick; nor did she ever kiss Yu on that spot. Because she was too proud to admit that another woman had kissed her husband, Yuyuan covered up the unhappiness in her heart—after all, it was her wedding night. Not until the next morning did that red lipstick mark involuntarily come back to her mind. At that time she was a bit numb, and presumed that the woman must have been an audacious tramp who intentionally left it on Yu when he wasn't paying attention—otherwise Yu Kerun would have never brought this shameless mark back home with him.

Yu Kerun believed he was playing the part of Casanova. In order to let Yuyuan see his outstanding qualities, during their honeymoon he paraded before her the several dozen love letters he had collected. Most of these had been written by pure and innocent female students—there were university students, middle-school students, even a little girl who said she was an elementary-school student about to graduate. Naturally, there were also letters from older women—some of these were self-introduction letters in which they offered themselves as his lover; others were from women playing matchmaker for their daughters in hope of becoming his mother-in-law. Anti-Japanese sentiment among Chinese had never been as strong as it was in 1937, nor had it ever been as romantic. As he was an outstanding pilot, Yu Kerun's name appeared in the newspapers on more than one occasion. The formation leader during the unbelievable air show for Chiang Kai-shek's birthday celebration, Yu Kerun, the "national hero," became a virtual household name overnight.

Halfway through their honeymoon, Yuyuan discovered a similar lipstick mark on Yu Kerun's shirt collar. Yu had drunk himself silly, and he instantly admitted that the female server at the inn had left it. He and a few old classmates from the Aviation Academy had gone out drinking, and when it was time to settle the bill someone suggested that they let the waitress give Yu a kiss for a 20 percent discount. Yu Kerun let the girl plant a kiss on him, and they indeed got a discount on the bill—but ended up having to leave a fatter tip.

The deep love that the people felt for pilots could also be seen in their enthusiastic rush to purchase aviation lottery tickets. On the eve of the Second Sino-Japanese War, the Nationalist government's aviation lottery tickets, which totaled more than three million *yuan*, were already on their thirty-eighth draw. The war between China and Japan had yet to break out, but everyone understood that during the coming battles the air force would play a very important role. No wonder that during an inspection in early 1937, when a reporter asked an official from the Philippines about his feelings during his trip, the official seemed deeply moved as he replied, "Your country's aviation lottery ticket system is truly without flaw." When the reporter asked him to elaborate, the official couldn't give an answer. He just kept repeating: "Your dear country's aviation lottery ticket system is indeed without flaw." The reporter pointed out that this lottery-ticket fever perhaps illustrated that the Chinese people had already made preparations for full-scale war. That is because purchasing aviation lottery tickets is basically donating money to buy war planes. The reporter continued, "The Chinese are a peace-loving people, but if someone already has a knife to their throat, the Chinese people cannot help but rise up in resistance." The reporter told this Philippine official that the reason Chinese were all running out to purchase aviation lottery tickets had nothing to do with winning that 250,000-*yuan* grand prize. The Chinese have a saying, "Once your skin is gone, how can your hair survive?"—with national survival and destruction hanging in the balance, all the Chinese people could do was use their flesh and blood to construct a new Great Wall. The reporter's words brought sensitive international problems into their interview. He did not actually mention the word "Japan," but it was impossible that this Philippine official from a British colony did not understand what the reporter was referring to. As a foreigner, the Philippine official could only ramble ambiguously to avoid directly answering the question.

II

On the day of Old Ren Bojin's sixtieth birthday celebration, Chiang Kai-shek, who was all the way in Fenghua in Zhejiang province taking a vacation, sent someone on a special trip to present Old Ren with a hanging plaque inscribed with the four characters *junjie qisu*, or "Renowned Elder of the Military." The Generalissimo's inscribed words meant that this birthday celebration was destined to be quite a bash. Ren Bojin had been a serviceman his entire life. Although he had never had any real military power or actually led any troops in battle, because he never followed any of the warlord factions and had loyal students and allies in each of the various military camps, Ren Bojin was looked upon with extremely high regard in military circles. Amid national calamity, all should be kept simple, but even if they wanted to keep the birthday party for the noble and respected Ren Bojin simple, it stubbornly wouldn't stay that way. Well-wishers came and went in succession. After a reception at the Ren house, the true celebration was held at Six Splendid Springs near the Temple of Confucius. It was such a large-scale affair that the people who lived in the area all thought something really important was happening. One after another, famous figures from every arena flocked to the banquet; private cars formed a long line outside; in the end they had no choice but to telephone the police department and have them send someone to maintain order.

There were two people who accidentally got the day of Old Ren's birthday mixed up. One of them was Ding Wenyu. When Ding first saw the congratulatory announcement in the newspaper, the first thing that came to his mind was that he would have another opportunity to see Yuyuan. Ever since he had attended Yuyuan's wedding, he couldn't stop thinking of her. The pure image of Yuyuan was continually dancing back and forth before his eyes; no matter what he did he couldn't make it go away. He decided almost instantly that he would attend Old Ren's birthday celebration, but because he was a bit too anxious he ended up rashly showing up a day early. No one expected him to confuse the date, including Ding himself—at first he simply couldn't understand why the place was so dead. The most disheartening thing was that he couldn't see the woman whom he had yearned for day and night, Yuyuan. Not until he said his good-byes and dawdled out of the place did he finally realize that he had gotten the date mixed up. The entire Ren family was quite entertained by Ding Wenyu's mistake. Ding Wenyu had always been the butt of their jokes, and this time he provided them with fresh comic material. This mistake, however, was not necessarily that serious for Ding Wenyu, for while he was there he inadvertently heard some good news: Yuyuan had already telephoned; she would arrive first thing the following day.

Yu Kerun was the other person who screwed up the date. He absentmindedly pushed the celebration back a day. The result was that in his scheduling was a huge mistake of unforgivable proportions. His immediate superior was to accompany some government big shot to Fenghua to deliver a work report to the Generalissimo. This big shot fingered Yu Kerun as the man he wanted to fly the plane. He wanted to get a first hand taste of Yu's special acrobatic flying skills. Yu Kerun's superior hinted that this was an excellent opportunity and with the support of this figure, Yu's future in the air force would be boundless. Because at the time, the country was in dire need of outstanding young talent like Yu, his superior estimated that his first promotion would be to the level of assistant chancellor of the Aviation Academy. Yu Kerun naturally could not give up such an opportunity. However, only after they had settled on a time did he suddenly realize he had mixed up the date of his father-in-law's birthday. His superior had already taken into consideration that fact that Yu Kerun had to attend the birthday celebration, but because Yu had told him the wrong date there was nothing he could do. Yu Kerun had no choice but to rush to the celebration and express perfunctory congratulations before flying off to Fenghua. It was as if he came just to show his face for the official morning roll call. After mingling briefly with the Ren family, he left as quickly as he had arrived.

The ever-attentive Lady Miyako could tell with one look that her headstrong daughter Yuyuan's honeymoon had not gone too smoothly. Yuyuan acted as if she didn't care about her husband's abrupt departure, but actually, deep down she couldn't forgive his behavior, not only because this was her father's birthday but also because this was the first time she had returned to her parents' home since getting married. When the Ren sisters all got together, they expressed their anger at Yu Kerun for coming and going so hastily. Yuyuan's third sister Yujiao had a quick tongue, and as soon as Yuyuan tried to say something in defense of her husband, she cut her off quite sharply: "No matter how busy Yu Kerun is, he can't be busier than the Generalissimo. Even the Generalissimo has time for vacations; isn't he still on recuperation holiday right now?" Yuyuan swallowed her temper and said seriously, "It seems that at times Kerun is indeed busier than the Generalissimo!" Everyone burst out laughing at her refutation. Even Yuyuan herself couldn't help but giggle. Her face turned bright red.

As the sisters were carrying on endlessly about Yu Kerun's absence, Lady Miyako changed the topic of conversation by asking Yuchan about America. Yuchan, who had recently rushed home from the States, had already spent seven years abroad. Seven years before, she had married a diplomat, after her first husband, who was from Sichuan, died in the civil war; Yuchan had carried out the vows of a widow for three years. During those years, one after another, all three of her husband's concubines married. After thinking about it, she decided there was no need to remain a widow. Her mother-in-law was an old-style conservative, and they did not get along at all. Yuchan left her three children by her first husband with her mother-in-law and remarried without ever looking back. Her new husband, a military attaché stationed abroad, was a widower. Because by the time they remarried neither of them was a spring chicken, they decided not to have any more children. Yuchan and her second husband got on extremely well, and their time spent in America went fairly smoothly.

The topic of conversation quickly moved from everyday life in America to Ding Wenyu. Whenever someone in the Ren family mentioned Ding Wenyu, everyone perked up. Because for the last two days in a row, Ding's old distraught self had appeared at the Ren compound, everyone started talking about him with a feeling of nostalgia. Ding was the kind of person women love to gossip about, rambling on and on; their words gradually became quite unbridled. Already reaching middle age, Yuchan eventually turned red at her sisters' brazen gossip. She pretended that she was going to get angry but actually wasn't even close to losing her temper. She felt a need to say something in Ding Wenyu's defense: "Back then, he was still a child." Yuyuan grabbed hold of her sister's words and wouldn't let go. With a hidden meaning behind her words she asked, "But the question is whether or not he's *still* a child?" After uttering this she couldn't help but blush. Although she had yet to be dragged into the conversation about Ding, Yuyuan already had a premonition that sooner of later that day would come. Yuchan was left speechless by Yuyuan's line of questioning. These sisters were always extremely close and could joke about anything. Yuchan looked at her still-honeymooning sister Yuyuan and with her face turning red added, "Of course he isn't a child, but what exactly are you hooting about? Back then *you* were still sleeping in the cradle!"

Yujiao felt that she had the strongest credentials to discuss Ding Wenyu. Although she had already exhausted most of her stories about him, she repeated them with great relish. She imitated the way Ding Wenyu had helplessly stared at Yuchan all those years ago and once again drew thunderous laughter from her sisters. Lady Miyako was beside them and as she tried to control her laughter, waved her hand for Yujiao to stop her Ding impersonation. She was, after all, a benevolent mother and felt that her daughters shouldn't laugh at another person's expense. No matter what, there was nothing funny about falling in love. Love has never been any kind of terrible mistake. Lady Miyako had an intuition that Ding Wenyu was not the kind of person her daughters had made him out to be, always brooding over Yuchan, unable to forget his childhood love. Lady Miyako noticed that now, when he was around Yuchan he was completely normal. There was not even a hint of him making a fool of himself or causing a scene. When he greeted her, it was obvious that he had already forgotten the Ding Wenyu of his adolescence. As if it were nothing, he joked a bit with Yuchan and then turned away to busy himself elsewhere.

It was clear that Ding Wenyu had not come because of Yuchan—not only did the observer Lady Miyako have this feeling, but even Yuchan, the alleged object of affection, could tell. Yuchan almost immediately noticed Ding Wenyu's inattentive manner. It was as if he had something on his mind and was in a strange mood. The image of the innocent adolescent boy of so many years before had been cast to the wind, and everywhere there were rumors that Ding had transformed into a playboy. These rumors had even made their way to Yuchan stateside. However, since the moment of their reunion, Yuchan understood that bygones were indeed bygones and past love was no more. No matter what his intention might have been, there was absolutely no way that Ding Wenyu would again try to seduce her, as everyone seemed to fear. He was no longer the old Ding Wenyu.

Yuchan took the lead in approaching Ding to greet him. She was afraid that he would be uncomfortable seeing her, but actually *she* was the one who was uncomfortable. When she asked how he was doing, her face turned crimson and it was as if she had gone back twenty years. "It's a shame that I returned to China so late and missed Yuyuan's wedding. Did you know that that we met a storm on the way?" Yuchan blurted out. "We got stuck at sea for quite some time." Not knowing quite what to say, she could not control the quivering in her voice when she spoke: "Time really flies; twenty years ago Yuyuan was still a baby in a rocking cradle and now she is already a new bride!" This comment led Ding Wenyu into deep thought, but not about Yuchan, over whom he had lost his head those twenty years ago, but rather about that innocent baby, Yuyuan. For now, the only impression Yuyuan left on him was her big, round eyes. These eyes had once directly gazed at him; her stare was innocent and un-affected with a touch of cunning. Yuchan and her sister Yuyuan really did not have anything in common. Their facial appearances were completely different and because of the great disparity in their ages, when together they looked more like mother and daughter than two sisters.

Ding Wenyu did not pay the slightest attention to the numerous peo-ple secretly taking note of his expression as Yuchan greeted him. With her his actions were quite reserved, so much so that he left his audience disappointed. The only topic of conversation that seemed to spark his interest was Yuyuan. That ardent look in his eyes as he spoke to Yuchan was born out of hope that she would continue talking about Yuyuan. Ding Wenyu's opportunities to be alone with Yuyuan on the day of Old Ren Bojin's birthday could hardly have been any fewer. He was contin-ually trying to find the perfect moment, but in a place as large as the Ren compound it wasn't easy to find Yuyuan, much less an opportunity to be alone with her. Ren Bojin had six daughters, and with them all there to-gether, in addition to the constant flow of guests, it was quite a specta-cle. Yuyuan was like a fleeting shadow; she would appear before Ding Wenyu and then, in the blink of an eye, would disappear without a trace. Then, quite rudely, Ding Wenyu abruptly left Yuchan; from the corner of his eye he had caught sight of Yuyuan walking to the eastern wing of the compound. Without taking the possible repercussions into consid-eration, he rashly pursued her. In the end, however, he discovered he had gotten the wrong person. She merely resembled Yuyuan a bit from the back. His erratic manner once again created a misunderstanding among others, but Ding Wenyu was never one to fear making a fool of himself. He had always had thick skin. He felt that since he had bothered to come, he might as well make the best of it and try to be alone with Yuyuan.

On the day of Old Ren Bojin's birthday Ding Wenyu had set out first thing in the morning. In his diary he recorded the ridiculous scene from the day before when he had mixed up the date. In Ding's eyes this was an amusing little mistake; like the saying goes, "true love indeed never come easy." Because of Yuyuan, Ding Wenyu even began to start warming up to Old Ren Bojin. In the past he had the impression that Ren was always stuffy and serious, his mind constantly filled with national affairs that had nothing to do with Ding. But now, all at once, he changed his habit of avoiding lively parties and prepared a generous—perhaps too generous— gift for Old Ren Bojin. Ding arrived a bit too early, and as a result had no choice but to accompany Old Ren into the study for a long conversation. What surprised Ding was that what this old military man spent most of his time pondering was national defense. All his life Ren Bojin had been thinking about ways to build up a modern national defense. He chatted with Ding Wenyu about European military affairs, the American navy, and the Spanish civil war. Ren Bojin was already an old man. For his entire life he had been an armchair strategist, and now during his final days there was no one really left who had the patience to listen to his ramblings. Before their conversation ended, Old Ren had Ding Wenyu take a moment to admire his last will and testament on the table. This testament had been composed a few years earlier, but each year during his birthday Ren Bojin felt compelled to respectfully recopy it:

> I have devoted my life to the military, holding ever firm to the principle of willingness to die for my country. Although China and Japan are destined to eventually come to blows, I am already frail and can no longer hope to die on the battlefield wrapped in a horse's hide. For this I feel great regret. Without resistance against Japan there is no way to save China. If we desire to resist Japan we must have absolute sincerity in rallying together. No matter what, we must not stand divided with each group maintaining their own opinions. We must unite with the outside. Russia along with Britain, France, and

America can all become our friendly allies; only with Germany, owing to its unusual relationship with Japan, must we proceed with caution. The Nationalist government currently relies heavily upon German military advisers; from the standpoint of national defense, this is a concern. Besides this, as the threat of war is breathing down our necks, we should not hesitate to borrow more in foreign loans. It is a shortcut to use the money of others to arm ourselves—this must always be remembered. At home we must carry out large-scale production and continue with the implementation of the New Life Movement, and most important, we must save our money and resources for the national defense. When I die there is no need to hold a public funeral, nor to see me off with an elaborate ceremony. When I die simply bury me. Do not erect a tombstone, simply plant a few trees. When these trees grow into timber, make them into a table and chair and it will be fine, just as long as they can be of use to someone. This shall express that even after death, my soul still longs to repay the great debt of gratitude toward the nation for rearing me.

During the mammoth birthday celebration, Ren Bojin, at someone's request to say a few words, once again restated the contents of his testament to his well-wishers. At first everyone responded with shock; this was followed quickly by thunderous applause. Ding Wenyu repeatedly scoured the room for a trace of Yuyuan. It was a rarity for his eyes to meet with Yuyuan's, but even a fleeting match proved enough to start a spark. From the look in Ding Wenyu's eyes, Yuyuan could sense a kind of unrestrained passion, a kind of madness that heeded no bounds. She thought that this guy who once insanely pursued her elder sister indeed had no shame. She thought back to her own wedding, when they first met, and how he tightly grasped her hand while uttering those audacious words. This skirt-chasing bookworm had far too much gall. Just thinking of him made Yuyuan feel both infuriated and amused. As everyone was drinking, she couldn't help but casually turn around on occasion in hope of catching a glimpse of Ding. If Ding Wenyu happened to be looking at her at that moment she would quickly turn away; if he wasn't, her gaze would only remain a moment because before too long, Ding Wenyu was bound to cast his eyes back at her.

It was also at this birthday celebration that for the first time, Ding Wenyu removed his red nightcap in public. This red nightcap had always been his symbol of trying to cajole the public with claptrap; no matter what kind of engagement he was attending, no one ever even dreamed of making him remove that hat. Since he had returned home from abroad, this was the first time that Ding Wenyu hoped *not* to attract attention in public. His sole desire was for people to pay him no heed so he could secretly admire Yuyuan to his heart's content. He drank glass after glass of wine to cheer himself up, but even after he was quite drunk he did not forget himself. After a few rounds of drinks the hall started to grow chaotic. Ding Wenyu, raising his glass of wine, staggered over to the table Yuyuan and her sisters were sitting at in hope of toasting each person there. When he got to Yuyuan, she took notice of his sottish appearance and said coldly, "I'm sorry, but I don't drink."

Ding Wenyu was flabbergasted and replied by saying, "Don't drink, that's okay, I'll drink for you!" He threw his head back, emptying the glass, and then extended it for more. Yujiao took his glass and filled it to the brim with wine. Ding Wenyu took that glass and, gazing straight ahead with a forced smile, abruptly downed the alcohol. All of the sisters applauded successively, and with a drunken lisp Ding Wenyu declared: "There's no such thing as people who 'don't drink,' there are only those who don't dare to drink! If you want me to drink, I can still drink more." No one asked him to drink more, so he wobbled back to his original seat and waved triumphantly to Yuyuan. Yuyuan flashed him a disdainful look. Turning back to the table, she discovered her big sister Yuchan had been staring at her the whole time with a fixed gaze.

When Ding Wenyu left he was so drunk he could barely tell which cane was his. As he looked in the mirror to put his nightcap back on, he couldn't help but make a funny face. The female hostess beside him couldn't hold in her laughter. Although he had already drunk more than he could handle and began to feel his stomach churning, he seemingly didn't care—he simply stood in the doorway staring blankly toward Yuyuan, desperately hoping to catch one last glimpse of her. When he had first arrived, he had noticed that the groom Yu Kerun was not present; Ding Wenyu felt this was a most interesting sign. He felt himself more than a bit selfish and base; he even secretly hoped that from that day forward Yu Kerun would never again appear. As flock after flock of well-wishers who had attended the celebration made their way outside, Ren Bojin's daughters and sons-in-law stood at the door bidding everyone farewell. The only one missing was Yuyuan. By the time most of the guests had left, Yuyuan still had not showed her face, and Ding Wenyu began to wonder how she could simply disappear without a trace.

The Temple of Confucius was desolate in the afternoon. Those who had come for morning tea had long since left; the prostitutes were still asleep and the johns had yet to hit the streets. Many of the shops were practically deserted. Although the end of the lunar year was approaching, the people of Nanjing had yet to start their busy preparation for the Spring Festival. Ever since the Generalissimo Chiang Kai-shek had put forth the New Life Movement, the Spring Festival, declared obsolete, was seemingly of negligible importance. The people still felt that they should celebrate it, but government officials were doing their best to change this custom and make the western New Year into an important holiday. Ding Wenyu staggered across the avenue and, finally finding a steel garbage can, began to vomit his heart out. A couple of children not far away watched as rivers overturned and seas raged upside down in Ding's stomach, and the seven meats and eight vegetables all forced their way out. When he was finally done vomiting, he panted heavily, trying to catch his breath, and gently used his fist to massage his back. Strand after strand of tears and snot dripped down his face.

III

Ding Wenyu couldn't figure out how he ended up going to Miss Chen's apartment. Although he frequented the Temple of Confucius, especially those famous prostitution lanes, Ding Wenyu never really knew his way around the area. Each time Ding went there it was Monk who enthusiastically led the way. He had been to Miss Chen's place many times, but if you asked Ding to find her apartment on his own it would still be a difficult task for him. When Ding Wenyu emerged from the birthday celebration at Six Splendid Springs and vomited his heart out into that metal garbage can, he suddenly caught sight of a familiar bridge not far away. The apartment where Miss Chen was temporarily staying was just under that bridge.

Miss Chen was shocked by Ding's battered appearance. When he showed up at her door Miss Chen thought that this bookworm must have been beaten and mugged by a bunch of thugs on the street. Ding Wenyu looked pitiful. Raising that cane of his, he looked lifelessly at her—it seemed like forever before he finally opened his mouth. Miss Chen approached him, anxiously asking what had happened and whether or not he was hurt. Ding Wenyu gave a wry smile before he finally began to speak. He told Miss Chen that he had merely had too much to drink. At that moment Miss Chen's painted face immediately lost its color: "What do you know, all along you were having your fun with some other woman! What the hell did you even bother coming here for?"

Ding Wenyu could feel his head pounding; it was as if there were an army of countless ants crawling through his brain. Almost pleading, he told Miss Chen that all he wanted was to borrow her bed to get a bit of shut-eye. Miss Chen was infuriated. She said, "You intend to drag that filthy and disgusting body of yours into *my* bed?! If you want to sleep, go sleep in the maid's bed." It was clear that since the number of visits he paid to Miss Chen since New Year's had dramatically declined, she had a bellyful of pent-up anger. Ding Wenyu felt so uncomfortable that he didn't have time to worry about all that. With a belch, he headed for the housemaid Auntie Wu's bed. Pulling a long face, Miss Chen stopped him before he got there. Seeing that he was truly in a bad way, Miss Chen couldn't bear to put him through anything else and led him into her room. She ordered Auntie Wu to quickly bring a basin of hot water and wash Ding Wenyu's face, neck, and hands. Then, after changing the water, Miss Chen herself got down and removed Ding's shoes to give him a hot footbath. After washing his feet, Miss Chen directed Auntie Wu to pour a bit of vinegar to sober Ding up. However, the second Ding Wenyu hit the bed he was out like a light.

By the time Ding Wenyu awoke it was already completely dark outside. Inside there was a table lamp emitting a soothing glow while the perfect silence of the room completely shut out the noises outside. At first he didn't know where he was, but there was Miss Chen sitting on the corner of the bed, gazing at him with tears running down her face. He sat up to discover he had been wrapped in a large, red comforter with silk lining, and his red nightcap hanging on an oval flower vase on Miss Chen's dresser, which resembled a face wearing a hat—it looked rather silly. Miss Chen had seemingly been waiting the whole time for Ding to awaken. Seeing him sit up, she grabbed a pillow to place behind his back. Finally, Ding Wenyu was starting to sober up. He turned his head to look at the clock and asked apologetically, "I've been sleeping all this time?"

"What do you think?" Miss Chen angrily replied.

It was quite chilly outside and although there was a small charcoal brazier against the door, it still was not enough to drive away the cold. Ding Wenyu noticed that Miss Chen was hugging a green hot-water bottle in her arms as if holding a doll; at almost the same time, he also felt a warm sensation near his feet and realized that wrapped in a cloth cover beside his feet was a purple, copper hot-water pot. Curled up on the blanket between him and Miss Chen was a white Persian cat. Ding Wenyu took another look at the clock on the dresser and said, "I'm indeed an embarrassment, I can't believe I really slept all this time!"

"Forget it," said Miss Chen. "Since when *weren't* you an embarrassment?"

With that comment, Ding Wenyu couldn't help but break out in laughter. Miss Chen also had trouble containing herself and let out a snicker. She wiped away the tears from the corners of her eyes and asked Ding if he was feeling hungry. She offered to have Auntie Wu cook something up for him. Ding Wenyu grabbed Miss Chen's hand, telling her he wasn't hungry; he then asked with concern what it was that made her so sad. Miss Chen pouted her lips and said, "What do I have to be sad about? You're the one who is sad!"

Ding Wenyu responded, "If you're not sad, then why are you crying?"

Miss Chen giggled and said, "What business is it of yours if I cry or not? I have plenty of time on my hands and nothing better to do. What's wrong with a girl letting some tears roll just for the fun of it?" Ding Wenyu knew that she was just saying this to let off steam and began to flippantly caress her face. This move, however, made Miss Chen even angrier. She made a fist and whacked Ding Wenyu's shoulder.

Under the care of Miss Chen, Ding Wenyu sat up in bed and ate a bowl of lotus rice soup. After he had finished, Miss Chen followed suit by having something to eat before joining Ding for some chitchat. After talking for a while, Ding Wenyu had to relieve himself. Because there was no bathroom in her apartment, Miss Chen was in a bit of a difficult situation; blushing, she said: "I'll go out for a second and you use the chamber pot." Ding Wenyu shot a glance at the red chamber pot in the corner and instantly shook his head, saying he was not accustomed to using those things. "That's fine," replied Miss Chen, "just hold it in then." Ding Wenyu was extremely uncomfortable; it seemed from the look on his face that he was about to pee in his pants. Miss Chen had no choice. She draped her jacket over Ding's shoulders and led him to the courtyard so that he could relieve himself in the sewer while she quickly ducked out of sight. When Ding Wenyu hopped back under the warm covers, he said with the utmost gratitude, "I never imagined that you, Miss Chen, also had your soft and caring side."

This made Miss Chen somewhat unhappy. She said that she was nothing but an already passé sing-song girl. Everyone knew about those sing-song girls on the banks of the Qinhuai River, and they were entitled to whatever opinions they wanted. There was no need for Ding Wenyu to show off his one-upmanship after having gotten the goodies, or call someone base after having taken advantage of them. There was indeed a difference between Miss Chen and those prostitutes who simply sold their bodies—although he was sleeping in her bed, this in no way meant that he had gotten her body. Ding Wenyu could not figure out why she should have such a furious temper on that day. But seeing how alluring she looked, it was obvious that while he was asleep she had taken the time to carefully make herself up. Ding couldn't control his urge to pounce forward and embrace her.

Miss Chen pushed him away and earnestly warned him: "Don't touch me! I'm warning you, I'm about to get married. You had your chance, but now it's already too late!"

Ding Wenyu thought that she was joking. Smilingly, he asked her whom she intended to marry. "Could it be *me*?" Ding asked.

"I originally did intend to marry you." Miss Chen said sternly. "But how could someone of your stature marry a woman like me? Moreover, you already have a wife." Ding Wenyu said that that didn't matter, he could always divorce his wife and remarry. "If you had said that earlier," Miss Chen uttered coldly, "I probably would have considered you. But now it is too late for that."

Ding Wenyu listened to her words and took another look at her expression. It seemed she really was going to tie the knot with somebody. Deep down, part of him still didn't want to believe it, so he again inquired who she was going to marry. Miss Chen threw out a name. It was familiar to Ding Wenyu—he was a Nanjing contractor who did business in building materials; not long ago, he and Ding frequently shared the same mah-jongg table. Ding Wenyu told her, "If it was someone else I might believe you, but no way if it's him."

Miss Chen asked why he didn't believe her, was it that this fellow was too much of a philistine? Ding Wenyu didn't answer, but he was wondering how the high and noble Miss Chen could fall for a rustic lout like this fellow. It was clear that Miss Chen could tell what was on Ding's mind, and she asked him who else an outdated sing-song girl like her could marry. "During your time at the top, those people with power and influence will, at the very most, take you as their kept woman, but once you start downhill they take quickly to their heels. What's more, even if I were to marry one of those powerful and influential men, they are still unreliable. I have seen enough of those in my day and frankly speaking, they would never fall for me, nor would I fall for them. Who doesn't know about those rich bigwig types who take up with sing-song girls like me? Actually it is hard to say whether we simply hoax them—you can never tell just who is playing with whom." Seeing that the more she spoke the angrier she became, Ding didn't dare interrupt. After Miss Chen had said a mouthful she sighed and continued, "Do you know why I'm so good to you?" Ding Wenyu stared at her blankly with bulging eyes and repeatedly shook his head. Miss Chen extended her index finger and tapped him lightly on the forehead. Her face turned red as she told him, "Although you're a playboy, you are not in the least bit annoying."

Ding Wenyu laughingly replied, "No, Miss Chen, you are wrong. I'm a bit annoying, but not at all a playboy."

Miss Chen said, "That's right, you *are* a bit annoying!"

"You see," said Ding, "a moment ago you said something else and now at the drop of a hat you go and change your story!"

Although Ding Wenyu had already spent a huge amount of time with Miss Chen since they had first met, the closeness between them that day was indeed a first. Miss Chen said that the reason she felt some affection toward Ding Wenyu was that he was different from those other men who spent all their time "chasing women and playing around." As the saying goes, "a true gentleman moves his mouth but not his hand"; on the basis of this alone, Ding didn't seem too bad. Ding Wenyu laughed as he said that she must have really gotten the wrong man, it was merely that she had never seen his bad side: "I'm afraid that besides you there is probably not another soul in the world who would take me for a decent man."

Hearing him say that, Miss Chen also laughed and said that her eyes had seen many of the bad men under heaven and no matter how bad Ding might have been, he wasn't going anywhere with his so-called "badness." Ding Wenyu was delighted by her words, but Miss Chen warned him not to get too carried away. "I know about your little trips to visit those tramps around the Temple of Confucius, so don't pretend I don't," she warned. Ding Wenyu didn't admit it or deny it, and Miss Chen went on to ask him just how many prostitutes he had made the acquaintance of in the Temple of Confucius area. Ding Wenyu giggled but would not answer. Miss Chen continued to pester him; she insisted on making him talk.

"What's the point of discussing this?" Ding Wenyu protested. "Even if I tell you, you won't necessarily like what you hear."

Miss Chen responded, "Men spend money and women make money. Everybody is happy and willing; it's not like I am your family, so what's there for me to be unhappy about?"

Ding Wenyu couldn't hold out against her persistent tactics and started to give Miss Chen a lecture on Prostitutes 101. As each of Miss Chen's questions became more and more detailed, Ding thought that she was indeed interested, so he opened up and began to tell her even more.

Miss Chen blushed as she listened. But suddenly she heaved a deep sigh and said, "What is it about men that makes them all so shameless?"

Ding Wenyu felt frustrated. "I didn't want to say anything and you forced me. Then once I open my mouth you get pissed off!"

"I'm not angry, so don't you go and get angry." Miss Chen said laughingly. "One of these days I'm also going to have a go at being a prostitute, then I'll really satisfy all you naughty men!"

Ding Wenyu saw from Miss Chen's manner that she really wasn't upset and went back to their earlier topic of conversation. He asked her if she was truly going to marry that building materials contractor. Miss Chen said that of course she was going to marry him; when had she ever pulled his leg? Naturally, there were times when Miss Chen *had* pulled Ding Wenyu's leg. However, judging from the honest look in her eyes, this time was different. Miss Chen said that she had long wanted to marry, but could never find a good one and was a bit unwilling to settle for a bad one. After picking and choosing, she finally decided on this Nanjing businessman. "People from Nanjing are relatively honest and kind. So after thinking about it, I decided it best to marry someone from here." Miss Chen made it clear to Ding Wenyu that this was not only the first night he would stay over, it would also be the last. Since she had already promised herself to another in marriage, she had no choice but to take back her heart and give all of her feelings to her future husband. Ding Wenyu again stared at her dumbfounded with a pair of blank, fish-like eyes. Miss Chen couldn't help but break out in another fit of laughter and told him, "Don't get any crazy ideas. I'm only having you spend the night because you were drunk and nothing else—don't you dare try to take advantage of the situation! I'll tell you now, as it so happens, I have my period today, otherwise there is no way I would dare keep you. With this shielding me from you, I'm not afraid of you!"

Without their realizing it, the time had crept by, and Ding Wenyu got back up to go out to the courtyard to relieve himself again. He seemed to be getting hungry again, so Miss Chen called Auntie Wu out of her warm bed to make them a midnight snack. After they ate, Miss Chen washed up, drove that white Persian cat from the bed, and placed another comforter on the bed. She said that in order to keep Ding Wenyu from trying any funny stuff, tonight it was one blanket per person. Ding Wenyu's temper began to flare a bit, and he threw the comforter into the corner of the room. "Don't tell me that you think I'll lose control the second we crawl into the same blanket! Well, let me tell you, although I may be a playboy, I have my days when I can sit in the arms of a beautiful girl and still not be moved!" Ding Wenyu's indignant stance won over Miss Chen, and she crawled into the same blanket with him. With a sorrowful tone Ding Wenyu said, "We have known each other for quite some time. You should really leave me with something as a token of our friendship."

Dazed, Miss Chen thought for a moment before she propped herself up in bed and removed a small envelope from the drawer at the nightstand. From the envelope she pulled out a three-inch-square photograph and handed it to Ding Wenyu without hesitation. Ding Wenyu was shocked when he looked at the photo—it was a frontal nude of a woman—but then upon closer scrutiny, he realized that the woman was none other than Miss Chen. In the photo she had just emerged from a bathtub and was drying her soaking-wet hair with a bath towel. Miss

Chen said that there was a long story behind the photo. Way back when, it had been surreptitiously taken by Dai Li, chief of the Nationalists' military intelligence organization. On the occasion in question, Dai Li arranged to meet her at the Fuchang Hotel. At the time Miss Chen was at the peak of her popularity, and Dai Li worshiped her to the point that he was ready to jump through hoops of fire for her. They often met secretly at the big Nanjing luxury hotels. Because they were afraid of being discovered, they always checked into separate rooms. Sometimes they even intentionally asked for rooms on different floors. Miss Chen told Ding Wenyu that all together there were only two photos like this; Dai Li kept one for himself, and this was the other one. She originally had intended to burn this photo because if the man who was about to become her husband were to see it, he would no doubt go into a jealous rage.

"That's right!" said Ding Wenyu, grimacing. "You don't even need to mention your husband; even *I* get uncomfortable looking at it."

Miss Chen turned to give him a whack, planting her fist right on his shoulder.

Ding Wenyu made a pleading gesture and then fixed his gaze on that photo. Miss Chen asked him what he was so anxious about: "When you go home you'll have all the time in the world to look at it." Ding Wenyu replied that when he got home he would naturally slowly go over it, but right now he wanted to get his kicks. As he spoke he brought the photo to his lips and kissed it. Grinding her teeth, Miss Chen gave him another whack on the shoulder. With a fixed stare, Ding Wenyu continued to admire that photo. Miss Chen said, "I'm not paying any more attention to you. I'm tired, go to sleep whenever it suits your fancy." With that, she took off her outer garments and slipped under the covers. Ding Wenyu looked at the photo a while longer before he set it on the nightstand and turned off the light. In the darkness he took off his clothes, and when he was mostly undressed, he got under the covers and reached over to hold Miss Chen. Miss Chen pushed his hand away, saying, "We already agreed, no fooling around! Otherwise I'll throw you right out the door!"

Ding Wenyu whispered, "What, we can't even hug each other? You're really something." As he spoke he had already placed his hand on Miss Chen's breast. Miss Chen yawned and said, "Okay, but that's as far as you go. I'm really tired. Let's keep our word, all right?" With that, Ding Wenyu really did abandon all further plans. Before long Miss Chen fell asleep and began to gently snore. At first Ding Wenyu wasn't a bit tired; he turned around to lie with his back facing Miss Chen—and then he suddenly thought of Yuyuan. Her image appeared vividly before his eyes. Ding Wenyu wondered what Yuyuan would think if she could see what he was doing now. For a moment he felt he was utterly sordid and despicable; how could a girl as pure as Yuyuan possibly think about him? Ding Wenyu then thought about what it would be like to sleep in the same bed next to Yuyuan. That would be simply too good to be true! He had had relations with so many different women, but not one of them could be compared with Yuyuan. She made him feel passion of an intensity he had never known. She was truly a naturally outstanding creature, a fairy sent down into the mortal world, a cure for all diseases, and a light on a dark night. Gradually, an exhausted Ding Wenyu curled up and, longing for Yuyuan, began to drift into dreamland.

When he awoke it was already light outside. Ding Wenyu rolled over to discover that Miss Chen was still asleep. He had traces of the hangover from the day before, but Miss Chen was sleeping like a baby, her lips slightly open. He reached over and began to gently caress her. Having been awakened by him, Miss Chen hit him twice, but seeing it was of no use, she had no choice but to let him do as he pleased. He fondled her breasts, feeling their size as well as the shape and hardness of her nipples. Then he suddenly changed direction and quickly headed downward. Miss Chen tried to stop him but it was no use—it was already too late. Ding Wenyu directly reached his target to discover that Miss Chen had tried to deceive him—she didn't have her period after all. Instantly, Ding Wenyu felt an uncontrollable excitement arising within him. Heaven never seals off all exits. Now there was nothing that Miss Chen could say to stop him. Even if there were, it wouldn't matter: Ding Wenyu had the upper hand and wasn't about to give in. Victory was in the palm of his hand. Because of his vast experience, the art of sex had long been engraved in Ding's mind. He knew when to go in for the kill and how to make a woman quickly lose her sense of shame. Under attack by an old hand like Ding Wenyu, Miss Chen quickly groaned as she lost her final line of defense. She sighed, explaining that she honestly hadn't been trying to deceive him. She indeed had had her period; the sanitary belt she had changed was still soaking in the foot basin. Miss Chen heaved deeply, barely able to catch her breath; Ding Wenyu, however, appeared rather indifferent. He moved mechanically and then suddenly, at that most untimely of moments, Yuyuan entered his mind.

IV

February 12, 1937 was the day of the Spring Festival, the Chinese lunar new year. Ding Wenyu found an excuse not to return to Shanghai for this traditional festival; he instead shut himself up alone in his university apartment and pondered the mistakes of his past. On the night before the Chinese New Year's Eve he attended Miss Chen's wedding. It was quite a scene; the newspapers had run wedding announcements three days in advance. On the day of the wedding, the bride and groom hired a spanking-new British Austin decorated with large red silk strips and ostentatiously drove around the main streets of the capital. Miss Chen had the aura of being reborn as a new person. The satin cheongsam she was wearing was a deep crimson, but she was so cold wearing it that clear mucus kept dripping from her nose. The groom was much older than Miss Chen; he was wearing a short fur coat outside his cotton gown. He appeared honest and good-natured, carefully waiting on her, lest he incur the smallest iota of dissatisfaction from his new bride.

Seeing Miss Chen exposed to the cold like that, Ding Wenyu felt a bit sorry for her; he could also understand why she should want to take the trouble to have such a grand and extravagant wedding. Usually, people only have nasty things to say behind the backs of sing-song girls who get married. If you listen to what comes out of some people's mouths, you would think that on the banks of the Qinhuai River, "sing-song girl" was virtually synonymous with "prostitute." Miss Chen hoped to use the extravagance of her wedding to defy the scorn that others felt toward her. For many years now, Ding Wenyu had seemingly settled into his role as playboy. Never once did he wonder what a woman was thinking, let alone attempt to put himself in a woman's shoes. However, since he had laid eyes on Yuyuan, Ding Wenyu seemed more attentive to women; he became somewhat meticulous in his actions and even a bit garrulous in his speech. When he shook hands with the bride and groom to bid them farewell, he appeared quite concerned as he exhorted Miss Chen not to rush right into the bridal chamber when she got home, but first have a bowl of ginger soup to drive away her shivers.

Because no one imagined that Ding Wenyu would spend the Spring Festival alone in his university apartment, naturally no one came to call on him New Year's Day, as was the custom. Ding Wenyu did not get out of bed until quite late; at the crack of dawn he was awakened several times by the thunderous explosions of firecrackers. Not long after he had gotten up, bored out of his mind, an idle Ding Wenyu simply crashed back into bed—he spent the entire day in a muddy, partly comatose state. After the explosive sound of the larger firecrackers had died down, all that was left was the intermittent sounds of small firecrackers. The children next door were setting them off beside the courtyard wall; occasionally he could hear their cackling jabber. Ding Wenyu lay in bed as his mind drifted off into space. He thought of Yuyuan. He thought of her with a kind of inexplicable longing, with seemingly no rhyme or reason; he couldn't get her off his mind. Time after time, Yuyuan's facial features, voice, and smile appeared before his eyes. Ding Wenyu realized that, inconceivable as it might be, he had already fallen in love with her.

This was truly an experience that he had never before encountered. Ding Wenyu was confident in his role as an old hand in the game of love. He had experienced more women than he could count, women of all different colors, nationalities, ages, and classes; some were married, some were single, and there were even some who weren't of the legal age! There were so many shameless acts in his past that Ding simply didn't have the time or patience to recollect. There was a certain small coastal city in India that attracted swarms of pleasure seekers who came out of a yearning admiration for the fledgling young prostitutes there. All you had to do was pay a tiny sum of money to the pimp at the hotel and he would present you with a young girl still in the bud of youth. Although those young girls' breasts had just begun to develop, as far as their sexual techniques went, they were just as mature as any of the older, more experienced prostitutes. In the past, whenever Ding Wenyu had occasionally looked back on his exploits, he did so with a hedonistic feeling of intoxication—as a man in this world, he had felt that he indeed had not lived in vain.

Yet whenever Yuyuan's image appeared before him, Ding Wenyu began to feel a kind of unspeakable guilt. He suddenly realized that he was wretched, dirty, and absolutely shameless. For Ding Wenyu, this was a terribly strange feeling. Besides those days when she was still in the cradle, he had seen Yuyuan only twice: once when he attended her wedding and once on the day of Old Ren Bojin's birthday. They had had virtually no direct contact and, during the little contact they did have, they had only exchanged a few words. Moreover, that conversation had been far from congenial; from the start, Yuyuan looked at him with cold and indifferent eyes. Ding Wenyu, on the other hand, had never before been so passionately attracted to a woman. Calling the event of so many years before, when Ding Wenyu lost his head for Yuyuan's big sister Yuchan, an example of fanatic love would not be as accurate as saying it was a kind of adolescent chivalry. That is because, at the time, Ding Wenyu did not truly understand if he was actually after Yuchan's hand in marriage or if he merely wanted to rescue her from the hands of an evil and despotic warlord. Without understanding the way things worked, he naïvely felt that he should go out and boldly do something for her.

His love for Yuyuan was a completely new feeling. Ding Wenyu didn't seem to have any ulterior thoughts. He simply hoped he could love her. His mind was extremely clear and simple; what he felt was a kind of adoration of the utmost purity. It was pure giving without even the slightest care for any kind of reciprocity or outcome. As long as he could love he would be content, as long as he could love all other thoughts would turn to ash. As a man, Ding Wenyu always had thought of how he could get what he wanted, but this time he earnestly wanted to give, he wanted to give with every last bit of his heart and soul. For the time being, he felt that besides his love for Yuyuan he had no other desires. As long as she approved of his love for her, it would be more than enough. Ding Wenyu spent an enormous amount of time trying to figure out how to arrange a third meeting with Yuyuan. He prepared a whole slew of words that he might use during their next conversation, trying to envisage exactly how to express his feelings. However, he was overcome by a feeling of irresoluteness. It was obvious that no matter what acrobatics his tongue might pull, there was still no way Yuyuan would be able to immediately grasp his feelings. He needed to be careful, extremely careful. But all the while, he knew that no matter how careful he was, his words were still certain to scare the wits out of her—if she wasn't scared out of her wits, now *that* would be strange. No matter what happened, though, there was one sentence that

Ding Wenyu was determined to say to Yuyuan—even if doing so meant the complete and absolute violation of a taboo: "I just hope that you will allow me to have the right to pursue this love. This is a right that belongs to me just as it belongs to the rest of humanity." He had already quietly gone over this sentence in his head innumerable times. No matter what he did, this sentence preoccupied him and until he was able to get it out, he felt as if a fishbone were stuck in his throat.

On the second day of the Chinese New Year, Ding Wenyu strolled over to Monk's place. He really didn't know if Monk would be willing to take him down to Ren Bojin's house—there were more than a few rickshaw coolies who were unwilling to work during the holiday. Monk lived in a multifamily compound in an alley not far from the university. Ding Wenyu had already been there on more than one occasion. He was surprised to find an angry Monk cursing somebody under his breath as he sat squatting under a Chinese locust tree near the gate to his compound. The moment he laid eyes on Ding Wenyu, Monk's temper seemed to flare even greater. He abruptly stood up and charged at some family's front gate, uttering vicious obscenities. That gate suddenly opened and out walked a pretty woman about forty years old who yelled to Monk: "Hey dopey! Do you plan on staying pissed at me forever?"

Monk angrily retorted, "Well, if I'm so 'dopey' than I guess I will!"

The pretty woman was about to say something else, but seeing Ding Wenyu she swallowed her words. Monk's temper seemed to quell a bit. He brushed the scraps of exploded firecrackers off his rickshaw and told Ding Wenyu that they could get going. The pretty woman followed on Monk's tail, asking him if he would be coming home to eat. Monk sternly told her that whether or not he came back was none of her business. The pretty woman said, "How is it that a bastard like you suddenly becomes so damn hard to wait on?"

Without even bothering to turn around, Monk responded, " 'Boss' will be eating out tonight!" The pretty woman chased after him, asking him where he expected to find a restaurant open on the New Year. Monk said that if there were no restaurants open he would just go hungry on the streets. Losing her patience with him, the pretty woman screamed: "You bastard! If you were half a man then you'd never come back!"

Sitting in the rickshaw, Ding Wenyu couldn't help but giggle; he could sense the special nature of the relationship between Monk and this pretty woman—not your everyday, run-of-the-mill affair. It was obvious that the woman was much older than Monk. With one look you could also tell that she was not the type of woman who was overly honest and dutiful. As she squinted at Ding Wenyu, her eyes filled with an aura of wanton flirtatiousness. Ding Wenyu was only all too familiar with those kinds of eyes. Laughing, he wanted to joke with Monk about it, but Monk had already beaten him to the punch and begun to impatiently complain about her. He did so without holding even the slightest bit back. "Mr. Ding, sluts like her can't be trusted. She promised her daughter to me in marriage, and now she's going back on her word." Monk spoke casually, his temper already mostly subsided.

Ding listened with interest and said, "Oh, so it's her daughter you are after." Monk replied frivolously that of course he was after the daughter—the mother was a bit too old for him.

On the second day of the Chinese New Year, Yuyuan didn't return to her parents' home as was the custom. Too shy to open his mouth and ask when she would return, Ding Wenyu had to contain himself. Showing up rashly on the Rens' doorstep was already a bit ridiculous and quite enough to induce several unnecessary misunderstandings. There was really nothing to be said. After sitting for really no time at all and not even touching his tea, he awkwardly took his leave. As he left the Rcn compound, Ding Wenyu figured that since he had already caused a scene, he might as well see things through to the end—so he decided to go directly to Yu Kexia's residence. Because Yuyuan and Yu Kerun's bridal chamber was set up at Yu's brother's house, Ding Wenyu thought there was no harm in visiting Yuyuan under the pretext of calling on his old classmate. This was a most bold and assertive move on Ding's part, but you could say that he was "launching an assault with a just cause and remained perfectly justified in his conduct." Anyway, Ding Wenyu almost never considered the consequences of his actions.

As it happened, Yu Kexia was on his way out the door with his wife. Yu never imagined that Ding Wenyu would show up, but upon seeing him, he kept repeating, "You came at just the right time, I had some matters I'd been meaning to discuss with you." Seeing his rushed manner, Ding Wenyu couldn't imagine what Yu had on his mind. With the utmost urgency, Yu Kexia said, "Don't worry, I won't feed poison to an old classmate. Just let me have a few words and I'll be finished." Ding Wenyu said that he wasn't at all worried, but after hearing Yu's comment he started to think that maybe he should be. Yu Kexia told Ding Wenyu to relax; he simply wanted to give his old classmate a chance to share in a lucrative deal he had on the burner.

Ding Wenyu asked, "Now that you're the talk of the town among the Nanjing officialdom, what kind of deal would you want to let me in on?" Yu Kexia didn't have the time to keep Ding dangling, so, with a flighty look, he said straight out that he was setting up a Military Council and when the time came he would be sure to have Ding take a titular post.

"So far I've already recruited quite a few big names for this council. There is also no need for you to do any real work. There's really nothing you have to do except show up for a couple of dinners." Yu Kexia still appeared restless with anxiety as he incessantly looked at his watch; it seemed like he couldn't care less about the confused expression on Ding Wenyu's face. "It has already been decided that Tang Shengzhi will be the chairman of the board. Tang Shengzhi is the inspector-general of military training; he couldn't be more suitable for the job. Don't laugh, there was nothing we could do about this 'chairman of the board' title. I know it doesn't sound quite right, but Ding, you really don't know what it's like doing business these days. You can't play around with these names and titles. Since we have Generalissimo Chaing Kai-shek and Premier Wang Jingwei, we can't go off and rashly adopt titles like 'generalissimo' and 'premier.' We'll just have to make do with 'chairman of the board' until something better comes along."

As Yu Kexia rushed out the door, Ding Wenyu still didn't understand just what this Military Council was all about. All he knew was that Yu Kexia was to be the secretary-general of this soon-to-be-born council, and besides himself, those holding titular posts would include Ren Bojin and the vice-chairman of the National Military Council, Feng Yuxiang.

During 1937 in the capital of Nanjing, names of associations and committees were flying around everywhere; there were the famous Air Defense Association, the Women's Reformation Association, the Sanitation Association, the Insect Extermination and Waste Management Association, the Aviation Committee, the Central Committee for Managing Disaster Relief Funds, and the celebrated New Life Movement Committee. Between the governmental and privately run committees and associations, there were so many that no one could make heads or tails of them. Countless people had the title of committee chair or vice-chair printed on their name cards. In the end, the Nationalist government had no choice but to respond by ordering a restriction on all titles that could easily lead to misunderstandings. The capital was without question home to China's largest circle of officialdom at the time. All kinds of people went there looking for opportunities. However, when they had no success, they tried something different and threw together a bunch of empty titles to give themselves an undeserved reputation to deceive people.

What made Ding Wenyu's spirit soar was that Yu Kexia's rushed departure had provided him with the kind of golden opportunity that only comes around once in a blue moon. For fear that his old classmate would feel lonely, Yu Kexia ran into his little brother's room and called his sister-in-law Yuyuan out to keep Ding Wenyu company. Since this was the first time that Ding Wenyu had called on him, Yu Kexia couldn't help feeling bad about his abrupt exit. He repeatedly expressed that he would return shortly and told Ding that no matter what, he simply must stay for dinner. He said that he had already instructed the chef to make a few extra dishes, and when he returned they would all drink to their hearts' content. Deep down Ding Wenyu's heart called out in approval. He could not hold back the look of utter joy on his face. Yet he acted as though being respectful was not as good as simply following orders and politely accepted Yu Kexia's invitation. What Ding Wenyu truly rejoiced in was not just the departure of Yu Kexia and his wife but the fact that heaven had been on his side in ensuring that Yu Kerun wasn't home.

Left behind with Ding Wenyu and Yuyuan were Yu Kexia's eight-year-old son and three-year-old daughter. It was impossible that this situation not evoke the scene that had transpired some twenty years before between Ding Wenyu and Yuchan at the Ren compound. Yu Kexia's home was brimming with the *nouveau riche* scent of officialdom—they had just finished work on the house, and the pungent smell of paint still lingered in the air. 1937 was the year for large-scale construction among Nanjing officials. Even though everyone was shouting anti-Japanese slogans and the newspapers repeatedly ran articles that spurred on anti-Japanese sentiment, no one in Nanjing that year anticipated the actual arrival of the war. People had not even the slightest premonition of the impending catastrophe. Everyone was engaged in idle theorizing; as far as the people of Nanjing in 1937 were concerned, war couldn't be further away. It was off in the four fallen Manchurian provinces, off in North China or in distant Suiyuan. That year was nevertheless the heyday of the Nationalist period; in everyone's minds it was the best time for purchasing real estate.

During that year Nanjing underwent startling expansion. The city government encouraged people to build new, modern, custom-designed houses in the remote northern section of the city. Just a few years before, the Drum Tower, which now rests in the center of the city, had been one of the northernmost points in the entire city proper. It didn't matter if you set out north or northwest from the Drum Tower, you were bound to run into nothing but burial mounds. At the time, plot after plot of this land was being sold, and virtually every day there were announcements in the newspapers indicating which graves were being moved. The day you bought a plot of land, you could run an announcement in the newspaper. If within a specified period of time, the caretaker of the grave in question did not come to relocate it, you as the owner of the land had the right to assume that the deceased had no living relatives and could simply pay to have the grave moved. This boom in large-scale construction caused Nanjing to take on, for the very first time, the true spirit of a capital. Nanjing began to transform into a flourishing urban center. One after another, unique little western-style buildings shot up. These beautiful little buildings combined both Chinese and western architectural styles. Almost all of them were designed by engineers who had returned from studying abroad. There were a variety of different styles, including Euro-American and Oriental; moreover, amid some of the Euro-American buildings there were also traces of Northern and Western European influences. This development craze caused Shanxi Road and Yihe Road to intersect where they never had before; moreover, they crisscrossed and curved in a most irregular manner. In the end the neighborhood around the intersection became as confusing and chaotic as a labyrinth. Many people would get completely confused and lose their bearings when they went there. Owing to the fact that most people came and went in automobiles, when the owners of these homes had to occasionally set out on foot, they sometimes found that after only a few blocks, they couldn't even find their own front door!

The splendor of this flourishing city seemed to open the eyes of virtually everyone in Nanjing. Besides knowing endless inside gossip about party VIPs, Nanjing people greatly relished loud, empty, and bombastic talk. Where so-and-so lives, how much money so-and-so's home cost, so-and-so's hiding a killer beauty in his magnificent house—with one mention of any of these topics, people became excited beyond belief. Far away in Shanghai, Ding Wenyu's father couldn't resist the temptation to get in on this construction fever. With a brain brimming with business cells, this banker presciently realized that in the rise of real estate prices, land prices always go up before the prices of houses, so he didn't rush off to build a small, luxury western house; instead he made a one-time investment and bought a very large plot of land in his son's name. The area of the land was enough to build more than a dozen homes. Its value later exploded, nearly doubling that very same year.

With Yuyuan accompanying him, Ding Wenyu was full of zest as he looked around Yu Kexia's new house—this tour was the special activity arranged by Yu Kexia just before he left. Yu deeply regretted that he could not personally show Ding Wenyu around, but he was extremely anxious to hear Ding's comments about his new house. Ever since construction had finished, Yu Kexia had been waiting to hear a word of praise from someone. "We don't lock any of the rooms here, so you can see everything." Just as he was going out the door, Yu Kexia instructed his sister-in-law: "Yuyuan, you take Ding Wenyu for a look around and have him tell you what he thinks. He has seen a lot of nice homes; let's see how this old thatched hut of mine sits with him."

V

Many years later when Yuyuan would reminisce about Ding Wenyu she couldn't help but think of this day alone with him—nor could she help but think back to that premonition of Miss Chen's that Ding had relayed to her that day. This face-to-face meeting turned out to be of unusual significance. Until that moment Ding Wenyu had been someone who had barely any connection with her; there was nothing between them. Yuyuan knew Ding's story; she had heard all the jokes about him, including all types of slanderous gossip. He was simply a lovesick lunatic who had once gone after her big sister Yuchan. He was just pretending to go mad in his cups when he offended Yuyuan with those crude words at her wedding and when he maliciously made eyes at her during Ren Bojin's birthday celebration. As far as Yuyuan was concerned, Ding Wenyu had already gone as far as he could. She couldn't imagine what else he could possibly have up his sleeve. Ding Wenyu was just someone you heard about in stories; he was the object of everyone's laughter. There is no way that Yuyuan could have imagined that a ridiculous clown like Ding could take things a step further with her.

Ding Wenyu did not offer the slightest comment about Yu Kexia's new home, but when Yuyuan refused to take him in to see her bridal chamber he became unexpectedly stubborn. "I can't imagine what reason you would have for refusing to let me see your room." Ding sounded like an elder trying to milk his years for all he could. He then childishly stood outside her bridal chamber, unwilling to budge, until Yu Kexia's eight-year-old son took the lead, pushing open the door to his auntie's room. Yuyuan wanted to stop him but she was too late; Ding Wenyu was already standing in the doorway, diligently examining the room's furnishings. After gazing around the room for a while, he didn't wait for Yuyuan's invitation and strutted directly in. Anticipating Yuyuan's dissatisfaction with his rash behavior, Ding intentionally put up a careless front while deep down he actually felt quite guilty for going in. To his delight he noticed that all Yuyuan did was laugh in her sleeve.

"So, here is the handsome young fellow who makes everyone jealous," Ding Wenyu said seriously as he looked at the portrait photo of Yu Kerun hanging on the wall.

Yuyuan's face instantly turned red, and the scene from her wedding day flashed before her eyes. She seemed to be able to hear those dubious words that Ding Wenyu had uttered in Japanese echoing in her ears. She tried her best to act like nothing was wrong, but she wasn't very experienced and had a difficult time hiding her true feelings. She realized the very real probability that this outrageous man in front of her might go on with his disgraceful ramblings. Ding Wenyu had been looking around as if nothing was going on when he suddenly turned and began staring straight at Yuyuan. Under his shamelessly daring gaze, Yuyuan was at even more of a loss as to what to do. She didn't dare directly meet Ding's gaze, yet at the same time, she thought it would be rude to make him uncomfortable by giving him a sour look. Since Ding Wenyu was her brother-in-law's guest, and it was his house, Yuyuan really didn't know how she should react. She knew that her brother-in-law Yu Kexia very much admired Ding and would often talk openly about him at the dinner table. Moreover, how could she rashly throw out a visitor who came calling on the Chinese New Year holiday?

When Yu Kexia spoke of Ding Wenyu it was usually with a tone of boundless adulation. In order to squeeze his way through the official world, Yu Kexia relied upon his Ding Wenyu stories to show off his outstanding foreign study background. Through his praise of Ding, he was actually praising himself. Besides, he also needed to compare himself to Ding in order to highlight just how far he had advanced in his career. Whether to brag about his past achievements or to flaunt his present status, Yu Kexia had to get the most use out of Ding Wenyu. "Back when we were in Europe . . ." Yu Kexia would say at the drop of a hat. He would always criticize the young people of today, saying that they had no way of imagining what he and his buddies had gone through back in the old days. "Don't just look at the fact that we have all made big names for ourselves. Back then things weren't easy for us." He would ramble on and on, not forgetting to occasionally throw in a few well-placed sighs. Those were sighs of jealousy directed at all those old fellow students he knew from Europe who were much more adept at getting by and getting rich.

"In officialdom, it is always those incompetent people who end up really making out." Often at the dinner table Yu Kexia would suddenly sigh with emotion, "In the end it's Ding Wenyu who's got the last laugh. With one look he saw right through the whole game."

Yu Kexia's wife disdainfully said, "How could you expect a bookworm like him to become an official?"

Yu laughed at his wife's lack of knowledge. "Don't tell me that there is anything easier than becoming an official."

Yu Kexia made Ding Wenyu out to be a great literati genius brimming with talent. People often envy those who rise to a realm they could never hope to attain themselves. Yu Kexia could never look as indifferently at fame and wealth as Ding Wenyu did. He envied Ding Wenyu's family background, and he envied that nonchalant attitude of Ding's where nothing seemed to matter. After his unusual visit that day, and even after Ding Wenyu's maniacal pursuit of Yuyuan had become an untidy bit of common knowledge, Yu Kexia continued, by either accident or design, to bring up Ding Wenyu during meals. At the dinner table, everyone seemed to repeat the most unnecessary and trivial things; discussing Ding Wenyu just happened to be one of those topics that often got repeated. Actually, after this unusual one-on-one meeting, Yuyuan didn't object to discussing Ding Wenyu. Moreover, it was precisely her unconscious enchantment when listening to stories about Ding that seemed to inspire Yu Kexia to rattle on like a broken record.

That day, besides boldly expressing his hope that Yuyuan would permit his love, Ding Wenyu did not make any other excessive moves. His words and actions all demonstrated an unbelievably gentlemanly quality. He straightened his clothes and sat up properly on the couch and, as if consoling a child, began to speak tirelessly, calmly telling Yuyuan that this was merely a spiritual game of his and he had not the slightest immoral objective. Ding was simply in search of a kind of spiritual consolation; he did not want to receive anything, and the last thing that he wanted was for Yuyuan to sacrifice anything for him. She could act as if she didn't understand a single word he said. She could take him as a lovesick lunatic, a strange idiot, or even a worthless sexual pervert. She could pretend that absolutely nothing had happened between them, and that this unusual conversation had never taken place. Ding Wenyu repeatedly avowed that all he was looking for was something purely metaphysical. For Ding, this conversation was the result of much careful thought and consideration. He spoke eloquently at length, as if he were discussing some play or American movie—something that had absolutely nothing to do with him.

Yuyuan's reaction was not very strong. It wasn't that she was unwilling to make a scene, she simply didn't have time to. In sharp contrast to Ding Wenyu's full preparation, Yuyuan didn't even have time to put her guard up, let alone for it to work. She was left completely stupefied by Ding Wenyu's bold, brazen move. For a long time she just passively thought that Ding Wenyu was way out of line, that he was truly a sex-crazed maniac. How could someone be so shameless? What Yuyuan regretted most was that she didn't give him a harsh scolding and throw him out on the spot. At the time they were sitting in the living room speaking, the teapot on the stove had already begun to boil, spitting out a stream of whistling steam. Yu Kexia's eight-year-old son was rolling around on the leather sofa; he took advantage of the confusion to wolf down all the candies placed upon the coffee table, throwing the wrappers everywhere as he consumed his plunder. Yu Kexia's three-year-old daughter periodically pestered her new auntie to tell her stories. The atmosphere in the living room was anything but harmonious as Ding Wenyu went on speaking with fervor and assurance—he paid absolutely no attention to the fact that the more he spoke, the more contorted the look on Yuyuan's face became.

"Please don't say any more. Mr. Ding, your words are truly a bit ludicrous." Yuyuan gave Ding Wenyu a warning. However, in front of the two children she was a bit afraid that her every word would be picked up by them and relayed back to their parents. Because of this she had no choice but to pay strict attention to her attitude and to avoid using any sharp words that would surprise the children. After all, this was not her home, so Yuyuan couldn't do as she pleased or say what was really on her mind. Her marriage clearly had been a bit rushed. She never imagined that she would end up moving into her brother-in-law's house. However, since her bridal chamber had been set up there, she had no choice. As soon as she moved in, she noticed the look of inconceivable fear in her new sister-in-law's eyes. Trying to assess the situation, her sister-in-law often asked Yu Kerun where he planned to settle down. Yu Kerun ignored these questions that were obviously nothing more than a hint for them to pack their bags. He had already grown accustomed to relying upon his brother. This so-called marriage was nothing more than a way to bring another person into the family. In reality a young man his age would very rarely take the time to think about setting up a warm and happy family. He was completely confident about his future and believed that as long his official career was a success, all other problems would be readily resolved. Moreover, Yu had never given the slightest thought to how to live independently, away from his brother and sister-in-law—as far as he was concerned, under his present conditions, a family life could be nothing but a burden.

Yu Kerun's eight-year-old nephew would often mis-transmit strange things he had heard and unexpectedly create some family quarrels. For example, on one occasion Yuyuan casually complained to Yu Kerun that their family servant's cooking wasn't very good: she didn't add ginger, scallions, or even wine to the fish she made—the fishy smell was so strong that Yuyuan couldn't bear even to touch the dish with her chopsticks. Through the little mouth of Yuyuan's nephew, this comment made its way to Yu Kerun's wife's ears; she instantly took it to be a sign that her sister-in-law was attempting to steal her position as the mistress of the house. While they were eating, she said quite magnanimously—actually she was quite serious—that she would be more than willing to turn the household over to Yuyuan. She then continued with a barrage of words that left Yuyuan extremely embarrassed. At the time Yuyuan felt as if she had been terribly wronged but didn't quite know how to handle this awkward situation. In the end, her sister-in-law took Yuyuan's uncomfortable silence as proof that she indeed harbored malicious intentions.

Having been doted on by her parents ever since she was little, Yuyuan had had the feeling that she was merely living under somebody else's roof ever since she moved in, that she didn't belong. It was precisely this guest mentality that provided Ding Wenyu with the opportunity to pour out his heart. Even though they were still on their honeymoon, Yu Kerun would often neglect Yuyuan, leaving her all alone in the bridal chamber. He always had so much to do—this minute it would be some meeting, the next minute it would be some congratulatory ceremony, and then there were all those different activities to "resist Japan and save the dying nation." Always having his hand in numerous projects at once, he at the same time made sure always to be the one to liven things up on the social scene. Because virtually every female reporter in Nanjing seemed to know him, Yu Kerun's name repeatedly appeared in all the tabloids. Yu Kerun couldn't get enough and felt happier by the minute. Early on he expressed his apologies to Yuyuan for never being around, but after so many apologies even he got sick of them. Eventually, his apologies turned into complaints. In the end, each time Yu Kerun showed his face after having gone out, Yuyuan had to sit through a barrage of complaints and accusations.

Yuyuan couldn't help but raise her head to look at the clock, hoping that Yu Kexia and his wife would return soon. For a while she wasn't even listening to whatever Ding Wenyu was babbling. She couldn't care less what he said, it was all a bunch of nonsense anyway—nothing but the nonsensical ravings of a lunatic. She genuinely felt that this guest of her brother-in-law was simply too annoying to bear. She imagined what her husband would do if he knew what impudent remarks this Ding Wenyu had uttered. There was no question that Yu Kerun would teach this flighty playboy a lesson he would never forget; he would beat him until Ding had a bloody nose and a swollen face, and was on the ground begging for mercy. Every pilot in the Chinese air force was in great shape, and they were all experts when it came to fighting. Yu Kerun once described to Yuyuan how he had gotten into a huge fight with a complete stranger in a bar. He nonchalantly told her that he just hit the guy lightly and the guy fell to the floor holding his face. Even when Yu Kerun and his buddies were leaving the bar, that man was still on the floor, unable even to drag himself to his feet.

Even though Yuyuan's face displayed a full array of annoyed expressions, Ding Wenyu didn't pick up on a single one. Bold and assured, he continued and gradually, even he himself was deeply moved by his own dull words. He expressed to Yuyuan the feeling of happiness he had after having discovered this love. For all these years he had been a poor orphan that love had forgotten. While he roamed a cold, desolate world, his heart had grown numb and his thoughts were already dead. But spring came to this withered tree and it sprouted new life. Ding Wenyu thanked Yuyuan from the bottom of his heart for giving him a new lease on life. He repeatedly stressed the fact that she had enabled him to grasp the significance of this rebirth. "You gave a man on the brink of death reason to live." He was extremely worked up as he continued, "A small boat drifting on the vast boundless ocean has finally caught sight of the shore."

If Yuyuan hadn't suddenly rushed off in a huff, undoubtedly Ding Wenyu would have kept on like a broken record, as if acting in some never-ending play. But finally Yuyuan couldn't take it anymore. She glared at him with a look of abhorrent disgust, left him behind with the two children, and angrily rushed back into her room, slamming the door behind her. "You bastard!" Yuyuan cursed him under her breath, beside herself with anger. She felt utterly insulted and couldn't imagine that in this world there was anyone this shamelessly audacious. Ding Wenyu sat there stunned, not knowing what to do. Suddenly he realized that he had gone too far. Even though he had thought everything through beforehand and put his best foot forward—for a fleeting moment he actually believed that he had succeeded in striking a chord in Yuyuan's heart—he suddenly became conscious of the fact that things had gotten out of control. Although Yuyuan had already staggered off, the living room seemed to bear the remains of her angry breath. Shaking with fright, Ding Wenyu abruptly stood up before Yu Kexia and his wife could have a chance to return; as he did so, every last drop of courage seemed to escape through the soles of his feet. As if he had brought about a disaster that could not be remedied, Ding Wenyu hastily abandoned the two children and skulked away.

Chapter Four

I

During the first lunar month of 1937, just as the untimely opening of his emotional floodgates hurled the lovesick lunatic Ding Wenyu
headlong into a dead-end obsession with Yuyuan, Jiang Qing, the woman
who thirty years later would make a huge name for herself on the political scene, became an overnight star known all over Shanghai. At the time,
Jiang Qing's stage name was Lan Ping. Her performance in the play *The
Thunderstorm*, which had been the rage for some time, had been an
enormous success. The Russian writer Alexander Ostrovsky's modern
stage play had created an even bigger stir than when it had first been performed in Russia. When the news hit Nanjing, one of the new leading
impresarios in theatrical circles decided to send someone to Shanghai to
invite the troupe to Nanjing for a performance. Nanjing was the capital,
it was the economic and cultural center, and the play could only be called
a true success if it won over the audiences there. Deeply committed to

this performance, the impresario began to put all he had into advertising for *The Thunderstorm*.

FAMOUS RUSSIAN PLAY:

THE THUNDERSTORM

DIRECTOR: Zhang Min

STARRING: The new pop superstar—Miss Lan Ping

MUSIC: New School Composer Xian Xinghai

THEMES: Sexual frustration, the vexation of the flesh, the loneliness of the heart, and the pursuit of the soul.

CHARACTERISTICS: Describes a young woman's longing for love that rages like a fire. Carves an unforgettable portrait of a despotic tyrant that will move one to tears.

Naturally, these advertisements ran in all the newspapers. In those days printing methods were not anything fabulous; the text came out okay, but that was not the case when they tried to run photos. Although lavish previews had made Lan Ping out to be one of the most beautiful women in the country, you couldn't tell what was so dazzling about her from that dark, blurry picture. The small tabloid presses went on at length, singing the praises of the play. Everyone had prepared to get an eyeful when the play was suddenly canceled for some unknown reason. In the end, the people of Nanjing got all excited over nothing. According to some inside rumors that were floating around, the female lead had a problem of some sort with someone and wasn't willing to come. Immediately there were people writing essays in the newspapers criticizing the terrible professional ethics of modern-style actresses. It was the middle of the Spring Festival, yet they still went back on their word after everything had been agreed on. It was true that Nanjing audiences were honest and kind, but that did not mean they could be kicked around. Through the grapevine, there were also reports that the troupe looked down upon Nanjing for being too old, too conservative. Although Nanjing was the capital, it couldn't accept anything western. And so the newspaper editorials became even more enraged—the troupe wasn't simply playing with the people of Nanjing, it was outright insulting them.

Since *The Thunderstorm* did not make it to Nanjing, the production that turned out to be the major success during the first lunar month of

1937 was Dr. Mei Lanfang's *Farewell My Concubine*. The decisive stage battle between the new and the old, the Chinese and the western that everyone had been waiting for never happened. The nation's traditional stage art, Bejing opera, won the Nanjing stage without even a battle. Since there were no new plays to be seen, the people swarmed to the theater to see classics like *Farewell My Concubine*, *The Fisherman's Revenge*, and *Resisting the Tungusie Soldiers*. Suddenly, tickets became hard to come by. Nanjing people always loved to follow the excitement of the crowd, so all at once the streets were flooded with people talking about Mei Lanfang. Even those people who normally never even watched Beijing opera went with the flow and started talking with a Beijing accent as if they were all amateur opera performers.

It was during a performance of *Farewell My Concubine* that Ding Wenyu again ran into Yu Kexia and his wife. He couldn't help but feel both anxious and excited. Because they hadn't noticed him, Ding Wenyu couldn't decide whether to actually approach them. He was afraid that Yuyuan had already told them everything that had happened, in which case all that would be waiting for him would be a reprimand. Although Ding Wenyu was always thick-skinned and self-assured, never one to be bound by etiquette, he did in fact have something of a guilty conscience. It was only natural that the old maxim, "Thy friend's wife, one shall not take advantage of," should also apply to a friend's sister-in-law. What made Ding Wenyu's heart pound was the premonition that Yuyuan had probably also come to the opera. Thinking that he would again see his beloved, Ding Wenyu suddenly turned indifferent to everything else. Yuyuan's image seemed to take over every inch of his brain. He didn't have the slightest interest in watching the rest of the opera; instead he kept turning around in his seat to scope out the theater. Forgetting himself, he at one point even stood up to look around, completely disregarding complaints from those sitting behind him. It was clear that Yuyuan hadn't come, because sitting around Yu Kexia and his wife were a bunch of elderly people who didn't seem to have any connection with them. During the intermission, Ding Wenyu's impatience got the best of him and he ran over to Mr. and Mrs. Yu Kexia. In an attempt to catch them off guard with his sudden display of initiative, he expressed his greetings to both of them.

Yu Kexia's overwhelmingly enthusiastic reaction amply illustrated his complete ignorance about what had happened between Ding and his sister-in-law. That day, many important officials from the Nationalist government had come to see the opera. During the intermission, this group of big shots became the center of everyone's attention and admiration. One after another, the people in the back rows all got up on their tiptoes, some even shamelessly standing on their seats. The entire theater was in a clamorous uproar. It was so loud that Yu Kexia had to practically scream to ask Ding Wenyu why he hadn't waited for him to return that day. He warmly invited Ding to his house again for dinner. Ding Wenyu noticed that Yu Kexia's attention was not focused on him. Yu's eyes continually shot over to an official not far from them—as he rambled his perfunctory remarks to Ding, he waited for that official to turn around. He mentioned that the Military Council that he had spoken to Ding about establishing had already gotten the green light from several government organs. Everything was ready, and he was just waiting for the eastern wind to blow in his direction. They had only to get the red stamp of approval from a certain department; then their announcements could appear in the newspapers. When that official finally turned around, Yu Kexia jumped as if he had been given an electric shock, and, with a sudden leap forward, ended up right in front of him. Yu acted as if he had just run into an old friend. He smiled and wanted to shake the man's hand. This made the official quite uncomfortable, but he couldn't help but go through the motions and extend his hand to Yu.

"Mr. Ding, how come you don't bring your wife to the capital to live?" Mrs. Yu asked casually when she saw that her husband had blown both Ding and her off in order to get close to that bureaucrat.

Ding Wenyu smiled but didn't answer. The performance was about to resume, and one by one the audience members made their way back to their seats. Mrs. Yu continued to speak to Ding Wenyu about his wife. It seemed like the more Ding withheld, the more prying Mrs. Yu became. Ding Wenyu, however, simply toughened up and continued to avoid her questions. He was truly in no rush to think about his wife Peitao—she was simply an unwanted gift from his father. Mrs. Yu was really too untactful. How wonderful it would be if she were talking about Yuyuan instead of Ding's wife.

Yu Kexia rushed to conclude his conversation with the official, and, with an air of mystery, came over to tell Ding Wenyu that the bureaucrat he had just been talking with was the Generalissimo's most popular aide. The house lights suddenly dimmed, signaling that the performance was about to resume. Yu Kexia called his wife to quickly return to her seat. Ding Wenyu sullenly returned to his seat but wasn't in the mood to continue watching the performance. Only in its second half did the opera truly reach its climatic moment. After the audience had called for him repeatedly, Dr. Mei Lanfang finally strolled on stage to display his true talent. When the stage lights lit up and the house suddenly became quiet, Ding Wenyu got confused; he thought something had gone wrong. All he heard was the sound of a delicate voice singing backstage; then, wearing a traditional costume, Dr. Mei Lanfang slowly made his way to center stage doing his trademark *yangko* dance, which he had single-handedly developed and made famous. Slim and graceful, he struck a pose there on the stage, and the audience broke out into a round of thunderous applause. Ding Wenyu couldn't help but follow along and clap with them—if he didn't applaud it would have been proof that he was an opera layman, and that would have meant that he had wasted his time in coming.

Ding Wenyu crept out of the theater before the opera was even finished. Dr. Mei's performance wasn't bad, but Ding Wenyu couldn't get over the fact that this was a man dressed as a woman. In fact, he had absolutely no interest in Beijing opera. Not only did he dislike the so-called quintessence of Chinese culture, but while in Europe he was also not at all fond of its western counterpart, which the Europeans seemed to go crazy for. One year while Ding was in Rome, a Chinese art student sold off two of his sketches to scrape together enough money to buy a pair of opera tickets for Ding and another friend. He brought them to the theater and gestured for them to go in. He said that he had already seen the opera and didn't want to watch it again; instead he'd just wait for them at the entrance. Ding Wenyu felt the whole thing was quite odd. He thought that the art student was just looking for an excuse, because in actuality he also didn't have the slightest taste for western opera. Halfway through the opera the painter's other friend leaned over to tell Ding that the art student waiting outside was a fanatical opera buff. Because the student was currently hard up and opera tickets were so expensive, he had no choice but to give up on seeing it himself. In the end, Ding Wenyu watched the entire opera without the slightest interest. He couldn't help but admit that he had forced himself to get through it. If he hadn't watched the whole thing, he would not have done right by the young student who had gone through so much to invite him. Ding Wenyu felt that he was watching the opera completely out of friendship. After the performance was over and they came out, the art student who had been waiting outside rushed up to them brimming with enthusiasm and eagerly asked what they thought. "Besides Leonardo da Vinci, this is the greatest stuff in Italy!" He couldn't stop praising this opera, as if *he* were the one who had just seen it. "Only an Italian tenor is a true tenor. The most wonderful music in the world is produced from the human throat. When the ancients said, 'The melody lingers on and for three days I knew not the taste of meat,' this was exactly what they were talking about."

That evening they ended up sauntering the streets all night. It was a rarity for Ding Wenyu to be short of cash, but as luck would have it, that day he had barely a dime in his pocket. They spent their very last copper on some cheap spirits and were forced to repeatedly drive off the prostitutes who kept pestering them. At dawn they arrived at a hotel. The art student pointed out a room with a light on up on the second floor and told Ding Wenyu that there was a female painter living there named Huang. She wasn't much of a painter, but she was fun to be around. And so they boldly decided to call on her. The female painter, who had been up all night, was just preparing to go to sleep when they arrived and wasn't terribly willing to entertain them. Naturally, there was no way that Ding Wenyu could know that this Ms. Huang Yifan was the mother of the woman who would later make quite a name for herself on the literary scene—Eileen Chang. Ms. Huang was a divorcée who, having left behind her daughter and son, had gone all alone to Europe to study art. She resembled a Malaysian more than a Chinese. Rather good-looking and a bit dark-skinned, she was a woman of few words. The topic of conversation that morning was still the Italian opera that was being performed. Actually, all of Rome was talking about that opera that day. Ms. Huang finally showed them her newest painting, and Ding Wenyu insincerely praised it to the skies. Mrs. Huang probably saw through his superficial compliments and did not seem to take them much to heart.

As Ding Wenyu walked alone along the broad streets, the scene outside the theater was bustling with excitement. From time to time rickshaw coolies approached him looking for business, repeatedly interrupting his nostalgic recollections. According to police department estimates, there were all together more than 2,000 rickshaw companies in the capital and more than 12,000 rickshaw pullers. Ding Wenyu had already grown accustomed to taking Monk's rickshaw when he went out. If Monk wasn't around he would rather walk. Automobiles belonging to government officials were parked all over the street around the theater entrance while rickshaws were ordered to line up at a spot relatively farther from the entrance. Five days after the Spring Festival, those wineshops and dance halls around the Temple of Confucius that had been closed for the holiday had already reopened, and the men who sought their pleasures in "flowers and willows" came out soon after. Without walking too far, Ding Wenyu could arrive at those exciting places. Through the cracks in the doors that were not entirely closed, he could hear strains of graceful dance music and merry song. Then there was a peculiarly dressed woman with thick rouge who emerged from the darkness to grab prospective johns in the most primitive manner. These types were the lowest-class prostitutes on the Qinhuai River banks. They all came from the countryside and had thick provincial accents. Nine out of ten times they returned from the hunt empty-handed.

On this lonely night Ding Wenyu was unwilling to return all alone to his apartment, but of course he was also not willing to give up without a fight and simply become the prize for some lowly prostitute. He had already resolved to mend his ways and never again screw around at those places of disrepute, wasting the golden years of his life. Alone, roaming through the streets of debauchery flooded by the red lanterns and green wine, he thought of Yuyuan and was filled with feelings of tenderness. He remembered what she had looked like when he had first laid eyes on her and compared her beauty when wearing her uniform with how she looked in ordinary clothes. No matter what this lovely woman wore, it moved him. In uniform she appeared bright and brave, in everyday clothes she looked natural and poised. No matter what she did, no matter what she wore, Yuyuan was always stunning. Ding Wenyu's entire mind was occupied by the shadow of her graceful beauty. As Ding Wenyu walked through the streets he couldn't help but mumble Yuyuan's name; over and over again he nauseatingly pledged his love to her.

Ding Wenyu lingered blindly around the banks of the Qinhuai River for more than an hour before he got so cold that, shivering, he made his way home. He knew that what awaited him was a long sleepless night.

During this hour or so, he was continually thinking of Yuyuan. He thought of the way she acted, moved, knitted her brows, and laughed, he closed his eyes and visualized her expression when she was happy and even when she was mad. He had already offended her, and heaven only knew how much she dreaded him at that moment. Gaily painted pleasure boats periodically rowed past him; the lights aboard were bright and the sounds of laughter from the boat hostesses and their guests reverberated into the night. Even though the police department had already proclaimed pleasure boats "public places strictly prohibited from gambling," without exception, every boat that passed had a mah-jongg table set up. Disregard for orders and prohibitions was one of the distinguishing peculiarities of 1937. Despite constant appeals in the newspapers, warnings from the departments in charge, and the nonstop issuing of all kinds of articles and prohibitions, hardly anyone seriously carried them out. During the Spring Festival everything gave way to the power of indulgence, and the boat-keepers took advantage of the opportunity to make an extra buck. It was already deep into the night and Ding Wenyu felt very cold. He picked a stone up off the street and forcefully threw it into the Qinhuai River.

II

Yuyuan thought that she would be quite angry but, not long after slamming the door shut, she realized that her temper had more or less calmed down. She did not hold on to her anger and resentment as Ding had feared she would. Yuyuan had already made Ding Wenyu uncomfortable enough. By putting him through the wringer, she had made it clear that she was not at all fond of hearing his nonsensical ramblings. No matter how much smug nonsense he spewed, it was still no use. Yuyuan was never the kind of person to be hard on someone once she got the upper hand. Her sole regret was that she did not put on a grave face and, with perfect justification and assurance, ask Ding Wenyu to leave instead of letting things go as far as they did. Running from the battlefield defeated made it look as if she were guilty of some wrongdoing.

Never before had a man so boldly and flagrantly expressed his love for her. Never even in the pages of those pulp romance novels that Yuyuan normally enjoyed reading had she encountered such scorching, naked confessions, such lectures on love, or such utterly nonsensical, absurd logic. Not even the boldest and most brazen men from those romance novels could hold a candle to Ding Wenyu. For a time, Yuyuan did not know how she should deal with this secret. She couldn't make up her mind if she should tell her husband Yu Kerun or first go home and tell her sisters. There was no question that it would be a most entertaining topic for conversation. Moreover, Yuyuan was obviously innocent of all wrongdoing. Because everyone knew what kind of a jerk Ding Wenyu was, she was certain that there would be no misunderstandings. Yuyuan was sure that Ding Wenyu also behaved this way with other women; this thought instantly made her feel more than a bit lost.

Yu Kerun had absolutely no interest in hearing about Ding Wenyu's antics with his wife. The moment Yuyuan began to tell him her story about what had happened with Ding, Yu Kerun impatiently interrupted her.

"Don't pay any attention to him. That guy's a clown!" Yu Kerun said with a look of seriousness.

Yuyuan was terribly disappointed; Yu Kerun's tone carried a hint of contempt for Ding Wenyu. He also seemed to be reminding Yuyuan not to be too conceited or get too fanciful. Yuyuan immediately felt as though she had been insulted and wanted to set things straight with Yu Kerun. He asked what there was to fuss about—if she felt he had said something wrong then he would take it back. With that, Yuyuan felt even more insulted. Trying to gloss things over to avoid a quarrel, Yu Kerun asked if she was trying to make him jealous. If she was, there was no way Yu Kerun was going to get jealous over a clown like Ding. If she wasn't trying to make him jealous, than what was the point in telling him at all? Yu Kerun said that whenever he went out there were always countless women after him, but never once did he allow them to arouse his desire. Who the hell was this Ding Wenyu anyway, wearing that red woolen nightcap, neither a country bumpkin nor a westernized dandy? An eccentric mess. His only fear seemed to be that that others didn't know that he had once spent a few years muddling about abroad. What's more, he was a man who was already old but refused to accept it; he didn't even stop to think about his own age—for God's sake, he was old enough to be Yuyuan's father.

Yu Kerun always had way too much confidence in himself; never for a moment did he stop to consider that he might be harming someone else's self-respect. Perhaps because everything came so easily for him, he treasured nothing—including Yuyuan. When they had first met, he hadn't aggressively pursued her; all they did was dance a number together. But afterward, everyone seemed to take them for a match made in heaven and enthusiastically paired them up. When someone asked his first impression of Yuyuan, Yu Kerun answered nonchalantly, "That girl, well, frankly speaking, she's not bad." Yu Kerun also looked down on her job. In his eyes, female confidential secretaries at the army headquarters were nothing but a bunch of pretty flower arrangements kept around for their good looks rather than their abilities. Their purpose was simply to brighten up those decrepit and muddleheaded officials and make them feel a bit younger. No matter where he was, Yu Kerun always felt the need to show off the superiority of the air force. His leather boots were eternally polished and shining bright; when his iron-soled shoes walked on the cement floor they made a clear and sharp sound—it was as if unless he did these things he would not be able to bring out the special qualities of a pilot. Moreover, Yuyuan and Yu Kerun hadn't had much time alone with each other before they got married. Young people in 1937, even those fashionable enough to resist arranged marriages, still had their very conservative side. For example, in order not to cause any unnecessary misunderstandings when they went out, each of them always brought along their friends.

When Yu Kerun told Yuyuan of his plans for marriage, Yuyuan agreed with a barely a second thought. The reason they moved so fast was simply that they both thought that was the only way they could be perfectly justified in being alone together. Since they had already formalized their relationship, marriage was simply a matter of time. Yuyuan didn't really have any experience with the opposite sex and she was somewhat at a loss as to what to do once they got to the nuptial chamber. Like always, Yu Kerun maintained his haughty attitude; he appeared calm and unhurried as he sat on the edge of the bed. He stared at her, and harbored within his sly smirk were his malicious intentions. His grimace made Yuyuan feel embarrassed and shy; at the same time, it also made her furious. By the time the sun came up the next morning, Yuyuan and Yu Kerun both felt a kind of indescribable melancholy. The reason for Yuyuan's sorrow was that she felt that she had dazedly departed from the days of her youth. She had given her most precious possession to Yu Kerun, yet he not only didn't appreciate it, he didn't even seem to feel an ounce of satisfaction. For a long time, Yuyuan didn't understand why Yu Kerun was unsatisfied. Seeing his trancelike manner, she couldn't figure out what she had done wrong. But her purity was unquestioned, and it was clear Yu Kerun had no suspicions in that department. Yuyuan didn't know why he looked so crestfallen. He was so depressed that it appeared as if he had just taken a staggering blow from someone's cane. Although Yu Kerun shared the same bed with her, for several days after that he was like a shy boy—not daring to even lay a single finger upon her.

In the beginning Yuyuan wondered if Yu Kerun had something wrong with him. Back even before they were married, Yuyuan had heard rumors concerning the improper conduct of pilots; besides hearing endless gossip about their promiscuity, she overheard her sisters talking about male impotence. There were no secrets among the Ren sisters. Once they got together, they would go on chatting as if there was no tomorrow. Yuyuan's fourth brother-in-law suffered from premature ejaculation. Every time he and his wife were intimate, he would hastily spill his pudding the second he got in the door. Whenever Yuyuan's fourth sister talked about men she was unable to restrain her dissatisfaction. She always said that just because a man was big and strong didn't necessarily mean that he was anything to write home about. Her husband was the perfect example: out of all the sons-in-law who married into the Ren family, he gave the impression of being the strongest and healthiest. By the same token, just because a man is weak and skinny doesn't mean that he isn't any good. Yuyuan's eldest sister's first husband might have been short, but he was a regular Don Juan in the bedroom. This undersized warlord from Sichuan was a modern version of the legendary lover Ximen Qing. He often had enough spunk in him to drive two women out of their minds in a single night—their screaming and moaning went on endlessly as if he were slaughtering a pig.

As a newlywed it was impossible for Yuyuan to discuss her own sex life unscrupulously the way her sisters did. Upon her return to her parents' home shortly after her wedding, her sisters asked how *it* felt. However, as soon as this topic came out in the open, Yuyuan quite skillfully swept it right back under the rug. Although she didn't want to discuss it, Yu Kerun's awkward fear of sex remained a constant enigma to Yuyuan. As a woman she couldn't be too aggressive, yet at the same time, to bashfully pretend that she had absolutely no interest in sex would be going against her nature. Things had barely begun, and Yuyuan was confused as to what she actually wanted. Making love was not necessarily what she was yearning for, but it was her honeymoon, after all. She needed a man to caress her, she needed her husband's firm embrace—otherwise it would be simply too strange. A newlywed couple lying together and sleeping in the same bed like two strangers was absurd. She wasn't exactly sure what a honeymoon was supposed to be like, but she knew that it wasn't supposed to be like this.

Completely out of instinct, Yuyuan wondered if there could be another woman—any woman in her shoes would probably have thought the same thing. Even though the mere thought of another woman would inevitably damage the self-respect of someone with Yuyuan's haughty disposition, what else could she do? Yuyuan secretly kept on the lookout for any trace of a woman on Yu Kerun. She noticed the little notes in his pockets, the scent of perfume on his clothes, and the lipstick marks left by other women. Sometimes Yuyuan was overcome with jealousy at the mere thought of her own husband brazenly screwing around with other women on her honeymoon that she gnashed her teeth in hatred. At other times she felt that she was just being overly suspicious. After all, there was more than enough conclusive evidence to prove that it was impossible that Yu Kerun could have been having an affair. There were indeed an ample number of young girls who took a liking to him; he also enjoyed hanging around the women. However, when it came down to it, Yuyuan was convinced that Yu Kerun was the kind of man who could check his passions before they went over the line of propriety.

Only one day toward the end of their honeymoon did Yu Kerun inadvertently let out the secret reason behind his fear of intimacy with Yuyuan. The flames of passion were obviously torturing him, because lying beside a gorgeous woman like Yuyuan and not being moved was something quite unimaginable. It was the day after the anniversary of the January 28 Anti-Japanese Incident,* when all of the major military organs

---

*Increased anti-Japanese sentiment and boycotts of Japanese goods in the wake of the Mukden Incident came to a head on January 28, 1932, when Japanese forces engaged in battle with the Chinese Nineteenth Army in Zhabei, which was in the northern section of Shanghai, just east of the International Settlement. The incident escalated into an undeclared war that raged around Shanghai until March of that year, when both sides agreed to an armistice.

were holding commemoration activities, that Yu Kerun and Yuyuan once again stole the show on the dance floor. They exhausted their passion in dance, and after the music stopped and the crowds had left, the two of them held each other in the moonlight, returning alone to their little love nest. The dark shadow that engulfed their honeymoon seemed no longer to exist. The moment the door closed, Yu Kerun could not restrain himself and embraced Yuyuan. Their passionate kisses quickly developed to the point where they were removing each other's clothes. One after another, articles of clothing were tossed in all different directions; by the time they slid under the covers, a messy disarray of clothes, shoes, and socks covered the entire floor.

Things moved so quickly that Yuyuan didn't have time to think of anything else; all of a sudden it began, it lasted for a while, and then it ended. Yu Kerun's breathing went from an urgent panting to a steady breath. Like a child who had been wronged, Yu gently nibbled on Yuyuan's shoulder. Yuyuan was at a loss and didn't know quite what she should do; it was as if she were jogging and had fallen behind. Deep down she wanted nothing more than to catch up, but no matter how she tried she couldn't pick up any speed. As they chatted about insignificant matters, the moonlight rushed in through the window like a stream of quicksilver. As they spoke, Yu Kerun's hand kept sliding up and down Yuyuan's body. He caressed her neck, her round shoulders, and then rubbed back and forth on her stomach and firmly grabbed her breasts. Finally he staunchly began his downward exploration, his hand sliding down between Yuyuan's legs.

"How come you don't have any hair here?" he delicately whispered in Yuyuan's ear. Yuyuan couldn't help but giggle from the warm, ticklish breath. Although this question had come from her own husband's lips, it was indeed the first time a man had asked her this, and Yuyuan felt quite embarrassed. Having just gotten married, Yuyuan had yet to grow comfortable enough to discuss such things with her husband. Yu Kerun, however, was obviously waiting for her answer. His naughty hand continued to play with her; he used the strength of his fingers to force her to immediately reply to his question.

"How should I know?" Yuyuan said, almost laughing.

Under the caresses of Yu Kerun, Yuyuan stretched out like a kitten, repeatedly arching her body. Again Yu Kerun's lips approached Yuyuan's ear as he asked her if all the women in her family were all clean and smooth, without any hair. This was another absurd question. If it had been any other time, Yuyuan would have probably lost her temper; after all, what did the secrets of the women in her family have to do with him? But during this intimate moment, Yuyuan not only responded to this question but entered into a good-humored conversation with him about it. Yuyuan clearly had inherited her Japanese mother's special trait, because her two oldest half-sisters who were born of another mother both had thick, black pubic hair. Her other sisters' pubic hair was rather sparse, but she alone had none at all. Only in Yuyuan's mother's old age did she finally feel comfortable disrobing in front of her daughters; before that time, everyone always thought that Yuyuan was so strange, they would always make fun of her while bathing.

As for this amusing little inquiry into pubic hair, it was enough to once again ignite Yu Kerun's passion—meanwhile, he also sensed that Yuyuan's passion was blazing even more fiercely than his own. It was virtually inevitable that this would restart everything, however, this time it lasted for a very long time. Yu Kerun's technique was more mature the second time around. As if he were an old, experienced lover, he moved slowly and deliberately, completely intoxicated by the sound of her constrained panting. As far as their sex life went, this was the first—and only—time that they had achieved perfection. They were soaked in sweat as if they had been running naked in a boundless desert where the blazing crimson sun tempted them from far away. Not knowing exhaustion, they ran and ran toward that sun, but just as they seemed to come to the end, something happened that exceeded their expectations and everything began all over again.

The next night they tried to revisit their happiness of the evening before, but Yu Kerun ruined everything. The topic of conversation went back to the previous night, when Yu Kerun carelessly asked Yuyuan if she knew what a "white tiger" was. Yuyuan shook her head, saying that she didn't know, and so Yu Kerun told her that women like her without any pubic hair are called "white tigers." Legend has it that white tigers have the power to harm men. Because of this, in the past, generals on the battlefield, high rollers who played mercilessly in the gambling halls, and businessmen who went head to head in the market would all obstinately refuse to have anything to do with white tigers. If they did, they were bound to be struck by bad luck before they even knew what hit them. Yu Kerun told Yuyuan an anecdotal story about a warlord who had the habit of deflowering virgins anytime something didn't go his way. Once while he was in the Henan region he went four rounds in a row at the gambling table without winning a single hand. In a fit of anger, he had his underlings immediately go out to find him a young girl. After she arrived, this warlord brought the trembling girl into an adjoining wing and quickly removed her clothing. Suddenly he screamed aloud is if he had run into the devil himself. His gambling partners were dumbstruck; they heard the warlord's furious stamping and incessant cursing but did not dare go in to try to calm him down. Finally they heard a gunshot and rushed into the room to see the girl lying naked on the floor with blood gushing from her stomach. Panting with rage, the warlord was still cursing. He said no wonder he was having such bad luck, it was due to the dirty tricks of this damned white tiger!

Yuyuan obviously wasn't in a very good mood after hearing this, and Yu Kerun began to realize that it was a mistake to tell her a story like that at such an inopportune time—an extremely stupid mistake at that. Yu kept swearing that he hadn't made the story up, assuring Yuyuan that he had read it in some tabloid. He continued with his uncalled-for explanation, saying that that girl must have still been developing, because it is said that genuine naturally hairless women are extremely rare. He obviously could sense Yuyuan's dissatisfaction with his story and wanted to make up for his indiscreet remarks. The result, however, was that he hurt Yuyuan even more deeply. Yu Kerun pretended that the belief did not bother him one bit by saying, "My fate is already set in stone, so I'm not at all afraid that you will harm me!"

Yuyuan laughed grimly and said, "*You* might not be afraid, but now *I'm* a bit afraid."

Yu Kerun tried to use a joke to end this increasingly glum conversation, but his tasteless jokes came off quite awkward and oafish. Not even he could laugh at them. He realized that he was quite clumsy in speech and no matter what he said, he couldn't seem to get on Yuyuan's good side. Nor was Yuyuan the kind of naïve woman likely to be won over with a little humoring. Yu Kerun discovered that he had fallen into very awkward straits. He tried to console Yuyuan with his caresses, using his old ways to get back that old feeling, but she didn't have the slightest reaction. In order to show that she wasn't angry and that she could care less about those things her husband had said, Yuyuan forced herself not to resist his fondling. She even made herself imagine the passion of the night before. She didn't want to disappoint her husband or make him feel uncomfortable, but it was useless. She didn't have a trace of ecstasy, nor even of passion. She came off even more anxious than on her wedding night. This was one very uninteresting battle. Having exhausted all his tricks, Yu Kerun couldn't help but admit defeat; he hastily went to finish what he had started. Lying on top of Yuyuan and carrying a bellyful of resentment, he fell asleep.

III

When Yuyuan received Ding Wenyu's first love letter, she was in an extremely complicated state of mind. Strictly speaking, this was not an actual love letter but an apology letter. In it Ding used an extremely remorseful tone to express his deepest apologies. He told Yuyuan that he had not intended to offend her in any way. Seeing her angry terrified him, leaving him on tenterhooks for several days. Upsetting Yuyuan was the last thing that Ding Wenyu wanted to do, and it was only after seeing how distressed she was that he felt compelled to write such a letter. Ding Wenyu said that he had already pondered it for several days but could not come up with a better way of redressing the situation.

The letter was delivered by Monk. An unknown rickshaw coolie standing mysteriously in the lane outside her house calling her name—as soon as he removed the letter from his inside jacket pocket, Yuyuan realized that this was another one of Ding Wenyu's tricks. The first thing that came to her mind was that she shouldn't accept the letter, but Monk simply stuffed it in her hand and strutted off. The whole delivery happened in the blink of an eye. As he was leaving, Monk turned to say something to Yuyuan, but before she could catch it, he was already far off. By the time Yuyuan had collected herself and was about to call him to stop, he had already turned the corner of the lane. If Monk hadn't left so abruptly, Yuyuan would have torn up the letter in front of his face— but since he had already disappeared without a trace, throwing the letter away would have been a wasted effort. No one had seen her receive it, and if she were to throw it away on the street, some good samaritan would probably think she had dropped it and would hand it back to her. Then again, maybe someone would deliver it to her house, or even open it right up and read it. Thinking of all these possibilities, Yuyuan stuffed the letter into her pocket.

This was a letter without an addressee or signature; besides the two people involved, probably nobody else would be able to understand its meaning. It wasn't overly affectionate or too philosophical, it was a simple apology letter. Besides sincerity, there wasn't any part of the letter that exceeded the proper decorum. Between the pages were two slightly withered but still fragrant plum blossom petals. This was a letter brimming with inhibitions. You could tell that the writer had much to say, but because he was afraid of once again offending the one he held to be his goddess, he took the words back as soon as they got to the tip of his pen. Yuyuan knew this letter was written merely to test the waters. If perchance she were to accept it, Ding Wenyu would become even more brazen.

Indeed, three days later Monk used the same method to deliver a second letter to her in the same place. Yuyuan, however, did not refuse to accept the letter as she had originally intended; instead, she suddenly had the urge to see exactly just what kinds of shameless things Ding had to say. That night, as if nothing had happened, she ate dinner and sat with Yu Kexia and his family in the dining room for a bit before shutting herself up in her little room where, full of zest, she began reading the letter. With this letter, Ding Wenyu started to get a bit out of hand. Besides reiterating the love lecture he had delivered when they were alone, he expressed some mild complaints. Ding Wenyu hinted that his endless longing had already become the most important component of his life. Love is a kind of right, a right that no one has the power to interfere with. The right to love and be loved should be entitled to ample freedom.

Three days after that, Yuyuan received a third letter. Just like in the second letter, Ding Wenyu played his little tricks; the countless letters that followed were in the same set pattern. Because he was afraid the letter would fall into the wrong hands and bring about unnecessary trouble, Ding Wenyu gave himself a pseudonym. He gave Yuyuan one as well. Each time he used two envelopes, one within the other, and would write "Ren Yuyuan please forward to Miss B" on the outside envelope. In his third letter Ding Wenyu expressed his deepest apologies over the resentful tone of his second letter. Deeply moved, Ding Wenyu said that just thinking that her beautiful eyes were reading his unworthy words, he already felt enormous satisfaction. What more could he want? How could he shamelessly desire those things to which he clearly had no right?

Letter after letter made its way into Yuyuan's hands. In the beginning it was one letter every three days, but very quickly it developed to the point that she was getting letters virtually every day—sometimes she would even receive two or more in a single day. The method and place of delivery also changed. They were still delivered face to face by Monk, but instead of in the lane across from Yuyuan's front door, they were given to her while she was on her way to work at the army headquarters. In the very beginning, Yuyuan kept thinking that each letter would be the last, but after receiving one she would instantly realize the inevitability of a follow-up. Gradually she developed somewhat of an interest in this secret little game. Since the letters were not written to her but to a certain nonexistent Miss B, Yuyuan felt that receiving them would probably not be seen as too improper.

Ding Wenyu continually thought up new tricks. Before long Yuyuan found that just as she received a letter from Monk, the postman would deliver the same letter via mail. At first she couldn't figure out what was going on. Perhaps Ding Wenyu realized that he could not continue using Monk as his private mailman forever, so he tried the post office. Because he was afraid that something would go wrong, after finishing a letter, besides saving his draft copy, Ding Wenyu would make two extra copies. This "double safety" method was a bit much, but as long as Ding Wenyu remained unable to verify whether or not Yuyuan received his letters from the postman, he insisted that Monk continue to deliver them. He repeatedly asked Yuyuan to give him some kind of indication whether or not she had received his letters through the post office; that way he wouldn't have to make two fair copies.

Yuyuan naturally did not pay any heed to Ding Wenyu—no matter what her reaction, it would be enough to illustrate that she was reading his letters. She realized that the best response would be to continue ignoring him. Receiving two copies of the same letter was a bit ridiculous. She already had more than enough letters from Ding. Monk was also becoming consistently more annoying, making Yuyuan somewhat irritated.

On one occasion Yuyuan crumpled a letter up and threw it into the curbside sewer right in front of Monk's face. She immediately regretted her rather drastic reaction. Monk seemed to be able to read her mind and simply turned and left without the slightest response. From that point onward all letters came from the post office. What Yuyuan couldn't understand was, after not receiving any kind of reply, why did Ding Wenyu continue writing all those silly letters? Could it be that he truly intended to continue like that, writing for all eternity?

Actually, these secret letters were not really a secret. Back when Yuyuan had received the first few letters she had thought about seeing what kind of reaction Yu Kerun would have. She intentionally put the letters in an unlocked drawer. One time she even deliberately left them on the table, but Yu Kerun couldn't care less about her little secret. He was always so busy, forever coming and going like the wind, complaining nonstop about this and that. Even when Yuyuan hinted to him that these were love letters, he still had no reaction. "There is nothing at all strange if a woman like you receives a couple of letters from men expressing their interest." Yu Kerun came off quite magnanimous. All he did was look at the words written on the envelope.

Yuyuan said, "I never said that these letters were written to me."

With that Yu Kerun became even more aloof; he couldn't think of any reason why he should go and read other people's love letters. In the most serious manner he told Yuyuan that as an educated person, even if someone did write her love letters, he still wouldn't read them. Reading other people's letters is not a very polite thing to do. He respected his wife's freedom of correspondence and had absolute trust in her. At the same time, he also felt that the recipient should not carelessly show the love letters to others to read, for it was a form of disrespect to the letter writer. Yu Kerun didn't pay attention to the red tide that overtook Yuyuan's face. Yu had completely forgotten about all those times he had waved *his* old love letters in Yuyuan's face.

There were no words that could describe Yuyuan's feeling of depression. The youthful and spirited Yu Kerun was brimming with a feeling of superiority; this was the common flaw of all Chinese pilots in 1937. They always felt that they were the pride of heaven, and believed that every woman under the sky was bound to fall in love with them. Yuyuan, proud and haughty in disposition, felt that she had suffered a gratuitous injury and wanted to have it out with Yu Kerun. Yu Kerun, however, had absolutely no idea how he had offended her. On the contrary, he felt he was quite generous in the way he handled the situation. He thought she was simply angry with him for always being too busy, so he gave her a hug and a kiss and promised that he would take her to Plum Blossom Mountain next week in time to catch the flowers in bloom. The newspapers said that the early flowers on Plum Blossom Mountain were already in bud. Yuyuan discovered that there was nothing more for her to say. If she were to continue with her rash actions in the face of Yu Kerun's efforts to make up, she would only appear to be making an unreasonable ruckus.

Although she knew that she had many admirers, unlike Yu Kerun, Yuyuan had never before received any love letters. Back when she was in middle school, no matter if it was in class or during after-school activities, there was always a handful of boys who secretly stared at her. On her way home after school, there would always be at least one boy hanging around the intersection waiting for Yuyuan to make her appearance. Except for the dissolute and debonair Yu Kerun, Yuyuan's experience with the opposite sex was virtually zero. Perhaps the only time she went just a little bit out of line was on April Fool's Day when she was seventeen. A boy who had been hiding in a doorway suddenly jumped out as she walked by and gave her a soaking wet rose. Afterward he took quick to his heels down the street like a thief. The thorn on the rose stem pricked Yuyuan's hand, drawing blood. She didn't have an ounce of affection for the kid who gave her the flower, but oh, did she like that red rose. And so she took the flower home, filled a glass bottle with tap water, and put the rose in it.

Since Yu Kerun didn't have any interest in those secret letters, Yuyuan planned to bring them home to her parents' house and share them with her sisters. Actually, well before this, Yuyuan's female colleagues had been fortunate enough to enjoy an advance hint of her secret. They made all kinds of frivolous remarks and criticisms about Ding Wenyu, and went on and on giving Yuyuan all kinds of rotten ideas. They encouraged Yuyuan to write a letter to Ding Wenyu, an ambiguous letter that would lead Ding to bite down even harder on the hook and bring him even deeper into the marshland of love. They wanted Yuyuan to daringly arrange a date with Ding Wenyu, while they, as if watching a comedy, hid off to one side to catch a first-hand glimpse of this lovesick lunatic in action. There was nothing more interesting or engaging than this type of love game. They firmly opposed Yuyuan's idea to reject Ding Wenyu's letters outright. They all assumed that having a little fun at Ding Wenyu's expense wouldn't tarnish Yuyuan's purity in the least bit.

Ding Wenyu's letters livened things up in the Ren household. Yuyuan's sisters started to pass around these secret letters, erupting in laughter as they read. They locked themselves up in Yuyuan's old boudoir, appraising certain phrases and sentences in the letters. It would be impossible not to link Ding Wenyu's current quest for Yuyuan with his fanatical pursuit of Yuchan way back when. One after another, all the sisters tried to get Yuchan to give her opinion. Full of zest and excitement, they listened once again to the retelling of that old story from Yuchan's youth and then discussed how they should deal with Ding Wenyu. They were all in agreement that there was absolutely no need to let Yu Kerun know about this; moreover, they felt that Yuyuan's idea to use Ding to make her husband jealous was extremely foolish. There isn't a husband in the world who would be happy to learn that his wife is being pursued by another man. Yuyuan's plan was nothing short of playing with fire. In this world there does not exist such a creature as a "lofty man."

The steady stream of continuous letters enabled Yuyuan, whose work was normally quite dull, to have an extra hobby to pass the time. There were more and more letters, so many you could make a book out of them. Ding Wenyu was obviously spellbound with infatuation. His letters became increasingly inclusive in content. From straightforward expressions of feelings to philosophical reflections on love, he discussed everything under the sun. Through pen and paper the sparks of the mind were consolidated into words and reached Yuyuan through the post office. More often than not, she felt that those florid words, nauseating outpourings of love, and endless confessions had little to do with her. Yuyuan always felt that these were letters to an unknown woman, someone completely unrelated to her—a nonexistent woman of Ding's imagination. As Ding Wenyu became more and more infatuated, his letters became increasingly eloquent, and increasingly long. Before one letter had even been mailed, he had already begun writing the next; because of this Yuyuan would often receive one overweight envelope with several different letters written on the same day.

Only when Ding Wenyu expressed his resolution to divorce his wife in a letter did Yuyuan become conscious of just how serious things had become. This rushed and stubborn decision had absolutely nothing to do with Yuyuan. She never made any promises or suggestions; she never once wrote even a single word to Ding Wenyu. What first came to Yuyuan's mind was the extreme stupidity of this move on Ding's part; it was clear that he was trying to use this divorce to put pressure on her. He wanted her to take responsibility for something that she should never have had responsibility for in the first place. Yuyuan felt that Ding Wenyu's actions were preposterous; it was as if he had gotten an inch and was now going for the mile. The ridiculous part was that he hadn't even gotten an inch.

After a period of anger, Yuyuan couldn't help but consider the seriousness of the situation. She didn't know if she should discuss this with her new husband. What's more, she was afraid that it was already too late, because no matter what kind of explanation she gave, she would still be unable to prove to Yu Kerun that she had absolutely nothing to do with this. If from the very start she had let him see the letters, if from the very start he had known the origin and development of the whole thing, then everything could have been clearly explained without any misunderstandings. But now that Ding Wenyu was declaring his resolution to divorce, not only Yuyuan's co-workers but even her own sisters began to have second thoughts about Yuyuan's innocence. They all felt that the final juncture had arrived and Yuyuan needed to take a stand.

IV

Ding Wenyu's decision to get a divorce caused a huge uproar. His father took a train out to Nanjing the very night he heard the news. Ding's father arrived in Nanjing the next morning with a livid face to give his son a ferocious tongue-lashing. As far as Mr. Ding was concerned, Ding Wenyu had committed an unforgivable mistake. His son indeed was no longer a three-year-old child who could do whatever he wished. How could someone from a family like his go and get divorced at the drop of a hat? Ding Wenyu was reprimanded by his father for a full day; afterward he was dragged back to Shanghai as if he were a wanted thief. In their first-class coach on the Blue Steel Express, Ding Wenyu's father's blood pressure shot way up because he was so agitated. He lay on the sleeper, groaning in pain. The first thing Ding Wenyu did when the train arrived in Shanghai was rush his father to the hospital.

Just as when he was in Nanjing, Ding Wenyu devoted huge amounts of time to letter writing while he was in Shanghai. He reported to Yuyuan his reasons and intentions for this trip, detailing all of the things that had already happened and those that were about to happen. Although getting a divorce was proving to be much more difficult than he had imagined, Ding Wenyu promised Yuyuan that his mind was already set and nothing could change it. Ding Wenyu told Yuyuan that for the time being, in order not to upset his father, he had decided to have a good long talk with his wife Peitao.

Peitao's answer was very simple, it was one word—"No!" Her reason for refusing was also very simple: she was set on never letting Ding Wenyu have his way so easily—especially if that meant getting a divorce. She coldly told Ding Wenyu that their divorce was most likely just a matter of time—but he had to wait until she was in the mood. If she was in the mood, they could have a lawyer come the next day with the divorce papers, but if she wasn't, it would be best for him to forget this dream for the rest of his life! The final say as far as the divorce went was safely Peitao's; she warned Ding Wenyu that even though he was a banker's son and had fiddled around abroad for all those years, he wasn't shrewd enough to pull this one off. He still didn't know how to get things done in China; if he wanted to divorce, well, frankly speaking, he wasn't going through with it at her expense.

The daughter of the Steel King was indeed much more formidable than Ding Wenyu had imagined. Almost instantly Peitao and Ding Wenyu's father formed a staunch united front. In at least one area they immediately came to the same conclusion—that there was no way they were going to sit back and let Ding Wenyu do as he pleased. It was impossible for them to have any kind of grandiose expectations for an immoral playboy like him. But if Ding wasn't satisfied with his shameless whoring and now wanted to play the divorce game as well, he would have to wait for Peitao to produce an heir to the family line before even thinking about the possibility. A legal marriage wasn't as easy to overturn as Ding Wenyu had thought. Ding Wenyu's father tried scaring Ding by telling him that if he was intent on defying the law, he would have no problem hiring the best lawyers to give his son a taste of the sanctity of the law. He warned his son that he would not only disinherit him but also make it so that he would never be able to get a foothold in society.

"I'm not some three-year-old child," Ding Wenyu blasted back, almost completely losing his temper. However, he was a bit fearful, since he knew that his father wasn't bluffing. He remembered the doctor's repeated warnings that under no circumstances could his father stand another shock.

In the letters he wrote to Yuyuan, Ding Wenyu exaggerated his courage in the face of battle; he also exaggerated his father's illness. He told Yuyuan that this divorce showed him for the first time since returning to China just how backward his mother country truly was. In order to better understand the possibility of bringing about his divorce, Ding Wenyu sought out the legal advice of a friend who had studied law in America. This friend was already a very well-known lawyer in Shanghai. He advised Ding Wenyu not to get tangled up in a never-ending struggle over a divorce. Over and over, divorce had become merely an excuse for conservatives to attack liberal young people. The conservatives advocate the taking of concubines, yet remained firmly opposed to divorce because, for a woman, divorce is nothing less than outright abandonment. In a family like Ding Wenyu's, liberalism was nothing but a surface phenomenon. Ding Wenyu's father, for example, was able to openly marry a trio of male heir-producing wives. As far as their character was concerned, deep down, all Chinese were traditionalists to the bone. On account of this, the lawyer recommended Ding Wenyu take a second wife rather than go through a divorce.

"I'm not willing to commit the crime of bigamy," Ding Wenyu said naïvely.

The lawyer laughed. "The laws of the Nationalist government can be interpreted in different ways. After all, did anyone investigate your esteemed father's case of bigamy?"

Ding Wenyu felt that the lawyer's suggestion was a great insult to Yuyuan. Whether Yuyuan would ever consider marrying him or not, Ding Wenyu never for a moment entertained the idea of making her his concubine. How could he subject her to that kind of humiliation? Yuyuan was an angelic idol; she was a fairy, a bodhisattva; she was the stars and the moon in the night sky. Although Yuyuan never made any kind of promise to him, Ding Wenyu felt that he already loved her with all his heart and that he must, without the slightest show of mercy, dismiss even the slightest trace of other women from his life. Only after he had made the acquaintance of the adorable Yuyuan did it for the first time enter Ding Wenyu's mind that women should be treated with absolute loyalty and faithfulness. True love should be simple and exclusive. To love is to be exclusive—and only when there is exclusivity is it true love.

Besides writing endless letters to Yuyuan, Ding Wenyu spent a huge amount of time during his ten days in Shanghai reading through newspapers. With his head lost in love, he had not read a newspaper in quite some time; it was as if the affairs of the country had absolutely nothing to do with him. Those clichés and hackneyed expressions were all too familiar, just as the variety of advertisements all had the same old flavor. Ding Wenyu suddenly became conscious of the fact that the war machine had already started its engine. The Japanese were carrying out military exercises as if there was no tomorrow; for a while they would be held in North China, then for a while in Qingdao. The newspapers used large, bold type at almost every turn to indicate developments: MORE FIELD OPERATIONS FOR JAPANESE ARMY IN TIANJIN, OVER SEVENTY JAPANESE WARSHIPS CONVERGE ON CHINESE WATER PREPARING FOR BATTLE. What astonished Ding Wenyu was that while he was in Shanghai, the Japanese marine battalion stationed there was practicing portal war maneuvers right in Shanghai's Hongkou District. No wonder the Chinese people were anxious—with the Japanese practicing with live ammunition right under their noses, it seemed as though China was already a colony of Japan.

Ding Wenyu's decision to divorce met with almost unanimous censure on the part of his friends. The nation was on the verge of disaster, but instead of taking some time to see what he could do to resist Japan and save his country, this "truly valiant man" was spending all his time immersed in love, fighting to get divorced, and tied up in a love triangle. He really had his head in the clouds! Even Ding Wenyu himself felt he had gone a bit too far. In his letter to Yuyuan his emotions suddenly became aroused and he began writing about resisting Japan. He was deeply terrified by his current mental state. With the country on the verge of no longer being a country, how could he even talk about his family? He told Yuyuan that if his request for divorce was not granted he would give up academia for a career as a soldier to defend his home and guard his country. As the saying goes, "A true man is eager to serve anywhere, willing to die on the battlefield wrapped in his horse's hide." Ding Wenyu truly believed that when the time came he would never scramble to save his skin on the battlefield.

With nothing but spare time on his hands, Ding Wenyu went to the Japanese concession to look up a Japanese friend of his who did business in China for a chat. Ding Wenyu's visit came as a pleasant surprise to his Japanese friend; after all, during 1937 almost all Chinese were extremely hostile to Japan. He said, "You Chinese are really too ungrateful. Don't you realize how much aid we Japanese have provided to you? If it hadn't been for us, how would your dear country's former president Sun Yat-sen have been able to establish the Revolutionary Alliance in Japan and overthrow the rule of the Qing government? What's more, didn't the top two officials in the Republic of China, Chiang Kai-shek and Wang Jingwei, both study in Japan? How is it that the moment your wings are stiff, you turn around and bite the hand the feeds you?"

Ding Wenyu replied, "Naturally, you are the ones in the wrong. Who asked you to come to our country and go around everywhere waving your guns? If the Chinese ever got in the habit of running over to Japan to conduct military exercises, what would you think?"

His Japanese friend laughed. "I see Mr. Ding really has quite a sense of humor. Frankly speaking, if China really had the power, there's no telling, we Japanese might even welcome you with open arms. The problem is that you *don't* have the power. All you do is whine about recovering the four lost Manchurian provinces, but do you have the ability? If you want to recover that lost territory, I'm afraid that only if we Japanese show our faces and help out will you be able to win it back."

Ding Wenyu was a bit angry and said that the only reason the four Manchurian provinces were lost in the first place was because of the sneaky tricks played by the Japanese! The two of them argued for quite some time, all the while switching back and forth between Japanese and Chinese. They each realized that they were both able to use Chinese and Japanese as fluently as their mother tongue. Finally, as their argument came to its end, Ding's Japanese friend said in Chinese: "Anyway, let's just forget it. Neither one of us is any kind of a real patriot anyway. Honestly speaking, I like this China of yours."

"Well, honestly speaking," Ding Wenyu replied in Japanese, "I don't like that Japan of yours."

Ding's friend invited him to a Japanese-run restaurant in the Japanese concession for dinner. To his great surprise, Ding Wenyu discovered that although he was still in China, his instincts told him that he wasn't. This was truly the stomping ground of the Japanese. All around were Japanese characters, Japanese soldiers, and military bunkers made from reinforced concrete. Ding's Japanese friend told him that Japanese residents in the area had been long prepared. When the day came that the bellicose Chinese attacked them, they would be able to assemble immediately; moreover, there was no way that their fighting capacity would be any weaker than that of a regular military battalion. "The day that combat breaks out, our country's army will quickly come to support us; we are quite capable of holding out until they arrive." Ding Wenyu almost smacked his Japanese friend over the head with his cane. Ding's friend sensed his unhappiness and finally changed the subject. They returned to the topic of Ding Wenyu's divorce. Laughing, the Japanese said, "This is the one thing that is wrong with you Chinese—you still haven't finished what's on your plate, yet you want to see what's in the pot. I've seen your wife, not bad at all. No wonder Japanese women don't like Chinese men. You don't know what it means to be faithful—instead you rush off to divorce and remarry without even a second thought."

There were many people whose views were virtually in sync with this Japanese friend's. They all reproached Ding Wenyu for his decision to divorce, blaming him for changing his feelings at the sight of someone new. One elder invited Ding Wenyu and his father to his home for a small banquet. Before they started drinking, the elder pointed to his old, ugly wife and said with the utmost seriousness, "The only reason I'm here today is because I've been able to stand by my old lady. There are countless beauties in this world, young man, but how do you expect to handle them if you run after every one that you set your eyes on?" Ding Wenyu couldn't help but laugh. The elder got angry and said, "You've got the nerve to laugh! Let me tell you, there is profound knowledge in these words. You'd better go back and take some time to think about what I said!"

In his letters to Yuyuan, Ding Wenyu gave a detailed report of his actions and whereabouts. He went to great pains to record everything, vividly describing people's reactions to his decision to get a divorce. The only time he was prudent was when writing about Peitao. He continually talked about how she had refused his pleas for a divorce and how she demanded that he and she produce an heir. At first Ding Wenyu didn't say whether or not he and Peitao slept in the same bed, but between the lines one could faintly tell that that was what was happening. Finally, seemingly unable to help himself, Ding Wenyu began to describe to Yuyuan the dejection of having sex without love. He said that he had already become nothing short of a "seed planter"; he had no choice but to perform his duty to breed. This was not done for love; on the contrary, it was done out of an utter lack of love. Ding Wenyu felt as if he had wronged Yuyuan; at the same time, he felt guilty about how he had treated Peitao. Whether or not Peitao could become pregnant became the key to whether or not he could get a divorce.

Ten days later, Ding Wenyu finally got the opportunity to escape from Shanghai. He was like a bird that had broken free from its cage to once again enjoy the taste of freedom. Although returning to Nanjing did not necessarily mean that he would be able to see Yuyuan, just thinking that the woman he loved was right there in the same city, gazing up at the same blue sky, he was immediately swept by a feeling of immense joy. That's where the secret of love lies—sometimes it is enough just to have love and to feel love. Ding Wenyu began his first letter to Yuyuan after returning to Nanjing with the following intensely passionate line: "Thinking about just how close you are to me, I feel a happiness unlike any I have ever known. This is a happiness that could only have been bestowed by heaven."

V

April 1, 1937 was April Fool's Day as observed in the West. That day somebody ran an article in the newspaper saying that the celebrated scholar Dr. Hu Shi had passed away. Dr. Hu's friends in Beijing thought the news was real, and one after another they telephoned the Hu residence and rushed straight over, hastening not to miss the funeral. Nanjing was also in an uproar. When Yu Kexia got wind of the rumor he immediately telephoned Ding Wenyu, who was just back from Shanghai, to arrange to place a joint condolence message in the newspaper. Ding Wenyu replied that if they wanted to express condolences they should send a telegram directly to the Hu residence. Why should they act ostentatiously by running an advertisement in the paper? Yu Kexia explained that they were both Hu Shi's friends; what was wrong with putting an ad in the paper? Ding Wenyu laughed and said, "To hell with your nonsense. I'm not any friend of Dr. Hu Shi, who the hell is he anyway? Why do I need him to be my friend? Haven't you heard everyone in the world going around bragging, 'my friend Hu Shi'? Anyway, I'm not about to ride on *his* coattails!" Ding Wenyu did, however, use this as a pretext to pay a visit to Yu Kexia's home. He hoped that he would be able to see Yuyuan, for whom he yearned both day and night. His wish, however, remained unfulfilled; Yuyuan and Yu Kerun were both out. It was a good thing that in the end Yu Kexia didn't place that condolence notice in the paper, because the truth behind this April Fool's prank was soon revealed. If they had run that ad it would have been a big embarrassment. This turned out to be Ding Wenyu's last visit to Yu Kexia's home. Not long afterward, Ding's pursuit of Yuyuan would be exposed. No matter how great Yu Kexia's tolerance might have been, there was still no way he could accept another man's attempts to seduce his sister-in-law.

On April third, Ding Wenyu received a short letter from Yuyuan. The letter was very straightforward, consisting of only a few dry sentences. She wanted to meet Ding Wenyu at Xuanwu Lake Park at one o'clock that afternoon. Ding reread the letter several dozen times, pondering over every word—even every punctuation mark. He was completely taken by surprise and couldn't tell if what awaited him was a blessing or a curse. Since he had returned from Shanghai, Ding Wenyu had been constantly trying to figure out a way to see Yuyuan. He had looked for all kinds of excuses and concocted all kinds of schemes to meet her, but now that the opportunity had arrived, Ding Wenyu unexpectedly found himself at a loss as to what to do. From the time he received the letter until he left to go to the meeting place, he couldn't control the wild pounding in his chest or focus his attention on any one thing. In front of the mirror in the washroom he took excessive care getting ready, even taking the time to mindfully pull out a few gray hairs around his temples. Who knows how many times he brushed his hair? For a while, he feared that his hair wasn't shiny enough and rubbed Vaseline into it like mad. A moment later he was afraid it was too shiny, so he rushed to find a towel to wipe it off. Finally he decided it would be best to stick to his usual appearance and just wear that red woolen nightcap. If he wasn't wearing that nightcap he didn't feel quite himself.

Ding Wenyu arrived at the meeting place, a small pavilion beside Xuanwu Lake, more than an hour early. During this time, he didn't know what to do with himself. Carrying the cane that never left his side, he suspiciously paced back and forth. The result was that more than a few tourists thought that he had a screw loose somewhere. His mouth wouldn't stop mumbling, but no one could understand what he was saying; not even *he* knew what he was saying. Many of his moves were made without a clear awareness of his actions. As the time approached, he had even more trouble getting hold of himself. Over and over again he looked at his watch. It was time, but Yuyuan had yet to appear. Ding Wenyu began to worry that he had mixed up the meeting place. But he immediately realized the impossibility of his getting it wrong. If anyone was confused it had to be Yuyuan; perhaps she got the wrong time or went to the wrong place. No matter what kind of mistake Yuyuan might have made, it could all be forgiven. After all, she was a young girl, and it was only appropriate that she make a few mistakes—they only made her more adorable. A cute angel like Yuyuan, there was no reason she should have to arrive on time to begin with. It was obvious that she was giving Ding Wenyu a little test. Just like the rehashed old plots in those romance novels, she would be sure to give Ding Wenyu ample opportunity to go through a few trials.

Yuyuan appeared just as Ding Wenyu was imagining how magnanimous he was. He suspected that she might not come at all, but not even in his dreams did he imagine that she would bring two people with her. These two women were Yuyuan's co-workers, but they attended this meeting in the capacity of her protectors. From the start Ding Wenyu sensed that these two protectors came with hostile intentions. Their attitude was quite unfriendly and overbearing, as if they had come on a punitive expedition against Ding. In an instant all of his beautiful fantasies disappeared and, before the awkward smile on Ding Wenyu's face had a chance to fade, he realized that there wasn't any blessing awaiting him on this day.

"Are you that thick-skinned weirdo who writes love letters to other people as if there were no tomorrow?" One of Yuyuan's two escorts was an extremely straightforward woman trapped in a man's body. She went straight to the point with her comment, "Heaven only knows just how your skin got so damn thick!"

All three women were dressed in military uniforms; each was full of spirit. From the get-go, their words seemed to carry the thick smell of gunpowder. Ding Wenyu's face still stubbornly held on to that awkward smile. Yuyuan's entire face turned red as she shyly avoided staring at Ding Wenyu. She wanted to say something but for the time being couldn't get any words out. In the end it was that woman who had already overtaken Ding with her earlier show of strength who came on with a hurricanelike scolding. With one mouthful she said so much. When she got tired she pointed her finger at Ding Wenyu and said, "How come you don't say anything?" Ding Wenyu shrugged his shoulders, making himself appear quite pathetic. Because he had his cane in one hand, he looked just like a surrendering soldier. This move instantly caused all three dashing women to break out in laughter.

Yuyuan's face turned even redder. She was somewhat angry, but at the same time she said with a pleading tone, "From this point on, please do not write any more of those letters!"

Ding Wenyu gazed unwaveringly at Yuyuan; written all over his face was his unwillingness to accept this decision. He used his silence as his weapon of defense. Yuyuan said that the purpose of their meeting today was to make it clear that that stupid game of his had to end. Ding Wenyu murmured his defense, saying that it wasn't a stupid game. The second the words left his mouth, a female escort hit him with a dose of bitter criticism. He didn't dare to say much more. Instead he just drooped his head and took his medicine as it came. Once again his appearance brought the three female soldiers to their knees with laughter.

That frank and outspoken woman said, "In any case, Mr. Ding, since you are a man of knowledge, why do you insist on acting like a clown? If you want to pursue a girl, you can't go about it as shamelessly as you have been."

Yuyuan felt that Ding Wenyu had already taken enough of a beating. She matter-of-factly told him that she didn't have an ounce of love for him. She explained to him that he needed to start respecting other people's feelings; since the other party had already so clearly spelled out her refusal, she hoped that from this point on he would end this harassment. Love is not something that can be forced. Never has forced love been real love—this was one principle that he should be able to understand. Ding Wenyu was rendered speechless. Tears welled up in his eyes and he looked like a small child who has been bullied. He looked at Yuyuan grievously. Yuyuan felt uncomfortable under his gaze and went a bit soft; at the same moment she felt an indescribable awkwardness. Ding Wenyu's tears really did roll down and, unafraid to make a fool of himself, he said, "I never asked that you love me, but . . ." He gazed steadfastly at Yuyuan. "But I love you. It is not forced, it is one hundred percent genuine, it is one hundred percent genuine love."

Hearing such nauseatingly melodramatic words escape from Ding Wenyu's lips, the three shocked female soldiers found themselves at a loss as to what to say next. Afterward, when the three of them brought up what happened that day, one of them smiled wryly as she told Yuyuan that she was truly moved by that damned weirdo. She said that as a woman, if there really were a man like him who loved her so deeply, she didn't think she would be able to hold out. Women and men are different. All men think about is how to love women, whereas women spend even more time thinking about how to win the affections of men. They all conducted a reevaluation of Ding Wenyu's moral character and agreed that he wasn't as bad as they had thought. "If you weren't married," Yuyuan's two friends reached the same irresponsible conclusion, "It might not have been a bad deal if you did marry him." A more presumptuous comment was made by the bold, outspoken friend. With a tone of jealousy she said, "At least one thing is for sure, this Mr. Ding loves you more than that Mr. Yu of yours."

"If the two of you really have such a good impression of this Mr. Ding," Yuyuan later said resentfully, "then why don't you let him fall in love with one of you?" Yuyuan felt like she had once again received a gratuitous insult. When she went to the park that day, she had nothing but good intentions—she simply wanted to keep Ding Wenyu from falling too deep into the quagmire of love. She wanted to put an end to Ding Wenyu's crazy ideas and convince him to give up on her; it was only out of compassion that she acted. Unlike her two friends, she didn't feel that Ding Wenyu loved her more than her own husband did—but that was only because she never once compared the two of them. The feelings each of them had for her were entirely different. Comparing them would indeed be just absurd. The reason she had asked her two friends to accompany her was not only to fulfill their curiosity; she wanted them to prove her own innocence, and she also wanted to get them to tell Ding all the things that she didn't have the nerve to say. At this critical juncture she needed her friends' help to make Ding Wenyu dismantle the unrealistic web of love he had snared himself in.

Yuyuan couldn't help but admire Ding Wenyu's crackerjack prowess in dealing with women. According to the social customs at the time, most young people were a bit embarrassed to go out alone with their partner if they were not yet married. If they went on a date they would always bring a friend with them. Although Yu Kerun was handsome and debonair, he didn't leave Yuyuan's friends with a particularly good impression. He could never get rid of all the arrogant hang-ups that came with being the "pride of heaven." "All of those pilots think that they are always flying through the sky. Even when they're on the ground they act like they're up in the clouds." When Yuyuan's friends talked about Yu Kerun, they couldn't help but use a satirical tone to dig at Yu and his friends: "What makes them always so sure that everyone is going to fall in love with them?" Back when they used to go on outings, Yu Kerun and his buddies would show off their flair and charm to the female soldiers. They did whatever they could to please the ladies, even going so far as flirting with complete strangers.

Ding Wenyu, on the other hand, had the air of a polite and cultivated gentleman. On the surface he admittedly appeared quite ridiculous; nevertheless, one could not but acknowledge that he had excellent manners. The bad impression that he left on people was always only temporary. Whenever someone took the time to really get to know him, they would immediately find that he wasn't at all a disagreeable fellow. That day at Xuanwu Lake after receiving a face-to-face rejection from Yuyuan, drowning in depression, Ding Wenyu picked himself up and insisted on accompanying the three female soldiers on a tour around the lake. "I know that I don't deserve to enjoy a kind of unrealistic love, but please do not deny me this opportunity to accompany you three ladies for the afternoon." He raised his walking stick, motioning for one of the pleasure boats. All at once, several of those small tour boats rushed over, trying to pick up this bit of business.

Yuyuan told her friends that she didn't want to go, especially not with Ding Wenyu. But one of her friends replied, "What's there to be afraid of with us around?"

As it happened, it was exactly that time of year when the peach blossoms were just coming into bloom. The banks of the lake were covered with crimson peach blossoms and emerald willows, bringing swarms of tourists who came to admire the beautiful sight. There was an endless stream of heavy traffic at the main entrance to the park. Yuyuan and her friends had intended to go to Xuanwu Lake that day, and by arranging to meet Ding Wenyu they wanted to kill two birds with one stone. Now that they had said everything that needed to be said, what was wrong with spending the day together on the lake?

When they had first arrived at the park, there were already a few flippant, dandy-looking teenagers who tried talking to them, offering to accompany them around the park. Each one in the bunch was wearing a brand-new school uniform with the three characters *zhi*, *ren*, *yong*, or "wisdom, benevolence, and courage" embroidered on the front. But not one of them was in school studying like they were supposed to. Instead they were running all over the city accosting respectable women. Because of the trouble these youngsters caused at Xuanwu Lake Park, desperate appeals like the following appeared in the newspapers:

WOULD THE AUTHORITIES PLEASE FIND A WAY TO STOP THE RAMPAGE OF THE XUANWU "LAKE BANDITS"

As Yuyuan and her friends' pleasure boat reached the center of the lake, two boats filled with those frivolous teenagers approached them. The students acted as if they couldn't control the direction of their boat, and intentionally came on a crash course toward the boat Yuyuan and her companions were in. One of Yuyuan's friends was so scared that she began to wail like a baby. Yuyuan was so nervous that she held her breath and grabbed the side of the boat with both hands, waiting for the banging sound of the impending crash. Ding Wenyu suddenly stood up in the front of the boat and waved his cane, angrily trying to scare away those up-to-no-good teenagers. As their boat got closer, Ding Wenyu mercilessly waved his cane to hit the kids. Seeing that things weren't going their way, the teenagers laughed it off, turned tail, and fled. One of them even used his oar to splash water onto Ding, soaking his western suit. Ding Wenyu wasn't close enough to hit them; all he could do was stand at the bow and curse "Bastards, bastards!" He went on and on cursing them, but all he could do was repeat that same word. Those teenagers snickered as they paddled away, going off to ram some other unsuspecting female pleasure-boat passengers. Ding Wenyu's chivalrous bravery made Yuyuan and her friends rock back and forth with laughter. During their whole time on the lake, he didn't lay so much as a single finger on the oar. The way he periodically waved his cane made him look like the spitting image of a serious general; at the same time, he also had a side that seemed closer to a spirited child. It was impossible to see any sign of overt unhappiness in him; it seemed as if he had already forgotten all about Yuyuan's rejection. Only when their tour of the lake was coming to an end did that look of desperate sadness once again return to his face.

Almost pleading, he said, "Although I may be asking a bit too much, I would still like to invite you three ladies to have dinner with me!"

Yuyuan may have been softhearted, but she definitely didn't want to eat with Ding Wenyu; she already felt that the lake tour was a mistake. If they kept going like this, the whole affair would become a complete mess. Her friends put on airs and said that it was indeed a bit much to ask them to dinner, but if Yuyuan wasn't against it, they saw no harm in coming along. Yuyuan immediately voiced her refusal and turned to leave. Ding Wenyu had no choice but to abandon his request and eagerly rush after Yuyuan and her friends. As they emerged from the park gate, Ding Wenyu hailed a car to take them home. Although the women didn't necessarily endorse the idea, he had already stopped a car, so they took it. On the way, Yuyuan's two friends were the only ones who spoke giddily— Yuyuan stared out the window and didn't make a sound; neither did Ding. At one point Yuyuan inadvertently turned around and saw his dejected expression and drooping head—it looked as if he was in the utmost pain. He held on to his cane with both hands as his entire body jolted back and forth with the movements of the car. The red nightcap on his head sat crookedly to one side.

When the car arrived at its destination, Ding Wenyu jumped out, opened the door for the three women, and courteously helped them out. No longer could he hold back his desperation and sadness. At that moment, Ding Wenyu surprisingly lost the courage even to face Yuyuan. With a trembling voice, he simply uttered good-bye, crawled back into the car, and signaled for the driver to go. His miserable appearance left the three female soldiers speechless. Yuyuan was filled with resentment;

she felt that this entire disastrous day could be blamed on her friends' rotten idea. Now that the whole affair was finished, she took a deep breath and headed home alone.

VI

When Yu Kerun finally learned the story of Ding Wenyu's painstaking pursuit of his wife, his violent reaction took Yuyuan completely by surprise. Even though in the beginning he acted as though he couldn't care less, as if he wasn't even willing to waste time on this issue or seriously entertain the possibility that such a thing could happen, once he sat himself down and carefully read through those passionate love letters, a volcano of jealousy violently erupted within him. It was clear that things had already gone far beyond the level that could be tolerated. He sternly criticized Yuyuan, interrogating her as if she were a criminal. But no matter what she said, he refused to accept it. He didn't believe for a moment that Yuyuan had never once responded to Ding. Ding Wenyu's pile of letters was already more than enough to show that their relationship was anything but average. "I don't even want to imagine just how far things went between you two!" After a barrage of criticisms, Yu Kerun mumbled to himself: "Just what the hell else did you do behind my back?"

"Just what the hell do you think we did?" Infuriated, Yuyuan was filled with a sense of being treated unfairly.

Yu Kerun didn't really believe that anything improper had happened between Yuyuan and Ding Wenyu. If it had, Yuyuan would not have naïvely handed over all those letters. However, just because his wife hadn't slept with Ding, he wasn't going to let the whole thing slip by. There was nothing strange about another man pursuing his beautiful wife. What was strange was the way that Yuyuan kept all of those nauseating letters, as if she were carrying out the preservation of some rare cultural relics. The reason she kept them, however, was to prove her innocence to Yu Kerun. Just as Yuyuan, furious, was getting ready to burn those damn love letters right there on the spot, Yu Kerun smiled coldly and accused her of taking advantage of the opportunity to destroy the evidence of her guilt. If she was truly as innocent as she made herself out to be, there should be no reason for her to be afraid of this material evidence. Yuyuan quickly realized that all she was doing was providing Yu Kerun with an excuse to have an argument. This gave them both an opportunity to vent all those grievances that they had pent up against each other. Although they had already been joined in holy matrimony as husband and wife, in actuality, they were closer to a pair of high school sweethearts. Neither of them was very mature, nor did they really understand each other. As time went on, all they discovered was just how far their partner was from the kind of person they had originally thought. All that Ding's love letters did was provide them with an opportunity to take off their masks and fully expose themselves—and each other—for who they really were. From then on, Yu Kerun came up with an explanation why he was never home; he shamelessly took advantage of the situation and said that he was just "trying to make things convenient for them by leaving."

Yuyuan asked Yu Kerun to explain just who he was referring to by "them" and just what kind of "convenience" he was trying to provide. Yu Kerun said that he had already made things as clear as could be and didn't feel a need to go into details. And so the young couple began their game of endless quarreling. Neither of them was willing to give an inch—they could go on arguing all day over the meaning of a single unclear word. They adopted a tactical method of attack that allowed them to alternate; while one party took the defensive, the other would ferociously charge ahead. By the time the first party had had about all they could take and rose up to counterattack, the other would quickly put up their guard. Since day one, the battle between them had been carried out like a campaign of protracted warfare; neither wanted to admit defeat— thus neither could ever be the victor. Sometimes when one of them was tired but the other still didn't want to let the matter rest, the exhausted one would suddenly get a second wind and heroically resist and completely turn the tables! At first, Yuyuan's desire was quite simple: all she wanted was for Yu Kerun to let her off the hook. She felt that since she was the woman, it was only natural for the man to give in. Yu Kerun's stance was also quite simple: since he felt like he had done nothing wrong and had the goods on her, why should *he* give in?

When Yu Kexia and his wife got involved, the whole thing became even more complicated. At first each couple holed themselves up in their rooms, nagging away only for each other's ears to hear, but gradually things came out in the open. It seemed that a bout of tangled warfare would be inevitable, even though in all probability no one really wanted to argue and make such a mess out of a simple affair. Yu Kexia's wife shouted at her husband: "Didn't you ever hear the saying 'Thy friend's wife, one shall not take advantage of?' This shameless friend of yours really is something! You treat him like he is some kind of little treasure, when actually you're inviting a wolf into your home!" Yu Kexia told his wife to keep her voice down so his brother and sister-in-law wouldn't overhear them, but this only made her angrier. Unwilling to be told what to do, she screamed at him: "This is my house, why the hell should I keep my voice down?"

The sound of their bickering made its way to Yuyuan's room, and for a moment the young couple was struck with an almost indescribable embarrassment. Yu Kerun smugly gloated over his wife's situation, saying, "After your 'glorious romps,' how do you expect to be able to face people?" Outside Yu Kexia and his wife were screaming their guts out at each other, while behind the closed door of their room Yu Kerun and Yuyuan continued their bickering on a quieter level. Finally, Yuyuan got so angry that she almost stormed out of her room to interrogate her sister-in-law—this was because she heard Mrs. Yu mumbling that "flies are only attracted to cracked eggs." Yu Kerun wouldn't let his wife leave their room, and Yuyuan asked him why she couldn't go and find out just exactly what her sister-in-law meant. Yu Kerun said that what she meant couldn't have been more clear, so there was no reason for her to go out and make a scene. Yuyuan saw her husband and her sister-in-law shared the same opinion and exploded with fury. She forcefully pushed her husband out of the way, opened the door, and strutted into the large parlor.

"Sister-in-law, I don't want to argue with you. If you feel that there is no place for me here, just tell me and I'll move out—but don't you dare hang an innocent person!" Afterward Yuyuan was filled with regret; she never should have tried to go head to head with a housewife, but at the time she really couldn't help herself. Her tears poured down; not since she came into this world had the pampered and spoiled Yuyuan been so insulted and felt so wronged. She knew that this nosey sister-in-law of hers would never admit she was wrong, but she had to get this off her chest. There was no way Yuyuan could stand by and let her sister-in-law go on insulting her for no reason. Standing beside them, Yu Kexia felt extremely awkward. In the end, all he could do was take the side of the injured party and scold his wife, telling her that she had indeed gone a bit overboard and was being unreasonable.

Seeing her man helping his sister-in-law, Mrs. Yu's flaming temper increased threefold. Stamping her foot with anger, she asked, "If it was that derelict friend of yours sticking up for her, I would take it. But what the hell are *you* taking her side for?"

Yu Kexia was afraid that his wife would keep going and say something even more inappropriate, so he gave her a wicked slap across the face. It had come to the point where the boss of the house needed to stand up and assert his authority. Mrs. Yu was struck silly; only after a moment of shock did she break out with an earsplitting wail. Yuyuan at once felt that the whole thing was ridiculous. She still didn't know what to say when she turned to the still-furious Yu Kexia. With a perniciously vile tone, Yu Kexia said, "What the hell are you up to? Go back to your room!" Still Mrs. Yu didn't let the matter rest; amid her sobs as she left the parlor, she grumbled all kinds of complaints under her breath. As she walked past Yu Kerun and Yuyuan's room, she tearfully complained how terrible her fate was and how useless the man she married was. She grumbled that all she did was suffer for most of her marriage and it wasn't until recently that things had finally started to turn around. Besides beating his wife, her man didn't have any other skills. Her aim was quite simple—she just wanted to let her brother-in-law know that her husband had hit her.

After that incident, it was a full day before you could hear people talking in the Yu household—besides, of course, the sound of the two children playing. Everyone was filled with resentment. When the servant announced that dinner was ready, Yuyuan said that she wasn't hungry and wouldn't come out. When Yu Kerun finally left the room to eat, he didn't utter a word the entire meal. Everyone ate in silence, and after he was finished, Yu Kerun went back to his room, changed clothes, and went out. He returned in the middle of the night a drunken mess and fell asleep the moment he hit the sheets. The next day he pulled himself out of bed only to brave another night of drinking. Once again he didn't return until early the following morning. This went on for the next three days, after which Yuyuan was near the end of her rope. She pulled Yu Kerun up from the bed and with tears in her eyes said, "There is no reason for you to show yourself in such a pitiful state to others. Act like a real man and give me a good slap like your brother did to his wife, and everything will be okay. What you are doing is even more painful than if you were to hit me."

"I've got a heavy hand," said Yu Kerun. "If I were to hit you, you wouldn't be able to take it."

Yuyuan grabbed hold of his hand and tried to force him to slap her. Yu Kerun refused to hit her. He said that if she insisted on fighting, then she could hit him. After pushing each other back and forth for a while, the young couple basically made up for a few days. They both felt that carrying on like that wasn't going to solve anything. After they calmed down and thought things over, everyone realized that they had gone a bit overboard. For things to have gone so far, everyone had some responsibility. Lying under the covers, Yuyuan came to a sudden realization and said, "From now on I'm not making a fuss over anything. If they make me angry again I'll simply move into the dormitory at the army headquarters. Your sister-in-law was right, this is her home, not ours."

Yu Kerun knew that the main thing eating at Yuyuan was being forced to live under somebody else's roof. Time and time again, Yuyuan hinted that they should move out and get their own place. She felt it would be best if they could buy some land and build a new house; otherwise they should just rent one. However, deep down, Yu Kerun wasn't a bit happy with this idea. Although he was a married man, in his heart he still felt like a bachelor and was unwilling to be tied down with a house and family. It seemed as if there was always something not right between him and Yuyuan. Yuyuan's intuition told her that she wasn't Yu Kerun's ideal wife. As far as he was concerned, their little two-person family wasn't of the least importance. He claimed that he didn't believe in the superstitious sayings about "white tigers," but in actuality he took them quite seriously. Whenever he was scheduled to fly, Yu Kerun made sure not to have intercourse with Yuyuan the night before. Yu Kerun claimed that this was a pilot guild regulation set up for pilots to save strength and conserve energy. But then one day at the pilots' club, Yuyuan overheard a conversation over coffee. According to those pilots, the greatest misfortune that could befall them was to be without the comfort of a woman before a flight.

Yu Kerun's self-imposed celibacy wasn't restricted to just before flying; he would also avoid intimacy with his wife before other important events. Whenever things didn't go quite his way, he would begin his endless complaints about how he had run into bad luck. Yuyuan discovered that Yu Kerun was extremely superstitious. There were so many taboos he was afraid of violating that it was enough to make you laugh. She would often find little fortune-telling books under his pillow. Moreover, whenever he talked to Yuyuan about other women, he would always quote all kinds of fortune-telling theories to express his opinion. When their sister-in-law came up, Yu Kerun would sternly warn his wife not to look down on her just because she had been born into a poor family; from the shape of her cheeks you could tell that she was destined to bring good fortune to her husband. "My brother got engaged to sister-in-law before he went abroad. From then on he has had nothing but smooth sailing." Yu Kerun used his hands to push his cheeks together to show Yuyuan. "The fortune-telling book says that people with full cheeks will have great happiness and wealth."

Yuyuan suddenly broke out with a sarcastic comment that surprised even herself: "Maybe you should ask your brother if sister-in-law has any pubic hair!"

Yu Kerun's face instantly flushed with anger. "How could you be so filthy!"

Not caring what might happen next, Yuyuan replied, "That's right, I'm filthy. Not only am I filthy, I'm a 'white tiger'! You regret that you married me, don't you?" In the end, however, she was the one who regretted saying such a thing—because her accusation meant that *she* in some way had forced Yu into getting married. After all, whether or not she had pubic hair was a simple biological phenomenon; the only thing strange was Yu Kerun's superstitious beliefs and taboos. Yuyuan suddenly realized how ashamed she would be if this thing got out. She remembered how Yu Kexia's wife had once come into the bathroom to get something while she was in the shower. It was a good thing that her sister-in-law didn't take a close look at Yuyuan; otherwise, who knew what she would have thought? When Yuyuan imagined Mrs. Yu discussing her private affairs with Yu Kexia as if she had just discovered a new world, her face instantly turned red and goose bumps popped up all over her body.

Chapter Five

I

April 1937 was Nanjing's tenth anniversary as the capital of the Nationalist government. The city government wanted to take full advantage of the celebration and began preparing all kinds of different exhibitions; detailed protocol was sent down spelling out the specifics for each event. After three months and five days of organizing their data, the census bureau released their population statistics for the capital, placing Nanjing's population at 945,544. The New Life Movement was still the number one political movement, and the Nationalist government called for everyone to continue studying the Generalissimo's essay, "The Significance of the New Life Movement." The result of various government research organizations' inquiries into prostitution came out, and they all concluded that prostitution should be banned outright. Moreover, they demanded that the police department draw up plans for the implementation of this ban and the Social Welfare Bureau research the issue of getting former prostitutes back on their feet in society.

The Insect Extermination Movement began with a bang. The entire city was divided into six districts, and twenty insect extermination teams conducted an initial probe into the city's public bathrooms. A full month earlier, Chiang Kai-shek had taken some time from his busy schedule to personally write to Mayor Ma to find a way to beautify the Nanjing cityscape as soon as possible. Chiang also had the Public Works Bureau draw up a detailed proposal and a feasible method for carrying it out. The city's central sanitation unit put up urgent notices banning litter from being thrown in ponds and lakes. The Capital Committee for the Eradication of Pine Moths was also formally established. The Sanitation Department warned Nanjing citizens that several early cases of meningitis had broken out in the city and that all residents should hasten to get their immunization shots. Starting on April 1 the Epidemic Prevention Movement took off like a raging fire; the newspapers ran public service announcements by way of large, eye-catching, bold print headlines: UNLESS YOU WANT THE POX, RUSH TO GET YOUR SHOTS. Accurate counts for the numbers of contagious diseases were released for the most recent week. There were two cases of typhoid fever, and both patients died. There were four cases of dysentery and two cases of smallpox; one patient died. There were eighteen incidents of diphtheria, in which eight people died. There were also four cases of meningitis and four cases of scarlet fever.

Nanjing's very first crematorium had been open for four months but had so far only cremated two foreign women. It was obvious that the citizens in the capital had yet to grasp the significance of funerary reform. The "China Funeral Home" on Equitable Road ran ads in the newspaper almost every day. On account of its inauspicious name, its advertisements inspired wave after wave of complaints from the people. Finally the city government issued a formal declaration ordering that names found insulting to the country be changed within a specific period of time. Other names ordered to be changed along with the funeral parlor's were "The National Meat Shop" and "The Capital Committee for Marrying Prostitutes."

During March and April of 1937 Nanjing was extraordinarily lively. It seemed as if before Chiang Kai-shek had time to fully recover from the exhaustion and shock of the Xi'an Incident, an excess of compulsory dinner parties and other obligations were already damaging his health. After examining his physical condition, Chiang's doctor decided that the Generalissimo should take some time off to conserve his strength and rest. And so the Standing Committee of the Central Committee held their fourteenth meeting to deal especially with this matter. The motion they reached read as follows:

> The Generalissimo Chiang Kai-shek has sent a wire requesting an additional two months of leave in order to regain his health. We pass the resolution that Comrade Chiang, suffering from exhaustion after having long taken the country's responsibilities upon himself, hereby be given an additional two-month recuperation period. During the Generalissimo's absence, Comrade Wang Chonghui shall act on his behalf, fulfilling all regular duties in the Executive Yuan. Hereby the motion is passed. We hope that, for the sake of the country, the Generalissimo protects his health and is able to recover soon.

Flocks of party VIPs followed the example of the Generalissimo and left Nanjing. The Government Chairman Lin Sen went to inspect the provinces of Guangdong and Guangxi. Just back from Europe, Wang Jingwei flew to Suiyuan to commemorate officers lost fighting the Japanese. As it happened, while spending time recuperating at his hometown, Chiang Kai-shek had to bury his recently deceased elder brother, Chiang Kai-ch'ing. Led by Feng Yuxiang, virtually all the party big shots came out to Fenghua to take part in the funeral procession. Among the important officials who attended were T. V. Soong, Chen Guofu, and He Yingqin; even Chen Bulei and Zhang Zhizhong came. On the surface, it truly looked like a peaceful scene. Just four months later, however, on August 13, fighting would break out in Shanghai. From this point on, it was full-scale war with Japan. Zhang Zhizhong would serve as the commander-in-chief during the Shanghai battle. No one imagined that sometime during April while Chiang Kai-shek was supposed to be resting at his home in Fenghua, he was actually secretly discussing with his beloved general, Zhang Zhizhong, a plan to go head-to-head with the Japanese in Shanghai at the proper time. They researched all the specific problems that might arise during battle and analyzed the potentially disastrous consequences. A brutal battle in Shanghai would be difficult to avoid. Even before the Xi'an Incident, the Central Army's crack 36th Division, as well as the 87th and 88th Divisions, all secretly converged near Shanghai. According to the humiliating Treaty of Nanjing signed by the Qing government, Chinese troops were not permitted to be stationed anywhere near Shanghai. However, in order to get the upper hand for the impending military resistance, it was imperative that they deliver a swift, fatal blow to the Japanese concession in Shanghai the moment the first shot was fired. The war machines of both sides were already rumbling. The surface aura of peace could no longer conceal the reality of impending war.

Meanwhile, the citizens of Nanjing were reveling in the semblance of peace that surrounded them. April 4 was Children's Day as established by the Nationalist government. The first place winner of that year's Capital Children's Day Chinese Speech Contest was Ning Beidi of Shanxi Road Elementary School. The title of his speech was "Laugh not when it is contrary to propriety; weep not when it is contrary to propriety." The National Arts Exhibition was held just a few days after Children's Day. Students of the Drama Academy premiered two comedies in the People's Assembly Hall. The Shanghai Ministry of Works Orchestra organized a concert in Nanjing; there was also a fashion show, which ended with the participants leading the audience in a chorus of "March of the Volunteers." Each university, middle school, and elementary school organized different commemoration activities to celebrate Nanjing's ten-year anniversary as the capital. Nanjing intellectuals held a fervent debate tracing the true meaning and significance of Nanjing's imperial destiny. In the newspapers, the Japanese continued inciting unrest all over China, and it was clear that the Nationalist regime's attitude toward the Japanese government had toughened.

The university where Ding Wenyu taught organized a lecture series. A group of famous professors used it as an opportunity to expound upon their scholarly views. Because of the peculiar atmosphere at the time, most university students were not particularly enthusiastic about attending academic lectures. This was not a year for academics, and there were many professors who, for the first time, learned what it was like to speak to an empty room. A few of the lectures in the series were stopped halfway through due to poor attendance. Those that were too specialized not only were uninteresting but also seemed completely disconnected from the exciting, everyday events going on right outside the campus gates. A handful of professors tried adapting to the situation by changing their lecture topics to "National Defense Chemistry" or "A History of Warfare During the Great Tang"—but still only a petty few even bothered coming to listen. A few radical students incited strikes, calling for all students to join the National Student Alliance's Association to Save the Nation. The government didn't acknowledge this National Student Alliance because it had no legal status; it was eventually labeled an illegal organization. Then campus authorities punished strikers with one-year suspensions and forced them to delay all make-up examinations until spring of the following year.

Under these circumstances, Ding Wenyu's lecture met with unanticipated success. His topic was "A Comparison of Chinese and Western Prostitution Traditions." Although the university was filled with an atmosphere of academic freedom, when his chosen topic was reported to the campus authorities, they couldn't help but have a few reservations. This subject was obviously out of step with the times. Before the lecture even began, the large classroom where it was to be held was already packed with bodies. No one could have imagined that this lecture would break all previous university lecture attendance records. There were people crowded along the hallway alongside the classroom and even outside the windows. Students roared with laughter as they listened. Once the lecture ended, jubilant students broke out in a thunder of applause and hoots. During his lecture, Ding Wenyu wagged his tongue, offering a penetrating analysis and comparison of Chinese and Western prostitution. He hit the nail on the head by pointing out the fundamental difference in the origins of each tradition. According to Ding Wenyu, prostitution did not start with money; nor were there any evil or immoral connotations associated with the practice early on. Western prostitution was a product of religion, whereas Chinese prostitution was a product of love. Western prostitution began when women shamelessly lay at the temple gate, fulfilling the basic desires of soldiers setting off for battle. Chinese prostitutes, on the other hand, were acting in defiance of traditional arranged marriages. Because the Chinese intelligentsia left no place for love in the feudal marriage system, they had no choice but to look for love in the brothels. The most marvelous part of Ding Wenyu's lecture was the way in which he separated love and desire with knifelike precision. Western prostitution began with desire, while Chinese prostitution ended with love. Men driven by desire are ruthless and warlike, whereas men who seek their ends in love become increasingly tender and soft.

Some of the radical students felt that Ding Wenyu's lecture was offensive and corrupting. After it had concluded, students divided into different camps and turned red in the face debating just what kind of person Ding Wenyu was. Those who opposed him felt that there was absolutely no reason a playboy like Ding Wenyu should ever set foot in a university lecture hall. With professors like him, it would be a wonder if China *didn't* fall to the Japanese. Luckily Ding Wenyu couldn't care less about the students' reactions. Without the slightest scruple, he blurted out whatever came to his mind; then when he finished his lecture, he simply returned to his apartment to write more love letters to Yuyuan.

Later that night, as Ding Wenyu was leaning over his desk writing a letter, he was scared out of his wits by a knocking sound on his window. Through the glass, Ding Wenyu recognized Monk. As Monk motioned for Ding to open the window, he placed his finger over his lips signaling him to keep quiet.

"Don't let anyone know that I'm here." Utterly flustered, Monk closed the window blinds. Monk's face was pale and his eyes were blank; with a quivering voice he continued, "I've done something terrible!"

It had already been some time since Ding Wenyu had taken Monk's rickshaw. Monk had been forced to take some time off work in order to participate in obligatory military training for city residents. Ding Wenyu had seen Monk at the university athletic field receiving his training. He was all done up in a tidy gray conscription uniform with leggings and an army cap, and was holding a rifle with a bayonet. Monk appeared proud and confident as he practiced bayoneting the straw targets. For the past few years, the city government had held firmly to their policy of providing citizens with military training. The fellows who worked the abacus in stores, the coolies and petty vendors who carried their loads on shoulder poles down the streets, and the idle drifters who had no steady job all took turns receiving military training. Almost every day the university athletic field near Ding Wenyu's apartment held training exercises for citizen draftees. When he had first moved in, Ding would often be awakened by the commands and slogans shouted by those conscripts. After not seeing him for so long, Ding Wenyu was a bit taken aback when Monk suddenly showed up on his doorstep like a scared rabbit.

"Mr. Ding, I think I killed someone," Monk said dejectedly as he raised his eyes and gazed at Ding with a pleading look.

Again, Ding Wenyu was scared out of his wits. Murder isn't something you joke about, and from Monk's panic-stricken expression it didn't seem that he was joking. Moreover, Ding Wenyu was by no means the kind of person with that sense of humor. He and Monk were quite close, but their relationship was still that of an employer and employee. Monk was always most respectful toward Ding, and even if he occasionally told a few jokes, they never exceeded what was proper. In Monk's eyes Ding Wenyu was simply a man with money, status, and knowledge who was a bit on the lustful side and enjoyed spending a lot of energy on women. The reason he came running to Ding Wenyu was that he was so desperate he couldn't think of anyone else to go to. He had already spent quite a bit of time absentmindedly pacing around the university campus. He had come to the end of his rope when he unintentionally raised his head and saw a light on in Ding Wenyu's apartment. And so, without considering the consequences, he tapped on Ding's window.

Not knowing what to do, Ding Wenyu looked at Monk, hoping that he would explain exactly what had happened. Monk looked Ding Wenyu in the eyes and said, stuttering, "This time I . . . I really killed someone."

"Who did you kill?" Ding Wenyu was even more flustered than Monk.

"I killed Little Moon. I took a claw hammer and hit her a whole bunch of times on the head. . . ." Monk's pale face began to turn red. He swallowed the saliva in his mouth but could not bring himself to continue.

Ding Wenyu didn't even know who Little Moon was, let alone why Monk would want to kill her. Since he had murdered someone and was now at Ding Wenyu's apartment, from a legal perspective, this was indeed a very awkward situation. Ding Wenyu instantly realized that this affair was going to be trouble—after all, it was illegal to harbor a murderer. With this in mind Ding Wenyu, virtually without hesitation, told Monk to turn himself in immediately. Monk said that he still wasn't sure if the person he killed had actually died. If she was already dead then he would have to pay with his life—turning himself in would be nothing short of suicide. After hearing that, Ding Wenyu was even more confused about what to do. Monk kept repeating himself. He described how confused he was as he hit her on the head with his claw hammer until she passed out. After she lost consciousness he got scared and ran off without taking the time to actually see how she was. Listening to Monk anxiously retell what had happened, Ding Wenyu discovered that there was a huge hole in his story. It was obvious that Monk had lost himself in the moment, and it was very probable that the results were not nearly as serious as he had imagined.

Under Ding Wenyu's consolation, Monk was eventually persuaded that there was a possibility that luck was on his side; perhaps he hadn't killed anyone after all. Ding Wenyu changed clothes and immediately set out for Little Moon's house to see what he could find out. By then Ding had figured out who Little Moon was. He remembered that he had seen this barely seventeen-year-old girl with the big eyes when he went to Monk's place to hire his rickshaw. Just before leaving, Ding Wenyu told Monk not to be nervous; he'd see what happened and come right back. Luckily Monk's place was not very far away. As soon as Ding stepped into the alley where Monk lived, he could see a group of people still crowded around. As he got closer he could hear an uproar of gossip with everyone trying to get their two cents in. He pretended that he was just passing by and asked curiously what had happened. No one was willing to answer Ding Wenyu's inquiries; they all just continued, enraptured in their own gossip. Then Ding Wenyu caught a glimpse of two policemen searching Monk's room, and instantly his lax mood tensed up. It didn't look so good. From another open door Ding heard a woman shrieking with sorrow. He walked over and saw that the woman wailing was that same pretty woman he had once seen Monk arguing with. The pretty woman cursed Monk through her sobs. One glance at that room and Ding Wenyu knew that things were pretty serious.

II

A few days before the big "enlisted man marathon," where uniformed soldiers raced around the city, Yuyuan decided to move into the dormitory at the army headquarters. She had been considering packing her bags for quite some time. Her patience with her sister-in-law's complaints and restrictions was growing thinner and thinner. She gave Yu Kerun an ultimatum: if he didn't find a house for them, she would move into the army dormitory. There was no way she wanted to go on living under someone else's roof. In order not to make the situation too awkward, Yuyuan didn't rashly move out in anger, with everyone upset. Instead she found an excuse. She said that the army headquarters was going to increase study time for confidential personnel and it would be more convenient for her to simply stay in the dormitory. It was easy to see that her excuse for moving out wouldn't hold up. Yu Kerun's sister-in-law was elated that Yuyuan was finally moving out, but also worried about being stuck with the charge of not putting up with her—so she insisted that Yuyuan must have a hidden purpose. Yu Kerun knew that his wife didn't want to go on living in his brother's house, but he couldn't bring himself to say anything bad about his sister-in-law; instead he blamed Yuyuan for lacking patience and not being conciliatory enough. Yu Kerun explained that his sister-in-law was a woman who had never received much of an education and asked Yuyuan why she insisted on making things so difficult with her. He told Yuyuan that moving out would only give his sister-in-law something to gossip about.

Although the young couple was desperately trying to avoid an argument, they were both filled with resentment. Yuyuan knew that her husband didn't want to offend his brother and sister-in-law, so there was nothing he could do but direct his anger at someone else. Yu Kerun was dying to accuse his wife of moving out simply to make it more convenient for her to receive Ding Wenyu's letters and give Ding an opportunity to get close to her. However, it was precisely because he didn't say what he felt that Yuyuan could sense his bottled-up anger. She discovered that a cold war between them could be even more hurtful and destructive than a heated argument where they both turned red with anger. Yu Kerun often acted as if he didn't care about a thing in the world; however, it was precisely this attitude that proved he did indeed care. When Yuyuan decided that she wanted to move out, he drove her to the army headquarters. On the way there Yu Kerun intentionally gave her the silent treatment, all the while driving as fast as the wind.

"Be careful not to run anybody over!" Yuyuan coldly warned him.

Yu Kerun put his foot down even harder on the gas, and Yuyuan noticed the shocked looked on pedestrians' faces as they watched the car go whistling by. Even though Yu Kerun was a most adept driver, he was in no mood to milk his driving skills. Before them was an old man sluggishly crossing the street, and Yu Kerun had no choice but to slam on the brakes. The jeep came to a screeching halt and Yuyuan's body was thrown forward, her head almost hitting the windshield—it was a good thing that she had been tightly holding onto the door handle the whole ride. She turned to look at Yu Kerun, but he was simply holding the steering wheel with both hands as if he had not even noticed the shock Yuyuan had just undergone. At first Yuyuan wanted to have it out with him about his driving, but after seeing his expression she wasn't even willing to open her mouth. Yu Kerun was waiting for Yuyuan's reprimand, and her silence left him somewhat dejected.

Outside it was a sunny and enchanting spring scene with bright and beautiful girls filling the streets. Roses in the flower terraces were blooming like a blazing fire. Neither Yuyuan or Yu Kerun felt that marriage had bridged the innate distance between them; it instead seemed to have had the opposite effect, and they became more and more like strangers. They were both conscious of the rift in their relationship—actually, this rift had probably existed long before. They were equally full of themselves. Whenever there was a disagreement, each of them hoped that the other party would give way and let them off without losing face. As their car soared over the asphalt roads of 1937 Nanjing, they both seemed to be pondering the same question at the same time—whether or not their marriage had been too hasty. Their relationship had grown fragile and weak. Marriage had brought them together, but any little incident was enough to make them question just whether or not their union was even worth the trouble. Sometimes they seemed intentionally to sow discord, like when Yu Kerun deliberately exaggerated Ding Wenyu's role in driving them apart. At the same time, Yuyuan blamed every unhappy event that transpired between them on the evildoing of their sister-in-law.

"Since I have already moved out, I'll tell you frankly, I'm living under my own roof from now on. Never will I move back into your brother's house!" Yuyuan was like a small bird that had escaped from its cage and expressed her clear-cut stance to Yu Kerun. "Don't tell me I don't deserve to have a house of my own."

Yu Kerun said, "I don't necessarily feel that staying at my brother's place is living under somebody else's roof."

"Well, *I* do," Yuyuan adamantly responded.

Yuyuan's stance won the unanimous support of her friends—they all had been against her moving into Yu Kerun's brother's house in the first place. Her friends felt that a young pilot like Yu Kerun, even if for the time being he couldn't afford a house, should at least rent one. It was necessary to have a place of one's own. Yu Kerun was a little bird who was always flying around; all he needed was a place to rest his feet while on the ground. Yuyuan was different from him, she wouldn't stand for being treated like a thing to be stored at someone else's place. When Yu Kerun came to drop Yuyuan off at the dormitory, Yuyuan's friends had a frank discussion with him. They said that leaving Yuyuan with them was an expedient measure that needed to be taken for the time being and they would take good care of her.

"There is no fee for us looking after her, but you better hurry up and find a house for Yuyuan!" Yuyuan's friends were all on close terms with Yu Kerun. As their mouths went nonstop with their stern reprimands, they didn't forget to throw in a few good-humored jokes every now and then. All of the girls who worked in the army headquarters had been around the block—they were quite a bunch. Yu Kerun pretended to listen diligently; he gave people the impression that he was going to rush right out and rent a house, when actually that was the last thing on his mind. Yu Kerun was an instructor at the Aviation Academy. This type of instructor was much different from teachers at other schools because the place of instruction was not a room but the boundless, blue sky. As conflicts between China and Japan increased, so did the pressing need for training pilots who could engage in aerial combat. Chiang Kai-shek had long known just how weak the Chinese air force was, and he not only served as the director of the Aeronautical Committee but also had his wife Soong May-ling act as its secretary general. Actually, all of the instructors at the Aviation Academy had dual responsibilities. While they had their teaching commitments, they had to be constantly prepared for an attack by the Japanese air force.

Yu Kerun figured out a way to satisfy both himself and Yuyuan. Whenever the opportunity presented itself, they would stay a night in a hotel. At first this idea seemed a bit ridiculous; however, it quickly proved to be extremely innovative. For the hotel industry in Nanjing, 1937 was a flourishing era of growth. Floods of people came to the capital in search of work; unable to immediately find suitable housing, they took rooms in one of the city's many hotels. The profusion of hotels kept prices down, and the average hotel was not at all expensive. Since Yuyuan refused to return to Yu Kexia's residence and Yu Kerun was unwilling to go with Yuyuan back to her parents' home, hotels became the perfect place for their secret rendezvous. The hotel they frequented most often was near Daxing Palace. It was close to the main street and only a ten-minute walk from Yuyuan's dormitory.

Their first stay in the hotel came by chance. Three days after Yuyuan had moved into the dormitory, Yu Kerun came to visit her. The two of them left the main gate of the army headquarters and walked south as if they were a pair of homeless children. Not far away was the OMEA compound, the place they had been married just over four months earlier. Gazing at the palacelike architecture of the compound rooftops, they were both struck with an unspeakable melancholy. And so the two of them turned the corner and walked west in the direction of Daxing Palace. On the way, the spring breeze stroked their faces. The large French parasol trees were beginning to sprout delicate buds. Originally they had just planned to eat out, but as they passed a hotel, Yu Kerun suddenly got a strange idea and invited Yuyuan to go in with him for a look around. At first Yu Kerun said he was thinking of renting a long-term room in the hotel and wanted to go in to check out the price. The owner of the hotel warmly took care of them. In order to make sure he got this bit of business, he promised them the best possible deal and even offered them a complimentary night. He brought them to the easternmost room on the second floor and opened the window that overlooked the street to allow them to admire the view.

"This is our best room." The owner pointed to a small restaurant bustling with business across the street. "If the two of you want to eat, all you have to do is wave your hand and they'll send something right up."

That night they indeed stayed in that room; moreover, they followed the owner's instructions and called the boy from the restaurant across the street over to deliver their dinner. Eating in that hotel room was really something new. They watched the street scene as they ate, and when they finished the boy came back up to collect the plates and chopsticks. Yuyuan felt it was perhaps their most exciting and refreshing experience together, when she suddenly realized that it all must have been planned in advance by Yu Kerun. From the way he and the owner spoke, this obviously wasn't the first time that Yu had booked a room. She instantly thought it highly possible that he had brought other women here—it might not have been this hotel, but it could have been somewhere else. She giggled and asked Yu Kerun, trying to get him to confirm her suspicions. This line of questioning made Yu Kerun extremely uncomfortable and even a bit temperamental. He wouldn't admit to it, but he wouldn't deny it either. He simply refused to respond to any of his wife's ridiculous suppositions.

Yuyuan laughed. The last thing she wanted was an affirmation or a denial. No matter what kind of answer she got, she still wouldn't be satisfied. How could she expect Yu Kerun to speak the truth? Keeping his mouth shut was the most intelligent response. She felt that she was quite foolish—how could she suddenly bring up such a dampening topic at a time when they were supposed to be so happy? She shouldn't have ruined the mood that night. Yuyuan thought back to the way the hotel owner looked at her when they first entered the hotel; it was obvious that he took them for a pair of lovers. There was absolutely nothing strange about this. How could the owner be expected to believe that that they were legally married? Yu Kerun couldn't figure out why Yuyuan kept on snickering. It didn't seem like her laughter had any bad intentions, but her giggling indeed left him uncomfortable. In order to cover up his awkwardness, Yu Kerun also started to giggle.

"What are you laughing at?" Yuyuan asked him, while continuing with her girlish giggling.

Yu Kerun retorted by asking her what *she* was laughing about. This was also an unanswerable question that didn't need to be addressed. It was a rarity to have such a warm, intimate night together. From the sidewalk on the street below a young girl shouted with a faint voice, "Flowers for sale!" Yu Kerun called the flower girl up and bought Yuyuan a few roses. Since they didn't have anywhere to put the flowers, Yuyuan filled a drinking glass with tap water, stuck the roses in it, and placed it on the nightstand beside the bed. Neither of them knew how they should spend the rest of the evening. It seemed a bit too early to go to bed, so they sat next to the window and watched the street scene. The pedestrians began to thin out, but the restaurant across the way was still bustling. There were a few people making a hubbub as they played finger-guessing games over their ale. At the restaurant entrance there was someone peddling peanuts and sunflower seeds; that flower girl had also made her way to the restaurant to try to bag some extra business. There was a fashionably dressed young woman pacing back and forth around the hotel entrance. Not far away under the electric pole was another chic young woman wearing a cheongsam. It only took one look to figure out what line of work these girls were in.

The hotel room was filled with the fragrance of the roses. Yuyuan and Yu Kerun both knew what was coming next—neither of them needed to say anything. As they casually chatted, Yuyuan noticed a man who staggered out of the restaurant and took out some money to buy some flowers from the flower girl. It was at that moment that Yu Kerun suddenly turned off the electric lamp and embraced Yuyuan from behind. The time they had spent in anticipation seemed a bit drawn out. By the time she felt Yu Kerun's restless hands fondling her body, Yuyuan also could wait no longer and pushed Yu Kerun down on the bed. Her movements were so raw and savage that even she herself thought them a bit comic. She wanted to be aggressive, but she went too far, to the point that Yu Kerun misunderstood her intentions. Yu Kerun thought that she couldn't wait for it. Yuyuan's abnormal aggressiveness spurred Yu Kerun to also take things too far and overreact.

The roses on the nightstand beside the bed were knocked over, spilling the water in the glass all over the floor. Yuyuan felt a kind of indescribable perplexity. Yu Kerun was obviously putting on quite a performance, but for some reason she couldn't keep herself in the moment. She was like a lost child at her wit's end, completely in the dark as to what she should actually do. Her excitement was more than a bit forced; in order not to disappoint Yu Kerun (and in order not to let Yu Kerun see how disappointed she was), Yuyuan had no choice but to mechanically hold him close to her body. How wonderful it would have been if the two of them could have just spent the night talking or sitting there leisurely admiring the night scene outside the window. When it comes to affairs of men and women, why does everything have to end the moment they get into bed? Once again, the very real possibility that Yu Kerun had spent the night with other women in hotel rooms just like this crossed Yuyuan's mind. The second this thought came to her, Yuyuan warned herself that this was not the time or place to be thinking of this. She should be thinking about some happy things, like the joy she felt when she and Yu Kerun had first met. It was then that Yu Kerun took her for her very first ride in a jeep. They had driven straight toward the outskirts of the city. Crossing hills and dales, they at one point even drove the jeep off the road into the fields.

Yu Kerun once promised that he would take her for a plane ride. Taking Yuyuan flying was actually something that came up quite often while they were still dating—a pity that he never mentioned the subject again after they were married. Sitting in an airplane as you soared through the sky must have been quite a thrilling experience. For a time, Yuyuan often dreamed about what it would be like to fly. She imagined herself shuttling back and forth between the blue sky and the white clouds, the moon and stars all within an arm's reach. She dreamed of her plane spinning in the sky, diving rapidly from the heights of heaven down toward the ground. On this special evening, Yu Kerun had long since fallen fast asleep, yet Yuyuan still wasn't even a bit drowsy. Although he didn't snore, Yuyuan was all too familiar with the sound of his even breathing as he slept. There were more than a few times that Yuyuan was tempted to wake him up to revisit the issue of him taking her flying. In the end she didn't have the heart to wake him. Yuyuan knew that even if she did it was still no use; he would simply mock her and her crazy ideas. Every time Yuyuan brought up something that was a bit unrealistic, Yu Kerun would snicker at her for what seemed like an eternity. He would continue until Yuyuan was thoroughly embarrassed.

"Who ever said that I wanted to go flying with him anyway?" Yuyuan mumbled to herself, lying in the dark.

Deep in the night it began to drizzle, bringing in the first call of spring thunder. Yuyuan was just beginning to groggily drift asleep when the first light of dawn began to shine down and she was disturbed by the bustling sound of voices coming in through the window. She leaned over the windowsill to look but could only see crowds of people on both sides of the street and a few police officers maintaining order. Everyone was on their tiptoes looking east. Every now and then someone would even slide into the street and extend their neck to get a better look. The police officers waved their nightsticks to scare the people who had slipped into the street back to their place on the sidewalk. Suddenly someone yelled: "They're coming!" Instantly the crowd became excited and everyone's necks extended even farther. Yu Kerun was awakened by the noise and joined Yuyuan at the window to see what was happening. It was a clear day after a rain; the sun had just risen and the ground was still damp. Far off in the east there was a group of people running toward them. They got closer and closer as they ran until Yuyuan and Yu Kerun were finally able to see them clearly. It was a couple of fully uniformed soldiers.

In order to commemorate Nanjing's ten-year anniversary as the capital, the city government and the military co-sponsored an "enlisted man marathon." Leading the race were a group of students from the Military Academy. There was quite a large gap between the leaders and the large group that lagged behind. It was some time before the majority of the participants finally thundered past the hotel window. Besides soldiers, students and conscripted men in training took part in the race. Among the crowd of racers, Yuyuan finally recognized a few of her co-workers from the army headquarters. All she noticed was that they were soaked in sweat. As they jogged by, they wiped the sweat dripping from their foreheads. A lot of people took part in the "enlisted man marathon"; they were all in high spirits and full of stamina. It looked as if each one had an unlimited supply of energy. From time to time, two reporters ran out into the middle of the street to take photos. One of the soldiers lost a shoe and came running by wearing just one. A reporter ran behind him, trying to get a shot of this one-shoed runner, but that soldier flew right past and, in an instant, there were already other runners behind him. Who knows if that reporter ever got his shot?

III

At first Ding Wenyu never imagined that Monk could bring him any kind of trouble. It was completely out of curiosity that he went to the quadrangle compound where Monk lived with a number of other families to see what he could find out. As far as outsiders are concerned, murder always carries with it a peculiar kind of attraction. After he returned home and told Monk that Little Moon was indeed dead, Monk's face showed not the slightest reaction. He stared blankly at Ding Wenyu as if this affair had absolutely nothing to do with him. Ding explained to Monk that as they spoke, there was still a pair of police officers searching

Monk's room, and that pretty woman was still weeping. But still, Monk didn't seem to react. Ding Wenyu was somewhat confused by Monk's odd expression. He should understand the seriousness of the matter. Someone had died, this was no longer just a little careless mistake. For the time being, the police probably wouldn't trace Monk's whereabouts to Ding's apartment, but where else could he run? Ding Wenyu tried to convince Monk to turn himself in the next morning. Since it was just an accident, perhaps the courts would treat him with leniency if he voluntarily surrendered.

Ding Wenyu couldn't figure out just what could be going through Monk's head. At that moment Monk's mind was a complete blank. He had been somewhat out of control ever since he had decided that he was going to teach Little Moon a lesson. That afternoon, with the claw hammer tucked away under his jacket, he paced back and forth outside that pretty woman, Mrs. Zhang's front door. He kept raving to himself, saying that something bad was going to happen that day. He realized that he very much wanted to pull off something big, something no one would ever expect from him. Monk's father had passed away not long after he was born. Then before he even came of age, Monk's mother died from an illness. The orphaned Monk's temper was never very good, and whenever he ran into trouble he backed himself into a corner. Ever since Mrs. Zhang had approved of giving Little Moon's hand to Monk in marriage, he had looked at Little Moon as his little bride-to-be. When Mrs. Zhang made this promise, Little Moon was but nine years old, a chit of a girl. From that point on, however, Monk always took this bit of pillow talk to heart.

"Don't tell me that besides Little Moon there's no other girl in the world who is suitable?" Later Mrs. Zhang wanted to go back on her promise, but it was already a bit too late—Monk was already dead set on this affair. He was like a hunter; for years he had hidden in secret, waiting, constantly keeping one eye open on his prize—Little Moon. He took notice of even the slightest changes in her. He watched as her breasts gradually began to develop—he once even spied on her taking a bath. Mrs. Zhang was having a hard time with the way Monk "kept an eye on the pot while still eating from his bowl," but there was nothing she could do about it.

"You'd better keep your word!" Monk stubbornly warned her.

Mrs. Zhang responded, "Don't tell me that you intend to share the same bed with both mother and daughter?"

Monk said that he wasn't concerned with that. All he knew was that Little Moon was supposed to become his wife. Everything began one summer day when he was sixteen years old. Mrs. Zhang called Monk over from across the way to help her empty out the bath water and invited him into her small kitchen. She had just taken a bath and her body emitted the fragrant scent of soap. She had Monk carry the water basin outside to empty it; she gazed at him as she brushed her hair. Monk, then in the bud of youth with thoughts of love filling his mind, was clumsily rushing about with the water when Mrs. Zhang called him into her room. She undid her clothes and had Monk rub perfumed toilet water on her back. She extended her neck and pulled her shirt collar open to either side as far as it could go. Every muscle in her body was trembling. Monk's hands started to get a bit naughty; he hesitated as he moved from her backside around her body to grab her full breasts. Mrs. Zhang's face suddenly turned stern and she said, "And I thought you were still just a kid—how can you touch me there?" Not knowing what to do, Monk stood there stupefied with that tall bottle of toilet water in his hand—he looked like a statue. The room was blistering and Monk's face looked blackened, not because he was naturally dark-skinned but because he was dirty. The sweat dripping from his brow left tracks across his face. If Mrs. Zhang hadn't grabbed hold of him he probably would have run off. But Mrs. Zhang seized him as if she were catching a thief. Not only that but, without the slightest hesitation, she reached out to grab that member of his that was already sticking up. Under Mrs. Zhang's firm, unbridled grasp, Monk was even more confused. He felt like he could barely breathe; he tried to hold Mrs. Zhang back with one hand as he continued to grasp that bottle of perfumed toilet water with the other. He grabbed Mrs. Zhang's hand with the intention of stopping her, but he almost instantly gave up on the idea when their hands met. His whole body seemed to tremble as he firmly held Mrs. Zhang's naughty hand. Finally, not able to take it anymore, Monk pushed Mrs. Zhang down onto a chair.

When it was over, Monk lay in Mrs. Zhang's bed, facing the wall and weeping like a child. No matter how Mrs. Zhang tried to console him, Monk still couldn't get his deceased mother's warning out of his head. Once when his mother discovered he was unwilling to get out from under the covers she tried to scare Monk by telling him that kids who played with their "little birdies" would end up "shooting the load"—and "shooting the load" was as lethal as playing with a loaded gun. What happened to Monk's "little birdie" that day had already occurred many times before, but only in his dreams. In those obscene adolescent dreams, Monk had already had a go with Mrs. Zhang. The encounter with her scared him half out of his wits; he dreaded what would happen as a result. It was quite a feat on Mrs. Zhang's part to finally get Monk to stop crying. She tried to console him by telling him that there were men his age who were already fathers. That night Mrs. Zhang cooked a nice dinner for Monk, and she even kept him over to have a bath. After this out-of-the-ordinary incident, Monk became Mrs. Zhang's godson. No longer did he have to wash his own clothes, and he often ate over at Mrs. Zhang's house.

It wasn't long at all before Monk truly matured. He became a rickshaw puller, and while waiting for his next bit of business he would often hear all kinds of man talk from his fellow rickshaw coolies. The coolies would brag about all kinds of sexual encounters they had had—and others that they had completely made up. They taught young Monk how to take advantage of those lonely female passengers who were all too willing to give themselves over to a strong young man. If business was good, rickshaw coolies would usually head down to the brothels for a good time—that's how their logic of life went. On more than one occasion they tried to drag Monk with them down to the whorehouses. After the Republic established the capital in Nanjing, all brothels were technically outlawed. In order to do better business, virtually all rickshaw pullers had to know how to get their customers to those shady places where their desires could be satisfied. Without any difficulty, Monk learned how to milk those generous pleasure seekers; moreover, with one look he could tell which women he pulled weren't straitlaced. One day Monk took a prostitute to the home of a retired police official. They agreed that she would pay later that afternoon when Monk came to pick her up. However, it was that prostitute who ended up taking Monk for a ride. She told Monk that that police official hadn't even paid her. "If the old man doesn't pay me, how am I supposed to pay you?" Bold and assured, that young prostitute sat in the rickshaw unwilling to budge. "Why don't you just accept your bad luck!" She didn't pay and yet she was still so terribly rude—other than a prostitute, no woman would dare to take such liberties. Monk didn't bother wasting his breath arguing; he simply took off. When the prostitute realized he wasn't taking her home, she asked him where he was taking her. Monk turned and said, "Shit, I'm not taking you anywhere! *I'm* going home!" The prostitute suspected that he wasn't harboring any good intentions and tried to jump down off the rickshaw, but because she was wearing a tight cheongsam she had to give up after several attempts. When they arrived at Monk's home he ferociously barked at her: "Get the hell out of here and don't let me run into you again!"

Monk told this story to his godmother Mrs. Zhang, and she couldn't help but offer a grim sneer. She asked Monk why he didn't invite her in—after all, he had already gone to the trouble of bringing her all the way to his doorstep. How could he bear to part with her so easily? "With a godmother like you, what do I need to bring other women home for?"

Mrs. Zhang turned red and replied, "Bullshit, just who do you take your godmother for?" It was that very night, after some affectionate hanky-panky, that Mrs. Zhang promised Monk that, as long as he didn't go after any other women, Little Moon would be his when she got older. Mrs. Zhang told him, "When the time comes, I won't be your godmother, I'll be your mother-in-law." Mrs. Zhang didn't really take this promise seriously. In her eyes Monk, a treasure as he was, was still a boy. It had already been many years since Mrs. Zhang's husband had left; heaven only knew where he went. There were people who came to report that he had died a stranger in some faraway land; then there were others who reported that he was still alive. During her early days with Monk, Mrs. Zhang was constantly pondering what she could do to tie him down. She knew that she was getting older and it would only be a matter of time before her beauty would fade—and so she resorted to using her own daughter to rope him in.

"Why do you have to keep letting that disgusting guy into our house?" When Little Moon was fourteen she had once asked her mother this with disdain. She had long known about the relationship between her mother and Monk. Each time Monk came by, Little Moon would crawl up to the attic, refusing to come down until he left. At first Mrs. Zhang thought that Monk must had done something to Little Moon to scare her like that, but later she learned that he had simply given her a new bookbag. Naturally, Monk's intentions behind this gift were far from lofty. Little

Moon took out a pair of scissors from her mom's sewing box and, clenching her teeth, cut the bookbag into shreds. In the face of her daughter's anger, Mrs. Zhang felt the ultimate humiliation. As she stared silently at her daughter cutting up that bookbag, she could feel an invisible, shapeless hand slapping her face. Once her daughter started to calm down a bit, Mrs. Zhang sighed; she knew that Little Moon was probably right. She promised that she would listen to her daughter and immediately break it off with Monk. She used a string of apologies and self-censure to console her daughter's pain—she even gave herself a pair of sharp slaps across the face.

Mrs. Zhang used this incident as an excuse to get into an all-out argument with Monk and broke up with him for three months. During these three months Mrs. Zhang became a pure and chaste widow, refusing Monk's several attempts to reconcile. Finally one night Monk came in through the window and crawled into Mrs. Zhang's bed. Still, Mrs. Zhang didn't lose her bearing; she wrestled with Monk on the bed until he finally got anxious. Monk lowered his voice and said, "What the fuck are you doing playing the saint? Are you really unwilling to do it, or are you just playing hard to get?"

Mrs. Zhang responded, "I'm not going to let you lay a finger on me unless you give up on marrying Little Moon." In an instant Monk's shame transformed into rage, and he heartlessly hit Mrs. Zhang in the face before crawling back out through the window. The next day she had a large black-and-blue mark on her face. Mrs. Zhang sobbed silently as she gazed at her swollen face in the mirror. Mrs. Zhang's mother-in-law was a blind old lady and, living in the next room, had long known of her daughter-in-law's illicit actions. As Mrs. Zhang was sobbing to herself before the mirror, her mother-in-law suddenly appeared beside her like a phantom. With unspoken intentions behind her words, the old lady asked her daughter-in-law if a thief had visited the night before.

"No, last night my lover came by and tried to get into my bed!" Mrs. Zhang resentfully replied.

The blind old lady was rendered speechless by Mrs. Zhang's response. This unbridled and shameless daughter-in-law of hers had already brought her to the end of her rope. She gazed blankly with her sightless eyes, mumbling under her breath. For a long time both of them were silent, but finally it was the old lady who spoke. She told Mrs. Zhang not to forget that "*You're* the one who said there was a lover in your bed, not me! I'm blind, I can't tell whether or not there was a man running around." Gritting her teeth, Mrs. Zhang smiled wryly and said, "It's a good thing you can't see him! You probably wouldn't be able to stand the sight of him! If you really want to know what it feels like, I'll find an old man for you!"

The blind old lady almost fainted in anger. As Mrs. Zhang stood up and passed by her, she grabbed hold of a small stool and swung it fiercely at Mrs. Zhang. With one swipe, she hit Mrs. Zhang directly on her lower back; the pain was so sharp that it knocked the wind out of her. "I'll kill you, you dirty whore!" the old lady viciously cursed.

Like a child, Mrs. Zhang burst into tears. The more she cried the sadder she became; in the end she wailed with more sorrow than when she had first heard the rumor that her husband had died. At first she cried because of the sharp pain in her back, but after a while her tears seemed to be more out of self-pity than anything else. She hated herself for what she had done; she had let down her husband, she had let down her daughter Little Moon, and she had let down her blind old mother-in-law. Hearing her daughter-in-law's unending weeping, the blind old lady began to feel a bit unsure if she had done the right thing by hitting her. After all, it was her daughter-in-law upon whom the whole family relied. In her younger days the old lady had also had a lover; back then she was on fire with passion—"a wolf at thirty and a tiger at forty," as the popular saying went. She wasn't really angry at her daughter-in-law, and the more Mrs. Zhang cried the more the old lady felt she should give her an opportunity to get off easy. Finally, the old lady said, "It would be great if you could find yourself a good man. But let me tell you, that godson of yours isn't anything to write home about." Mrs. Zhang knew that although the old lady was blind she knew exactly what was going on. Mrs. Zhang and Monk's on-and-off affair continued for several years after that. On the surface it appeared that they had broken up, but secretly it continued—of course, from time to time they really would break up, only to get back together shortly thereafter. Monk didn't care whether or not Mrs. Zhang went back on her word; as far as he was concerned, Little Moon was already his fiancée. While never refusing Mrs. Zhang's nightly affections, he was drooling over the thought of being with his Little Moon. Mrs. Zhang took notice and began to grow anxious, so she secretly arranged for Little Moon to marry someone else. Little Moon didn't want to go on living at home either. So after only a single meeting with her prospective suitor, a middle school graduate fresh out of school, Little Moon immediately agreed to marry him.

By the time Monk caught wind of things, Little Moon was already engaged. In order to cover up her guilt, Mrs. Zhang tried to be as warm and considerate to Monk as possible. Monk grew increasingly angry until he finally couldn't take it any more. In order to express his anger, he began to visit the brothels and tell Mrs. Zhang about all the repulsive things those whores did to him. He paid no heed to Mrs. Zhang. He swore that he would one day make her eat her words—he would make her regret going back on her promise for the rest of her life. One day in the courtyard where they lived Monk stopped Little Moon and asked her what she was so giggly about. Monk said, "Your mother is despicable, promising you to me and then going and allowing you to be matched up with someone else." Giving him a look of disdain, Little Moon turned and walked away. Monk pursued her, yelling, "What the hell are you so uppity about? From day one you were supposed to be *my* wife! Don't think for a second that you can get rid of me so easy!"

Monk only intended to teach Little Moon a little lesson. He wanted to make a fool of her and make Mrs. Zhang miserable for the rest of her life. When he stopped Little Moon a second time at the courtyard entrance, Monk had that claw hammer hidden under his jacket—he realized that things might get out of hand, but he didn't have the slightest intention of murdering anyone. All he did was grab that hammer on his way out the door in order to scare Little Moon. Like before, Little Moon paid no heed to him, but with a wry smile Monk told her, "I know that you despise me because of what went on between your mother and me. But the only reason I was willing to be with your mother was for you." Little Moon turned to go home, but Monk grabbed hold of her and wouldn't let go. With one strong push, Little Moon brushed him aside and ran toward her house. Putting everything on the line, Monk pursued her inside. Mrs. Zhang had gone out and only the blind old lady was home. Seeing that Monk indeed had the nerve to follow her inside, Little Moon crawled up into the attic. The old lady heard Little Moon's footsteps and asked with alarm, "Little Moon, who's that talking to you?"

Little Moon responded, "Nobody."

The old lady continued: "I know I heard you talking to someone."

Little Moon answered, "Don't worry, I was just talking to myself."

Monk unexpectedly crawled up to the attic after her. Lowering his voice, he warned her: "Don't you play good girl with me. Actually, you're a slut just like your mother!" Little Moon raised her hand and slapped him across the face. Monk's anger exploded and he grabbed hold of her. Little Moon tried to scream, but Monk forcefully clenched her throat. The two of them rolled around the attic, locked in struggle.

The blind old lady yelled from downstairs, "What's going on?"

Catching her breath, Little Moon screamed, "Monk, get the hell out, you fucking hoodlum!"

Monk started to panic. He removed the claw hammer from his jacket to show Little Moon before beginning to dejectedly descend the stairs. It was at that moment that the old lady began her unbridled cursing. She called Monk an animal, a womanizer, a shameless piece of meat. The more Monk listened to the old lady's curses, the more explosive his temper became. He stood in the doorway listening to her admonishments, all the while wishing he could rush over and give her a few good whacks with his claw hammer. The old lady thought he had left and after a few minutes stopped her yelling. Suddenly Monk was struck with an evil idea, and as quiet as he could be, snuck back inside and silently crept back up the stairs.

Before Little Moon had a chance to realize what was happening, Monk raised his claw hammer and hit her with three consecutive blows on the back of the head. With her arms wrapped around her head, Little Moon's body fell to the ground. Afraid that she would scream, Monk rushed over to gag her mouth with his hand. Once things got to this point, Monk started to get bold. He noticed that Little Moon's eyes were open but had a faint, dead look. He released his hand from her mouth and, seeing that she didn't make a sound, told her, "I though you were a tough cookie. Well, you don't look so tough now!" Little Moon didn't have the slightest reaction and Monk, feeling that he still hadn't gotten even with her, began to grumble to himself: "What are you gonna do if I want to have my way with you, huh?" What happened next he had already thought about for a long time. In his dreams he had already acted it out step by step, innumerable times. He carefully pulled off one of her pant legs, undid his own pants, and slid them down to his knees. At this critical moment he discovered that he had completely lost control of himself and couldn't help what he was doing. He realized that he didn't even really want to do it. For a moment everything was quiet, but suddenly the blind old lady called from downstairs. Monk became even more panicky. He tried to contain himself, but he lost control and that dirty fluid spurted out of him onto the floor. In a fluster Monk scooped it up off the floor with his finger and, in an desperate attempt to mend the fold even after his sheep had gotten out, wiped it on Little Moon's vagina. It was at that moment that he discovered that there was a pool of blood seeping from Little Moon's head. The blood was spreading out on the floor like a red snake slithering forward, dripping down through the cracks in the floor. The blood dripped downstairs onto the blind woman's face. The old woman wiped it with her hand, placed it under her nose to smell it, and began to scream in terror.

IV

Ding Wenyu listened in suspended disbelief as Monk told his tale. By the time Monk had stammered through his story it was already the middle of the night. Ding Wenyu could sense his hair standing on end. Monk spoke in a completely composed and detached manner, as if the whole event had nothing to do with him. Already, the anxious tone he had first expressed had completely dissipated, and it seemed that his sole fear was that Ding Wenyu would disbelieve some of the details. When it came to these details, Monk carefully repeated them over and over. He meticulously described the claw hammer that he had used; it was one of the tools he used to repair his rickshaw. He made hand gestures to show the size and weight of the hammer and then, once again, he described the hammer's effect when it smashed down on the back of Little Moon's skull. Sighing, he explained that he never wanted to kill Little Moon, he just wanted to teach her a lesson. He never imagined that things would go as far as they did. He told Ding Wenyu that he was truly fond of that girl Little Moon.

"Well, you took your fondness too far." Ding Wenyu said quietly.

"What do you mean, I took it too far?" Not agreeing with Ding's view, Monk protested, "What's more, she was supposed to be my wife from the beginning."

Ding Wenyu didn't know what else he could say to try to change Monk's mind. All Ding could do was tell him that he had committed a terrible, unforgivable crime. He explained to Monk that the charge of murder combined with necrophilia was much more severe than straight murder. Monk immediately denied his guilt; he naively explained to Ding that he didn't really finish doing it. "Mr. Ding, you said before that whether or not she was dead or not made all the difference in the world— so naturally it should also matter if I finished or not." Monk refused Ding's recommendation that he turn himself in. With a wry look on his face he said, "Mr. Ding, are you saying you want me to simply throw my life away?" Already in way over his head, Monk was at a complete loss as to what his next move should be. He hoped that Ding could provide him with some way out rather than turning himself in. After all, Ding Wenyu was a man of learning; if anyone could help Monk, he could.

It was deep into the night when Ding Wenyu suddenly remembered that last letter to Yuyuan he hadn't finished writing. He had class first thing the next morning and wasn't in the mood to continue being tied up with Monk's problems. A life for a life—Ding Wenyu felt that if Monk had the courage to kill someone he should have the courage to face the reality of the consequences. Monk took notice of Ding's impatience and mumbled to himself that he regretted not joining the army. "Everyone's saying that we're about to go to war with Japan. Had I known, I would've signed up to fight the Japs rather than end up like this." Ding Wenyu wasn't in the mood to respond to this comment. Instead he sat down under the desk lamp to complete his letter to Yuyuan. After writing a few words he turned around to tell Monk that he could sleep on the couch and they would talk in the morning. Monk knew that Ding didn't want to listen to any more of his ramblings, so he sat down on the couch and stared into space. All Ding was concerned with was the writing of his letter. He couldn't help but yawn as he wrote. When he finished, Monk was still sitting there in a trancelike state. Ding Wenyu quietly returned to his bedroom to sleep.

First thing the next morning Ding Wenyu went to campus. At the university gate he mailed his letter to Yuyuan. It wasn't until the middle of class that he suddenly thought of his houseguest Monk and what he had done. As he was distracted by his thoughts, Ding's lecture that day was terrible. He kept abruptly pausing, and all of the students sitting in front stared at him in confused silence. He was tempted to raise the preposterous question to his students of whether or not a person could possibly kill for love. But just as the words were on the tip of his tongue, he stopped himself. This was not an appropriate matter to be discussed in class; moreover, Monk's actions were in no way motivated by love. What motivated Monk was a lack of love—love and murder should never be mentioned in the same breath. Ding's thoughts were in utter disarray and he decided to announce that they would end class early.

In the faculty lounge Ding Wenyu dashed off another letter to Yuyuan. He felt he should discuss Monk's actions and motivations with her. Yuyuan was the sole person he could share this with; moreover, only discussing it with her had any meaning. When writing to Yuyuan, Ding never ran out of things to say—actually, whenever he picked up his pen to write her he felt his thoughts flowing like a surging spring. It didn't matter the time or place, virtually any set of circumstances could inspire his longing for Yuyuan. Whenever he came upon something new, his first impulse was always to share it with her. He imagined what kind of response Yuyuan might have—whether she would approve or disapprove, what she would look like laughing or touched with a tinge of anger. As he wrote he thought of Little Moon, whose body probably had yet to grow cold. He told Yuyuan that he had once seen this girl; she was a radiant and comely girl whom everyone liked. As soon as Ding pictured her, he was suddenly struck by the truly unforgivable nature of Monk's crime.

Halfway through his letter to Yuyuan, Ding Wenyu was forced to put it aside and rush to his second class. This was a fairly common occurrence. Writing to Yuyuan had already become an integral part of his life. Even though she never answered his letters, hopelessly lovesick Ding Wenyu never once felt that they were like stones thrown into the sea. Writing love letters was the most ancient and interesting way of expressing one's love. Ding Wenyu had grown accustomed to stopping halfway through his letters and doing something else—that way he could maintain an air of love in whatever he did. In his next class Ding Wenyu began an all-out discussion of Scandinavian fairy tales. Quoting left and right, he kept his students in awe. Ding's students were all upperclassmen majoring in foreign languages, so Ding always lectured in English. Sometimes, however, in order to accurately express the original flavor of the Scandinavian fairy tales he couldn't help but quote long passages in Swedish.

After class Ding didn't go directly home—he went to the post office. Leaning against the mailbox, he finished up his last letter to Yuyuan and stuffed it in. However, the very moment he slipped the letter into the box, Ding realized that there was still more he wanted to say. Being in love is truly an inexpressible feeling; because he was in love, Ding Wenyu felt a fulfillment unlike any he had ever known. Whether or not Yuyuan loved him back wasn't really that important—Ding felt that being able to truly love someone the way he loved Yuyuan was in itself a form of extreme happiness. This was the first time in his life that Ding Wenyu had found true love. It was such a substantial feeling; love was everywhere and flowed through everything he did. It was as if the scent of love had inundated the very air he breathed—all Ding had to do was reach out his hand and he could touch it.

By the time Ding Wenyu returned home, Monk had already taken his leave. It was obvious that someone had been through his apartment. Ding Wenyu never imagined that Monk would run off with his valuables. At first he couldn't figure out what had actually happened, but after he opened the drawer in which he kept his money, he discovered that all the money he usually kept stashed away in a small cardboard box was missing. He questioned his maid about it, but she said that she hadn't seen anyone in the apartment. She said that when she came to clean the apartment the place was already empty. Ding Wenyu forced a wry smile. He figured that Monk must have taken the money and run before the maid even arrived. But after thinking about it, Ding realized his assumption was wrong—his money must have been stolen after the apartment was cleaned because when the maid arrived nothing had been out of place. Ding Wenyu thought of reporting this to the police but instantly gave up on the idea. It was a very complicated situation, and the police would certainly accuse him of harboring a murder suspect. In the end he had only himself to blame for the robbery.

As he was reading the paper over dinner, Ding Wenyu saw the first report about Monk's case of murder and necrophilia. It was extremely sketchy and consisted of only a few sentences. The deliberately exaggerated headline said that the murderer was on the run and that the police were doing everything in their power to bring him to justice. Starting with this report and continuing for several days, all of Nanjing's newspapers ran articles about the murder. Monk's case eventually became the hottest topic among the people of Nanjing during the spring of 1937. Reporters got their news from all kinds of sources. The phrase: "According to an anonymous source . . ." often appeared in their articles. As time went on, the reports became more and more ridiculous and the story became ever more incredible. Three days later, the police apprehended Monk at the Nanjing harbor. At first Monk was unwilling to confess where he had gotten all the money he had on him, but after repeated interrogation he finally admitted that he had stolen the money from Ding Wenyu.

Because of this change in events, Ding Wenyu's name also began to appear in the newspapers. A police investigator paid a visit to Ding Wenyu and requested he relate everything he knew about Monk. Ding was asked why he had harbored a murderer and failed to report the robbery. Ding Wenyu was not entirely willing to accommodate the investigator's line of questioning. He was in somewhat of a tough position because he didn't want to sell out Monk. Ding Wenyu wasn't fond of that police investigator and his never-ending questions. The investigator acted like a know-it-all who had everything in the palm of his hand. He kept stopping halfway through his sentences, hoping that Ding would finish his sentence and fall into his trap. He constantly harped on whether Monk had stolen Ding's money or Ding had willingly given Monk the cash. Ding Wenyu indeed fell right into one of the inspector's little traps when he foolishly admitted that he gave the money to Monk— he thought by doing this at least the theft charges against Monk could be dropped. By the time Ding realized what he had done, it was already too late. That astute inspector immediately grabbed hold of him, insistinged that Ding Wenyu explain the motive behind his actions. Suddenly the inspector's intentions became clear—he was hinting at the possibility that Ding might be an accomplice in this murder.

Ding Wenyu, who had been rendered speechless, flew into a rage. Waving his fist in the air, Ding asked this haughty detective to leave immediately. He told the investigator that he was no longer welcome in his home and angrily opened the door to show him out. Ding said that if the detective did not leave in the next minute he would have no choice but to step out for a moment himself. The investigator's belly was filled with anger, but he was helpless to do anything. He attempted to scare Ding with the charge of obstruction of justice, but a furious Ding Wenyu was in no mood to talk anymore. Instead he simply stamped outside, slamming the door behind him. As Ding was a famous university professor with an unconventional disposition, the inspector's threats were doomed to have the opposite effect of what was intended. The news of Ding Wenyu admonishing a police official somehow leaked out and embellished reports appeared in a gossip column the next day. Who knows how the reporters got hold of this bit of news, but worth noting was one quote that Ding never said—but wished he had: "A complete idiot would make a better detective than this arrogant buffoon."

For over a month afterward Ding Wenyu had to undergo innumerable interrogations; he was even forced to serve as a court witness. Monk's murder and necrophilia case became a public sensation of unprecedented scale and scope. The newspapers ran photos of Monk, Little Moon wearing her student uniform, and even the pretty Mrs. Zhang. Reporters recorded Monk's courtroom confession—those portions recounting the details of his affair, the murder, and the subsequent act of rape were repeatedly quoted in various newspapers. Ding Wenyu's name also frequently appeared. The press even dug up scandalous stories about how Monk used to take Ding to visit prostitutes. Although they only used his surname in these reports, anyone who knew Ding Wenyu would know exactly who this "certain famous professor by the name of Ding" was.

Realizing that Yuyuan might get upset when she saw what was written in the papers, Ding Wenyu openly admitted the errors of his old ways to her in a letter. With the deepest sincerity, he explained that the only reason he was able to recognize them was that he now had love in his heart. Love had led Ding Wenyu to reflect upon the ridiculous behavior of his past. In this world there are many mistakes committed due to a lack of love, but love has the power to purify. It can make someone forget themselves and all their inhibitions. Before he had met Yuyuan, Ding Wenyu was a pathetic orphan, lost in a desert without an oasis in sight; he didn't know from where he had come or where he was going. Orphans to love are stranded at an eternal impasse; to pursue a woman without love will never quell the loneliness in one's heart. Love is both humankind's starting point and its final resting place.

Monk's case suddenly grew quite complex when Mrs. Zhang, who hated that "godson" of hers more than anyone else in the world, unexpectedly changed her stance in court. She began to soberly reflect and came to the realization that she also had an irrefutable responsibility for this tragedy. She realized that, indirectly, she herself was also a kind of murderer. Since her only daughter Little Moon was already gone, she decided that she didn't want to lose her godson. As long as Monk was willing to take an oath to take care of her for the rest of her life, Mrs. Zhang would beg the court not to serve him with the death sentence. Her request caused an explosive uproar in the courtroom. Immediately, the pity people had slowly built up for her disappeared into thin air. In the next day's newspaper, a reporter printed the following news in large, boldface print:

WANTON MOTHER SHAMELESSLY DREAMS OF
REKINDLING HER ROMANCE
MURDERER HAS HOPE FOR RELEASE?!?!

Scores of good-natured citizens were moved to anger, complaining that releasing Monk would be nothing less than the most serious defilement of the law. Virtually on the spot, the court threw out Mrs. Zhang's request. Her tearful appeal at best was nothing more then a public display of the shame she had brought on herself. When she nauseatingly addressed Monk as her "godson," the public audience in the courtroom was first shocked, and then, realizing what she meant, immediately broke out in a wave of unfavorable commentary. The audience found it both shocking and ridiculous that their ears should be subjected to such shameless words in a court of law. People started to whisper among themselves, occasionally breaking into laughter. Even though she had suffered the pain of losing her daughter, the middle-aged Mrs. Zhang didn't forget to do herself up. Her hair was combed straight and neat and her clothes were sparkling clean. As she sat there in silence, people in the courtroom felt that she not only still had her charm, but, for a middle-aged woman, was actually quite stunning. From Mrs. Zhang's handsome appearance, people could infer that the now deceased Little Moon must have been one outstanding beauty. It was a shame that Mrs. Zhang's plea to spare Monk destroyed the wonderful impression she had left on everyone—instantly, dozens of people in the courtroom audience began to think of the wantonness hidden behind her beauty. They immediately began to imagine all the shameless things this very wanton woman was capable of.

V

During the late spring and early summer of 1937, Ding Wenyu's name frequently graced the newspapers—but not always in connection with Monk's case. What really stuck in peoples' minds were the divorce announcements that he ran in all the major newspapers. The battle over his divorce that year not only exhausted all of Ding Wenyu's energy but also made him look like an idiot on more than one occasion. Because he did not return to Shanghai and carry out his responsibility as the "seed planter," as had been agreed, Ding's father sent him three rush telegrams in a row. By the time the third telegram made it into Ding's hand, Peitao had already bought a train ticket to Nanjing. Ding Wenyu was caught by surprise and had no choice but to pick up Peitao from the station. After she casually emerged from the Blue Steel Express's first-class car and laid eyes on Ding Wenyu, she made her first request—she wanted to see the dirty tramp that Ding had been sleeping with.

"I am at least entitled to this, aren't I?" This was Peitao's first trip to Nanjing since their marriage. Her moodiness left Ding completely in the dark as to her actual intentions. It was already dark when her train arrived in Nanjing, and before they went back to Ding Wenyu's apartment, Peitao requested they go for a drive so she could see what the city looked like at night. There were barely a handful of people out roaming those dark streets—naturally, Nanjing's nightlife couldn't compare with the splendor of Shanghai. Peitao gazed out the car window at the cityscape and complained with a hint of sarcasm, "So this is the capital? What's so great about Nanjing?" After she stepped into Ding's university apartment she became even more fastidious. She wasted no time in searching Ding's bedroom in an attempt to find traces left behind by another woman. Ding Wenyu realized that Peitao's trip to Nanjing was obviously carefully planned; there was no way that she simply came to cause trouble.

Ding Wenyu's young maid was clearly uncomfortable under Peitao's unfriendly gaze. During dinner Peitao gave a terribly low appraisal of the maid's cooking and asked Ding why he didn't find a maid who was a better cook. "On the other hand, I'm sure you're reluctant to part with her," she said sarcastically. Almost immediately Peitao changed the subject. "I've been thinking I should stay here a bit longer with you this time." Ding Wenyu couldn't help but shudder. Taking notice of his reaction, Peitao said coldly, "I know that you don't like me, but legally I'm still your wife!" Although Peitao said that she wasn't satisfied with the maid's cooking, she had quite a hearty appetite. As Peitao slowly gobbled down her dinner, she looked for all kinds of topics to provoke Ding with.

The university found out that Ding Wenyu's wife had arrived and sent a representative to welcome her. The wife of Ding's department chair was an elementary school classmate of Peitao, and when she learned that Peitao was in Nanjing she insisted on inviting Mr. and Mrs. Ding Wenyu to dinner. Several other professors and their wives were also invited, which led to a whole series of dinners. During her two weeks in Nanjing, barely a day went by that Peitao wasn't invited out or didn't treat someone to dinner. When out with others, Peitao came off as a poised woman from a wealthy family, leaving everyone with the impression of being virtuous and elegant. Everyone had long ago caught wind of Ding Wenyu's plans to divorce, but after seeing Mrs. Ding they were at a loss to do anything but compliment him on his wife and bombard her with endless flattery to win her over. They said in jest that Ding Wenyu had already lost focus of what was in his own best interest, because all that time he spent abroad had gone to his head.

"*I'm* the one who doesn't know what's best for myself," Peitao replied with complete composure. "Mr. Ding wanted to leave me, yet I brazenly came all the way to Nanjing after him."

Peitao would always taunt Ding by playfully mentioning his divorce plans at the most inopportune of times. She pulled away that thin veil, leaving Ding Wenyu, and everyone present at the table, feeling extremely awkward. This was quite a move on her part. Listening to her tone of voice, one would think that she and Ding had gotten past all of their marital hurdles. Everyone had a wonderful impression of Peitao. They all felt she was a most tolerant woman to put up with her husband's escapades without getting jealous. With grace and ease, Peitao managed to continually transform run-of-the-mill dinner parties into impressive social events. She moved through the upper echelons of Nanjing society like a fish through water. Peitao even enthusiastically donated money to help university students driven out of Manchuria by the Japanese and veterans wounded in Suiyuan. Ding Wenyu quickly realized that Peitao's entire public act was just a show—she was a marvelous actress. The way she displayed herself, everyone took her for a one-in-a-million wife. Everywhere she went, she intentionally displayed the inviolable legitimacy of her marriage and her magnanimity and manners. When she was alone with Ding Wenyu, however, she transformed into a completely different person—she became an utterly terrifying woman.

They slept in the same bed at night, and it was at this time that they became true enemies. They slept in the same bed, but each of them had their own thoughts, desires, and dreams. For a time Ding Wenyu had questioned whether he should continue to fulfill his responsibility as the "seed planter." However, each time Ding started to lose control over himself, Peitao would not fail to coldly warn him that if he had even an ounce of self-respect he should conduct himself with dignity and stop climbing onto the body of a woman he despised. She told him it was one thing if he didn't want to respect himself, but he should at least respect other people. Her words made Ding completely lose heart, leaving him too ashamed to face her. In a letter to Yuyuan, Ding Wenyu despairingly admitted that although he felt no love for Peitao, he couldn't bring himself to hate her. Peitao, on the other hand, not only had no love for Ding but had a hatred for him that cut down to the bone.

Ultimately, with her unmatched sensitivity, Peitao sniffed out the source of Ding Wenyu's insanely impassioned love. She read through an unfinished letter to Yuyuan that Ding had hidden—moreover, she came across Yuyuan's address. That day, for the first time, Peitao completely lost her temper with the cleaning woman and threw her out, cursing her with the harshest possible words. Gritting her teeth, she smashed a flower vase onto the floor in the living room and tore up the landscape painting hanging on the wall. After she got this bout of girlish anger out of her system, Peitao immediately went about fixing herself up. She then called a car and headed straight to the army headquarters. On the way there Peitao considered what she should say once she came face to face with Yuyuan, carefully weighing the pros and cons of all the possible scenarios. By the time she arrived at her destination, Peitao had yet to decide on her course of action. She didn't know if it would be better to have a reasonable talk with Yuyuan or simply play her hand and make a fool out of her.

The army headquarters was in the middle of a meeting between high-ranking military cadres. Peitao was stopped outside the entrance gate and, no matter what she said, the gate sentry firmly refused to deliver any messages for her.

He Yingqin chaired the meeting that day. Everyone realized the inevitability of a Sino-Japanese war, and they were deliberating on the impending conflict. During the meeting a dark shadow loomed over many of the participants, all of whom believed that defeat was inevitable. Pessimism was clearly the mood of the day. After an analysis of the two countries' current military strength, the conclusion was that it would be a no-win battle for China. The Nationalist army's revised statistics on infantry firepower revealed that the Japanese army's horizontal and curved firepower was 3.7 times greater than that of the Nationalist infantry. On average, each Japanese infantry battalion was equipped with 89 20-millimeter cannons, 27 37-millimeter quick-firing guns, and 400 grenade launchers—while the Nationalist army had absolutely none of this weaponry. As far as firepower went, mountain artillery was the sole area where the Nationalists could hold a candle to the Japanese—but even then each Chinese division was allotted a mere 12 mountain guns, as opposed to 36 for every Japanese division. Besides this, the Japanese military had twice as many heavy machine guns and light machine guns as the Nationalists.

This comparison, however, dealt solely with the well-equipped Central Nationalist Army and the Japanese Army. If one were to take into consideration China's countless inferior local units, which had been ravaged by the Civil War, China's position as the underdog would have been even more pronounced. There were many local units whose artillery was composed of a collection of old, beat-up guns of various barrel sizes; in combat this could create an extremely grave problem when it came to supplying ammunition. However, regardless of the fact that they were the unquestionable underdogs and pessimistic sentiments had taken over, the majority of the generals present were still in favor of going to war with Japan. An army is nurtured for a thousand days, all for a single moment of battle. To fight takes courage, and the Chinese people were not afraid of war. Since the Japanese already had their guns to China's head, there was nothing wrong with people venting their anger and putting up a fight. Military intelligence had already conducted a most thorough analysis of the Chinese army's morale. He Yingqin pointed out that as high-ranking military generals it was imperative they have a clear sense of their enemy's dominant position—however, for the time being this information was to be regarded as a classified military secret and could not be made public for fear of damaging morale. According to intelligence reports at the time, the Japanese military's primary future target was not China but Russia. Moreover, if the Japanese navy wanted to conquer the Pacific, a direct conflict with America would be inevitable. Japan's plan was nothing more than wishful thinking. With minimum military pressure, they wanted to force China into submission and, bit by bit, nibble away until China broke apart and collapsed. This incessant nibbling was precisely what the Nationalist government feared most. Like the saying goes, "Fear not being swallowed by a whale, fear only being nibbled away by the silkworm." China, a country of vast territory, abundant resources, and an immense population could never be swallowed by Japan, no matter how powerful she might be. Certain death by choking was the inevitable consequence facing whoever dreamed of swallowing China in one gulp.

According to the national policy in 1937, China was already at the point of no return. The Japanese had placed China's head on the chopping block, leaving her no path but fervent resistance. Their sole option to stop Japan from slowly "nibbling away" the whole country from north China was to wait for the right time and open up a secondary front in Shanghai, cutting off the Japanese vanguard from the rear.

It was just as they were in the midst of discussing this issue at the meeting that Peitao started to make a scene outside the army headquarters gate. Peitao's rash behavior eventually got to the point where she tried to barge inside. The sentry telephoned security, and several officers soon arrived. The military police didn't listen to any of Peitao's explanations; instead, they suspected her of attempting to sneak into a military affairs organ to steal state secrets and detained her. Peitao was held until nightfall, when the military police finally escorted her back to the university apartment complex. If Peitao hadn't shouted out the name of a certain government big shot, she probably would have been held for several days. However, after the military police telephoned this bigwig, he ordered her immediate release.

After expressing their apologies to Ding Wenyu, the military police officers swaggered off. Instantly, Ding Wenyu realized how serious things had become—this realization had nothing to do with Peitao being detained for an entire day, nor was it because his secret love for Yuyuan had been exposed. The first thing that crossed Ding's mind was the possibility that Yuyuan was somehow embarrassed or put on the spot by Peitao's actions—this was by far his greatest fear. The moment he heard that Peitao was unable to see Yuyuan he felt as if a weight had been lifted from his chest. In Ding's mind, Yuyuan was sacred and inviolable. It was for this reason that Ding didn't rush to console Peitao when he saw her, nor did he try to explain things to her; instead he harshly admonished her by saying that she had absolutely no right to do what she did. A detestable woman like her didn't even deserve to speak with Yuyuan, let alone defile her ears with foul words and empty accusations. Ding Wenyu had never hit his wife, but suddenly he felt the urge. He couldn't care less about Peitao being detained; stamping with fury, he told her to take herself back to Shanghai.

Never one to be outdone, Peitao responded with a most simple and powerful defense—before Ding had a chance to make a move, she gave him a mean slap across the face. Ding Wenyu was struck silly; standing there rubbing his sore cheek, he completely forgot to hit her back—actually, he didn't even have the slightest inclination to hit her back. Instead he ruthlessly cursed her in foreign languages she didn't understand, berating her with a barrage of dirty slang only popular among the dregs of European society.

"I already know that you lived abroad," Peitao responded, "so stop showing off with your annoying chirping!"

It suddenly dawned on Ding Wenyu that all his tricks were exhausted. He realized that he was no match for Peitao. He couldn't imagine what he could possibly do to get her to give up her plan to meet with Yuyuan. This wife of his was indeed a woman who stopped at nothing to get what she wanted. Just thinking of the kind of insult Yuyuan might be subjected to, Ding Wenyu felt a sharp pain deep in his heart. Naturally a woman like Peitao would never believe that what he felt for Yuyuan was purely spiritual love; nor would she believe that Yuyuan had absolutely no hand in any of this. Without a better plan, Ding Wenyu took out the pile of his draft letters. Randomly pulling out a few, Ding read a few sentences aloud that could prove that Yuyuan never responded to a single one of his letters. He gave his word to Peitao that Yuyuan was a pure and absolutely trustworthy woman; she not only was innocent but was of impeccable character. With language bordering on melodramatic, Ding began to sing Yuyuan's praises. The more he spoke, the more emotional and unrestrained he became. Peitao listened with complete composure; for a while it even seemed as if she was moved by Ding Wenyu's sweet ramblings. Ding Wenyu got completely carried away. Pretending she wanted to read it for herself, Peitao took the letter draft from Ding's hand and suddenly ripped it to shreds. A stunned Ding Wenyu immediately tried to pull it away from her, but Peitao went for the pile of love letters on the nightstand and tore them with all her might. The letters she couldn't rip she threw into the air, leaving Ding's bedroom covered with a layer of scattered pages.

VI

When Yuyuan learned that Ding Wenyu's wife had come to see her on a "punitive expedition," her first impression was relief. She figured that this would be her chance to finally set the record straight. Yuyuan firmly believed in those sayings, "Stand upright and fear not a crooked shadow," and "If you haven't done anything wrong in the daylight, there will be no reason to fear ghosts coming for you in the night." With full assurance that she was doing the right thing, Yuyuan would be able to tell Ding's wife that it was that thick-skinned husband of hers who wouldn't leave her alone. She would explain that Ding Wenyu had sent these disgustingly nauseating letters to her—if Peitao wanted to square up with somebody, it should be with her own husband. Yuyuan could confidently tell Peitao to keep a leash on her man and recommend that she think twice about why not even her own husband could find her attractive. Yuyuan had already made full preparations for Peitao's assault. Although the whole situation would be quite embarrassing and there was a very good possibility that Yuyuan might be made a fool of in public, she had a clear conscience and wasn't in the least bit afraid.

In his letters to Yuyuan, a terrified Ding Wenyu repeatedly expressed his apologies. He felt terribly guilty for the problems he had caused her. In these letters Ding never once placed even an ounce of blame on his wife Peitao; instead, he continually reproached himself. His fear that Yuyuan might suffer because of his actions appeared vividly. It was clear that Peitao was unwilling to give up on her planned meeting with Yuyuan. Since there was no way out, Ding Wenyu wrote to Yuyuan recommending they meet at Xuanwu Park like last time. He said that Yuyuan could bring along a few of her girlfriends just like before and they could all grab a bite to eat—just one hasty meeting should take care of everything. Not even for a second did Yuyuan entertain the thought of taking Ding up on his preposterous proposition. It seemed as though he was contradicting himself: he was afraid that his ruthless wife would hurt Yuyuan, but at the same time he cooked up this silly idea to openly introduce them. In his next letter, Ding Wenyu presumptuously stated that he had already decided on a place. They were to meet at the Six Splendid Springs near the Temple of Confucius. He chose this place because it was where, during Old Ren's birthday celebration, Ding Wenyu had gotten drunk over Yuyuan. Although Yuyuan never once wrote back to him, Ding Wenyu was convinced that she read every letter he wrote her. He wasn't sure if she would attend, so he said that for the next three days he and his wife would be there waiting for her.

There was no way to describe Yuyuan's anger. Ding Wenyu's behavior was truly outrageous. Her first impulse was to give Ding a good lesson to his face. He had absolutely no right to invite her anywhere in such a discourteous fashion. First off, she wanted to ask what made him think that she even received his letters—let alone read them? And second, she wanted to tell him that she wasn't afraid of attending this stupid meeting, the only reason she wasn't going was simply that she didn't want to go. If however, she were to rashly attend and lash out at Ding, the first question would be rendered superfluous. If, on the other hand, she did not attend, it would show she had a guilty conscience and was afraid to face Mrs. Ding. Without even realizing it, Ding Wenyu had stuck innocent Yuyuan between a rock and a hard place.

Yuyuan decided to play with fire. She didn't look up her "protectors"—bringing them along sometimes had the tendency to mess things up. The loneliness of dormitory life made Yuyuan thirst for some excitement to relieve her boredom. Yuyuan was the kind of girl who was always ready to take on a challenge; she didn't feel that anything could happen to her if she attended a simple meeting. Perhaps her most appropriate escort would be her husband Yu Kerun. Yuyuan imagined all kinds of different scenarios for their meeting; she wondered how Ding Wenyu's wife would react should she lay eyes on her own handsome husband. There was no question that Peitao would be struck with a sense of inferiority and realize that she was getting jealous over the wrong person. Mrs. Ding's husband was by no means any great catch—there were plenty of men in the world who outshone him. At the most, Ding Wenyu was just a lunatic who would do anything for love. Yuyuan compared Yu Kerun with Ding Wenyu and discovered that in most areas Yu had the upper hand. Even if she were given the chance to choose all over again, without hesitation Yuyuan would pick Yu Kerun. In 1937 Nanjing, an outstanding pilot like Yu Kerun was like a knight in shining armor in the minds of countless young girls. How could Ding Wenyu be placed on a par with him?

However, there was one important detail that Yuyuan overlooked—just as Mrs. Ding wanted to meet her, she too was dying to see just exactly who it was she was dealing with. This was due to a kind of odd yet uncontrollable curiosity. From Ding Wenyu's letters, Yuyuan already had a rough idea about the kind of person that Peitao was. Yuyuan knew that this overbearing and arrogant daughter of the so-called Steel King was no knock-'em-dead beauty; nor was she a very virtuous wife. The reason Ding Wenyu wanted to divorce Peitao wasn't that she was bad looking; nor was it a typical case of a rich man abandoning his wife once they had gotten through hard times. The sole reason Ding wanted a divorce was that he did not love his wife. Theoretically, bringing a loveless marriage to a close should be a good thing. Just as Ding Wenyu had repeatedly stressed in his letters, Yuyuan was not some kind of ringleader who masterminded Ding's divorce, she was merely the catalyst for an inevitable chemical reaction. Yuyuan never once uttered a single comment about their divorce—even on those few occasions when she and Ding Wenyu had talked, she'd never had the opportunity to say more than a few words. Yuyuan thought of herself as nothing more than a mailbox that indifferently received letters from Ding Wenyu. She felt that Peitao had absolutely no right to criticize her. Yuyuan was completely innocent; she was free of any wrongdoing and fully able to stand up to any of Peitao's attacks.

Then there was another important detail that Yuyuan overlooked—besides wanting to risk a meeting with Peitao, she wanted to see Ding Wenyu again. Although she believed that ultimately she would still be unmoved by him, after receiving Ding Wenyu's countless sincere love letters, without even realizing it, Yuyuan was undergoing a subtle, almost imperceptible change. In fact, Ding Wenyu's letters and the nauseating words that they were imbued with had already become a part of Yuyuan's everyday life—far from an indispensable part, but they were at the very least a terribly entertaining part. Yuyuan couldn't really say that she was moved by Ding Wenyu's honeyed words, but she had to admit that sitting under her covers and reading his letters before she went to bed at night was indeed a great pleasure. Ding Wenyu's letters were like a series of mirrors through which Yuyuan could admire how charming she herself really was. There isn't a woman in the world who doesn't like hearing compliments from men—from day one women have always been the object of men's affection.

Only on the third day did Yuyuan finally show up by herself for the game of mousetrap that Ding Wenyu had set up for her. It wasn't that she was irresolute about attending, she just wanted to see if Ding Wenyu and his wife were really willing to go so far as to wait three days for her at Six Splendid Springs. The whole idea was preposterous from the start; naturally, the outcome couldn't be much better. Because he was still the target of investigations related to the Monk case, Ding Wenyu was in a terrible mood those three days. The papers kept rehashing those old stories about him, even reprinting an article about how Monk used to take Ding all over the city in search of carnal excitement. This led to a huge argument with Peitao. By the third and final day Ding Wenyu had already given up on Yuyuan coming, and Peitao seemed finally to begin to understand that Ding's so-called affair was actually nothing but a case of unrequited love. Saying that Peitao was waiting at Six Splendid Springs for Yuyuan to show up would not be as accurate as saying that she was waiting to see just how far Ding Wenyu would go in making a fool of himself. Ding Wenyu stood anxiously at the main entrance, distracted by each and every pretty girl who walked past him.

Yuyuan's sudden appearance shocked both Ding Wenyu and Peitao. It was a highly dramatic scene as Ding stared dumbfounded at Yuyuan. His eyes filled with a look of appreciation. Lost for the moment, he not only forgot to introduce Peitao but didn't even think to greet Yuyuan. Waiting for Ding to say something, both Peitao and Yuyuan were left in an extremely awkward situation. For a moment, neither woman knew how to react. In the end it was Peitao who came around and said in a most haughty tone, "What are you standing there for? Have a seat and let's eat!"

Ding Wenyu snapped out of his dreamlike trance and eagerly motioned for Yuyuan to sit. His overattentiveness and obvious anxiety that Yuyuan would be put in a bad situation made Peitao extremely jealous—and Yuyuan terribly uncomfortable. Since Ding Wenyu was in such an anxious flurry, he never should have arranged such a meeting in the first place. Perhaps when he had written Yuyuan to invite her, Ding had completely overlooked the potential consequences. His sole thought was to see Yuyuan again, and nothing else seemed to matter. Ding must have subconsciously thought that Yuyuan would never come because when she did finally arrive, he was completely unprepared. He was rendered speechless and appeared quite ridiculous as he peered around like a complete outsider—it seemed as if he had come solely to hear just what these two women had to say to each other. Yuyuan suddenly became conscious of how absurd the risk she had taken in coming was; however, it was already too late for regret.

The only one of them who was able to maintain her composure was Peitao. Deep down she had to admit that Yuyuan was indeed a beautiful girl; however, other than her beauty, Peitao didn't feel there was anything else very special about her. What Peitao found even more laughable was the fact that Yuyuan was wearing a military uniform. Heaven only knew what kind of crazy medicine Ding had taken to make this famous professor fall for a female soldier—a confidential secretary still wet behind the ears at that! Even though the Nationalist government had already banned polygamy, if Ding Wenyu had wanted to take a girl like Yuyuan as a concubine Peitao wouldn't necessarily have even been against it. However, the second that Ding Wenyu's intention to *divorce* her over this girl came to Peitao's mind, she couldn't help feeling that Ding must have been out of his mind.

"Miss Ren"—after toasting Yuyuan, Peitao smiled at her and got right to the point—"is there some advice you would like to offer concerning Wenyu and my divorce?"

Before the initial red wave of embarrassment had a chance to retreat from Yuyuan's face, she again turned a bright crimson. When she arrived, Yuyuan was brimming with curiosity, but now she was at a complete loss. She wasn't in the least prepared to express her opinion on their divorce. Suddenly Peitao seemed to brighten, and she said coldly, "I'm going to go to the hospital for an examination. If it turns out I'm pregnant then Wenyu and I will go ahead with the divorce. To tell you frankly, I'm more than happy to let the two of you have your happiness." Immediately both Ding Wenyu's and Yuyuan's faces expressed varying degrees of shock as Ding gave Peitao a confused glare. Peitao glanced at him for a moment before turning her gaze toward Yuyuan. "Miss Ren, if Wenyu and I divorce, do you really intend to marry him?"

Stammering, Ding Wenyu interrupted. "We never discussed any intention of getting married."

Peitao waved her hand signaling for Ding not to interrupt. Like a haughty princess with a disdainful attitude, Peitao awaited Yuyuan's answer. Yuyuan implored Peitao not to get the wrong idea. She solemnly declared that there was absolutely nothing going on between her and Ding Wenyu. She told Peitao that the only reason she had come was to declare her innocence.

Peitao wasn't in the least bit interested in Yuyuan's declaration. Instead she pushed Yuyuan to respond to her question of whether or not she intended to marry Ding Wenyu. Yuyuan offered a cool smile as she said that this question wasn't even worth answering. Peitao asked why and Yuyuan responded, "That's simple. I've already got a husband with whom I'm very much in love."

This time it was Peitao's turn to be surprised. Never had she heard any mention of Yuyuan being married. Ding Wenyu never mentioned this tidbit to his estranged wife. Never in her wildest dreams could Peitao have imagined that her own husband could fall in love with a married woman.

Chapter Six

I

The doctor at the Nanjing University Hospital who administered Peitao's pregnancy test was an American named Robert Wilson. This blue-eyed, big-nosed foreigner not only was an acquaintance of Ding Wenyu's father but also knew Peitao's father, the Steel King. A surgeon by training, Dr. Wilson agreed to see her only because of his relationship with Peitao's father. Ding Wenyu couldn't understand why Peitao had to choose a male foreign doctor to examine her; nor could he figure out why *he* had to go with her. Although they had made an appointment the day before, Dr. Wilson was up to his eyes in work when they arrived. The maternity ward was so huge it looked like an auditorium; almost forty beds were set up in two rows against the walls. Just as the Dings entered, the nurses had pulled back the sheets to expose all of the lying-in women naked from the waist down. Dr. Wilson handed Ding Wenyu a long white gown so that he would look like a doctor. To get to Dr. Wilson's office, one had to walk through that auditorium-size maternity ward. As he walked, Ding Wenyu couldn't help but curiously look around the ward. On his way to his office, Dr. Wilson occasionally stopped to examine his patients. He appeared quite stern as he repeatedly questioned pregnant women with his pidgin Chinese.

One young mother who had been forced to undergo a Caesarean section because her ilium was too narrow called out to Dr. Wilson. Dr. Wilson examined the incision on her abdomen and seemed quite satisfied with her progress. He told her what things she should watch out for and recommended that she consider getting up and attempting to walk around a bit. Ding Wenyu noticed how pretty this new mother was and how unabashed she was about exposing herself. It seemed as if she wasn't in the least bit conscious that Ding Wenyu was actually a wolf in doctor's clothes. Ding Wenyu muttered something to Dr. Wilson in English, but the doctor was concentrating on his examination and didn't pay attention to what Ding said. Standing beside them, Peitao kept a stern expression without uttering a single word. She looked away, but when she noticed that dirty look in Ding Wenyu's eye she couldn't help but firmly tug on Ding's gown. Ding Wenyu thought that she wanted to tell him something, but when he turned around she wasn't even willing to look at him.

Finally it was Peitao's turn to undress and lie down for Dr. Wilson to examine her. The entire scene was quite ridiculous. Lying there with her pale, white skin, Peitao resembled a fish on a chopping block waiting to be scaled. Wearing a pair of surgical gloves, Dr. Wilson, without the slightest show of emotion, began to feel around Peitao's vagina and inserted a small instrument into her body. As Ding Wenyu stood beside the white partition, a sudden thought flashed through his brain and he wondered if what Dr. Wilson was doing was ethically correct. Only at that moment did Ding seem to finally realize that the woman lying before him was his wife—the same wife he had no love for and was planning to divorce. Ding suddenly felt a kind of unspeakable uneasiness. Every so often Peitao let out a faint grunt; obviously Dr. Wilson had done something that hurt her. Ding Wenyu couldn't bear any more; he left the examination area and walked toward the other end of the office. On Dr. Wilson's desk was a glass vase containing a pair of freshly cut Chinese roses. A nurse rushed into the office to grab a patient's chart from the desk and quickly made her way out. Just as she was going out the door, the nurse looked somewhat curiously at Ding Wenyu. He gave her a faint smile.

As Dr. Wilson offered Peitao his congratulations, her only response was a bitter smile. Peitao was on the verge of tears. As she sat up and got dressed, she quietly expressed her thanks to Dr. Wilson. Finally, under the confused watch of the doctor, Peitao walked over to Ding Wenyu and told him they should go. Dr. Wilson had removed his surgical gloves and was washing his hands in the sink when Ding Wenyu went over to ask about the results. Peitao, however, rudely interrupted him, pulling Ding away. Ding Wenyu had no choice but to hurriedly offer his thanks to the doctor and follow Peitao out through the maternity ward into the street. Outside on the deserted street he urgently asked whether or not the doctor said she was pregnant. Peitao gave Ding a cold stare but wouldn't answer; instead she rhetorically asked, "Did *you* hear the doctor say I was pregnant?" From the time they left the hospital until that night when they went to bed, Peitao wouldn't say a word about the doctor's diagnosis. Each of the several times Ding asked her about it, she simply pretended she didn't hear him. Then in the middle of the night, Peitao suddenly woke a groggy, half-asleep Ding Wenyu and, pinching his ear, asked him if he was really set on getting a divorce.

"So, that mean's you're already pregnant?" A look of delight appeared on Ding Wenyu's sleepy face.

Peitao forced Ding to answer her question first. She wanted to know if he was really prepared to part company the day she produced a heir for the Ding family—she wanted to know for sure whether her pregnancy marked the end of their destined time together. Ding Wenyu felt there was no need to answer Peitao's question. Of course this was the end. Moreover, this was precisely the day he had been waiting for. Although this was not the kind of topic one takes pleasure in discussing, the worst was seemingly over—Peitao and Yuyuan had come face to face without making a big scene or making anyone lose face. The serenity of the meeting even struck Ding Wenyu as a bit out of the ordinary. He couldn't help but be surprised by how reserved Peitao was; she didn't even reveal any major hostility toward Yuyuan.

"That's right, I'm pregnant, all right." Peitao noticed the happiness written all over Ding's face—not because he was about to become a father, but because he could finally shed the shackles of his unhappy marriage and had an excuse to abandon Peitao. As she realized the reason for Ding's ecstatic smile, anger instantly flared up inside Peitao. The fact that getting a divorce could bring Ding Wenyu so much happiness made her grit her teeth in rage. Her hatred brought her to the point of utter disheartenment. She stared unflinchingly at Ding and said coldly, "But, I've changed my mind. Let me tell you, Ding Wenyu, you're not home free yet. There's no way I'm letting you get away with this." A perplexed look appeared on Ding Wenyu's face. Peitao turned away from him as she announced her newest decision: "There's no way I'm letting some girl off the street take my place that easily."

Pregnancy didn't make Peitao more soft and loving; just the opposite, it made her even more unbridled and unbearable. In the face of Ding's stupefied silence, she began to use the vilest of language in her nightlong string of indiscriminate bombing. By equal turns, Peitao mocked, ridiculed, and damned Ding Wenyu and Yuyuan. On this night, she transformed into a devilish fiend—and also on this night, every last bit of tenderness and guilt that Ding had left disappeared into thin air. Peitao completely lost all sense of reason. She was in an overly agitated state of mind. She angrily denounced Ding Wenyu's maniacal love for Yuyuan as nothing more than shameless carousing and whoring. Peitao barraged Ding with virtually every curse word in the book—not even in the brothels had Ding Wenyu heard such filthy language. Peitao didn't have any scruples about her attack, nor did she know exhaustion as, time and time again, she awakened Ding Wenyu just as he was attempting to get some shut-eye. Pinching his ear, pulling his hair, she did everything she could to keep him from sleeping. As dawn approached, Ding Wenyu could no longer understand just what Peitao was muttering about. He was thoroughly exhausted; squinting at her through half-shut eyes, Ding could have fallen asleep at the drop of a hat.

The next day, Ding Wenyu still had class to teach. He arrived at the classroom yawning, and the first thing he told his class was that he hardly gotten any sleep because his wife, whom he was unfortunately still married to, barraged him with vicious insults the whole night through. The students burst out in laughter; some of the female students laughed so hard that they were in tears. Ding Wenyu realized that if it hadn't been for his need to get away from Peitao, he never would have even shown up. During class Ding Wenyu couldn't control his incessant yawning. He was a man with an unconventional air, and if he was going to yawn, there was no way he was going to go about it half-assed, he was going to do it right and *really* yawn. Every so often his mouth would extend open as far as it could go and his exaggerated yawns would follow one after another. He thought of Peitao, who also hadn't had a wink of sleep the night before—he was sure she must be in bed fast asleep, saving up her strength in preparation for a second bout of protracted battle. The instant this came to his mind, Ding couldn't help but shudder with hatred and fear. He knew that Peitao wasn't going to let him off easy.

After class, Ding Wenyu went directly to the editorial office of the nearest newspaper. Rushing into the advertisement division, he asked them to immediately run a divorce announcement. He had already gone over this move several times in his head and had long ago settled on the wording and diction. Now it was time to take action. He asked someone in the office for paper and pen and, leaning on the advertising division manager's desk, he wrote out what he wanted to print. Moreover, he stressed that they had to run it in the largest boldface print available.

DING WENYU HEREBY URGENTLY POSTS: IN ORDER TO PRE-VENT FUTURE MUTUAL SUFFERING, WENYU IS ANNOUNCING HIS DIVORCE FROM MS. HAO PEITAO DUE TO IRRECONCILABLE DIFFERENCES. FROM THIS POINT ON, WENYU AND MS. HAO WILL NO LONGER TAKE PART IN EACH OTHER'S AFFAIRS.

After placing his advertisement, Ding Wenyu felt a wave of relief. Suddenly he had a burst of energy and didn't feel a bit drowsy. He want-ed to go straight to Yuyuan and tell her everything. Then, on second thought, he thought it best if Yuyuan saw the ad for herself after it ran. He imagined the different kind of reactions Yuyuan might have. Lost in thought, he smiled to himself, and deep down he felt a wave of satisfac-tion. Ding also wondered whether or not her should tell Peitao. It seemed only reasonable that he give her a warning—if only to prevent the shock when she saw the ad. Peitao would undoubtedly explode like a volcano. Ding Wenyu could almost hear her roaring voice ringing in his ears. Without question she was bound to go into a terrible fit; however, no matter what Peitao might think, or even whether or not his divorce announcement carried any legal weight, Ding Wenyu had made up his mind that he was through with Peitao. Their life together had begun as a confused, muddled mess, and thus should it end.

Ding Wenyu never imagined that Peitao would have already returned to Shanghai. As he arrived back at his apartment, all he was thinking about was how to deal with Peitao's temper. As he was prepared for another dose of insults, Peitao's sudden departure left Ding Wenyu with an almost indescribable melancholy. Having been spared additional wrath, Ding was left with the uneasy feeling of having an unpaid debt. Naturally, Peitao's departure was a good thing. Although he was starving, Ding Wenyu decided he should first go to bed and catch up on his lost sleep. He took off his shoes and started snoring the second he hit the mattress. Ding slept until the sun was about to set behind the mountain. After he woke up, he had a glass of milk and a few slices of bread and went to the telephone office to place a long-distance phone call to Shanghai through the operator there. He wasn't telephoning his family in Shanghai, but directly phoning the advertising division of the largest Shanghai newspaper, *Shenbao*. He dictated the full text of his ad and asked them to print it as soon as possible. Three days later, the most important newspapers in Nanjing and Shanghai had all run Ding Wenyu's divorce announcement. One paper even misprinted Peitao's name so instead of "Jade Peach," she became Pei*dao* or "Jade Patty." Ding Wenyu instantly thought about how angry Peitao would probably be after she saw it.

There was no major uproar or fallout as Ding Wenyu had anticipated. Everything takes time. Usually no one gives these kinds of announcements a second glance. Moreover, Ding Wenyu's divorce wasn't something that happened overnight. The first person to feel the heat over it was not Ding Wenyu but his father in Shanghai. Peitao forced her father-in-law to explain the meaning of this announcement. Secure in the knowledge that she had strong backing, she waved the newspaper around, screaming at her elderly father-in-law, hysterically using suicide to threaten the old man. Still not recovered from the ecstatic news of his daughter-in-law's pregnancy, Ding's father suddenly found himself on the verge of collapse. The Steel King's spoiled daughter could care less about preserving face; repeatedly broadcasting threats to take her own life, she proclaimed that she would jump off the Bank of China's high-rise office building.

"If you Dings don't deserve to have your family line cut off, then I don't know who does!" This was the last word she spoke to Ding's father just before, in a flush of anger, violent-tempered Peitao moved back to her parents' home.

Ding Wenyu's father was struck with another attack of high blood pressure—however, this time it wasn't on account of his own precious son; he was choking with anger over Peitao. No one had ever dared speak to him in such a vile tone. The old man was so angry that he was shaking all over. After Peitao strutted off, he clattered around the house, smashing things to relieve his anger. His three concubines were all pale with fear but didn't know what they should say to calm him down. The three of them knew that whenever the old man was angry at his son, he was actually also angry at them. He despised the way they all flowered without ever truly blooming. He hated them for being nothing but a barren wasteland. No matter how diligently he worked "planting his seeds," none of them could produce a heir to replace Ding Wenyu.

"Just what sins have I committed in my past life to deserve this?" Ding Wenyu's father began to wail like a small child. He ripped the newspaper that ran Ding Wenyu's divorce announcement into tiny shreds; he then had one of his concubines throw the scraps into the fireplace and burn them. It seemed to suddenly dawn on him that he was already one foot in the grave. He realized that the next time he closed his eyes could very well be his last. If his son was set on making a mess of his marriage, let him, but the old man was not going to waste any more time worrying about who would inherit his great family wealth. He took solace in the old saying: "If good fortune awaits there is no reason to hide—if disaster awaits there will be no place to hide." If Peitao was indeed pregnant as she said, then his son's announcement of their divorce wasn't really going against their agreement. It would be best to simply let things take their course. If the two of them were set on making a big ruckus, they could do whatever their hearts desired, but Ding Wenyu's father washed his hands of his son's affairs.

II

During the days immediately following the publication of his divorce announcement, Ding Wenyu was struck with a kind of helpless panic. He felt that something was wrong; everything was just too quiet.

During class his students constantly exchanged whispered comments. Ding Wenyu thought they were talking about his divorce announcement, but in the end, he discovered they were only discussing the Japanese war games being played out on the Qingdao peninsula. Anti-Japanese sentiment continued to intensify and Wang Jingwei, who had continually been suspected of sympathizing with the Japanese, articulated the Chinese government's stiff policy toward Japan in a recent meeting. Wang stressed that although China was resisting Japan, they were not anti-Japanese. There was only a one-word difference between *resisting* Japan and being *anti*-Japan, but this one word made all the difference in the world. The Chinese government had already made massive concessions; however, in the face of ever-increasing Japanese pressure and deliberate, repeated provocations on the part of the Japanese military, the Chinese government had no choice but to declare a position of resistance. The essence of resistance was standing up in opposition—there was no way that the Chinese people would sit back and become a piece of meat on Japan's chopping block.

What left Ding Wenyu most anxious and fidgety, however, was having no way of knowing Yuyuan's reaction after she had read his divorce announcement. The weather was gradually heating up, and anti-Japanese sentiment in the capital Nanjing was rising with the temperature. The Municipal Air Defense Association held screenings of educational films about gas defense and organized all kinds of lectures on air defense. Mayor Ma delivered a radio address on the citizens' role in air defense, employees of the Air Defense Association hit the streets to spread propaganda to the people, and even schools made knowledge of air defense a mandatory part of the curriculum for the boy and girl scouts. Before showing feature films, movie theaters throughout the city all ran a series of air defense slide shows. Gas masks, offered for around 10 *yuan*, were sold directly by the Municipal Air Defense Association. It was reported that there was a rapid increase in businessmen cashing in on this wave of resistance against Japan. Ding Wenyu was unsure whether to go and look for Yuyuan; he continued to write her letters but felt increasingly anxious about never having received any kind of feedback. When he first began to write to Yuyuan, Ding Wenyu felt a deep satisfaction just in writing the letters; later he began to hope that Yuyuan would receive and read them. People are never satisfied. Ding Wenyu was now struck with a pressing desire to know Yuyuan's attitude.

One after another, Ding Wenyu shot off letters to Yuyuan. He requested to meet her face to face in order to explain why he printed that divorce announcement. He repeatedly provided her with a clear time and place to meet, but Yuyuan never showed up. All of his letters seemed to be nothing more than stones thrown into the sea. Finally one day Ding Wenyu received a short letter from Ren Bojin, wherein the old man set up a time to meet Ding. The letter was extremely succinct, and Ding Wenyu couldn't tell if it was a blessing or a curse. He nevertheless went without hesitation. At the least, he would be able to get a bit of information about Yuyuan. Although he was dying to see her, an ominous feeling weighed down his heart. He realized that there was no way he would see Yuyuan during his visit. Waiting for him instead was an unbearable lecture from Old Ren.

As luck would have it, it was pouring outside the day Ding went to the Ren house—this was a omen of sorts. It was obvious that Ding Wenyu was not terribly welcome at the Rens'. He smiled as he walked in, but instantly his smile froze on his face. No one in the house returned his courteous smile; even the always-affable Lady Miyako greeted him with a stiff, straight face. Because Ding Wenyu's maniacal pursuit of Yuyuan had long been an open secret in the Ren household, everyone from the servants on up intentionally gave him the cold shoulder and gazed at him with knowing eyes. Ding Wenyu was shown to Old Ren Bojin's study. The old man put down the ancient classic that he had been reading and looked at Ding. After a long period of silence, Old Ren pointed to an empty chair and motioned for Ding to sit down.

Ding Wenyu suddenly realized that he had yet to pay his respects to the old man. He most awkwardly expressed his best wishes to Old Ren, but the old man responded with a sigh and solemnly got right to the point. "Wenyu, you've spent many years abroad and are an educated man who knows the rules of propriety. I asked you here today to have a good talk with you."

Ding Wenyu made as if he was ready to respectfully listen to whatever instructions Old Ren had to offer.

"My youngest daughter is already a married woman; you are also a man with a family," Old Ren began. "The Dings and the Rens have a family friendship spanning several generations. I see no reason for you to continue carrying on as you have. Even your own dear father has been brought to the end of his rope with your actions. The country is in the midst of national calamity. As an educated man, how can you waste your precious energy on a childish love affair? What's this, running a divorce ad in the newspapers? What are you trying to do? How can you take the solemn institution of marriage as a game? I don't care how modern that brain of yours is, you still can't carry on like this!"

Throughout his stay in Ren Bojin's study, Ding Wenyu didn't make the slightest effort to defend himself—opening his mouth only would have made things worse. Declining a challenge is always the most effective form of defense. Everyone at the Ren house felt that there was something not right about Ding Wenyu. He didn't say a word, and no one knew what to do with him. Yuyuan's oldest sister Yuchan had already gone back to the States with her husband, so Yuyuan's third sister, Yujiao, was elected the family representative to give Ding a second lecture. She looked at this crestfallen Ding Wenyu and thought him both infuriating and ridiculous. Twenty years ago he had madly pursued her older sister Yuchan; now he was at it again, only this time, her little sister was his target. She wondered who would be next.

With the utmost sincerity, Ding Wenyu explained that his pursuit of Yuyuan and her older sister were two completely different affairs. "From the outside they might appear the same, but actually the difference is as clear as black and white." Ding Wenyu spoke to Yujiao with the utmost sincerity, as if he were discussing some serious academic issue or instructing his students during class. "Back when I fell in love with your eldest sister, I still didn't even know what love was. In regard to my feelings for Yuyuan, however, I couldn't be more clear about the meaning of love!"

Yujiao shook her head. "Hey, there's a word I don't think you ever heard before. . . ."

Ding Wenyu stared at Yujiao, waiting for her to finish.

"The word is 'shameless'!" Yujiao continued. "What is it, don't you have this word in your vocabulary?"

In her frank and outspoken way, Yujiao gave Ding Wenyu quite a lecture. The scene unfolded as if the whole thing had been prepared in advance. Yujiao spoke plausibly and volubly, harshly criticizing Ding Wenyu's behavior. Although she was in a rather strange position, she still got right into her role as Ding's admonisher. The first thing that she so irrationally pointed out was that, had he really fallen so pathetically in love with Yuyuan as he had said, he never should have gotten married in the first place. Moreover, he shouldn't have waited until after Yuyuan wed before brazenly accosting her. Yujiao's blame was indiscriminate. Although she was quite stirred up, she was still far from feeling any kind of genuine indignation. In the end, however, no matter what she said to Ding Wenyu, she was wasting her breath—he was simply too thick-skinned to actually take to heart anything she said. When it came to relations with women, Ding was inevitably somewhat of a jerk. All he seemed to know how to do was shamelessly chase after other men's wives, never for a moment stopping to consider how impractical his actions might be. Ding Wenyu was simply a lovesick lunatic with a couple of screws loose—emotionally, he had long been destroyed, but now he wanted to bring someone else down with him.

Ding Wenyu withstood Yujiao's attacks, all the while stubbornly believing that he hadn't been destroyed. Love has the power to save, to deliver—never could love destroy a person, Ding protested. "But don't you understand?" Yujiao argued. "Love is precisely what is being destroyed here!" As Yujiao added fuel to her assault, Ding Wenyu stared at her unfalteringly. He hoped to make out some trace of Yuyuan's features in her sister's face. All of the Ren daughters were stunning beauties. Ding couldn't help but think how wonderful it would be if standing before him was not Yujiao but his beloved Yuyuan. How truly magnificent it would be if Yuyuan were standing so close to him! The second Yuyuan crossed Ding's mind, his heart filled with tender, warm feelings. If only he could be with her, Ding would be more than willing to face these endless reprimands. If only he were able to be with Yuyuan, Ding Wenyu would have absolutely no problem climbing a mountain of knives or descending into a sea of fire. For a moment Yuyuan's brilliant image took up every space in Ding Wenyu's heart and soul. And for that moment, Yuyuan seemed to be everywhere.

Amid Yujiao's endless string of reprimands, Ding Wenyu finally realized that he had done something wrong. It finally dawned on him that he had indeed brought Yuyuan a fair share of trouble. Besides the two of them, there was probably not another living soul willing to believe that they were both innocent of any wrongdoing. Even the Ren family couldn't figure out just how far they had taken their so-called affair. Ding Wenyu's brazen pursuit of Yuyuan had already become a true scandal.

The possibility of his actions bringing Yuyuan some problems had indeed crossed Ding Wenyu's mind; however, he never imagined things would become so serious—and when they finally did, he was reluctant to spend too much time really thinking about it.

"You said before that love could never destroy a person or hurt a person. But in actuality, Yuyuan has already been hurt." Yujiao cautioned Ding Wenyu to start paying attention to his actions. Because of his interference, Yuyuan and her husband had separated. "Shouldn't you think twice about the damage you have done?"

"So tell me, just what harm *have* I done?" Ding Wenyu mumbled, still unconvinced. Although his lips uttered protests, deep down Ding realized that Yujiao was right. His heart was suddenly struck with a heavy burden. Just thinking that Yuyuan was suffering because of him caused a deep feeling of regret to well up inside him. Although Ding Wenyu was madly in love with Yuyuan and was almost constantly thinking of her, he still truly hoped that Yuyuan and her husband could love each other and have a happy marriage. As far as Ding was concerned, Yuyuan only had to acknowledge his love and that would be more than enough to satisfy him. What Ding Wenyu was after was a form of spiritual love—one's spirit never dies, and so, Ding hoped, his love would never die. There are many forms of love besides physical possession. True love is based on giving and not taking. Only a love based on giving is true love.

Ding Wenyu was asked to stay at the Ren's home for dinner that night. They didn't intend to invite him, but because Ding hung around without showing any intention of leaving, Lady Miyako merely extended an invitation out of politeness. One could always count on the ever-shameless Ding Wenyu to grab such an opportunity. Although it was clear that no one in the family welcomed him, just thinking that Yuyuan had grown up in that very house and that everything there was in some way connected to her—even the vegetation around the house seemed to carry her breath—Ding Wenyu felt wave after wave of unspeakable warmth. The Ren family didn't go out of their way to make Ding feel welcome, but that isn't to say that they had even the slightest hint of hostility toward him. In their eyes, Ding Wenyu was always a bit abnormal; they could never truly hate him, they just felt he was utterly ridiculous.

As the elder of the house, Ren Bojin drank and spoke at length with Ding about the seriousness of the current political situation over dinner.

The old man had paid constant and close attention to whether or not war would break out between China and Japan. In his estimation, the Sino-Japanese conflict had already reached a state of virtually unprecedented tension. Japan's drive to conquer China had not died, and all-out war was but a stone's throw away. The old man could already smell the musty scent of gunpowder and hear the metallic clanking and rumbling of the machinery of this impending war. What he thought was a true shame, however, was the fact that although Ding Wenyu was almost forty years old, he still acted like a child. "Every man carries some responsibility for the fate of his country," yet all that went through Ding Wenyu's mind were naïve thoughts of love and romance—it was an outrage. Even children were shouting slogans to resist Japan and save the dying nation. Everyone's hearts were united; high officials, notable figures, and people of the lower classes all rallied together against Japan. Only Ding Wenyu was still lost in his impractical daydream. The country was on the verge of being lost—how could one even think about one's private desires? How could Ding Wenyu not feel ashamed?

Not caring whether it was the right thing to do, Ding Wenyu took the opportunity of dinner with the Ren family to make a very awkward attempt to exculpate Yuyuan from any wrongdoing. He gave everyone the impression that he was trying to shoulder all the responsibility for everything that had happened. He had hoped that his words would move the Rens, but all his ambiguous speech actually did was make them even more confused. He had wanted to proclaim that nothing had ever happened between Yuyuan and himself; however, his clumsy attempt made it seem as if he was intentionally trying to cover something up. Ding left the Rens' feeling that he was a burglar calling "Stop thief!" Lady Miyako's eyes widened as she stared at Ding Wenyu with surprise. She was Yuyuan's mother, and no one knows a daughter like her mother. Lady Miyako knew that Yuyuan was not completely unmoved by Ding's pursuits, as Ding would like them to believe; she did not completely believe that this was a mere case of one-way unrequited love.

When Yuyuan mentioned Ding, she was no longer as blunt and unbridled as she once had been; nor did she seem to get disgusted whenever his name was mentioned and look at him like some kind of clown. Of late, Yuyuan would only reluctantly talk about Ding if someone else kept pushing her to. It was obvious that the situation had already changed.

Lady Miyako felt that Ding Wenyu's excessive explanation came off quite forced and artificial. She couldn't understand how Ding could keep up his show even after things had gone as far as they had. Not for a second did she believe the words that came out of his mouth. She felt that his speech was simply born of a sudden loss of nerve.

"If all you are after is 'spiritual love,' " Lady Miyako asked, "then what in the world did you divorce your wife for?"

Ding Wenyu's explanation was so awkward that he himself would have had a hard time believing it. He stuttered and muttered but couldn't explain. He probably never could.

Yujiao laughed as she interrupted, "Have you ever heard the saying, 'Plug your ears while stealing a bell'? You're really an idiot!"

III

What Ding Wenyu did that was even more idiotic was to go in person to explain things to Yu Kerun. He was trying to explain something that was impossible to explain. From start to finish, the whole scene couldn't have been more preposterous. By the time Ding stood face to face with Yu Kerun, Yu's first impression was that standing before him was a little clown in need of a good beating. Ding Wenyu confidently disclosed to Yu Kerun that he had fallen shamelessly in love with Yu's wife—but he had not the slightest ill intention. He nauseatingly sang the praises of another man's wife, using the most splendid and vivid words to describe Yuyuan. With perfect ease, Ding played the role of the innocent—it was as if Yu Kerun were the source of all the problems. Ding Wenyu even went so far as to threaten Yu not to misunderstand the nature of Ding's relationship with Yuyuan and to treat her right; otherwise Ding wouldn't be so polite.

"You've got yourself a wonderful woman. If you don't know how to take care of her, then you're nothing but a bastard!" Ding Wenyu waved his cane as if he were some gentlemanlike outsider stepping into a situation to restore justice.

Yu Kerun couldn't believe his ears. Although this ridiculous meeting was somewhat random, it hinted at something inevitable. Ding Wenyu had been hoping for an opportunity to meet with Yu Kerun for quite some time. It was clear that Ding had rehearsed countless times for this meeting, preparing a massive spiel. Ding Wenyu and Yu Kerun ran into each other completely by chance at the Provincial Public Recreation Center. During a heated basketball game, an utterly serious Ding Wenyu, without any regard for propriety, called Yu away from the action for this seemingly spontaneous but not entirely unplanned little chat. As far as Yu Kerun was concerned, the timing couldn't have been worse. The Provincial Public Recreation Center, which was situated just outside Tongji Gate, was blistering with shouts. The tide suddenly turned on the court and everyone started to cheer the underdog team. Yu Kerun's buddies, who had come with him to watch the game, kept an eye on Yu from their seats. They could see Ding Wenyu waving his cane around like a cocky bird. Among Yu's friends there were also a few women, and they all seemed to know who Ding Wenyu was. Yu Kerun was extremely irritated but kept a straight face; he asked whether they could go somewhere else for this damned discussion.

During 1937 in the capital, basketball was the most popular sport. Just before and after a big game, the streets and alleys would always be filled with chitchat about it. Nanjing at the time had two strong teams: one was the Central Military Academy basketball team and the other was the National Athletic College team. The Central Military Academy team was an old favorite. All over Nanjing they were virtually invincible, and in the people's hearts the players were all like heroes. The National Athletic College team was the new kid on the block; their main strength was two brothers named Zhang Changqing and Zhang Changjiang. Like a pair of newborn calves unafraid of tigers, they were young and fearless; during their previous game they had even beat the Central Military Academy in a major upset. After that, the two teams became sworn enemies, and their rematch became a major event in the eyes of Nanjing audiences, a clash of titans. Everyone knew that they were in for quite a show. In order to fully prepare for their rematch, each team did everything they could to recruit the best players around.

Students from the National Athletic College even organized a cheer-leading squad, and the school principal, Zhang Zhijiang, personally watched the game at courtside. The National Athletic College team, in their black tank tops and white shorts, were out to protect their crown, while the Central Military Academy were out for revenge. Although the

Central Military Academy didn't have a cheerleader squad, the school's director of education, Zhang Zhizhong, did zestfully rush over to supervise. Three months later, when the Shanghai Incident of August 13th broke out, bringing on full-scale war with Japan, Zhang Zhizhong would be the commander-in-chief of the bloody battle. However, during the game that day, he came off like a scholarly and dignified Confucian general, deferentially sitting there, his every gesture carrying the utmost elegance. With their white uniforms and uniformly shaved heads, the Central Military Academy's basketball team seemed to show off their serious side with their every move. As soon as the game began, both teams went all out—no one dared to slack off. It was a tight game, but gradually the tide seemed to turn in favor of the National Athletic College team. Then, one after another, the audience members started shouting slogans to spur on the Central Military Academy team.

It was precisely at this critical juncture in the game that Ding Wenyu called Yu Kerun aside. In order to get good seats, Yu and his pilot buddies had arrived more than an hour and a half early to squeeze themselves into the already packed bleachers. Accompanying Yu and his buddies were a pair of young girls. Both were students at Ginling College, and the one who took a particular liking to Yu Kerun, Miss Qu Manli, was the niece of an especially well-connected Nationalist official. Qu Manli majored in home economics in college and started to fall for Yu the moment she laid eyes on him. She knew that Yu Kerun was a married man, but that didn't stop her from launching her frequent forward assaults. Yu had no intention of refusing Miss Qu's advances. However, he still didn't want it to get out that Ding Wenyu was after his wife—especially not at the game that day. Yu tried as best he could to control his temper, hoping that Ding Wenyu would get the hell out of his sight.

Under wave after wave of enthusiastic roars from the audience, Yu Kerun suddenly lowered his voice and gave Ding Wenyu an unfriendly piece of advice. Yu warned Ding that if he planned to continue his attempts to seduce Yuyuan, he would only be asking for trouble. Yu then went on to warn him that he wasn't the kind of person Ding wanted to mess with—if Ding insisted on keeping it up, he wasn't going to get off easy. Ding Wenyu should take a good hard look at himself in his own piss to realize that he was nothing but an unworthy toad lusting after the flesh of a swan. Yu Kerun kept glancing over at the court; Miss Qu was anxiously awaiting his return. "I don't feel like wasting my breath talking to you today. But I'll tell you this: you're playing with fire! Perhaps you're sick of living?" With that, Yu Kerun turned to leave, but Ding stopped him, saying he still had some things he wanted to clear up. Ding's annoying relentlessness drove Yu to the end of his rope. Yu Kerun tightened his hand into a fist and took at good look at Ding's nose, itching for an excuse to plant a good solid punch on that proper little face.

Fighting to suppress his anger, Yu asked, "Just what the hell else do you want to say?"

"I don't intend to seduce your wife." Ding replied. "I admit that I love her, but it is entirely a one-sided infatuation and I don't plan on taking it any further."

Yu Kerun noticed that Ding Wenyu's insane confession was beginning to attract other people's attention. It was already blistering hot outside, and Ding Wenyu in his trim western suit appeared extremely strange. Wearing a gaudy tie, with every button on his suit tightly fastened up to the top, Ding looked like a butterfly shrimp as he bowed. No matter what he did, he continued to wave around his cane as if it were an officer's sword or something. But not for a second did Ding Wenyu feel himself ridiculous. It is usually only in the eyes of others that one appears so. Yu Kerun also realized that the longer he stood next to this clown, the more stupid he himself began to look. The basketball game roared on while Ding and Yu were bogged down in a stalemate at that corner near the edge of the bleachers. Trying to have a serious conversation about something no one really wants to discuss while surrounded by crowds of shouting fans is indeed futile.

"Don't force me to hit you!" Yu Kerun warned Ding.

Then suddenly, in the wink of an eye, Ding Wenyu felt a surge of incomparable bravery. Staring at Yu, he declared: "Go ahead then, hit me! Just try!"

Yu Kerun didn't know what to do; the basketball game was naturally not the appropriate place to get physical. Moreover, a young, strong serviceman like Yu striking a bookworm like Ding Wenyu in front of everyone would instantly make Yu out to be the bad guy—and besides, how would Yu Kerun explain his actions to his buddies? Qu Manli was already waving at Yu from her seat, signaling for him to hurry up and finish his boring conversation. Ding Wenyu, however, refused to let him go and raised the stakes on his challenge. It was as if Ding had been transformed into a knight from the Middle Ages who was ready to fight for his honor; waving his cane at Yu Kerun, he solemnly requested a chance to have it out with him. "You choose the place. We'll have a gun duel to decide who the winner is. I wish you the best of luck; hopefully you will win." Ding Wenyu gazed at Yu with a look bordering on outlandish; one could tell, however, that this was no joke.

Before Yu Kerun even had a chance to react, Ding Wenyu proudly strutted out of the gym as if he had been victorious. The game was still raging on—it had reached its climax. The Central Military Academy team had gotten back on its feet and was slowly beginning to turn the tide. Although the Military Academy came out victorious in the end, Ding Wenyu couldn't have cared less about the outcome of the game. The idea of a final duel to the death with Yu Kerun was tearing at him; he imagined how heroic he would be when the time came. Ding Wenyu visualized what he would look like with a smoking gun in hand, bravely charging at Yu. With his back straight and his head held high, he took big strides as he approached his foe—all in the name of love. Facing a battle he was destined to lose, Ding Wenyu walked firmly toward his own death. He didn't believe that he could win, nor did he hope to. With the elegance of an expert marksman, Yu Kerun raised his gun and pulled the trigger. At that final moment, Ding Wenyu didn't fire—he didn't intend to. It was a perfect ending. It was an ending that would leave everyone satisfied. Only as the bullet propeled toward him did Ding Wenyu finally see the distressed look of sadness in Yuyuan's eyes. Fantasizing about the look of distress on her face as he made the ultimate sacrifice for her, Ding Wenyu felt true contentment.

Ding Wenyu wracked his brains trying to figure out who could provide him with a weapon. There were no stores in Nanjing that sold guns. But then Ding remembered a small, nickel-plated, pocket-sized handgun that a Chinese-Colombian had given to him while he was studying in America. This hoodlum half-breed, who was said to have killed three people, had for a time been Ding's closest friend. His one-time buddy had told Ding that the secret to a duel lay in whether or not you dared to look death in the face. In most cases the lord of the underworld favors the cow-

ardly with a visit. In the end, victory or defeat are of the least consequence—all that matters is whether or not you show your courage. Nothing is more shameful than a coward facing a duel to the death. Ding's
Colombian friend told him that if he should pull the trigger and not hit
his opponent, it would not be because he wasn't a good shot; the only explanation would be that he had suddenly become scared. Perfect shots
exist only in the movies; even professional assassins sometimes get jittery
and completely miss their mark when they are only steps away.

For a time, Ding Wenyu had carried that little pocket-sized handgun
wherever he went—not to protect himself, but simply as an ornament to
show off. In the end, however, the little pistol was confiscated by customs. Ding Wenyu had no idea where he could get his hands on another gun. In the capital in 1937, it was against the law to carry weapons on
one's person. Never was it fashionable among the peaceful people of
Nanjing to keep a gun in the house for protection; moreover, a so-called
"duel to the death" was an outright joke—who in Nanjing had even
heard of such a thing? Ding Wenyu realized the possibility of his name
appearing in all the headlines. One could always read about violent
crimes in the papers, but most were murders and assassinations—a duel,
on the other hand, would be something brand new; it was bound to make
all the headlines. The legendary tale of Ding Wenyu's romance would be
transformed as it traveled from ear to ear all around the city. Ding imagined, once all the gossip had died down and his story had come to naught,
a dejected Yuyuan sitting alone beside her window shedding tears for her
lost lover.

Ding Wenyu wrote a decent-length letter to Yu Kerun. In it, Ding
again expressed his determination to die without the slightest regret.
Ding professed that he was already set on using his death to prove
Yuyuan's innocence. True love destroys nothing; love is a piece of white
jade that forever escapes defilement. Ding Wenyu felt deep regret over
the fact that he couldn't get hold of a gun; then, realizing that Yu Kerun
was a military man, Ding placed all his hopes on Yu. He hoped that Yu
Kerun would be able to tell him the time and place of the duel in advance; that way he could have ample time to make arrangements for his
own funeral. The gate of death was already open and, without the slightest hesitation, Ding Wenyu was fully prepared to extend his hand and
greet the lord of the underworld.

IV

Yuyuan wasn't the least bit surprised when she saw Ding Wenyu's divorce announcement in all the papers. She had learned from Ding's letters that this preposterous event was about to take place. Because she never returned his letters, there was no way she could or would have written for him to stop. And even if she had wanted to stop him, it was already too late; by the time Yuyuan received the news from Ding, the divorce announcement had already been typeset and sent off to the printers. Ding Wenyu had mentioned countless times in his letters that he would have to take drastic measures in order to end his marriage. He blabbered on and on, declaring to Yuyuan just what he was going to do. He could not care less about what her reaction might be; naturally he had absolutely no way of knowing just how she would react. Ding Wenyu was clearly isolated from everyone, and Yuyuan seemed to be but a mailbox that took care of his letters. She was simply a nonexistent, formless image that listened to his eternal ramblings and watched him run wild with his death-defying performance. It was as if everything he did had absolutely no real connection with her.

Yuyuan knew quite clearly, however, that everything that had been unfolding would have a direct effect on her. Just as Ding Wenyu became panic-stricken over the abnormal lack of response after his divorce announcement was first printed, Yuyuan also had a strange feeling; everything was just too quiet. She was waiting for people to ask her what had happened and admonish her; that way she could offer the proper response and fight back with a convincing explanation. But things went on as if nothing had happened. Besides Ding's mentions of the divorce in his letters, not a soul tried to find anything out about it from Yuyuan. It seemed like people were either completely ignorant about the divorce or wanted intentionally to stay away from the entire affair. There were a few times when Yuyuan saw her co-workers wrapped up in some conversation, and the second they realized she was around they held their tongues. Then after a period of awkward silence, they would start talking about some completely unrelated topic. It was obvious that this was their way of covering things up. Yuyuan quickly discovered that she was a superfluous participant in many of her co-workers' conversations.

Yuyuan wished she could run out to the street and scream her innocence. She needed an opportunity to explain herself; she hoped that someone would listen to her side of the story. She was hopelessly waiting; the longer she waited, the more furious and impatient she became. Finally one of her girlfriends arranged to meet with Yuyuan secretly. Yuyuan thought that her friend wanted to talk with her about Ding Wenyu's divorce announcement. Yuyuan had already prepared a response; she planned to tell her friend how everything was Ding Wenyu's fault and prove that she had no role in the matter. In the end, however, what her friend told her was that her husband Yu Kerun was hot on a girl named Qu Manli. Yuyuan's friend was shocked to learn that Yuyuan was still completely in the dark about the relationship. She then went on to spice up all the little details she had dug up about Qu Manli and gave Yuyuan a full report. Suddenly things started to make sense to Yuyuan; she instantly understood why her husband was so unmoved by Ding's divorce announcement in the paper.

"That Yu Kerun of yours is really no angel." Yuyuan's friend gave her a good-natured warning. "You need to be careful of men like him. I'm sure that he's dying to have something on you too!"

Yuyuan knew what her friend meant by this "something." Ding Wenyu's rabid pursuit of Yuyuan had long been an open secret between her and her friends. At first it was only a kind of game; they wanted to see just how insane a man could go for a woman. They had all been in on it right along with Yuyuan, but now the joke had gone too far and things were beginning to get out of control—almost to the point of no return. In the beginning all they wanted to do was get some kicks at Ding's expense, but suddenly they realized that Yuyuan's backyard was on fire. When the newly married Yuyuan moved back to her dormitory, these friends of hers, who had been adding fuel to the fire all along, immediately realized that things weren't going in the right direction. Although Yuyuan never told them about any of her problems with Yu, they could sense that there was already something wrong. After Yuyuan moved out, their marriage existed in name only; there wasn't even a trace of the intimacy shared by most newlyweds. Yuyuan's friends noticed the awkward formality in the way they greeted each other, as if they were simply friends. It was rare that Yu Kerun came to visit Yuyuan, and when he did, he didn't seem a bit happy. Sometimes he'd sit for a while and leave, sometimes he would take Yuyuan to a hotel, and sometimes he would awkwardly spend the night at the dormitory, disappearing first thing the next morning before anyone even knew he was there.

The fact that the political situation was unstable became Yu Kerun's perfect excuse for not settling down and buying a house. It wasn't that they didn't have the right opportunity or had financial problems. Some-one had offered them a plot of land at a great price and both of their fam-ilies offered to put up the money for the house, but Yu Kerun simply dis-missed the whole thing with a laugh. Not for one minute did he seriously consider settling down. He wasn't terribly satisfied with his present situ-ation; then again, you couldn't say that he was very dissatisfied either. Yu Kerun was not the kind of person you would call a family man. Although he was already married, he acted just as unrestrained and free as when he was single. He came and went as he pleased, getting excited one minute and losing his temper the next; he was like a spoiled child. When he was in a good mood, he would come off extremely open-minded and ask Yuyuan if that nerd named Ding was still writing love letters and chasing after her as if there were no tomorrow. If he wasn't in a good mood, Yu Kerun would suddenly change his mind and cancel his visit to Yuyuan, even though it might have been planned long in advance. Sometimes he wouldn't show his face for several weeks, and when he finally did, he wouldn't offer any kind of explanation for his behavior.

Once, when Yu Kerun seemed to be in a pretty good mood, he casu-ally told Yuyuan, "Maybe we should consider renting an apartment." Ac-tually, all he was trying to do was get on Yuyuan's good side. Heaven only knows how many times Yu Kerun had said things like that—but in the end, nothing ever came of these promises. During his visits, Yu Kerun would always feel frustrated by all of the inconveniences related to his wife living in a dormitory and would talk about setting up a little love nest of their own. Yu Kerun knew that Yuyuan was fed up with dorm life and longed to have a place of her own. When he came to visit there would often be a few unforeseeable issues that would pop up, making everyone uncomfortable. Although everyone in the dormitory knew to stay away, Yu Kerun and Yuyuan still had to use a certain amount of cau-tion. Who could predict when someone would barge in? Not having a place of their own made *everything* abnormal.

Sometimes, Yuyuan would accidentally discover a woman's embroidered handkerchief or a piece of fruit candy that women fancy in Yu's
pocket. His clothing was often marked with smudged lipstick and his
body often carried the fragrance of a woman's facial cream. Yuyuan got
the feeling that, whether he knew it or not, Yu Kerun couldn't help dropping clues about his relations with other women—it was as if he was trying to show off his spoils of war. The two of them seemed to always be
lacking a common language. Yu would either be dead silent or ramble on
and on about his fellow pilots' erotic encounters. He would tell Yuyuan
how those girls were only too willing to shamelessly give themselves to a
pilot. Ever since they had met, Yu Kerun couldn't help but show off his
superiority; he would always milk his loverboy charm. Whenever he noticed Yuyuan getting turned off by his bragging, he would talk instead
about the romantic adventures of his fellow pilots. He told these stories
with a tone of approval rather than criticism; he told Yuyuan how all the
young pilots were completely beside themselves as to how to deal with
the number of beautiful young girls throwing themselves at them.

Yu Kerun never had any set plans for his future. At times he thought
that he could have great prospects if he embarked on an official career,
and so he tried to make relevant plans for Yuyuan. He felt that she should
quit her job at the army headquarters and take up her role as a housewife.
In Yu's eyes, a female confidential secretary was not an ideal match for
him. In 1937, under the frantic shouts of "resist Japan and save the dying
nation," countless young girls longed to do something for their country.
Amid the nationalistic fervor of the times, a girl signing up for the army
was no cause for criticism, but over the long term, this career was still not
an option. It was as if Yuyuan was kept at the army headquarters more for
her good looks then anything else; because of this, Yu Kerun felt an indescribable, continuous uneasiness. Once, as Yu Kerun accompanied
Yuyuan down the main road leading to the heavily guarded army headquarters, they bumped into all kinds of commanding officers. Each and
every one of those upright and serious officers looked Yuyuan over with
an ill-intentioned gaze.

"Now I know why the Chinese army is in such terrible shape," Yu
Kerun said jokingly to Yuyuan as he announced his discovery, "because
all the officers are surrounded by too many pretty girls!" Yu Kerun did-
n't only tell this joke to Yuyuan—he also shared it with Yuyuan's female

co-workers. Yuyuan didn't know just what her husband was like when he was out flirting with other women; all she could do was deduce what she could from the way Yu horsed around with her female co-workers. One thing was without question: Yu Kerun was indeed the kind of guy who knew how to please a woman. Whenever he spoke, there was always a tinge of haughty confidence in his voice.

Since Yu Kerun didn't have the slightest reaction to Ding Wenyu's divorce announcement, Yuyuan decided to force him to take proper action. He shouldn't just ignore the whole thing as if it hadn't happened. Just when Yu Kerun least expected it, Yuyuan suddenly brought up the name Qu Manli. This time Yuyuan's reaction was completely out of character: no longer did she act indifferent; instead she demanded to know the exact nature of Yu Kerun's relationship with Qu Manli and just how far had it gone. "I don't understand why a popular and handsome guy like you should have rushed to marry me. You should have waited a while, heaven only knows just how many star-struck girls there are out there just dying to get their chance with you!" Yuyuan's self-restraint went out the window; brimming with jealousy, she glared at her shocked husband. The level of Yuyuan's anger exceeded not only Yu Kerun's expectations but even her own.

"We're just ordinary friends," Yu Kerun responded, trying to cover up the truth. Usually Yu didn't attempt to hide his relations with other women; the second he tried to lie his guilty conscience would show right through. In reality, Yu's relationship with Qu Manli was anything but ordinary; it had already undergone "substantial" development.

Not about to let her husband off easy, Yuyuan went on to ask him, "Just what do you mean by 'ordinary friends'?"

An obvious look of annoyance appeared on Yu Kerun's face. He suddenly thought of Ding Wenyu and the discussion they had had the day before. Yu Kerun's first reaction was that it must have been Ding Wenyu who'd revealed the secret that he was with Qu Manli. But then, he couldn't figure out how Ding Wenyu could have learned Qu's name. Yu Kerun didn't feel the slightest remorse under Yuyuan's persistent inquiries; just the opposite, he responded by turning his guilt into anger and flying into a rage. If it had been someone else who had revealed his secret, he perhaps would have been able to forgive them—but the second he imagined that bastard Ding Wenyu betraying him, anger seethed from his every pore. He couldn't bear to accept Ding Wenyu as his opponent. It would be a loss of status for Yu to admit that Ding Wenyu was even worthy of breathing the same air. Yu Kerun wondered in what ways Dingu vilified him to get on Yuyuan's good side.

"Well, it looks like you've already met with this love letter-writing admirer of yours," Yu Kerun said.

Yuyuan knew that he was just trying to change the subject. She was unsure if she should keep after her husband about Qu Manli or let him change the subject to Ding Wenyu. Yu Kerun's expression of mixed rage and panic proved that his relationship with Qu Manli was far from "ordinary." Yuyuan could feel her heart aching; in order to give her husband a taste of his own medicine, she went along with his empty accusations and declared that she had indeed met with Ding Wenyu. She decided to take a lesson from her husband and let *him* know what it feels like to be played the fool. For a moment, Yuyuan regretted not taking Ding up on his invitation to meet.

"What did I tell you?" said Yu. "I just knew that you had seen him."

Yuyuan didn't respond.

"I even know *when* the two of you met." Yu added.

Yuyuan waited for her husband to finish, but Yu Kerun seemed to have already said what he wanted to say. A conversation that had been brewing for a long time was already finished, since Yu wasn't willing to continue talking about his own affair or to talk about his wife's affair. Yuyuan had dreaded that things would come to this. Yu Kerun not only slyly protected himself by completely avoiding talking about his own relationship with Qu Manli but also showed off how forgiving he could be about the whole Ding Wenyu affair. Yu's magnanimity had nothing to do with his trust in his wife or anyone else, but with his overconfidence. Yu wasn't worried that his wife would cheat on him simply because he was so utterly carried away with himself. Yu Kerun's superiority complex as a pilot left him with the firm belief that Yuyuan falling for Ding Wenyu was impossible. The sun would have to set in the east before Yuyuan could fall for a weirdo like Ding Wenyu.

"Do you know that Ding Wenyu ran an announcement declaring that he divorced his wife?" Yuyuan was determined to continue this already half-finished conversation. Yu Kerun's eyes widened with shock, and Yuyuan glared at him, asking, "You really haven't heard? Or are you just pretending you haven't heard?"

Yu Kerun indeed hadn't known. He had absolutely no time to read the papers, and when he did occasionally thumb through one, the last thing he paid attention to was the classifieds. The only thing Yu Kerun looked at when reading the paper were those photos of female actresses in the movie preview section. Yu Kerun, however, did think it a bit strange that when they had met the day before, Ding Wenyu pledged to the heavens that Yuyuan was free of any blame; he went on and on like a broken record about proving Yuyuan's innocence. Ding even nauseatingly talked all about "spiritual love" and how he would never get in the way of some-one else's happy family. During their conversation, Ding Wenyu hadn't mentioned his divorce announcement; he made sure his own private affairs were kept completely under wraps. It was also during this conversation that Ding Wenyu had left Yu with the impression that he was quite high-minded by continually reminding Yu to be good to Yuyuan. He told Yu Kerun that Yuyuan was a priceless treasure and he needed to learn how to appreciate her; he needed to protect her as if she were life itself.

"Don't tell me that you don't even care?" Yuyuan asked.

"Don't care about what?" Yu Kerun responded.

"You don't care about me!" screamed Yuyuan.

"You tell me, what's the difference whether I care or not?" replied Yu Kerun. "I don't even know what it means to care about anyone anymore."

V

Like a lot of other pretty young college students, Qu Manli had her own set of rules when it came to selecting her future husband. It seemed like an unspoken law that girls who graduated with a degree in home economics were destined to marry somebody with money. Because of this, while in school most of their energy was spent on learning how to get their dream man—and tame him. The best-selling book of 1937 in Nanjing was the Generalissimo's *Two Weeks in Xi'an*. Not long after its publication, the book had already sold 430,000 copies. The newspapers used the most nauseating language in their rousing advertising campaign to push the book. The Department of Civic Affairs released an adminis-trative announcement ordering that all students have a copy of the book to read in their spare time. For a while, *Two Weeks in Xi'an* was the only place to look if you wanted to understand the Generalissimo's road to revolution, admire his grand character, or know his plan for saving China. Naïve schoolgirls especially loved to worshipfully thumb through the added chapter, "My Memoirs of the Xi'an Incident." This essay, written by Madame Chiang herself, moved the hearts of countless young girls.

Many female college students took Madame Chiang, Soong May-ling, as their idol, and with her lead, it became quite a popular trend for girls to marry significantly older men. Also because of this, old, successful officials had absolutely no problem remarrying young girl students after they divorced their wives. Pretty girls and successful men seemed to make countless matches made in heaven, and stories of old men with young wives were passed around with approval among the upper echelons of society. Being able to marry a young woman became the symbol of a man's success; choosing an older man was also the way in which women recognized and approved his career success. As a pretty young girl, Qu Manli couldn't help but follow the trend and hope to marry a successful man. If a woman's husband was successful then she was successful too. The right men, however, were few and far between—there were nowhere near enough of them to go around. Moreover, most of those who were successful were too old, old enough to be father or even grandfather to those girls. Men always marry too early; even a handsome young man like Yu Kerun couldn't wait to get hitched. The more Qu Manli learned at school about how to be a good wife, the more she realized how difficult it would be to find a satisfactory man.

Qu Manli knew that in order to catch a good husband she needed to chalk up some experience. You can only figure out what men are all about if you spend time with them. If she were to just sit around waiting, she knew that her Mr. Right would never knock on her door. She needed to find some men to practice on; of these romantic guinea pigs, Yu Kerun was not the first; nor would he be the last. Back when Yu had flown for the Generalissimo's birthday celebration, Qu Manli had already started to take notice of his name. Yu Kerun had caused quite a stir on that occasion, and more than a few adolescent young girls developed crushes on this star pilot. When they were alone with their girlfriends they would say how they dreamed of one day marrying a pilot like him. These pilots' one flaw was that they were all too young. The girl students would be old ladies by the time any of the pilots made anything of themselves. Qu

Manli had a long conversation with her classmates and decided to run her relationships according to a set of rules, in order to protect herself from one day being discarded by her future man. Qu Manli's number one rule dictated that she could flirt and play around with men like Yu Kerun all she wanted, but marriage was out of the question.

Yu Kerun first laid eyes on Qu Manli at an air force get-together. Yu Kerun attended all kinds of parties and had ample opportunity to meet plenty of pretty girls. Most of these girls had a wonderful impression of Yu; they would all circle around him as if he were the life of the party. It seemed as if every one of them was dying to be his bride—however, their interest never failed to dwindle the second they learned that he was already married. Qu Manli was the only exception. As soon as she heard that Yu Kerun had a beautiful young wife, she became even more aggressive in her pursuit. Almost immediately, she got the strange idea of using Yu Kerun to test the limits of her own charm. She wanted to prove herself even more outstanding than Yu Kerun's stunning wife. Qu Manli realized that if a handsome young newlywed like Yu Kerun could lose himself over her, any other man should be a piece of cake.

Qu Manli soon discovered that she had somehow gotten the short end of the stick. Not only didn't Yu Kerun lose himself over her, but she found herself completely taken in by Yu's smooth moves. Yu Kerun had many opportunities to meet women, but very few actually slept with him—flirting was one thing, making love was another. Qu Manli was quick to give Yu Kerun a shot at her, and without a second thought, Yu took her up on her offer. Naturally, it didn't matter who came out ahead; after all, it was simply a game that was destined to come to nothing. While Qu Manli tried to get even, Yu Kerun couldn't care less about the whole affair. Both of them had ulterior motives for being with each other, and their relationship was like a roller coaster—the whole thing was right out of a stage drama. They repeatedly appeared together at public events where they showed each other off and basked in each other's attention. Although it wouldn't qualify as an honor, it was something a bit out of the ordinary to have the beautiful Qu Manli accompany Yu Kerun to these events, because Qu's uncle was an important figure in the Nationalist government. Yu Kerun naturally had the desire to work his way up the ladder—he knew that he couldn't spend the rest of his life soaring through the heavens—and if he wanted a bright future, it would have to be as an official on the ground. There had been rumors that the position of vice-president of the Aviation Academy was going to be his, but the official word had yet to come down. The reason for the delay was quite simple: Yu Kerun still didn't have enough big shots in his corner. He needed a few people like Qu Manli's uncle to support him.

Finally, Qu Manli brought Yu Kerun to her uncle's house for dinner. The two of them had already gone out several times; all that was missing was this one formal step. There did, however, still seem to be a few minor obstacles in their way. Qu Manli's uncle's home was in the northern section of the city. The day of the dinner, Yu Kerun drove down to Ginling College to pick up Qu Manli and then headed north along Ninghai Road. Compared with the southern half of Nanjing, the north was much more desolate; all around there were green vegetable plots, willows, and small patches of bamboo. Around Shanxi Road there was a brand-new housing development where a lot of big officials lived; that was also where Yu's brother Yu Kexia lived. As Yu Kerun drove past his brother's small house, it was clear that it couldn't quite measure up to all the other luxury western-style homes in the neighborhood. With his hands on the steering wheel, Yu Kerun told Qu Manli about his brother. Qu Manli didn't seem very impressed. With a tone of arrogance she uttered, "What kind of future will your brother ever have if he just muddles around in educational circles?"

Yu Kerun explained that it wasn't that his brother was unwilling to leave academia; it was just that, with his educational background, there wasn't anything else he was qualified to do. Qu Manli sneered and said, "These days, what could be easier than working for the government? Besides, didn't you say your brother studied abroad? He should have no problem getting a lucrative post somewhere." When Yu Kerun said that perhaps his brother didn't want to work for the government, Qu Manli laughed even harder. She said there was no such thing as not wanting to work for the government, only not being able to. The only reason people said they didn't want an official life was that they couldn't get a job—or at least not the one they wanted. The whole car ride there, the two of them chatted and laughed as Qu Manli shared with Yu all kinds of interesting gossip about Nanjing officialdom. Yu Kerun never imagined that a female university student could know so much about what was going on behind the scenes in government circles; it was as if she had everything written on the back of her hand. As they chatted, the car zoomed past a new road; leaving the new development, they followed a dirt road deep into the distance—it seemed as if they were headed straight for the country. Then, far off, they caught sight of a row of country-style houses beside a dark green pond. The houses had white walls and black tile roofs, and were partly obscured by a bamboo forest—this was where Qu Manli's uncle lived.

Qu Manli's uncle was no spring chicken; it wasn't until later that Yu Kerun finally discovered that this "uncle" wasn't actually even a blood relative. He and Qu were only distantly related through a family marriage. Qu Manli's aunt, on the other hand, was comparatively young. Even though she was approaching middle age, she still had every bit of her charm and attractiveness; actually, *she* was Qu Manli's relative and her marriage enhanced Qu's relation with her uncle. Qu Manli's uncle had already heard his niece mention Yu Kerun, so when they met he was forced to put up a warm and hospitable front. Qu's uncle had served up north as an official for many years and had picked up a strong northern Mandarin accent. His words were brimming with evidence that he was a man of experience and knew his way around the block. Although Qu's uncle couldn't help but offer a few perfunctory words of encouragement to Yu Kerun, he obviously didn't have a very good impression of Yu. It was clear that inviting Yu over was all his wife's idea. The old man had barely any time with Yu Kerun before Qu Manli's aunt came into the living room and forced her husband to get some rest. "Yesterday at the Central Committee meeting, the old man got all worked up and said more than he should have—afterward he couldn't get a good bit of sleep the whole night through," Qu Manli's aunt explained to Yu Kerun before dragging her husband away. Afterward she came back to the living room to chat heartily with Yu Kerun. It was obvious how much she adored her niece; as she talked to Yu, every other word out of her mouth had to do with how wonderful her little Qu Manli was. Qu Manli also made sure to show that she indeed was the favorite of the family—she had no qualms about whining to her aunt (who couldn't have been more than a few years older than she was) or harshly berating the family maid for the most minor mistakes.

With Qu Manli as his guide, Yu Kerun was given a full tour of this country house, which, although it appeared rather rustic from the outside, was exquisitely decorated within. After the Nationalist government seat moved to Nanjing, untold numbers of luxury homes popped up all over the remote outskirts of the city. Qu Manli's uncle's house had a huge courtyard where they kept two watchdogs tied with a leather leash; they would start to bark and growl the second they caught sight of strangers. All around were fragrant flowers and chirping birds; the courtyard walls extended to the edge of the dark green lake. In the lake were small groups of ducks, divided into twos and threes as they played in the water under the shade of the trees. Beyond the pond were peasant farmers working the land, and not far off on a cleared patch of land were a few chickens pecking away at some insects. Yu Kerun and Qu Manli sat down on the homemade swing beside the pond. Gently rocking back and forth, they flirtatiously spoke about all kinds of inconsequential matters.

Yu Kerun realized that the mood was just like the old man of the house's temperament—although on the surface everything appeared relaxed and carefree, deep down there was a storm raging within. Although Yu Kerun had barely had the chance to exchange more than a few words with Qu Manli's uncle, during their short conversation the old man insisted that all he wanted was to retire to a quiet life in the country. However, Yu Kerun had a gut feeling that the old man was still a long way from losing interest in officialdom, as he seemed to want Yu to believe. Old as he was, he still harbored ambitions and restlessly schemed ways he could edge his way up the ladder.

Staying calm is a better tactic than hustling around; all of the plants and vegetation seemed to have a bunch of hidden dragons and crouching tigers lying in wait. In Chinese history, the motif of the country recluse has always carried with it a political undertone; there are countless stories in the history books about powerful officials who retreat to the country, only to come back to office even more powerful. Toward the end of the Qing dynasty, Qu Manli's uncle had already secured himself a decent government position; then, throughout Yuan Shikai's imperial restoration, the second revolution, and the reorganization of the Beiyang warlord regime, all the way up to the Nationalist revolutionary government, the old man couldn't keep his hands out of politics. He had so much knowledge of officialdom that he was like a walking encyclopedia; as far as politics went, he was indeed an old fox.

"If I really wanted to go somewhere with my official career, I can guarantee you that I wouldn't still be where I am today." During dinner Qu

Manli's uncle was in high spirits. As he downed cup after cup of yellow rice wine, he talked about his experience in government. He couldn't help but sigh as he uttered, "But don't forget that officialdom is like a battlefield. It doesn't matter if you are trying to get in or trying to retreat, your fate is sealed. The only way out of this vicious circle is to give up trying and simply resign oneself to the will of heaven—that's the only way you'll come out in one piece."

Yu Kerun didn't quite understand what the old man was talking about, so Qu Manli gave him an example by telling him about one of her uncle's most successful moves. During the fifteenth year of the Republic, at the height of the warlord period, the Nationalist government dispatched several divisions on the Northern Expedition. The former warlord Zhang Zuolin was appointed Grand Marshal, while Sun Chuanfang and Wu Peifu each took over huge areas of rich and strategically placed territory. In one week's time Qu Manli's uncle received three separate appointments—both the Nationalists and two different warlord factions wanted him to act as their Minister of Post and Telecommunications. Who would guess that such a coincidence could happen? It was as if in all of China, he were the only one qualified to serve as Minister of Post and Telecommunications. The old man, however, took his sweet time and, with those three appointment invitations spread out on his table, declared that he was ill and refused to see all guests. During those chaotic times it was virtually impossible to predict who would eventually come out on top, and so the old man simply hid out at home and let the warlords fight everything out with the Nationalists. Only after there was a winner did he finally come out of hiding and go to Nanjing to take up a halfway decent post that was there waiting for him.

"At the time my uncle was in Beijing, and if he had decided to serve as the Minister of Post and Telecommunications for the Nationalists, the Beiyang warlords never would have forgiven him. If, on the other hand, he had taken up the same post for the northern warlords, how could he have ever gotten to where he is today?" Qu Manli said without the least bit of naïveté—she wasn't at all concerned with the disappointed expression on Yu Kerun's face. Yu never imagined that Qu Manli's family could be so philistine and talk so plainly about life in government; in an instant, the initial reverence he had reserved for them disappeared without a trace. Young and talented, with his whole future ahead of him,

Yu Kerun started to feel uncomfortable the second he realized that he had actually come in hope of winning this decrepit old man's support. Qu Manli's crafty old scoundrel of an uncle and the man whom the newspapers constantly referred to as an "honest and sincere senior official" seemed to be two completely different people. In Yu Kerun's eyes, Qu's uncle was nothing but a petty puppet who cared for absolutely nothing besides his position. There were all too many of these types of people in the Nationalist government, and the capital of Nanjing was nothing but a big breeding ground for bureaucrats. In this kind of environment, senile but experienced old fogies precisely like Qu's uncle took like fish to water.

After dinner Yu Kerun drove Qu Manli back to her dormitory. Neither of them had anything to say the whole way there. There were a few times when Qu Manli raised her head to say something, but the conversation didn't seem to go anywhere. She didn't know why Yu was upset and, out of spite, ended up giving him the silent treatment. When they got to the college entrance, Yu Kerun pulled over for Qu to get out. Qu Manli felt like she had been made the bad guy for no reason and demanded that Yu explain exactly what was wrong and why the long face. Realizing that he had indeed given Qu the cold shoulder the whole ride home, Yu suddenly got an idea about how to remedy the situation. Yu didn't want to throw away the whole day, so he told Qu Manli that he was upset because he realized that she was about to leave him and he thought of how lonely he would be.

"What's there to feel lonely about?" Qu Manli whispered. "You can always go look up your wife."

"But I wanted to spend today with you," Yu Kerun told her.

"What are you talking about? You're really one nasty guy! I'm not talking to you from now on."

As Yu Kerun was waiting for Qu Manli to get out of the car, he kept thinking how wonderful it would be if she stayed with him; he figured if she stayed in the car, he'd have a chance to make his move. Qu Manli stroked her long hair draping down over her shoulders and turned around to face the streetlight that had just turned green before looking back at Yu Kerun. "I knew that you pilots all had a nasty side!" The way she used the word "nasty," it seemed to carry an especially rich meaning that could have several different interpretations.

Yu Kerun noticed the sparkling look in Qu Manli's eyes but didn't dare let his gaze stay on her too long; instead he warned her, "You're right, there are nothing but nasty thoughts going through my head—if you don't get out of the car soon, the consequences might be serious."

Qu Manli responded with a playful, "You nasty little boy." It was as if she intentionally didn't get out of the car out of spite, while at the same time it seemed as though she were looking for an excuse to stay with Yu. Whatever the case, Yu Kerun wasn't in the mood to give it much thought; with a sly look in his eye, he suddenly slammed down on the gas and the car took off. Qu Manli cried out; she knew all too well what Yu was up to and gently tapped his hand as he clenched the steering wheel. It was now too late to get out of the car—but that didn't matter, because she never intended to get out in the first place. Yu Kerun drove straight ahead, heading directly to one of those hotels he frequented. When they arrived, he gracefully helped Miss Qu out of the car. Qu Manli still wasn't completely resigned to what was about to happen, but she managed to straighten her shoulders, perk up her chest, and, with a look of ease and confidence, follow Yu Kerun into that hotel room.

VI

It wasn't until late June 1937 that Ding Wenyu and his wife Peitao finally signed their official divorce papers in Shanghai. Even though long before this Ding had placed his divorce announcements in all the Nanjing and Shanghai newspapers, the Ding and Hao families found out through their lawyers that Ding was only fooling himself with the announcements, which carried absolutely no legal weight. Since both families were of the upper class and divorce seemed inevitable, after much negotiation, lawyers for both sides agreed to sit Ding Wenyu and Hao Peitao down together and have them sign the official divorce papers. Before they signed, the judge asked Ding Wenyu to carefully reread the documents. Ding refused. As he did so, he flashed Peitao a euphoric glance. Peitao seemed once again to be moved to anger by Ding's smug expression; she grabbed the divorce papers and intentionally took her sweet time as she slowly went over each and every word. She tried to stretch the time as far as it could go—she knew that everyone was waiting for her and wanted to make them wrack their brains trying to figure out what she was up to.

"You're all just waiting for my signature, right?" Peitao said with an emotionless expression. "And what are you going to do to me if I don't sign?"

Ding Wenyu was afraid that his moody wife was going to change her mind again; she had already gone back on her word countless times. But then, like lightning, she picked up a pen and quickly signed her name. Then she impatiently grabbed Ding's copy and signed it as well. Ding Wenyu, on the other hand, seemed to be somewhat out of it as he affixed his signature. Afterward, he stared blankly at Peitao, unsure whether or not he should shake hands with her before they parted. Then, under everyone's gaze, Peitao unexpectedly extended her hand toward Ding. As she gracefully moved to shake his hand, she smiled. "Both of us made a big mistake; you shouldn't have taken me as your wife, but I made an even bigger mistake when I agreed to marry you." As she spoke her eyes turned red, and although that smile still hung on her lips, her tone of voice changed. "I never imagined that you were this much of a bastard! I hope you realize that you're really nothing but worthless scum!"

The people around them rushed over to pull Ding Wenyu and Peitao apart. Ding Wenyu knew all too well how ruthless Peitao could be and thought that she would go even further with her slanderous comments. Peitao, however, seemed to have already gotten everything off her chest and didn't say another word. She turned and headed toward the elevator. During those few days in Shanghai, Ding Wenyu had built up quite a tolerance for insults. Although he was almost forty years old, Ding had to spend all his days putting up with endless barrages of lectures and insults as if he were a naughty child. It seemed like everyone had the right to give Ding a good tongue-lashing: his father, his father-in-law, his soon-to-be-ex-wife Peitao, and even his three stepmothers all berated him endlessly. They all knew that Ding wasn't in the mood to listen, but still they couldn't help but open their mouths. They went on with their lectures until they were blue in the face and Ding was seeing stars; it got to the point that the second Ding saw someone's lips moving, he became convinced they were talking about him.

It started to get hot. Although it was only late June, the weather was already sweltering. As the cheongsams on all the fashionable young Shanghai girls got shorter, exposing more and more skin, the streets seemed to be filled with the aroma of flesh. During an interview with some Shanghai reporters, a famous Egyptian fortune-teller revealed a bold prediction about the future of the world political arena. This famous, globe-trotting swami made the shocking announcement of a large-scale, vicious, and unavoidable world war breaking out in 1938, which would drag humankind into unprecedented catastrophe and suffering. When a reporter asked about the possibility of China and "a certain country" coming to blows, the Egyptian fortune-teller immediately answered in the affirmative, stating that war would break out between them in 1938. In reality, war between China and Japan would explode a mere ten days later at the Marco Polo Bridge. In less than two months' time, Shanghai would already be a battlefield shrouded in constant gunsmoke.

After the formal signing of the divorce papers, the Ding and Hao families together held a large, high-class banquet at an upscale restaurant. The purpose of this banquet was to show everyone that although these two illustrious families were no longer joined through marriage, the alliance between the Banking Boss and the Steel King was still as strong as ever. All the big players from the Shanghai business world were invited; there were friends and competitors, compradors for foreign firms, presidents of large trading companies, triad bosses, successful and unsuccessful politicians, cultural elites, and military big shots. During the banquet Ding Wenyu's father walked over to toast Peitao and express his sincere wish that she not let the Ding family down and be sure to provide them with a strong heir to carry on the family line. "All of our hopes are with you now."

That was the last time Ding Wenyu saw Peitao. At the time Peitao was three months pregnant, but one still couldn't see any noticeable changes in her appearance. A few months later, on the eve of the fall of Shanghai, Ding Wenyu received a letter from his father saying that Peitao's pregnancy really looked like it was going somewhere. At the time, heated fighting was roaring on, and every day the Chinese army was suffering heavy losses. Ding's father urged his son to leave Nanjing immediately and follow the government to the interior. Amid this chaos, Ding Wenyu's father had already lost all faith in any kind of resolution to

China's predicament—the only two things he seemed to concern himself with were Peitao providing his family with a little Ding and his son's safety. Owing to the sudden change in the political climate, the old man went from being a firm believer that war would never break out to an all-out pessimist—he seemed like a completely different person from the Mr. Ding who had spoken so confidently at the banquet just a few months before. That day at the banquet, Ding Wenyu's father seemed quite at ease with himself as he clinked glasses with everyone there—the only person he didn't toast was that spoiled, disappointing son of his. Although Ding Wenyu's father had indeed lost virtually all hope in him, Wenyu was after all still Mr. Ding's only son, and he didn't want to embarrass him in front of everyone. Ding Wenyu would have to rush back to Nanjing that night immediately after the banquet, but he displayed not even the slightest trace of sadness. Not only was he not upset, Ding could barely conceal the utter bliss all over his face. He decided to casually ask the courteous Japanese guest sitting at his table what he thought of that traveling swami who was being talked about in all the newspapers, and get his opinion on the swami's prediction about the outbreak of war between China and Japan in 1938.

In fluent Chinese, the Japanese guest answered Ding, "Don't tell me that you actually believe that 'war' is the only way to settle things between China and Japan?"

All of the Chinese at the table were suddenly taken aback. No one spoke; they were all both stunned by the Japanese's fluency in Chinese and struck by the possible implications of his answer—perhaps he had a point. Ding Wenyu pondered the Japanese man's answer for a moment before hitting him with another question, only this time he spoke in Japanese. Ding was never willing to pass up an opportunity to show off his foreign language skills, but everyone at the table protested, demanding that Ding and the Japanese man speak in Chinese so they could all understand. Ding decided to drill the Japanese guest with a certain cliché that frequently appeared in the newspapers: "With the situation as bad as it is today, what other option do the Chinese people have but to rise up in resistance?"

"And what's wrong with China and Japan joining together?" the Japanese guest asked. "How come we can't work together to create a glorious future for Greater East Asia? What could be wrong with that?"

The table was in an uproar; everyone seemed to suddenly hate the Japanese guest for his impunity and twisted, self-righteous attitude. All of the Chinese present banged their hands on the table, gearing up for attack. This was indeed still China's territory. There was no reason for the Chinese to raise their voice since they were already in the right, but they couldn't help it, and everyone started talking at the same time, arguing about who was the bigger warmonger, China or Japan. After several rounds of wine, the consensus was that war should be avoided between China and Japan. Like the saying goes, "Peace is to be treasured"; naturally war is no day at the beach. The price of war is loss of blood, sacrifice, and deeper and deeper hatred. In order to prevent the Chinese surrounding him from getting too worked up, the Japanese man said that ever since the first Sino-Japanese War in 1895, when China lost miserably to Japan, the Chinese people had been longing to avenge the gross injustice of their past. Japan, however, had absolutely no intention of fighting—even if they did, their main opponent would never be China. The Japanese army's imaginary enemy was Russia, while the Japanese navy's imaginary enemy was America. As far as Japan was concerned, China was barely even worth wasting their time on. To his surprise, the Japanese guest's contemptuous attitude toward China once again left most of the Chinese at the table extremely uncomfortable. The man sitting next to Ding reminded the overconfident Japanese man to be careful; for the time being Japan might very well be the stronger of the two countries, but China's population and land mass were both several times greater. If in the end these two countries were to come to blows, China would, at the very least, utterly exhaust its tiny eastern neighbor.

Taking the night train back to Nanjing, Ding Wenyu made sure he had an ample supply of Chinese and foreign newspapers in his suitcase to relieve his boredom. He rarely ever read the paper, so even though most of the newspapers in his suitcase were old, he devoured them with great pleasure. As soon as he finished with each page, he would immediately toss it out the train window. The whole train ride went by with him reading his newspapers and throwing them out the window—how he relished the swooshing sound of newspapers being whisked away in the wind! Ever since he had fallen for Yuyuan, Ding Wenyu had been slow to pay heed to anything not directly related to his love for her.

Everything that happened in the world around him seemingly had nothing to do with him.

Then, for no apparent reason, the train was held up for some time just as it was nearing Suzhou station. The car suddenly became very stuffy, and Ding Wenyu opened his window to stick his head out. The train looked like a long, frozen insect quietly lying on the tracks. No one made any kind of announcement explaining the reason for the delay. Starting from the front, a track worker walked alongside the train, tapping the wheels with a small hammer as he went. The worker held a lantern in his other hand, and a ring of glowing yellow light rocked back and forth, following his body as he walked along the tracks. As the light shone on a wall not far from Ding, he suddenly noticed a huge advertisement painted on the wall. The ad, which featured a picture of a thin, slightly upturned moustache, was for Japanese Jintan, or Medicinal Breath Mints; back then you could see these posted in virtually every city in China.

Anti-Japanese sentiment was at an all-time high, and all around people were spontaneously boycotting Japanese goods, but even so, Japanese products still somehow managed to sneak into the Chinese market. Ding Wenyu had just read an article in the newspaper calling for a full boycott of Japanese goods. However, in the same day's paper he also saw a large advertisement for the Osaka-based Morishita Medicinal Breath Mint Corporation's "lucky drawing sweepstakes." Shanghai's *Shenbao* actually continued running ads for the Morishita Medicinal Breath Mint Corporation all the way up until July 7, when the Marco Polo Bridge Incident occurred.

A blinding light approached, followed by a rumbling sound that roared past—the whole time, Ding's train had been waiting for this other train to pass. Indeed, shortly after the other train scurried by, Ding's train started up again. The date was June 30, 1937, but, to be precise, July 1 was just a few minutes away. July 1937 has a special place in Chinese history. Sitting on that night train, Ding Wenyu wasn't in the least bit drowsy—and he still had not the faintest awareness of the impending war. Sitting on the train at that moment, he couldn't restrain his longing for Yuyuan. The moment she came into his mind, Ding Wenyu was filled with a warm, loving feeling. Summer break was just around the corner, and all Ding Wenyu was concerned with was the necessity of figuring out a way to see Yuyuan sometime during the coming vacation.

Chapter Seven

I

The reason Ding Wenyu had had to rush back to Nanjing was that his students had their final exam on July 2. As soon as that exam was finished, school would be out for summer recess. Because of the tense and unstable political situation, students were in no mood to study, so the school authorities had no choice but to use examinations as a way to straighten them out and maintain discipline. The yearly college entrance exams were about to begin, and from the registration numbers it was apparent that there would be many more applicants than in previous years. At least this showed that while on the one hand students seemed in no mood to study, both the kids and their parents still hoped that they would have ample opportunity to pursue a higher education even in these chaotic times. As the famous saying goes, "All under heaven is lowly; only scholarly pursuits are of a higher order." The university was the one place that seemed to constantly attract the young people—the classroom was still a pure, sacred land of almost religious significance.

Because examinations were mandatory, the school administration not only had to maintain a tight grip on students at the test sites but also had equally stringent requests for the teachers proctoring the exams. The administration organized a small team of proctors precisely for this purpose; like a group of street policemen trying to catch a thief, they circled around the test sites in search of little cheaters.

Ding Wenyu always had a relatively half-assed attitude toward exams; loads of students registered for his classes precisely because they wouldn't have to worry too much about tests. Ding Wenyu never once took grading exams seriously; he simply piled them up and gave out marks according to his own random formula. The highest grade Ding usually gave was a 90 and the lowest grade would be a 70. Naturally the first exam on the top of the pile would get a 90; Ding would then subtract two points from each of the following tests until he got down to 70, at which point he would start all over again. His preposterous grading method was always a big joke around campus, but Ding Wenyu was never concerned with what other people might think—even if they were all laughing at him behind his back. He felt that since taking exams was not the objective of an education, there was no reason to use them as a means to measure his students. Test scores could never truly represent the level of a student's performance. Because he was a big-name professor, the school administration's hands were tied. During the final exam, a small team of proctors came to his test site to catch cheaters. The team was supposed to deal with students, not teachers; Ding Wenyu, however, waved his cane in anger, ordering them to leave immediately. One of the proctors presented Ding with the university president's orders. An adamant Ding Wenyu told the proctors: "Stop trying to scare me with orders from the president! It's too hot for this nonsense! I'll tell you what, I'll give you an exam to take back to the president and let *him* try his luck!"

Knowing Ding Wenyu's stubborn temperament, the university president didn't push the issue. Big-name professors were like walking advertisements for the university, and the president didn't want to lose a talented member of the faculty—so he had no choice but to look the other way. On the Generalissimo's recommendation, the Nationalist government was preparing to hold a large-scale conference at Lushan to which notables from all fields were invited to have free discussions on state affairs. As a famous professor, Ding Wenyu was on the invitation list. To have one of their professors on this list was a great honor for the university. One after another, colleges and universities used the number of people on their faculty who were invited to this Lushan Conference to boost their prestige. Spending summer vacations at Lushan to get away from the scorching heat had always been enough to make people jealous. Since the Nationalist government had established their capital in Nanjing, July retreats to Lushan had become the rule. In the blistering Nanjing summers, virtually all the various government organs moved southeast to get their work done at this cool and scenic summer resort; Lushan was transformed into the Nanjing government's temporary palace. Top figures from each of the various government departments came by land, air, and sea, rushing to Lushan like a flock of migratory birds. On July 5, 1937, officials at the temporary summer government offices officially went to work at Lushan. The Executive Yuan held its first commemorative activity there; it was chaired by Chiang Kai-shek, who also gave a speech at the meeting entitled "The Issue of Chinese Education."

On July 9, Ding Wenyu boarded a direct steamer to Jiujiang, which lies not far from Lushan. On board the steamer were numerous people on their way to the Lushan Conference. A few of the passengers knew Ding and jabbered on endlessly the moment they caught sight of him. Although everyone had already gotten wind of the conflict two days earlier at the Marco Polo Bridge, also known as the July Seventh Incident, none of the people on board seemed to realize its seriousness. Naturally, they were even less likely to grasp the fact that this conflict was actually the official prelude to what would turn into an eight-year War of Resistance. Ever since the Mukden Incident in 1931, there had been not a moment's pause in Japan's incessant provocation of China. The Chinese people were numb; all they had left was hatred. They knew that if things kept going this way, a terrible war was only a matter of time. At first it was fairly common not to even take the July Seventh Incident to heart; most people didn't even bother bringing it up during discussions. It wasn't until July 9 that reports on the Marco Polo Bridge Incident started appearing in newspapers, and even then most people didn't read the early accounts.

The weather in Nanjing was just starting to get to the sweltering point; it wasn't until everyone boarded the steamer that they got a taste of the gentle river breeze. The steamship was moored at the river harbor as waves of wind came in, blowing over the passengers—but the heat was inescapable; even the river breeze was hot. It was just past one o'clock in the afternoon and the sun was glaring, flooding the docked steamship with its burning rays for what seemed like an eternity. As soon as passengers boarded the ship they felt as if they had entered a sizzling, stuffy steam pot. People naturally couldn't bear the heat in their cabins and all scurried down to the deck. Everyone stared impatiently at their watches, hoping that the steamship would hurry up and leave the port—the departure time had already passed and the roaring engine had been running for some time, but the ship simply refused to move. The longer the passengers waited, the more frustrated they became. Finally they began to dish out all of their complaints to the ship hands on deck. The deck was no wonderful place either—the open portions were too sunny and the shady areas were too muggy. Most of the passengers were VIPs and were not used to having to put up with such heat. Ultimately all of their manners went out the window; some of the men took off their long gowns, which made them indistinguishable from everyday workers. Others simply took off their shirts and, without even bothering to find out the asking price, called for the dockside vendors to send up palm-leaf fans. The women were also unbearably hot, soaked in sweat. Their runny makeup was unbearable to look at—it didn't take long at all for each of their pretty embroidered handkerchiefs to be sopping with perspiration. There was no end to everyone's complaints. They all rushed around the deck like a swarm of headless flies, as if it was the end of the world. Ding Wenyu's clothes were also drenched to the point that they needed to be wrung out. He was wearing pants and a long-sleeved, white silk shirt. Nearing his wit's end, Ding looked like a crow flapping its wings as he endlessly waved his black folding fan.

When the reason for the delay finally got out, it must have gone around the deck a hundred times. It was all because of a certain bigwig who was supposed to be on this boat to Jiujiang; although the departure time had long passed, there was still no sign of this man's car. Some people on deck said that this big shot was none other than Wang Jingwei, chair of the Executive Yuan; others said it was He Yingqin. And then there were some who held it was Gu Zhutong; everyone got worked up arguing over the identity of this mystery passenger. Nobody seemed to want the others on board to think that they weren't in the know. On the steamer there was no shortage of insiders when it came to local gossip, and it did-n't take long for a few of them to announce the impossibility of Wang Jingwei being the mystery passenger. Apparently someone had irrefutable proof that Wang Jingwei and his wife Chen Bijun, along with Chu Minyi and Zeng Zhongming, had boarded the *S. S. Founder* to Jiujiang several days earlier. Suppositions that the passenger was He Yingqin or Gu Zhutong were also refuted; He and Gu were both widely renowned figures in the Nationalist military, and there was no way they would put up with the torturously sluggish pace of a steamship. If they were going to go to Lushan they would without question fly there, just like Chiang Kai-shek.

The steamer waited a full three and a half hours before it finally left. As soon as the mystery passenger's black car pulled up to the dock, an attendant rushed over with an umbrella. The passengers on deck could only make out the man's black pants and short, fat, stumpy legs as he leisurely made his way out of the car. The attendant holding the umbrella was a tall, skinny guy; he kept himself bent like a shrimp over the big shot as if he was afraid someone would catch a glimpse of the mystery man's sweet little mug. The big shot managed to keep his face hidden beneath the umbrella, and even after he made it onto the deck, no one on board was able to figure out who he was. Of course a couple of people were able to sneak a glance at him, but when asked they were still unable to identify him. This meant that those few lucky witnesses were pretty green in official circles; at the same time it proved that this mystery man wasn't as famous as everyone had suspected. There were simply too many big officials in Nanjing; it was no easy task to recognize each and every one of them. Most of the people on board were pretty irritated; because of this guy under the umbrella, everyone on the steel deck had suffered more than three hours of torture.

"How are those officials supposed to be able to be concerned with the woes of the people? What happened today should be enough to prove this point," one passenger expressed with a sigh of frustration. The vast majority of those on board were fairly well known, and just like the late-coming mystery passenger, they were on their way to Lushan for the big meeting—naturally they were more than a bit agitated at having been kept waiting.

"Don't tell me that if this guy hadn't shown up they would have left us baking alive out here on the deck like a bunch of braised ducks?"

As soon as the steamer set off, the river breeze flooded the deck and the heat subsided dramatically. Suddenly relieved, everyone rushed into their cabins to wash their faces and change their clothes. Although there were a handful of washrooms on board, they were suddenly crowded as everyone rushed in at the same time. Luckily there was an unlimited supply of hot water; some quickly doused themselves, knowing that there would still be ample water to take more leisurely showers later on. Ding Wenyu lost track of how much he had sweated, but there was no doubt about the atrocious body odor that lingered around him. Being crammed into that public shower with a dozen other bare behinds was, it goes without saying, a kind of indescribable humiliation for Ding. One guy started screaming anxiously after his shower when he discovered that someone else had run off wearing his clean undershirt. The second he yelled, everyone rushed over to make sure that somebody else didn't mistakenly put on *their* clothes. The guy who had had his shirt taken wasn't about to let things go and started using all kinds of foul language to curse the man who took his shirt. His vulgar cursing attracted the attention of the people outside the shower room, who all rushed in to see the excitement. The shower room door opened, and a stark naked Ding Wenyu turned around to discover he and the others in the shower had already become the center of everyone's attention. Far off, there were even a few female passengers who shyly turned to steal a glance.

"Who would want to steal a lousy undershirt? Someone must have put it on by mistake."

This little incident was smoothed over when the guy who had his shirt stolen was forced to put his own dirty, wet clothes back on and angrily stomped out of the shower room, cursing under his breath. Ding Wenyu also managed to get through his half-assed shower. It was still rather hot inside the cabins, and after changing into a set of fresh clothes Ding Wenyu went back up to the deck. The ship was running full steam ahead on its western course and a strong river wind whistled over the deck, giving Ding Wenyu, who was nearing the end of his rope after his frustrating bout with the heat, a chance to get himself back together. While on deck, Ding Wenyu noticed that the women's shower room was also a chaotic mess. The revolving spring door didn't stop for a moment, and as it opened and closed one could see glimpses of bare arms inside. A little girl intentionally left the door open after her shower; she held the swinging door open with all her might and playfully yelled something to someone inside. The alarmed screams of women came from inside the shower room, leaving the little girl frozen there in shock; she had no idea what she had done wrong.

The sun was getting ready to set behind a far-off mountain, and everyone came out to the deck as the remains of the summer day held on. The wide-open surface of the river turned a blood red under the glow of the dying sun. Ding Wenyu was already fully prepared to admire the sunset; he put on a pair of sunglasses and stood like a proud peacock on the upper deck against the railing. From time to time, the steamer would pass a few small wooden rowboats. They kept fairly close to the riverbanks, and the massive waves caused by the steamer rocked them high and low, causing the terrified boatmen to adjust their rudders frantically to avoid being turned over. The men on each and every one of the little rowboats seemed to have the same startled reaction as they passed into Ding Wenyu's field of view. Ding Wenyu noticed that the vast majority of these small vessels were fishing boats; he could tell because most of them had nets on board, and they all seemed to have a raven-colored cormorant perched on the bow.

The steamer passed by a naked beach with a few scattered and bare willow trees; beneath these trees were seven or eight water buffaloes of varying sizes. A handful of small birds and a flock of crows glided up and down over the beach with the hooting sound of the steamer's spout. Ding Wenyu was just beginning to wonder whether or not anyone lived on this desolate shore when he suddenly caught sight of two peasant girls wearing red, unlined jackets. They were taking a rest under the shade of one of the willow trees. If it had not been for the eye-catching color of their jackets, Ding probably never would have seen them. The beach stretched on for quite a way, and Ding Wenyu noticed that the beach and riverbank started to separate as a narrow waterway ran between them. He even saw a tiny boat floating down this waterway. On shore at the far end of the beach was a small village and a group of naked little boys who were bathing in the muddy river water. They playfully horsed around as they washed; some of them were in the water while others stood on shore, futilely throwing stones at the passing steamer. Not far off was a large stone jetty where a group of women and young girls standing in the water with their pants rolled up washed silkworm cocoons. As the steamer passed by it sent out a series of huge waves, forcing the women to scurry back onto the jetty.

The summer sunset was extraordinarily peaceful; no longer would the threatening heat ravage the passengers. Everything seemed to give off an aura of calm; the Marco Polo Bridge Incident, which was still being felt up north, had yet to have any effect on this place. The steamer followed the main river path, suddenly veering left then quickly veering right; it never strayed far from the shore. Ding Wenyu was completely taken by the beautiful coastal scene as they went by. The scenic vistas on that bright day suddenly drew Ding's mind to Yuyuan. In an instant, longing for her consumed him and Ding seemed unable to think of anything else. He imagined how wonderful it would be if Yuyuan could be with him on his trip to Lushan; if only she were there to keep him company during this lonely journey. This unrealistic daydream led him to heave a deep sigh, and he lost himself in a moment of melancholy.

If it hadn't been for his growling stomach, Ding might very well have stayed there on the deck, reveling in his depression. Just as the curtain of night was about to descend, Ding Wenyu realized that the people who had been standing around him on deck had already been replaced by a whole different group of passengers. Ding decided he should go to the dining room to get himself something to eat. Just as he turned toward the stairway, he caught sight of the rear profile of a woman who looked just like Yuyuan. At first he couldn't help tensing up, but almost immediately he realized the utter impossibility of it being her and wrote the whole thing off, figuring that he simply must have gotten the wrong person. Things that good just don't happen in this world—Ding assumed that such good fortune could never be his. He stared blankly at the woman, refusing to believe his own eyes. But sometimes miracles really do happen. Standing not far away from him was indeed Yuyuan. There was no doubt about it. Ding Wenyu was flat out dumbstruck. He was taken completely off guard by this unexpected miracle. Yuyuan stood but a few paces away, silently staring at Ding; it was as if she was waiting for him to come over and greet her.

II

Yuyuan had noticed Ding Wenyu some time earlier—before they even set sail she had caught sight of the ever-eccentric Ding Wenyu amid the crowd of people on deck. Instantly she realized that this trip with her father to the Lushan Conference was destined to lead to some rather out-of-the-ordinary events. Just like Ding, she never imagined that they would end up on the same boat. Now the problem was clearly hanging over them; since they were both there, it was inevitable that something would happen between them. Yuyuan knew that Ding Wenyu wasn't going to let this opportunity slip through his fingers. Although she remained unmoved after all of Ding's letters and brazen attempts to pursue her, Yuyuan knew that he was not the kind of man who was so easy to resist. When Ding Wenyu finally noticed her, Yuyuan didn't bother taking advantage of his moment of shock by trying to run away. She simply wasn't willing to be the first one to make contact. Since they had run into each other, she didn't feel there was any reason to hide. She stood calmly on the deck against the setting sun with the river breeze blowing through her hair and skirt and tried her best to pretend that she had also just noticed Ding Wenyu. During that initial moment of contact, Ding Wenyu was the one who was taken off guard. This pleasant surprise went so far beyond anything that he could have possibly anticipated that he completely lost himself—he stood there in shock, forgetting to even say hello. His awkward hesitation also started to make Yuyuan feel ill at ease.

"I can't believe this is real," Ding Wenyu stammered.

Facing such an inappropriate greeting, Yuyuan was left speechless. She at once feared he would go off the deep end, while at the same time she secretly relished his quirky antics. In Yuyuan's mind Ding Wenyu was not someone who lived in the practical world. He looked absolutely ridiculous as he stood there with his stunned gaze and his mute, gaping mouth. Even at this moment, Ding Wenyu still was somewhat suspicious as to whether everything that was happening was real—he knew it couldn't be a mistake, yet he still couldn't help but be somewhat hesitant. He walked over to Yuyuan and boldly gestured to shake her hand. Yuyuan laughed as she looked at Ding's outstretched hand but refused to respond in kind.

When Ding Wenyu finally came around to the reality that was standing before him, he turned to look around and said, "The old man in heaven must have really been looking out for me to give me such a wonderful opportunity to see you! Miss Ren, it's simply amazing that something so extraordinary like this could happen!"

Yuyuan was in no mood to listen to his insane ramblings and re-sponded with a flat question: "Mr. Ding, are you also on your way to the Lushan Conference?"

"And to think that I came close to committing a great sin," Ding Wenyu answered with a sigh. "When I first received that conference in-vitation I didn't even want to go. Imagine what a terrible, terrible mis-take it would have been if I hadn't come!"

The 1937 Lushan Conference was of unprecedented scale; famous scholars from all fields were invited as guests of the government to pres-ent their personal opinions on the present circumstances. Ding Wenyu and Ren Bojin, whom Yuyuan was accompanying, could only qualify as two of the most common participants when compared with the other celebrity guests. This conference was generally viewed as a move on the part of the Nationalist government to truly listen to the voices of the people. It was also a concrete measure to prepare for leading the coun-try in the coming War of Resistance. On May 27 of that same year, be-fore his vacation period was even over, the Generalissimo took the lead and made an early arrival at Lushan. During his third day there, Chiang formally ended his vacation and reported back to work. On June 4 one of the key players in the Xi'an Incident, Yang Hucheng, went up to Lushan to call on the Generalissimo, as did Zhou Enlai, who was then serving as the chairman of the CCP delegation. The Nationalists' grow-ing resolution to resist Japan was becoming clearer by the day. One month later, on July 4, the first recruits of the Lushan Summer Training Corps formally began their instruction; more than 2,900 people took part in this two-week training program, including middle school princi-pals, several directors in the field of education, and various other ad-ministrators. After the term was over, Chiang Kai-shek personally awarded each participant with a diploma. Some of the scholars who had come to Lushan for the conference had the opportunity to witness the graduation ceremony; it was quite a grand affair. Under the glaring sun, the Generalissimo gave his famous lecture, "On National Reconstruc-tion." The Marco Polo Bridge Incident, which was still fresh in every-one's minds, had a huge influence on Generalissimo Chiang Kai-shek's resolution to go to war—the so-called final juncture had already arrived. The Generalissimo passionately expounded on the serious consequences of the incident.

On the day of Chiang's address, the scorching sun was beating down, and among the educators standing in the audience, more than a few fainted from the heat. Ding Wenyu and a handful of famous figures who were in town for the conference were invited to stand with the Generalissimo on the open-air rostrum, but they also could hardly bear the heat. It was a good thing that Ding was able to lean against the wall behind him—although he was exhausted and his vision was blurry as if he were in a drunken stupor, at least he didn't have to worry about falling down. What really won Ding Wenyu's admiration that day was the fact that although the Generalissimo was also standing directly under the glaring sun, as Chiang lectured in his thick Ningbo accent, he came off extraordinarily spirited and lively. He waved his arms as he addressed the graduates, becoming increasingly impassioned as he spoke. Ding Wenyu had no clue that, due to the Marco Polo Bridge Incident, an unavoidable, full-scale war between China and Japan was just around the corner. Because Yuyuan was there with him during this trip to Lushan, Ding Wenyu had nothing but love on his mind—not for a minute did he seriously consider the impending plight of his country. Ever since he had run into Yuyuan on the steamer, he had spent virtually every waking moment thinking about being with her; he ended up not getting enough sleep for the remainder of his river voyage. Other passengers couldn't sleep because of the rumbling noises of the steam engine; Ding's insomnia, however, was caused by the excitement of knowing that Yuyuan was right there on the very same boat with him.

During this trip, Ding Wenyu had an opportunity to be with Yuyuan for twelve full days; it was easy for their relationship to take a major leap forward during that period. From the looks of it, the old man in heaven really was going to let Ding Wenyu have his way this time. Before this, opportunities for Ding Wenyu to see Yuyuan had been rare—barring the fact that Ding had already written her countless letters, there still a huge divide between them. Their relationship had been nothing more than idle talk in letters, in which Ding made most of his painstaking pursuits. Yuyuan had long since grown accustomed to Ding's passionate words and usually didn't even give them a second thought. When face to face, the two of them were like a pair of soldiers engaged in hand-to-hand combat: everything changed instantly; everything was now straight and to the point; what was going to happen suddenly seemed inevitable.

Yuyuan was a bit worried that Ding Wenyu would get out of line, but was unsure just what exactly he would try to pull. While on the steamer, Ding Wenyu conducted himself completely within the boundaries of propriety; he even expressed his desire to go and pay his respects to Ren Bojin. Never expecting Ding Wenyu to be on the same boat, Old Ren was very surprised. Adding to Ren's surprise was the fact that Ding was accompanied by his own daughter Yuyuan; for a moment the old man was at a complete loss as to how to respond. After his visit with Old Ren was over, Yuyuan once again saw Ding out. Ding Wenyu was a bit reluctant to part, but Yuyuan paid him no heed; once they were outside the cabin, she turned and walked away.

First thing the next morning, Ding Wenyu was standing in the corridor outside Yuyuan's cabin door waiting for her. Just before they parted the day before, Ding had asked Yuyuan to get up early the next morning to watch the sunrise with him. Dawn came and went, but still no sign of Yuyuan. Even though Ding Wenyu was burning with anxiety, he dared not venture into the cabin to wake her. While he was waiting, he saw Old Ren leave the cabin, probably on his way to the dining room for breakfast. Ding didn't dare say hello; instead he quickly ducked out of sight. Only a long while after the old man had returned to his cabin did Yuyuan finally show her face. Ding couldn't help but rush up to greet her. He didn't dare complain about her being late; instead he simply flashed her a foolish smile. Yuyuan seemed to know that he had been waiting for her and told him how stubborn he was. "I never promised you that I'd be able to get up on time yesterday," Yuyuan teasingly said before asking Ding whether or not he had eaten breakfast. She hadn't yet brushed her hair, and it only took one glance to realize that she had just crawled out of bed. When Ding Wenyu saw her like that she suddenly became even more dear to him; it was as if he was now somehow even closer to the real Yuyuan. Yuyuan went back into her room to straighten up a bit. When she came out, she told Ding that her father had already eaten, so the two of them set out together toward the dining room. Breakfast consisted of coffee, milk, and a roll. Yuyuan wasn't used to eating this sort of food for breakfast and laughed as she asked Ding if this was the kind of stuff he lived on while he was studying abroad.

The way Yuyuan carried herself was much more relaxed and poised than Ding Wenyu could have imagined. In the past she had done whatever she could to avoid his harassment, but since she now had no way out, she suddenly became rather liberal in her dealings with him. The buzzing electric fan in the dining room blew the fragrance of Yuyuan's freshly applied perfume over to Ding Wenyu's nose. Unable to control himself, Ding Wenyu let his crazy, lovesick ramblings begin to sneak out. In a stern tone, Yuyuan told him that if he refused to behave himself and made any more improper remarks, she wouldn't have anything more to do with him for the remainder of the trip. She didn't seem to be against spending time with Ding, but she didn't find his blatant flirtations the least bit flattering. She warned Ding that he would have to control himself if he planned on maintaining their friendship.

As far as Ding Wenyu was concerned, Yuyuan's stipulation was more than agreeable—she had already granted him more leeway than he ever could have hoped for. For the next few days Ding Wenyu indeed carried himself like a true gentleman. He followed close behind her, saying whatever he could to make her happy and get on her good side while at the same time being especially careful not to act too rashly. Ding's only fear was that he might do something to disappoint Yuyuan. When they arrived at Lushan, they ended up staying not far from each other, at the guest facilities of an American-run school. When Ding opened the front window in his room, he could see the small building where Yuyuan and her father were staying. Yuyuan's only real obligation during her trip was to look after her elderly father. After they arrived at Lushan, Old Ren was busy entertaining the countless stream of people who came to call on him, leaving Yuyuan with more time on her hands than she knew what to do with. In the end, she couldn't resist Ding Wenyu's incessant invitations and went with him on a few scenic walks around the resort mountain. Before long, the two of them had visited virtually every famous scenic destination in the area, so Ding Wenyu took out several books about Lushan at a local library and led Yuyuan on a quest to find all the places talked about in those books that they hadn't yet visited. The two of them ended up having a wonderful time. By the end of their long mountain trek, Ding Wenyu was utterly exhausted, and Yuyuan started complaining that she couldn't take any more walking.

As long as there was a way to get out of those conference meetings, Ding Wenyu did whatever he had to to wiggle his way out of attending. It was a good thing that the meetings were run by people nothing at all like those shoddy university teachers who took attendance before each class. And although the conference was not canceled on account of the sudden development of the Marco Polo Bridge Incident, it was easy to tell that none of the high-ranking government leaders had conferences and meetings on their minds. On July 11, the Minister of the Board of Military Affairs, He Yingqin, made the announcement that the entire military was already operating in a state of war. A brutal, large-scale war was literally breathing down China's neck. Both the Generalissimo, Chiang Kai-shek, and Wang Jingwei gave speeches in which they took an uncompromising stance on the current state of affairs; these speeches meant that that the Chinese government would no longer give in to the Japanese military's overbearing demands. The Nationalist government, which had consistently taken a stance of appeasement toward Japan, had already made preparations for all possible scenarios. If when the time came there was no alternative, the Nationalists were now resolved to go to war and use their lives, their blood, to uphold the sanctity and honor of their country. Countless people were filled with apprehension about the future and fate of China. No matter what people were talking about, often halfway through conversations the topic would naturally drift to the most pressing issue of the day—how to wage war effectively against Japan. Everyone was talking about it, each person stubbornly sticking to his or her own opinion. People in academic circles held to the view that even if war broke out, all schools and universities should continue as normal. Representatives from some groups called for an immediate declaration of war, while others advocated a more conservative, sober-minded approach. Although the Nationalists had already taken an unprecedented stance against the Japanese, people still seemed to have doubts as to whether this was truly the beginning of an all-out war.

Ding Wenyu and Yuyuan were like a pair of truant school children. They also talked about the Marco Polo Bridge Incident and discussed the possibility of war with Japan, but these were just mentioned off the cuff as they enjoyed all the scenic spots around Lushan. The beautiful resort areas on the mountain were filled with pairs of young and energetic university students on their summer vacation. Whenever these students stopped to take a breather from their mountain hike, they almost instantly became wrapped up in serious political debates. The young students agreed almost unanimously that they should immediately fight back against Japan—even the sedan chair bearer they hired felt that they should go to war against the Japanese. As soon as someone even mentioned the atrocities committed by Japan in northern China, everyone was immediately blistering with anger. They craved an opportunity to teach those damn Japs a good lesson. Manchuria had already been lost, and northern China was in grave danger; if China didn't resist, its days would be numbered. Two of the students there actually had taken one of Ding Wenyu's classes; they quietly gossiped as they stared at Ding Wenyu's and Yuyuan's retreating silhouettes. Both Ding Wenyu and Yuyuan lost themselves in the moment—especially Yuyuan. Although she continuously reminded herself that she needed to maintain an appropriate distance when she was with him, in reality she was already starting to lose control of herself. She knew all too well what that pair of students was gossiping about.

Never before had Yuyuan spent so much time alone sightseeing with someone of the opposite sex. Her marriage to Yu Kerun had been too rushed; just thinking about it, she could feel the pangs of regret tugging at her. Before they were married, Yu Kerun rarely had the time to go anywhere with her, and the few times that he did Yuyuan always dragged her girlfriends along, making it a group activity. Then after they got married, Yu Kerun seemed to feel that there was no need for him to go out of his way to entertain her. His attention and energy didn't seem directed toward her; if he was going to go sightseeing, he'd always secretly take some other girl. Yuyuan had seen many photos that Yu Kerun had taken of these other women. Yu had a fancy German camera, and his skill as a photographer wasn't half bad. Whenever Yuyuan looked through his photos, he would tell her that one day he would take *her* picture too; not once were these promises fulfilled. People never treasure those things that come easy. Yuyuan had realized long ago that, since day one, Yu Kerun had viewed their marriage as being a bit too rushed. He was obviously the kind of man who should not be subject to the bonds of matrimony. He was married to Yuyuan, but his heart wasn't. Marriage didn't draw them together; just the opposite, it pushed them even further apart.

Yuyuan realized that her actions were somewhat out of line; she had more than ample opportunity to refuse Ding Wenyu, but she didn't. Not only did she not push him away, but when she went out with him she actually had a wonderful time. The two of them indulged themselves in fun, completely forgetting about the rest of the world. She seemed to return to the carefree days of her youth; they chatted and giggled, pushing all their worries to the back of their minds. Trekking up the mountain was not easy going, and Ding Wenyu hired a sedan chair to carry Yuyuan. The sedan coolies mistook Yuyuan for Ding's wife, and as the sedan chair creaked along they continually warned her: "Be careful! Sit tight, Madame." Yuyuan didn't seem to mind them calling her Madame; she actually found it somewhat amusing. Ding Wenyu, on the other hand, was a bit worried; he was scared that this misunderstanding would upset her and she would refuse to go sightseeing with him anymore out of spite. The two of them played to their hearts' content; Yuyuan loved to travel and wanted to see everything. Ding Wenyu gleefully followed close behind Yuyuan; he was so elated that he decided to hire a second sedan chair so each of them had their own. Carried by the sedan coolies, they went nonstop to each of the main scenic areas. Ding Wenyu really went overboard by skipping out of too many conference meetings. There were of course a handful he couldn't get out of and had to attend to say a few perfunctory remarks, leaving an idle Yuyuan to while the time away by herself. Stranded in her room, Yuyuan longed to get some rest but couldn't seem to fall asleep. She tried to read but couldn't get through a single passage. When she thought back to all the things that had happened over the past few days, she felt that she had acted completely out of line, but at the same time she also felt a rush of excitement.

III

The Ding Wenyu who spent all his time writing endless love letters to Yuyuan and the real life Ding Wenyu seemed to be two completely different people. That overly passionate, eternally off-center Ding Wenyu couldn't have been more compassionate and caring in the way he treated Yuyuan. This was the first time that Yuyuan had felt such loving care from a man—it was so real, so tangible, and it came so easily. Yuyuan suddenly realized that this was the kind of attention she had needed all along. Women always long for the affections and love of men—especially married women. Once they are married, they are much more likely to feel neglected and lonely—just as the rich are more keenly aware of how difficult life without money would be than the poor. Without consciously realizing it, Yuyuan seemed to be trying to make up for everything of which she had been deprived. It was clear that spending time with Ding Wenyu was playing with fire, but playing with fire is in itself quite an interesting game; with danger comes excitement.

One night as the two of them were strolling under the light of the silvery moon, Ding Wenyu heaved a deep sigh as he wondered out loud whether things would have turned out differently if the two of them had met earlier. Yuyuan was already used to paying no heed to these rather provocative questions. She knew that she should use her silence to deal with Ding Wenyu—silence is always the most effective weapon. On this occasion, however, there was nothing stopping Ding's words from going straight to her heart; Yuyuan couldn't help but be moved. Actually, she herself had, on more than one occasion, pondered all kinds of possible scenarios. The one thing that Yuyuan couldn't figure out was why she couldn't bring herself to hate Ding Wenyu. That didn't go just for her—no matter how much everyone in the Ren family might badmouth Ding, never once did they feel that he was a bad person. Whenever Yuyuan's big sister Yuchan mentioned Ding, she'd instantly turn red—she couldn't seem to help always sticking up for him and saying all kinds of nice things to cover up his defects. Ding Wenyu's unbridled pursuit of Yuyuan and her sister had caused quite a commotion at the Ren house. And although everyone thought that the entire affair was out of line, they seemed to spend even more time talking about how utterly ridiculous the whole thing was.

"You won't forget me one day like you forgot about my sister?" Yuyuan asked.

Ding Wenyu was caught somewhat off guard by this question. He had indeed long since forgotten about Yuchan. The moment Yuyuan jogged his memory, that long-lost, immature boy he'd once been suddenly reappeared before Ding's eyes. This time, however, Ding was completely unmoved. That boy of his youth was gone forever, an utter stranger to the now mature Ding Wenyu—likewise, the love he felt for Yuyuan was mature. Ding couldn't understand why Yuyuan would want to bring up her sister in such an untimely way. Taking notice of Ding Wenyu's awkward silence, she knew that he was upset and tried to smooth things over by saying, "Don't worry, I won't blame you if you one day forget me."

Completely enamored, Ding Wenyu assured Yuyuan, "You've already become a part of me—even if I should forget myself, I could still never forget you."

These words came off sounding nauseatingly pretentious, but for some reason Yuyuan was actually a bit moved by them. She knew that Ding Wenyu genuinely liked her. She had already read more than enough of his nauseating words in his letters, but to hear them coming directly from his mouth was indeed something different. She couldn't help comparing him to Yu Kerun; although this might not have been the most appropriate thing to do, she couldn't help herself. Yu Kerun, who always seemed to have a rather high opinion of himself, never really worried about anyone else. He only wanted people to like him, but never learned how to reach out to others. Ding Wenyu was different. Whether or not people liked him was rather inconsequential—all that seemed to matter was whether *he* knew what he liked, and Ding Wenyu couldn't have been more clear about that. He was set on Yuyuan. Without giving a second thought to the consequences, he pursued her with a relentless passion. When she was with Ding Wenyu, Yuyuan felt as if she were living in a fantasy world like the utopian Peach Blossom Spring. Coming out of Ding's mouth, virtually any old topic could instantly take on a fresh, new meaning. Ding Wenyu had seen a lot in his life and told her about all kinds of things she had never even heard of. The outside world was simply too large, and Yuyuan knew so little. The tediousness of military life had long begun to wear thin for Yuyuan and she suddenly realized that the best road to take would be to start over as a university student. Joining the army was an obvious mistake. Signing up for the military was not necessarily the only way that a young person could repay their country—female confidential secretaries like herself were not at all essential. The second she mentioned her plan, she won Ding Wenyu's instant approval.

"Miss Ren, if you want to, you could study abroad. I'll go with you." Ding Wenyu spoke with the utmost sincerity—one could tell that there were no ulterior motives hidden in his naïve proposal.

"Study abroad?"

"Why not? After living abroad for all those years, I can tell you that there's nothing really fantastic about living overseas, but compared to our situation at home, it's still a better idea. I think Europe would suit you best. Then again, there is the possibility that war might break out in Europe. With this in mind, you are probably better off going to America." It seemed from Ding Wenyu's tone that the whole thing was already decided. He told Yuyuan that he would write some letters to his friends in the States as soon as he got back to Nanjing.

It didn't take more than a second for Yuyuan to realize that all this talk about foreign study was nothing more than play; if she really wanted to study abroad, it wasn't going to be that easy. First off, Yu Kerun would never agree to let her go—not unless they got a divorce. Yu Kerun's ideal for his wife's future always seemed to change. Sometimes Yu wished that Yuyuan had a career of her own and could support herself like a modern woman; other times he hoped she would just stay home and be a good housewife; and then there were times when he wanted her to steal the limelight as the mistress of some big European-style salon. Men like Yu Kerun are destined to be somewhat unsatisfied with whatever women they end up with. No one in the Ren family would agree to let her go abroad either; there was no way they would be able to rest easy with their youngest daughter left to fend for herself all alone in some foreign country. Yuyuan would naturally not go abroad with Ding Wenyu—she never even considered this possibility. During those few short days in Lushan, Yuyuan discovered that she had nothing but good feelings toward Ding. If they really were to one day go abroad and spend every day together, she was afraid that that she indeed wouldn't be able to hold out for long against his advances.

They were supposed to return to Nanjing the next day, and one of Ding Wenyu's friends tried to get Ding to take a plane with him back. This buddy had some very close ties with the military; at the time only the highest-ranking officials had the opportunity to fly. However, Ding was all too willing to sacrifice this plane ride—even if someone had *given* him a plane, he wouldn't have wanted it if it meant missing out on a chance to be with Yuyuan. He politely refused the kindness of his friend; all he wanted was to be on the same boat with Yuyuan. However, there was a mix-up when they booked their steamer tickets, and Ding Wenyu ended up on a different vessel than Ren Bojin and his daughter. Ding's ship wouldn't leave until six hours after the Rens' steamer. Ding was like a cat on a hot tin roof, restlessly running all over the place in hope of changing his ticket. Yuyuan also felt a kind of unspeakable regret; if she had known earlier, she would have encouraged him to take that plane when he had the chance. No one was willing to trade tickets with Ding, especially since he had no really pressing reason to get on the earlier boat.

In the end, when he saw Ren Bojin and his daughter off, Ding Wenyu was so upset that one would think this was an eternal good-bye. Yuyuan did her best to put up an indifferent front, even though deep down she knew that the boring journey would have been much more interesting if she had had Ding by her side. She didn't want Ding to know that she was actually just as depressed as he was. Ding Wenyu saw the Rens on board and helped them get settled in their cabin. Ren Bojin looked at his watch and urged Ding Wenyu to hurry up and go. Ding Wenyu bade a dejected good-bye to Yuyuan and her father before drooping his head and dragging himself toward the dock. Yuyuan had offered to see him off, but Ding stopped her, saying that that would only make him more upset. Yuyuan couldn't help but laugh at his overly emotional mannerisms and insisted on walking him back to the dock. By the time the two of them reached the upper deck from the Rens' cabin, the roaring steamer was already preparing to leave port; a ship hand was just untying the cordage. With a look of utter despair, Ding Wenyu stepped onto the deck, but when he turned back to take a glance at Yuyuan, he suddenly decided not to get off. His luggage was still at a hotel in Jiujiang, but it was too late to worry about luggage. Yuyuan was anxious that Ding wouldn't have time to get off the ship and began to urge him to hurry up. But with a childish tone, Ding Wenyu simply turned to her and proclaimed: "Don't try and get rid of me; even if you threw me into the river I still wouldn't go back ashore."

Ding Wenyu had actually showed up at the port hours before the steamer was scheduled to leave in an attempt to switch his ticket, but the ship was already full and the ticket attendant flatly refused him. That steamer didn't waste any time in setting out. It was docked against the current, so the second the steamer blew its whistle it was already starting to turn around. Seeing that Ding Wenyu still hadn't made any effort to get off, Yuyuan didn't push the issue. She simply asked him what he planned to do about the luggage he had left behind in his hotel. Ding Wenyu replied, "What does luggage matter when I can be with you?" Yuyuan turned red the second Ding's response reached her ears. During the past few days Yuyuan had heard more than her fair share of similar compliments from Ding, but this time for some reason she couldn't help but shudder.

Ding Wenyu felt increasingly proud of himself as he saw the port fade farther and farther into the distance. He wondered why he hadn't thought of this move earlier. Since he was now on board, buying a ticket wouldn't be a problem—after all, they weren't going to throw him into the river. Anyway, he didn't request much; all he needed was a reclining chair to sleep in and he'd be fine. Yuyuan suddenly started to worry that her father would be upset if he found out what had happened. Old Ren Bojin thought that Ding had gotten off the ship long ago; if Ding were to abruptly reappear before him, Old Ren would probably think that Ding and his daughter were trying to put one over on him. Ding Wenyu didn't see much of a problem, since the old man spent most of his time in his room. All Ding had to do was stay out of Old Ren's sight and they'd be in the clear. However, things gradually ended up out of their hands. Yuyuan seemed to continually find excuses to sneak out of their cabin, and the old man couldn't help but grow suspicious. When it finally got to the point that they could no longer conceal their secret, Old Ren didn't bother asking too many questions. He just frowned and made it clear that he knew what was going on: "Just what the hell are the two of you up to?" Once everything came out, Yuyuan spent virtually all of her time in the cabin with her father. Seeing the shilly-shallying way his daughter was behaving, Old Ren wanted to remind her that she was a married woman and tell her to start paying attention to the impression they were leaving on people. However, the second these words got to the tip of his tongue, Old Ren reluctantly swallowed them. Ren Bojin had doted on his youngest daughter ever since she was a child and knew that she would never do anything out of line. Moreover, he didn't have any true dislike for Ding Wenyu; as far as Old Ren was concerned, Ding was simply a boy who'd never grown up. The seriousness of the Marco Polo Bridge Incident filled the old man with anxiety about China's fate. With the country on the verge of disaster, the one thing Old Ren couldn't understand was how these young people could run around chasing after each other as if absolutely nothing was wrong.

Ding Wenyu was like a headless fly, continually pacing in circles not far from Yuyuan's cabin door. Although he had arranged to meet her, Ding knew that he could not go barging in; at the same time, his suspicious behavior couldn't help but grab other people's attention. Someone who knew Ding shouted out a hearty greeting that immediately gave away his whereabouts. Then there was someone else who, seeing what was going on, intentionally played a little prank on him by calling out next to Yuyuan's cabin door: "Miss Ren, Mr. Ding is waiting outside for you!" Hearing that ill-hearted prankster's call, Ding didn't know whether to run or stay—it seemed like either way he was doomed. Ren Bojin was at his wit's end; all he could do was knit his brow and tell her daughter: "Get going, you don't want to make a fool of him by standing him up."

And so the two of them took the opportunity to spend time together openly—after all, everyone seemed to know anyway. The pair chatted and giggled, never leaving each other's side. People could say and think as they wished. When dinnertime came, Ding Wenyu ordered a full table of dishes and invited Ren Bojin and his daughter both to join him. They even had German beer on board; back when Ren Bojin was studying in Japan, he had learned that German beer was the best in the world. It was rather hot, and a cold beer was a great way to cool down—the perfect thirst quencher. This old military man who had spent the better part of his life engaged in idle theorizing talked openly about the coming War of Resistance as he sipped his German beer. Old Ren could talk about this forever and never get tired but, realizing that his listeners weren't necessarily keen on the subject, he changed to a somewhat dejected tone and criticized Ding's aloofness: "Every man has a share of the responsibility for the fate of his country. Imagine what state the country would be in if all young people were like you!"

Ding Wenyu quickly explained that he was no longer a "young person"; as he spoke he flashed a gaze over at Yuyuan, whose face was decorated with a charming smile. Ding Wenyu added, "Wouldn't it be a terrible waste if we were to send an adorable girl like Yuyuan to go head to head with the Japanese." Ding was afraid that Old Ren would be upset by what he said and quickly stole a glance at the old man. Yuyuan also motioned to Ding to stop with his wisecracks. Seeing Ding Wenyu and his daughter making eyes at each other, Old Ren had no choice but to pretend he didn't notice.

The steamer went by the strategically placed Madang Mountain Fortification as it passed into Anhui province. A depression began to overcome Ding Wenyu; how he truly wished that this steamer could forever go on rumbling down the river into eternity. Yuyuan couldn't figure out why Ding suddenly got so upset and thought she must have said something to offend him. Then Ding recited: " 'Difficult it is to meet you; but more difficult still to part.' Even today when we read this poem, it does something to your heart." With these words, even Yuyuan felt somewhat carried away and began to lose control over herself. At the very least, Ding Wenyu was an interesting travel companion. Yuyuan realized that she had already gone way overboard during this trip. That's not to mention the fact that she was a married woman; even if she were single, it still would have been a bit improper to have spent all this time with Ding Wenyu. Never before had she spent so much time with a man she knew so little about. Things that she never imagined she would do, she ended up doing as if they were second nature and there were not the slightest consequences. Only after it was all over did she start to get scared. Yuyuan was willing to bet that if she were to tell her friends about this trip, they would all be utterly dumbstruck.

As the steamer approached Nanjing, Yuyuan and Ding Wenyu made a three-point deal: they agreed that after they got back to Nanjing, everything would go back to way things were; Ding could continue writing her letters, but they would see no more of each other. During their conversation Yuyuan not only accidentally revealed the fact that she had received Ding's letters, but made it clear that she had carefully read each and every one. However, by this time there was no way that Ding Wenyu was going to be satisfied by the mere fact that Yuyuan had received his letters. With good-bye just around the corner, Ding Wenyu couldn't have been more depressed—his face was filled with a pained look of desperation. Not willing to let things go, he asked, "Why can't we still see each other?" Yuyuan knew about his stubborn temper and refused to cut him even an inch of slack. Unwilling to give up so easily, Ding told Yuyuan that he knew she hated him; he said that ever since he was born people had disliked him.

Yuyuan giggled as she said, "Since you know everyone dislikes you, then you should know better than to continue pestering them." Her tone of voice as she spoke was not terribly stern, and that gave Ding just enough leeway to keep on her like a big child.

"Let's stop here," said Yuyuan. "There is no way that what happened between us will ever come to anything."

Ding Wenyu replied with utmost sincerity, "I don't care about it ever coming to anything."

IV

Returning from the cool resort of Lushan to the intense summer heat of Nanjing made Ding Wenyu feel as if he had fallen from heaven straight down to the gates of hell. Nanjing was notorious for its sweltering summers; every year there were always at least a few days when you could practically die from the heat. The summer of 1937 was especially hot. The entire city was like a huge sweltering oven. Everyone said that this was a symbol of the impending war; it was going to be a year of crisis. Lengthy articles appeared in all the newspapers detailing the conflict in the north. There still seemed to be some last-minute hope for peacefully resolving the Marco Polo Bridge Incident. On July 20, the very day that the first round of talks concluded at Lushan, Chiang Kai-shek rushed back to Nanjing via plane. The newspapers reported that the Generalissimo was in high spirits and a relaxed mood; he was seemingly fully prepared to deal with the latest developments with Japan. One after another he received the ambassadors of America, Germany, and France and, as the situation in East Asia came to a head, provided them with the required explanations. Chiang even asked each ambassador to inform their respective governments that China's resolution to resist Japan was already set in stone. If Japan continued with its policy of aggression, the Chinese government would have to resist with force—as long as there was a single soldier standing on the battlefield, they were prepared to fight.

After the Marco Polo Bridge Incident, there was barely a person who wasn't filled with indignation—everyone in China was virtually spitting with anger. The officers and soldiers of the 29th Army, stationed at the conflict area, won waves of support. All kinds of organizations rushed to wire Song Zheyuan and his men to express their regards and encourage them to keep up the good work. University students who had stayed in Nanjing during the summer once again took to the streets to deliver passionate speeches and raise money for soldiers on the front lines. From high officials, respectable citizens, and rich women all the way down to beggars, rickshaw coolies, and maids, all made sure they gave at least something to show their support. Students even organized a summer theater troupe. They came up with their own anti-Japanese repertoire and took their show on the road, performing in all the villages around Nanjing. For a while, the tune of the War of Resistance became the single most important melody around. As the Marco Polo Bridge Incident was still unfolding, a script based on the affair, entitled *The Marco Polo Bridge Incident*, written by the famous playwright Tian Han and a star-studded group of artists, was being pumped out at blinding speed. A bunch of journalists based in the capital got a troupe together and began to rehearse at the Recreational Activity Center in hope of putting on a performance of *The Marco Polo Bridge Incident* to entertain the troops.

Even after he got back to Nanjing, Ding Wenyu was somewhat foggy about what was going to happen with Japan. Ever since the Mukden Incident when Manchuria fell, people had jumped at any opportunity to protest and make a big scene. Protest had already become a kind of social habit—it seemed as if anyone who didn't take to the streets was nothing better than a spineless chicken without an ounce of patriotism. Actually, nobody could predict how things would eventually turn out. All the official slogans had indeed gotten much tougher; it seemed as if the only way people were going to get those damn Japanese out of their system was with a fight. But in the end, the Chinese were still a peace-loving bunch. Even up north around the Marco Polo Bridge, as long as the Japanese kept their distance, an atmosphere of peace descended upon the area. Everyone knew that the Japanese were just trying to buy time while they waited for backup troops to be dispatched, but when there was no fighting on the front lines, everyone's enthusiasm seemed to fade. When Ding Wenyu got back to Nanjing, the most impassioned wave of anti-Japanese sentiment had just passed and people were beginning to doubt whether or not war was ever really going to break out. All they knew how to do was wiggle their lips and cry war slogans; when it came down to really fighting, they weren't in the least bit psychologically prepared.

Nanjing middle school students started a campaign to collect 50,000 towels to be donated to the troops. It stirred up quite a bit of attention and, one after another, all the newspapers rushed to cover the event. Because of the way tensions constantly fluctuated, a serious blow was delivered to the proresistance morale. The enthusiasm that inspired all of those programs meant to entertain the troops also ended rather poorly;

they came out of the gate like a lion and finished like a lamb. In the end, the 50,000 Towel Campaign, which had generated an impressive amount of attention, was only able to collect a measly 49 towels—a far cry from the declared target. And so the newspapers had no choice but to make a desperate plea on behalf of the students in hope that citizens of the capital would reach out and donate towels, which could then be sent to the soldiers on the front lines. Although the whole issue of donating towels didn't seem like much, it had a huge role in raising the people's morale.

The Municipal Party Headquarters called for an emergency expanded meeting where speeches were given on the need for implementing a military service law. The motive behind this meeting was to do away with the deeply entrenched belief among the people that "You don't make a nail out of a good piece of steel, you don't make a soldier out of a good man." If the people of this nation hoped to have equality, they must first be able to defend themselves; besides gaining financial and emotional support for the war against Japan, the Municipal Party Headquarters hoped that they could count on the citizens to rid themselves of fear and enthusiastically enlist to serve their country. In a capital city the size of Nanjing, only a mere 8 percent of the population were eligible for the draft lottery. Moreover, once this 8 percent were called in, the lottery was conducted and only one out of every hundred actually ended up in uniform. The proposed military service law clearly didn't meet with the welcome that it deserved; everyone seemed dissatisfied with the whole idea of having a lottery. Young men with hot blood running through their veins hated the fact that they couldn't just dash off to the front lines and kill their hated enemies while, at the same time, the average citizen took the attitude that it was best to be wise and play it safe, terrified that they might one day really be drafted.

Ding Wenyu never imagined that the day after he got back to Nanjing, Yu Kexia would show up strangely, looking for him. At the time, Ding's heart was still in Lushan; he couldn't get used to not having Yuyuan around. He was in particularly low spirits and didn't know how to pass the time. As it happened, Ding Wenyu was in the shower when Yu Kexia called on him. Yu Kexia called several times from outside the door, scaring the living daylights out of Ding, who was afraid that Yu had been specially dispatched on a punitive expedition to punish him for taking things too far with Yuyuan during their trip. Yu Kexia had actually ended his friendship with Ding after he found out about Ding's pursuit of his sister-in-law; this was the first time since then that he had seen his old friend. Ding Wenyu hid in the bathroom, refusing to come out. Finally, Yu Kexia was forced to announce the reason for his visit through the door. As it turned out, he wanted Ding to work with him on one of his business deals.

"Don't worry, there's no way I'll let you get taken in on this one." Yu Kexia got right to the point. He spoke in a tone completely unfamiliar to Ding; he sounded just like some old veteran businessman. "This is what we call loving our country and making money at the same time."

For a second, Ding Wenyu was somewhat confused and had no idea what Yu was talking about. As it turned out, the National Military Council, for which Yu Kexia served as secretary general, wanted to try making some money by selling "safety kits." These were little bags filled with the most basic emergency first aid medicine and supplies. Ding Wenyu emerged from the bathroom stark naked and hastened to get dressed. Yu Kexia waited for Ding to get his clothes on before formally handing him one of his flyers; the slogans on the flyer had been drawn up for the newspapers. Ding Wenyu took the paper and almost burst out in laughter when he read what it said. The entire flyer was covered with wonderfully crafted clichélike admonitions, for example: "Extreme Times Call for Extreme Measures," "When on the Verge of Chaos, Be Sure Not to Panic, Stay Calm in the Face of Emergency," "There Is No Finer Way to Support the Troops on the Front Line than Donating Safety Kits," "There Is No Better Way of Protecting Yourself than with a Safety Kit." The following line was printed in small type at the bottom of the page: "In order to ensure that safety kits are affordable and used by all citizens in this time of national calamity, safety kits are now on sale for an especially low price. Only 50 cents per kit or 45 dollars for a box of 100. Shipping and handling is only 20 cents for up to 6 kits and free for safety kits being donated to the front lines." As Yu Kexia watched Ding Wenyu diligently going over each and every word on the page, he picked up a palm-leaf hand fan to fan himself with and laughed, saying that unless something went terribly wrong, they were guaranteed to make a killing.

Ding Wenyu couldn't imagine what role Yu Kexia wanted him to play in this business of his; just thinking about those slogans on the flyer made

Ding snicker. Cashing in on patriotism was dressing like a nun and act-ing like a whore—it was truly an ingenious idea. The weather was simply too hot; just out of the shower, Ding Wenyu was already sweating. He also picked up a palm-leaf fan and began waving it back and forth to cool down. The Military Council usually only spoke a lot of empty words, but now it was time for them to finally take some action. What Yu Kexia wanted from Ding was simple: all he had to do was get his father's bank to grant a loan to the association. The factory was ready to go ahead with production; all they were waiting for was enough money to purchase the raw materials. The Military Council was essentially nothing but an empty frame; all they had to show people were the names of those big shot celebrities who had signed on. When it came down to actually put-ting anything into motion, they didn't have even a cent of funding. Ding Wenyu explained to Yu that he was not on very good terms with his fa-ther since his divorce and was afraid that going to him for a loan wasn't the best idea. Yu Kexia replied with a laugh, "Who do you have to de-pend on in this world besides your parents? All the old man has is this one precious son, there's no way he would leave him out in the cold." What's more, Ding Wenyu's father was a banker, and no one would be clearer than he about what investments were moneymakers. There was no way he could refuse a sure bet like this—although he was already mak-ing his share of profits with his bank, he wouldn't throw away an oppor-tunity to make some extra cash.

Ding Wenyu casually agreed to help him out. This perfunctory prom-ise was the only way to shut Yu up and get him out of his apartment. Ding Wenyu had already figured out how he would handle everything; in a few days when Yu came back to bug him, he would simply tell Yu that his fa-ther wasn't interested and there was nothing more he could do. Anyway, even if Yu Kexia didn't believe him, Ding knew there was still no way Yu would rush down to Shanghai to check his story. In his next letter to Yuyuan, Ding Wenyu described everything that had happened that day during Yu Kexia's visit. He made sure not to let even the slightest detail slip by, including how he emerged stark naked from the shower to greet Yu. After their trip to Lushan, the tone of Ding's letters changed some-what; he eased up a bit on his poetic romanticism, and his wording be-came markedly more down-to-earth. He rambled on and on, describing all the trivial things that had happened in his life, while doing his best to imagine what she was doing. He complained that that they shouldn't have left Lushan so soon. The summer heat in Nanjing was simply unbearable; it was hot enough to make him feel like he was trapped in a steamer. How wonderful it would be if at that moment they were still together in Lushan, spending days on end in each other's company. Although they had just parted, Ding Wenyu felt as if they had already been separated for what seemed like an eternity—he always had an endless array of things he wanted to tell her.

The newspapers said that the best place in Nanjing to beat the heat was in the southern part of the city along the Qinhuai River, near the Temple of Confucius. The bloody battle being fought up north near the Marco Polo Bridge didn't have the least bit of influence on the Qinhuai pleasure boats. The women of the Qinhuai knew not the sorrows of the dying nation; as long as there was a buck to be made, it was a holiday. Due to the swarms of people who came to the Qinhuai to escape the blistering heat, business had increased a hundredfold that summer. Even average low-class sing-song girls and unlicensed prostitutes became quite active, taking advantage of the opportunity to make a quick killing. The silken harmonies and gentle melodies carried on throughout the night. The pleasure boats made so much noise that the people who lived alongside the river couldn't sleep and rambled on with their complaints the whole night through. Finally the police department had no choice but to interfere. At first they went about the matter rather politely by pasting warnings, but after not getting any results they were forced to take action. They dispatched a police boat to patrol the river, which "disturbed the playful swallows and scared the lustful orioles" along the Qinhuai— on just one night they arrested forty singsong girls and other salacious women on the Qinhuai pleasure boats.

In the north of the city, the best place to escape from the heat was Xuanwu Lake Park. In order to give everyone a cool place to go in the evening, the park administration opened the gates and let the entire park become a seething, sleepless cauldron of laughter and fun that raged on into the night. Each year, as soon as summer rolled around, the people of Nanjing seemed to be incapable of doing anything respectable; they wore as little as they could get away with, never minding what was decent. One after another, all the men seemed to go bare-chested, while the women walked around in nothing but low-cut shirts. A poet had described it in a newspaper: "Summer in Nanjing was forever brimming with the poetic smell of flesh." Nanjing residents tried to get what sleep they could during the day, and when evening came, like a flock of night owls, they all came out to the park to cool off. Once they got started, they could gossip the whole night through. They talked about virtually everything under the sun, babbling on and on, especially about current affairs. Most of the conversations, however, didn't go much further than discussing whether or not all-out war would break out between China and Japan. Nobody seemed to see eye to eye. Each person thought he or she was right and sneered at everyone else's lack of knowledge. The pessimists were convinced that China was doomed, while the optimists took the position that Japan did not really want to fight China and that, although Japan had superior arms, their effectiveness in combat was not necessarily any stronger than China's. Because of the ongoing Chinese Civil War, the Chinese military was like a blade that was being constantly sharpened; the sharper the quicker, the more experience on the battlefield the more brave. Each and every Chinese soldier was a veteran fighter, unlike the Japanese army, who normally spent all their time doing nothing but drills and exercises; the only way they could scare people was by waving around those modern weapons they had gotten their hands on.

Between August and September 1937, as the Marco Polo Bridge Incident raged on in the north, the most uncomfortable event the municipal administration in the capital had to deal with was the adoption of a new centralized management plan for dealing with excrement. In light of the fact that there were very few public bathrooms in the city, most citizens tried to make things easier by simply digging pits and placing excrement vats in the ground. Then peasants from just outside the city would come in at specified times to collect the fertilizer. In order to improve public sanitation, that summer the municipal government began a comprehensive centralized management system for these excrement vats. Private vats that had been dug illegally were all to be filled in. However, this caused a major problem at the few remaining public toilets. The weather was blistering hot, and the few licensed public bathrooms were completely filled—in terms of both people *and* waste. Everyone was already in a bad mood due to the unbearable heat, and now with this new problem cries of discontent broke out everywhere. Admittedly the affairs of state are important, but one still can't overlook the everyday affairs of the people. For a time, the public's discontent with the centralized management of excrement seemed to be just as strong as their hatred of the Japanese. The municipal government had no choice but to organize an emergency sanitation squad to do whatever they could to increase the number of public toilets. The government also immediately met with the ringleaders of the various human waste collection organizations to work out a standard price for selling excrement as fertilizer. However, distant waters can't put out a burning fire; it's too late to mend the fold after the sheep have run away—the entire system was already too messed up to fix. Virtually every sparsely populated area around the city ended up stinking to high heaven, and all of this was caused by those irresponsible people who refused to do their jobs.

V

In the history books, the Marco Polo Bridge Incident of July 7 signals the official start of the Second Sino-Japanese War. However, at the time, there were quite a few people who didn't feel that way. As far as most people in Nanjing were concerned, the Marco Polo Bridge Incident was merely a war contained within the pages of the newspaper. The papers printed all kinds of stories about the conflict going on in the north; at the same time they also ran countless recruitment advertisements for universities and colleges. By the end of July, a flood of students had come to Nanjing to take the college entrance exams. Compared with past years, the number of registered applicants had greatly increased—this goes to show that, even in times of war, Chinese people still place a terrible amount of importance on a college diploma. Central University, Wuhan University, and Zhejiang University together organized a high-profile recruitment committee. All together, there were 8,600 students who had preregistered to take the entrance exams. Most of the tests would be administered in the gymnasium at Central University. Top professors from all the local universities were invited to proctor and grade the exams; Ding Wenyu had the honor of being among them. Just over 10 percent of the examinees were girls, and as Ding Wenyu watched them nervously fill out their exams, he couldn't help but think how wonderful it would be if Yuyuan could also take the entrance exams. After their time together in Lushan, Ding Wenyu knew that deep down Yuyuan really wanted to go to college.

Ding Wenyu's several attempts to see Yuyuan again had all ended in failure. But he didn't know that ever since her return to Nanjing, her marriage had been in a state of utter crisis. Yuyuan had gotten wind of the rather stunning rumors circulating about Yu Kerun's relationship with Qu Manli more than two months earlier. However, after coming back from Lushan, she was truly shocked to learn that not only had Yu Kerun failed to end his relationship with Qu, but they had actually taken it to the next level—the two of them had rented a house in the north part of the city and were secretly living together. No one could have imagined that things would go this far. Yu Kerun was no family man; he had planned simply to have his fun and let that be the end of it, but Qu Manli was unlike other girls. Never in his wildest dreams would Yu have imagined that he would be unable to get rid of her. Qu Manli didn't necessarily want Yu to marry her; the real reason she wanted to share a place with him was to use this stone cold fact as a wedge to pry Yu Kerun away from Yuyuan. She was a calculating girl and knew how effectively to trap Yu in her clutches. Yu Kerun suddenly realized that unless he wanted trouble, his only real choice was to go ahead and break off his relationship with Yuyuan.

Qu Manli frequently appeared with Yu Kerun at all kinds of upper-class functions; she brought him to call on her uncle's favorite former disciples and introduced him to an assortment of influential political and military figures. She took like a fish to water when associating with those high and mighty officials and notables—compared to the rather naïve Yuyuan, Qu Manli was much more experienced and knowledgeable. Yu Kerun understood that only a woman like Qu Manli would truly be able to support him and give his career the boost it needed. A fortune-teller had once told Yu Kerun that if he ever wanted his career to take off, he would have to rely upon a beautiful woman who would be not only his companion but also his most intimate friend. Ever since marrying Yuyuan, Yu Kerun had been constantly haunted by the fear that she would never bring him any good luck. Without a second thought, he had rushed into moving in with Qu Manli and concluded that this woman would somehow turn his luck around. Qu Manli picked out the house herself; it was obvious that this headstrong and cunning student wasn't satisfied living at either her dormitory or her uncle's house. Yu Kerun just happened to be the one she caught; she was never terribly satisfied with him, so she did whatever she could to tailor him to meet her standard.

Qu Manli's first offensive against Yu Kerun was pressing him to divorce his wife Yuyuan as soon as possible. Since Yu Kerun openly admitted his marriage to Yuyuan had been a bit rash, he should simply cut the Gordian knot and put an end to it. It was as if Yu Kerun were riding on a tiger's back with no way of getting down; he wished that Qu Manli could be like other girls and that they could simply have their fun and go their separate ways. Once she settled on a house, she telephoned everywhere trying to track down Yu, whom she hadn't seen for several days. Yu Kerun began to get scared. This little love game was getting out of hand—he realized that he had already been snared. If your hands are soaked and you dip them in a vat of flour, they're bound to turn white. Qu Manli didn't keep her feelings pent up inside like Yuyuan. She was a modern woman, a liberal thinker who didn't seem to give a second thought to sex, but at the same time she was like a traditional housewife who would continually threaten suicide unless her man did what she wanted. When she realized that Yu Kerun couldn't bring himself to make that final break with Yuyuan, she hid a pair of scissors under her pillow. When they made love that night, she suddenly pulled out the scissors and threatened that unless he gave in to her demand, she would kill herself right there in front of him. "I will not tolerate the man I love having a woman like her in his life." At the slightest provocation Qu Manli would suddenly blow up and become extremely aggressive. Her excuse for wanting Yu Kerun to get a divorce was not that she looked at Yuyuan as a threatening opponent; just the opposite, she felt that a girl soldier like Yuyuan didn't even *deserve* to be called her opponent. "You should have absolutely no problem finding a woman much better than her!"

Everything that Qu Manli knew about Yuyuan, she had learned indirectly from Yu Kerun. Arrogant girls seem to look down upon other women instinctively. So often the haughtiness of a woman works in strange ways; it usually stems from overconfidence. Just like every other unfaithful man, Yu Kerun exaggerated the rift between him and his wife to Qu Manli and, in the process, he even went so far as to make up several small incidents that never even happened. This little trick of Yu's had been put well to the test during the course of his relationships with a host of other women. However, he forgot one of the rules of the game: a smart man should be just as careful about bad-mouthing other women in front of his lover as he is about complimenting other women. In order to satisfy Qu Manli, Yu Kerun belittled Yuyuan constantly, sometimes without even realizing it. By the time he decided he had gone a bit overboard and tried lightening up the image of Yuyuan he had painted, it was too late. Qu Manli's impression of Yuyuan was already set in stone. When Yu tried to change his take on Yuyuan, Qu Manli simply thought that he was feeling guilty and took Yu Kerun for a spineless man who lacked the courage to end his loveless marriage. Yu Kerun couldn't bring himself to make the final decision, so Qu Manli decided to make it for him. She took the liberty of setting up a meeting with Yuyuan on behalf of Yu Kerun. She didn't bother telling Yu about it until the night before they were supposed to meet.

Even if Yu Kerun had wanted to bail out, it was too late. Qu Manli obviously went a bit far; she not only arranged this dramatic meeting but also made sure she was right there to observe the whole thing. Feeling she had every right to do so, she wanted to see exactly how Yu Kerun would handle things. For the longest time, the three of them were completely silent. Yuyuan couldn't help but steal a glance at Qu Manli; Qu had her head raised high with a disdainful look that seemed to say she wasn't even willing to waste her breath on Yuyuan. Yu Kerun could feel the prickles of anxiety scathing his back. It was hot to begin with, and in the short first few minutes of their meeting Yu had already broken into a full sweat. It took a while for Yuyuan to finally figure out what the purpose of this meeting was. She had just returned from Lushan and still felt a tad guilty for having gotten too close to Ding during her trip. In a way, things worked out for the best—now they were even. As if Qu Manli's imperious attitude wasn't bad enough, Yu Kerun's annoying silence made things worse and truly brought her to her wit's end. She couldn't help but think back to the other preposterously dramatic scene that had transpired several months before at Six Splendid Springs. It was almost the same situation, only the roles had changed—back then she was "the other woman," but now it was Qu Manli.

Finally Qu Manli went ahead and spelled out the reason for their meeting. She began her little talk as if she were launching an attack, leaving Yuyuan in utter shock. "Yu Kerun, if you want to end your loveless marriage with this woman, now is the time." Qu Manli's tone of voice made it sound as if she were reciting a line right out of a play; she delivered it with just the right rhythm and cadence. Yuyuan was stunned speechless. She turned to Yu Kerun, her eyes begging for an explanation. Yu, however, couldn't bring himself to face Yuyuan and simply pretended that he hadn't been listening. When Yuyuan finally realized what was happening, she was naturally extremely upset. Qu Manli had gone too far; it was not her place to say those things.

Yuyuan used one sentence to put a sharp stop to Qu Manli's arrogant ramblings. Glaring at her, Yuyuan furiously asked, "And who the hell are you?" Qu Manli was virtually tongue-tied, and Yuyuan turned to Yu Kerun to ask him the same question.

Yu Kerun shrugged his shoulders and stammered for what seemed like forever before he finally frowned and said, "Yuyuan, let me explain."

Yuyuan sat back to listen to what Yu had to say. But Yu Kerun's explanation proved fruitless; he kept talking in circles without ever getting anywhere. Yuyuan felt that there was absolutely no need for him to be so nervous—a real man should be able to face up to reality. Besides, Qu Manli had already let the cat out of the bag. Did he not arrange this meeting to simply put an end to their so-called "loveless marriage"? Yuyuan felt as if she had been stabbed in the heart with a dagger; she felt a sudden burst of pain followed by a dull numbness. Never in her wildest dreams had she given any thought to the question of whether or not there was love in their marriage. Yuyuan deeply believed that she was in love with Yu Kerun, just as she also believed that he loved her. The way Yu Kerun kept silent on the major issues while dwelling on the trivial not only left Yuyuan feeling disappointed, it also made her desperate. She had never before suffered such terrible pain.

"It looks like there are a few small problems that have cropped up between us . . ." Yu Kerun uttered.

Standing beside them, Qu Manli cut in with a harsh tone of dissatisfaction: "What do you mean, 'small problems'? Why don't you tell her who you're living with right now!"

Yuyuan was struck with a heaviness in her chest and could barely breathe. Yu Kerun found himself in a terribly difficult situation. It was obvious that he also felt that Qu Manli had gone too far, but she was already completely beyond his control—there was nothing he could do. Yu

Kerun decided to simply keep his mouth shut and let the two of them have it out any way they wanted. It didn't seem to matter since their little meeting was already way out of hand. Once Qu Manli got going she was virtually unstoppable; she spit out everything—including her secret living arrangement with Yu. This was a particularly tough blow for Yuyuan to take. She had wanted to have a house with Yu ever since their marriage. Even if they couldn't afford one, Yuyuan was more than willing to rent one for the time being. Never did she imagine that Yu Kerun would not only continually put the matter off, but in the end rent a house with another woman. This in itself was enough for Yuyuan to promise herself never to forgive Yu Kerun.

All the while Yu Kerun stood there without making a sound, as if what was going on had nothing to do with him. Yu's lack of participation was actually a silent admission that everything Qu Manli said was true. Qu Manli already had the upper hand. She noticed that Yuyuan's face was so red that her boiling blood seemed like it would burst out at any minute; the area around her eyes had also turned a bright crimson. Advancing on the crest of victory, Qu Manli decided to look for Yuyuan's soft spot by describing how much she and Yu Kerun were in love. Women always seem to know what to say to tear another woman apart; it's almost an inherent instinct. Taking her time, Qu Manli casually addressed Yuyuan: "I really don't understand how you could think that just because you have a lousy marriage license he belongs to you."

Yuyuan figured that at this point nothing she said would make much of a difference. She simply did her best to bear up and prevent her tears from showing. Qu Manli, as overbearing as she was, actually wanted to keep going, but Yu Kerun couldn't bear any more and tried to get her to knock it off. Since she was now in the driver's seat, the last thing Qu Manli wanted to do was let Yuyuan off easy: "Why the hell should I shut up? What, doesn't she have a mouth? She can talk back if she wants!" Yuyuan's hatred for Qu Manli went beyond words, but she didn't want to get in a shouting match with her. Fighting was never Yuyuan's strong point. Yuyuan just wished that Qu Manli would give her a minute alone with Yu Kerun so she could really talk to him. Yuyuan wanted to hear her husband's own take on this whole affair. Everything happened so fast that she didn't even have a chance to comprehend it all; she had no idea how to deal with what was unfolding before her very eyes.

Yu Kerun didn't seem to want to be stuck alone with her; Qu Manli had already ruined everything, and he felt that his best course of action would be to simply get out of there. He was never a very clever man, but under the circumstances he had no choice but to use a bit of cunning. Although he didn't want to be forced into personally telling Yuyuan that he wanted to end their marriage, he couldn't deny the fact that that was exactly the purpose of their meeting that day. The whole thing was quite ridiculous; he really felt that, in a way, Yuyuan wasn't worth losing over a woman like Qu Manli, but he had gone so far that it was already too late to turn back. Yu Kerun didn't really want to end his marriage but, because of Qu, he had no choice but to be a good little boy and get a divorce. Unlike Yuyuan, Qu Manli was capable of all kinds of shameful acts. When it came down to it, Yu Kerun and Yuyuan had the same problem—they were both too worried about losing face.

Qu Manli was indeed far from satisfied with Yu Kerun—especially after their little meeting with Yuyuan. Qu Manli could tell from the way that Yuyuan carried herself that she was the better of the two women. At the same time, Yu Kerun kept stammering, unwilling to make the final break; it was clear that he still had feelings for his wife. Qu Manli was ready to gnash her teeth in anger and, right then and there, she decided that Yu Kerun wasn't going to get off without a fight. As soon as he drove her home, he made up some excuse about having to go out to take care of some business. Qu Manli knew that if she let him out the door it would be days before he would show his face again. Yu Kerun's way to escape all problems was always: when the going got tough, Yu got going. If there was something he couldn't handle, he would simply hide out and not show his face. But Qu Manli was not the kind of woman to put up with his antics. She grabbed his arm and threatened, "If you even dare to walk out that door, you can consider it the end!" Yu Kerun immediately started to waver. Qu Manli's threat had a dual meaning: the first was that their relationship was finished; the second was that she was going to kill herself for Yu to see. Using suicide to threaten people really doesn't qualify as any kind of masterful stroke—but Yu Kerun was shaking in his boots and fell right for it. He couldn't tell if Qu Manli was serious or not, but *if* something should really happen, he knew his career would be finished.

Yu Kerun's back was against the wall; all he could do was try weaseling out by saying, "I'm not lying, I've really got some things to take care of."

Qu Manli responded, "I don't care if the heavens collapse, no matter what happens, don't you even think of going out today!"

Unable to dissuade her, Yu Kerun had no choice but to stay home and have dinner with her. While they were eating, Qu Manli casually told Yu that that if he really didn't want to divorce Yuyuan then he didn't have to. Yu Kerun thought it was strange that she should say such a thing, but just as he was beginning to heave a sigh of relief, dark clouds started to form around Qu Manli. Glaring at him, she said, "I knew that you were just waiting to hear me say that! Well, let me tell you, if you really don't want to divorce that wife of yours, nobody's going to force you. And even if you do divorce her, don't you go thinking that *I'll* marry you."

If she didn't want to marry him, Yu Kerun wondered why she even bothered forcing him to get divorced in the first place; but that's not what came out of his mouth. "Did I ever say that I wasn't going to divorce her?"

Qu Manli flashed him a cold smile and said, "You didn't need to say so—it's written all over your face!" Even someone who didn't have the slightest clue as to how to read someone's face would have been able to tell what Yu was thinking. Yu Kerun couldn't win with her—all he could do was heave a heavy sigh. With that, Qu Manli added, "What are you sighing about? Let me tell you, don't you go thinking that that wife of yours is anything special. Isn't her mother a Japanese? Who knows, maybe she's a Japanese spy. How could the army headquarters let a woman like her wiggle her way in?"

In the Nanjing of 1937, the worst thing you could call someone was a traitor or a spy. Yu Kerun knew that unless he let Qu Manli carry on with her vicious insults against Yuyuan, he would never hear the end of it. Deep down, however, he couldn't help but feel upset. Qu Manli's greatest skill must have been her ability to speak with all the assurance, uprightness, and justification in the world—even when she couldn't have been more wrong. A few days before, Yu Kerun had attended a ball with Qu Manli, and during a dance with Qu Manli's young aunt, Auntie Qu asked Yu when he planned on divorcing his wife: "It is a shame that our little Qu Manli has really fallen for you. It's terrible. Do you know how many big officials out there have their eyes on her? And let me tell you, there's not one of them that isn't a better catch than you!" Since Qu Manli's aunt was married to a considerably older man, she had no place to release all her energy, so as soon as she hit the dance floor there was no stopping her. She wrapped herself around Yu Kerun and wouldn't let go; afraid that Qu Manli might get jealous, she made sure to speak to him from the perspective of an older woman. Everything she said was naked and unabashed, and just before they left she made sure to leave Yu with an ultimatum. Yu Kerun was a bit frustrated. It wasn't because he didn't want to split with Yuyuan, nor because he was afraid Yuyuan wouldn't agree to a divorce; what really made him upset was Qu Manli's equivocal attitude. Qu Manli's aunt and Qu Manli herself had the same problem—all they knew how to do was push him, all they were interested in was splitting up Yu and his wife. But as for what was going to happen *after* Yu got his divorce, they never once gave him a straight answer. Who really knew if Qu Manli actually intended to marry him? The way Yu Kerun saw the situation was simple: since things had gotten to this stage, it was only natural he marry Qu Manli if he divorced his wife—otherwise, why even bother getting divorced?

Qu Manli had a natural knack for controlling men. She knew that after forcing Yu Kerun to stay home that night, she had to be nice to him—only by using the carrot and stick judiciously could she keep him in the palm of her hand. Just when Yu Kerun was worried that she was going to continue with her attacks against Yuyuan, she suddenly stopped pestering him about her. Yu Kerun was so relieved one would have thought he had just been granted clemency from a death sentence.

While they were eating, their maid boiled a large pot of water for them to wash up with. After everything was all set up, Qu Manli sent the maid away to do something else while she personally helped Yu with his bath. The weather was unbearably hot outside, so Yu Kerun couldn't help but break into a sweat while soaking in the bathtub; all the while, Qu Manli patiently sat beside him waving a fan to cool him off. After his bath she even helped him rub on some talcum powder. Yu Kerun was overwhelmed by how nice she was being, so much so he even felt a bit guilty and tried to repay her by fanning her. In a kind and pleasant tone, Qu Manli told him, "You don't have to do that, you just took a bath. Hurry up and go outside to find yourself a cool place to sit down and relax; otherwise you'll end up all sweaty again."

A bit later, Qu Manli also took a bath and, after applying an alluring perfume, went outside to sit down next to Yu Kerun. Because their house was on the outskirts of the city, they had a big open plot of land outside their front door. A bit farther up was a pond and two willow trees. With a large bamboo bed in the open space, there could be no better place to cool off on a hot summer night. The moon had already risen and the bright moonlight bathed the ground; far off one could even faintly make out a few stars. Yu Kerun was sure that Qu Manli was going to rehash all the things that had happened earlier that day with Yuyuan and they would end up getting into another argument. He never imagined that she would intentionally avoid the whole incident and, snuggling up close to him, start chatting about other things. As they talked, she continued to fan him. Finally, Yu Kerun couldn't take it and, heaving a deep sigh, brought up the meeting with Yuyuan. Qu immediately covered his mouth with her hand to stop him. Pulling her hand away, Yu Kerun said, "It's not that I don't want to bring this to a quick end, it's just that everything needs time. To be frank, she wasn't even the slightest bit prepared for what happened there today."

"Don't just think of her," Qu Manli responded. "You have to think about what's best for me too. What am *I* if you don't divorce her? Don't tell me you plan on keeping me as your mistress forever?"

VI

Ding Wenyu's several attempts to take Yuyuan out all ended in naught. He figured that she must have indeed meant what she said when she insisted that they see no more of each other after leaving Lushan. Just like that, it was all over. Ding Wenyu, however, was naturally not about to give up so easily. He honestly didn't feel that he had any kind of bad intentions—he simply felt a kind of indescribable happiness when he was with Yuyuan. And ever since their time together in Lushan, Ding Wenyu realized that his plight wasn't quite as hopeless as he had suspected.

Ding Wenyu was grading his stack of college entrance exams, and every time he came across a test booklet with smooth, graceful handwriting, he would assume that it must be the work of a beautiful young girl. The graceful words made him think about how wonderful it would be if Yuyuan were also able to attend college—that way he would have the opportunity to see her every day on campus. Like the saying goes, "Love me, love my dog"; Ding Wenyu couldn't bear to take away any points from those exams with the beautiful handwriting. With the country in the middle of a national calamity, it was almost impossible for students to buckle down and study. Although more students than ever took the entrance exams, their scores were not terribly good—only a measly three students scored a 70. Two were accepted by Central University and the third was accepted by Zhejiang University. Fewer than 50 students scored over 60, and Central University also admitted most of them.

After he was finished grading his share of the exams, all of Ding Wenyu's thoughts immediately returned to Yuyuan. Naturally he had to write to her every day. He had an endless array of things to tell her. Just as he would send out one letter, new things would immediately come to his mind, like a spring prairie constantly sprouting an inexhaustible army of new buds. Scenes from their time together in Lushan constantly reappeared before his eyes. At night he would return to Lushan in his dreams, and sometimes he would find himself unable to suppress his naughty thoughts. Because of this Ding Wenyu began to realize that there is never a time when a man can ever feel truly satisfied—this eternal craving seems to be what makes us human. At first he didn't want much: as long as Yuyuan was able to receive his letters he would have been more than happy; all he was originally looking for was a kind of spiritual love. Now, from the looks of it, he was only fooling himself with this so-called spiritual love. However, since he had begun to pursue Yuyuan, Ding Wenyu had indeed become much more lofty: he had already given up his bad habit of visiting prostitutes, and he had gotten rid of a lot of those strange practices that come with being a celebrity. Since falling in love with Yuyuan, Ding Wenyu was indeed no longer his old self.

When Ding Wenyu finally received a short letter from Yuyuan saying that she agreed to meet him, he was wild with joy. Immediately his stubborn heart started to pump again and he was unable to keep still—he hated not being able to run off that instant to find Yuyuan. In just a few days' time the political situation had grown markedly more serious; the Marco Polo Bridge Incident had already developed to the point of no return and, one by one, every last illusory hope for peace was shattered. The Japanese army took the port city of Tianjin and had already surrounded Beiping; it was only a matter of time before the former capital fell. It seemed as if this time the Nationalist government was really set on putting up a fight. One after another, political and military leaders from all over China converged on Nanjing; coming together in a time of national crisis, they discussed strategies for resisting Japan and saving the nation. Within a few short days, Shanxi's Yan Xishan, Canton's Yu Hanmou, Guangxi's Bai Chongxi, Sichuan's Liu Xiang, Hunan's He Jian, and Yunnan's Long Yun, as well as the Nationalist Party's old enemies, CCP representatives Zhu De and Ye Jianying, all rushed down to Nanjing. News of the meeting was all over the papers; reporters followed it closely, reporting on their every move. Never in Nanjing's history as the Nationalist capital had the city borne witness to such an impressive display of unity and political cohesiveness.

Back when Ding Wenyu was studying abroad in Germany, he had had some contact with Zhu De. During Zhu De's trip to the capital, some of his old classmates from Germany wanted to take him out to dinner. However, because so many big shots were waiting in line to take Zhu out, his classmates had to settle for taking him for some tea and drinks. During their little get-together, Zhu De, the healthy and glowing commander-in-chief of the Red Army, told Ding Wenyu a humorous anecdote about his trip that made everyone at the table burst into laughter. Living in Yan'an, Zhu De had long grown accustomed to a rather spartan lifestyle and ended up with an upset stomach from all the banquets he was been treated to during his trip to Nanjing. Just a few days before, while he was outside, Zhu suddenly started to feel uncomfortable and needed to find a bathroom. Since he didn't know his way around town and was anxious, he decided to simply rush back to his hotel. However, when he got back he discovered that he had accidentally locked his hotel room from the inside. It was only after struggling with the door for some time that he finally resolved the problem by having one of his assistants crawl through the transom window to unlock the door.

Although at the time the military conflict between China and Japan was still confined to the distant north, the atmosphere in the capital Nanjing was slowly becoming more warlike. The military were at that moment considering having the residents of Nanjing evacuate to the countryside, even forcing those unwilling to move; they wanted to leave just 200,000 rear personnel within the city proper. This proposal was instantly met with strong opposition because of the feared unrest such a large-scale migration would cause. The citizens were terrified enough as it was. Even though everyone was shouting their approval of resisting

Japan, when it came down to it, most people had no idea what they would do if war really broke out. Rumors of an impending life-and-death battle in Shanghai spread like wildfire and, one after another, people in Shanghai all flocked to the foreign concessions.

After his minireunion with his old classmates from Germany, Ding Wenyu still had some free time before his date with Yuyuan. It suddenly dawned on him that he should go down to the telecommunications office to make a long-distance call to his father in Shanghai. The office was unusually crowded as people lined up with anxious looks on their faces. It took forever to make it to a phone, and when they finally did they were forced to shout because of all the noise and hubbub inside the office.

Just before it was Ding Wenyu's turn, he gave up on calling. It was almost time to meet Yuyuan and he wasn't willing to make her wait. He grabbed a rickshaw and headed straight for where they were supposed to meet. Yuyuan was there already, waiting. Seized with panic, Ding Wenyu anxiously looked at his watch to discover that Yuyuan had arrived early. He couldn't help but feel somewhat surprised; he quickly paid the rickshaw coolie and rushed over to Yuyuan. Although he wasn't late, Ding couldn't forgive himself for not getting there first. Yuyuan didn't look good; it only took one glance to see that there was something on her mind that was making her upset. Ding Wenyu thought that she was angry he hadn't gotten there earlier and was about to apologize when Yuyuan unexpectedly apologized to him. Yuyuan told Ding that because they were having an important meeting at the army headquarters, she wouldn't be able to spend much time with him. The meeting came up so suddenly that she didn't have time to notify him, otherwise she would have rescheduled. After hearing this, Ding Wenyu was quite moved; he figured that Yuyuan must really understand his feelings. If she hadn't come to tell him, heaven only knows how long Ding Wenyu would have stood there waiting in vain for her.

Actually, shortly after Yuyuan sent out that short letter agreeing to meet him, she started to regret it. The only reason she had agreed to see him was that she needed someone to find Yu Kerun for her. She wanted Ding Wenyu to be her messenger. Yuyuan really felt that she needed to have a good conversation with Yu Kerun after that last damn meeting with Qu Manli. Ding Wenyu was clearly not the ideal candidate for the job, but in her grief, Yuyuan couldn't think of anyone better. She didn't want her girlfriends to know how upset she was, nor did she want her family to worry about her. Because everything had unfolded so quickly, Yuyuan was left with absolutely no idea how to cope with what was happening. She wanted to talk things over with Yu Kerun, but it was clear that he was trying to avoid her. Ever since they had gotten married, their time spent together always had to fit into Yu Kerun's schedule; he came and went as he pleased, never giving her even a moment's notice. Frankly, Yuyuan had no idea where she could find Yu. Qu Manli had said that they were already living together and had gotten a house somewhere in the city. But in a city as large as Nanjing, where was Yuyuan supposed to start looking?

Without the slightest hesitation, Ding Wenyu promised Yuyuan that he would find that heartless husband of hers. Since Yuyuan had so much faith in him, Ding Wenyu took it upon himself to do everything in his power to help her. Yuyuan looked like she was going to cry but didn't have any tears left; her pained appearance ignited Ding Wenyu's indignation—he couldn't understand how Yu Kerun could be such a bastard. Yu had such a wonderful wife, yet he didn't seem to have the slightest clue how to treat her. Yuyuan looked at her watch and, realizing that she had to go, quickly bade Ding farewell. Ding Wenyu awkwardly consoled her before stopping her a passing rickshaw. As she climbed in, he promised her that he would let her know the minute he had any news. Yuyuan forced a smile; she turned around as if she had something else to tell him, but the words never made it to her lips. Instead she simply waved goodbye. Ding Wenyu followed her for a few steps, but the rickshaw was going too fast; before she got too far away he called out to her, "Don't worry, I'll make sure that bastard gets what's coming to him!"

Yuyuan wasn't in the mood to hear that last comment; she knew that Ding was too much of a bookworm to back his threat up. However, she was already so far away that she could barely hear him, let alone object—she simply let his comments go and twisted herself back around in the rickshaw to face forward. Everything was already a mess; the situation couldn't get much worse than it already was. As Ding Wenyu gazed at Yuyuan's distant silhouette, he thought about Yu Kerun, and his hatred for him seemed to increase by the moment. As the atmosphere of war encapsulated the city and the Chinese hatred for Japanese militarism reached its pinnacle, so did Ding Wenyu's hatred for Yu Kerun, which ran at least as deep—if not deeper. Ding Wenyu took this favor to Yuyuan as a set of orders that must be carried out to the end. The problem was that he couldn't figure out how he was supposed to go about finding Yu Kerun. If Yu had been an easy man to find, Yuyuan never would have troubled him in the first place. Yu Kerun's dual status as both pilot and instructor at the Aviation Academy made him somewhat of a mysterious figure. No one could ever track him down because most of his time was spent at the airport, and the average person couldn't even get in. Security was especially tight now that China was on the verge of war; the military police would stop anyone before they got anywhere near the airport.

And so Ding Wenyu decided to go to Ginling College to look for Yu's live-in lover, Qu Manli. Ding rushed over to her campus only to discover that her school was out on holiday. Ding Wenyu had once given a lecture at Ginling College that had met with an unusually warm response. All the girls in the audience had grown accustomed to boring classes and felt that Ding's talk was extremely interesting and charmingly quirky. Ding Wenyu took his search seriously and, when the security guard at the campus gate tried to stop him from going in, Ding couldn't help but lose his temper. Ding raised his cane and waved it around wildly in the air, wanting to simply charge in. Unfortunately for Ding, the security guard also took *his* job seriously. The guard started to get worried and asked how Ding could possibly be so unreasonable. As it would happen, a music instructor Ding knew was crossing the street and, seeing what was happening, quickly came over to help smooth things over for Ding. That security guard insisted that he was in the right and wasn't about to let Ding off so easily. He kept nagging until the music instructor said sternly, "Professor Ding is an honored guest on our campus, how could you dare treat him like this?" The security guard was so scared that he didn't dare say another word. The music instructor gave the guard a few more words before telling Ding that her apartment was right around the corner and suggesting they simply go there since the campus was closed. Ding Wenyu felt that since he wouldn't be able to find out any news about Qu Manli, he'd best take a raincheck. It was so hot outside that after just standing there talking Ding was covered with sweat. Fearing that Ding Wenyu was still set on finding the girl he told her about, the music teacher took him to the girl's dormitory; indeed, all the doors and windows were bolted.

His next move was to see what he could find out from Yu Kexia. Deep down, Yu Kexia's house was the last place Ding Wenyu wanted to go; he was afraid he would once again get stuck talking about investing in those damn safety kits. For the past few days, Ding had been intentionally dodging him, but now he was going to walk directly into Yu's trap by going to his house. As expected, Yu Kexia was pleasantly surprised to see Ding. He gregariously greeted him as he came in and warmly escorted him directly to the living room. Ding Wenyu was kind of embarrassed by Yu's warm reception and was forced to beat around the bush by talking about some things that had nothing to do with the real reason for his visit. Yu Kexia was in high spirits and said happily, "It looks like we're really going to roll up our sleeves and get fighting! It's about time; how could a country as large as ours just sit back and be the punching bag for those little Japs?"

Ding Wenyu figured that under the circumstances he would have to say at least something about that whole safety kit affair. Slightly blushing, Ding Wenyu said that he had already talked over the loan with his father, but his old man insisted on taking some time to think it over before giving a definite answer. From the looks of it, Yu Kexia had already gotten his hands on some money elsewhere. His ego seemed to suddenly swell as he started bragging about how, with the way things were going, money should no longer be a problem—apparently there was already a virtual army of rich men who were just itching for a chance to get in on this deal. "Think about it, we've got the name of the Military Council to work under, the inspector general of military training; Tang Shengzhi has signed on to be the honorary chairman of the board, and the other board members are all big names. By investing in safety kits you're not only making money, you're doing something patriotic at the same time. You tell me, which of those profit-seeking businessmen wouldn't be tickled to death to have a play at this? Wenyu, we've been buddies for a long time, so please don't misunderstand; if your good father wants to get in on this and is able to help us out, we would naturally be happy to have him on board."

The two of them chatted awkwardly for a while before Ding Wenyu finally got around to mentioning Yu's brother, Yu Kerun. Yu Kexia was immediately taken aback—it seemed as if he suddenly remembered that it was precisely this old classmate of his who had a rather questionable relationship with his sister-in-law. He gazed at Ding Wenyu and, noticing the way that he dodged his eyes, asked, "What are you looking for my brother for?" Yu Kexia's tone carried some clear misgivings. Ding Wenyu smiled but didn't explain why; he knew that he would be in trouble no matter how he answered. Ding Wenyu was worried that Yu Kexia would keep questioning him until he got to the bottom of things. If Ding lied and said that he didn't really have anything particularly important to talk to Yu Kerun about, Yu Kexia would never tell Ding his brother's whereabouts and Ding's entire day would have been wasted. However, knowing Yu Kexia's temper, Ding also knew that if he answered by saying there was indeed something he needed to see Yu Kerun about, his brother would never give up until he knew exactly what this "something" was.

The suspicious look in Yu Kexia's eyes quickly disappeared as he continued talking about all the problems associated with his Military Council besides the production of those safety kits. He complained to Ding Wenyu about how busy he was as secretary general. When people complain about how busy they are, it is often a sign of how arrogant they are— to be frank, complaining is just another way to brag about your capability, as if the world couldn't get on without you. Although deep down Ding Wenyu couldn't take it anymore, he had no choice but to grin and bear it as Yu Kexia went on and on praising himself. Who would have guessed that after rambling on, Yu Kexia would suddenly stop to mention an event the Military Council was holding the following day at the YMCA assembly hall. They were organizing a lecture on air defense; all the newspapers had already run ads, and Yu wanted to know if Ding had seen them. Mayor Ma was going to be there in person to attend the lecture, and Yu Kerun was going to give a presentation to introduce the audience to the different models of Japanese aircraft and offer some basic tips on how to keep on the lookout for them. When Ding Wenyu heard this, his face lit up with happiness; he never imagined that he would find out what he needed so easily. After clarifying the exact time of the lecture, Ding Wenyu said a quick good-bye and got going—he didn't have time to worry about whether or not his hasty departure offended Yu. As Ding was heading out the door, Yu Kexia tried to convince him to stay for dinner but was again refused.

The next day Ding Wenyu arrived right on time at the YMCA assembly hall, only to find the place completely deserted. There were no electric fans in the hall, and those people who had arrived were standing outside chatting under the shade of a tree. Because too few people showed up, the organizers were afraid that Mayor Ma would be upset, so they ran off in a last-minute attempt to round up some more. In the end, the auditorium still resembled the gums of an old lady missing most of her teeth. When Mayor Ma finally arrived, he simply rushed through a few short introductory words and quickly left, setting the stage for the main speaker of the day, an official from the Air Defense Association who spoke with an annoying stutter. The Air Defense Association had much more pull than the Military Council, so during that official's speech, he didn't even bother to mention the various organizers from the Military Council. His speech was long, laborious, and torturously bad. He was all over the place, somehow jumping from England to France and then from Zhuge Liang, the famed statesman of the Three Kingdoms, to the Taiping Rebellion in the Qing dynasty. The audience was filled with long, bored faces; the speaker, on the other hand, seemed to get more energetic as he clamored on. He was sweating profusely and was forced to periodically interrupt himself to chug down water. The hall was filled with the sound of fans flapping and hushed chatter as audience members leaned over, whispering to each other. Ding Wenyu didn't stay long before he slipped outside to cool off under the shade of that tree. He had come to see Yu Kerun and didn't have the slightest interest in learning about air defense.

Yu Kerun finally made his appearance when the meeting was almost finished. Naturally, Qu Manli was with him. Because Yu arrived in such a hurry, even if Ding Wenyu had wanted to pull him aside, he wouldn't have had the chance. Yu Kerun was immediately rushed on stage as if he were the only one in the house who could put out a fire and began his speech amid a weak wave of applause. He wasn't a very good speaker, so his brother should be completely to blame for him rushing there to make a fool of himself. Qu Manli was also to blame for adding fuel to the flames—she seemed naturally disposed to any opportunity to show herself off in public. What Yu Kerun said as he stood there at the podium was not important; all that mattered was that everyone's eyes were on them. Yu Kerun spoke like a true expert, describing different types of airplanes and their respective properties. He talked about the types of bombs they usually carried and the potential destruction that these various bombs could inflict. His talk was actually *too* specialized; before long the entire audience was sick of listening to him.

Ding Wenyu quietly made his way over to Qu Manli and, sitting down beside her, asked bluntly, "Are you the woman who's shacking up with that chump on stage?"

Qu Manli was taken completely off guard. When Ding Wenyu's words finally hit her, she instantly blazed with a mixture of anger and shame. Never even in her dreams could she imagine being subjected to such verbal abuse—how could someone say such discourteous things to her face, berating her with such naked insults? The lecture was still dragging on, so she didn't dare speak too loudly; instead she lowered her voice and resentfully asked, "And who are you?"

"Don't worry about who I am," Ding Wenyu responded. "Just be so kind as to answer *my* question."

Qu Manli couldn't figure out who this guy was and asked why she should answer his question. As she spoke she stood up and switched to another seat. Without the slightest regard for the possible consequences, Ding Wenyu went after her. Realizing how stubborn this man was, she changed seats again—only this time to a spot where there was only one empty seat. Ding Wenyu couldn't continue harassing her and had no choice but to stand off to one side looking frustrated. Yu Kerun, who was in the middle of his speech, didn't know what had happened; he couldn't figure out why Qu Manli kept changing seats. But then he caught sight of Ding Wenyu, who was following her like a shady phantom. Yu Kerun bristled with anger but, since he was unable to release his rage, he ended up with his thoughts in utter disarray. The bored audience had barely been paying attention, but they noticed that something was wrong as soon as Yu started fumbling his words and they immediately perked up.

Yu Kerun's only recourse was to hastily bring his lecture to a conclusion. As he left the stage, someone in the front row who had saved a seat for him motioned for Yu to sit down. After he took his seat, Yu Kerun turned to Qu Manli and motioned for her to come over and sit next to him. Filled with anger, Qu Manli flashed him a cold glare, refusing to go over to him. Wondering what Ding Wenyu had said to her, Yu Kerun turned to Ding Wenyu and discovered that Ding was staring right at him. The lecture soon ended, and amid the audience's applause, Yu Kerun went over to Qu Manli and extended his elbow to walk arm and arm with her out of the auditorium. As they strolled outside, Qu Manli leaned over and grievously whispered something in Yu's ear. Yu Kerun seemed already to have a handle on what had happened. He looked shocked for a second as he turned back to glance at Ding Wenyu. By now they were already outside next to Yu's jeep; Ding Wenyu was following right behind them.

Suddenly picking up his pace, Ding Wenyu rushed up to them, calling out: "Hey, slow down, you two! I'd like to have a word with the two of you."

Yu Kerun pretended that he didn't hear him and told Qu Manli to get in the jeep as he climbed into the driver's seat. Ding Wenyu tried to stop them from leaving; Yu Kerun started the engine and said coldly, "If you've really got something to say, then get in and we'll find a place to have a good talk." This was exactly what Ding Wenyu had hoped for. He clumsily climbed into the open jeep and, before he even had a chance to sit down, the jeep whistled off. Ding Wenyu's behind was immediately thrust into the back seat. Sitting in the front, neither Qu Manli nor Yu Kerun uttered a sound. Yu Kerun paid attention to the road while Qu Manli stared blindly at the scenery outside the window. Ding Wenyu pondered how he should start the conversation; as if preparing some kind of big lecture, he periodically cleared his throat. Yu Kerun was obviously waiting for Ding to say something. Finally, he started to grow impatient and, looking into the rearview mirror, fiercely barked: "Hey! If you've got something to say, then spit it out!"

And so Ding Wenyu began to blame him for not treating Yuyuan better than he had been. He told Yu that Yuyuan not only loved him but never once had done anything dishonest behind his back. Any man married to a woman as angelic as Yuyuan should take it as his responsibility to bring her happiness, not grief. Once he got started, Ding Wenyu babbled on as if he were giving a public speech; his words poured out like an endless waterfall. Yu Kerun appeared unmoved as he drove, forging ahead toward the outskirts of the city. Finally coming to a desolate, off-the-map area, he slammed on the brakes and jumped out of the car. Pulling open the back door, he looked at Ding with a cold face and shouted: "Get the hell out!"

Ding Wenyu still hadn't come around from the speech he had been giving when he noticed Yu Kerun's red, glaring eyes—he looked like he were about to grab Ding and swallow him whole. "What are you doing?" Ding still didn't seem to understand what Yu was up to.

This time, however, Yu Kerun wasn't going to be polite. Pointing at Ding Wenyu's nose, Yu blasted: "I warned you not to let me set eyes on you again! It's about time you got what's coming to you! Hurry up and get the hell out!"

Ding Wenyu sat there without moving a muscle, so Yu Kerun grabbed him by his jacket and pulled him out as if he were picking up a baby chick. Ding Wenyu refused to be outdone and put up a fierce front: "You dare to lay a finger on me?" As he spoke, Ding raised his cane to hit Yu. Yu, however, ducked out of the way and, in one quick move, grabbed Ding's cane out of his hand, threw it to the ground, and delivered two blows to Ding's nose. Ding Wenyu was immediately knocked silly.

Yu Kerun said, " I wouldn't even waste my time on a bookworm like you." Standing off to one side watching, Qu Manli egged him on, telling Yu Kerun to teach him a good lesson. Ding Wenyu came around to realize that he was *not* in a position to take on Yu Kerun, but at the same time, he wasn't about to admit defeat. Ding Wenyu had never been in a fight in his life, and here he was rushing at Yu Kerun without the slightest concern as to what the consequences might be. Ding Wenyu looked like a girl as he wildly flung his arms, trying to grab Yu's face. This was the opportunity Yu Kerun had been waiting for—now he had an excuse to use full force. With a mixed attack of punches and kicks, Yu Kerun had Ding on the ground within a minute.

Panting with rage, Yu Kerun said to Ding, who was spread out on the ground, "I warned you! You must have a death wish or something!"

Just as she was gloating over Ding Wenyu's defeat, Qu Manli noticed that Yu Kerun's hand was bleeding. She quickly removed a silk handkerchief to wrap his hand, only to discover that it was actually Ding's blood. Ding Wenyu had lost every last ounce of his pride. As he lay on the ground groaning in pain, he had clearly reached his low point—he was indeed a sorry sight. Even so, Yu Kerun couldn't help but add a final insult by telling Ding that if it weren't for his age and the fact that he couldn't stand up to a beating, he would have beaten him until he was half dead.

Proud as a peacock, Qu Manli was still a bit confused about Ding's motivations and asked, "Just who the hell do you think you are? What in the world would possess you to stand up for *her?*" She didn't know the story about how Ding Wenyu had been after Yuyuan. Never in a million years would a conceited man like Yu Kerun let it get out that another man had fallen for his own wife. Qu Manli then arrogantly told Ding Wenyu to inform Yuyuan that if she had something to tell them, she had better come and say it in person—there was no need for her to send any more worthless messengers. Noticing a displeased look come over Yu's face, Qu stopped herself from going any further. Yu Kerun started up the jeep and motioned for Qu Manli to hurry up and get in. Yu stepped on the gas, leaving behind Ding Wenyu as they drove off into the distance.

Chapter Eight

I

A lot happened between July and August of 1937, more than anyone could ever have dreamed of. The sudden speed with which everything unfolded was just as startling as what actually unfolded. As far as the people of Nanjing were concerned, August 13, the day fighting broke out in Shanghai, was the day they finally realized that the war had truly begun. Even after the Marco Polo Bridge Incident, people more or less still thought there was some hope for peaceful resolution, but once there was bloodshed in Shanghai this hope was gone. As far as the army general headquarters was concerned, the war machine had long been in motion; it had picked up speed with the Marco Polo Bridge Incident, and by the time Tianjin and Beijing fell, a full-blown war was already inevitable. Armed resistance was now China's only course of action. On August 6, the Japanese government had ordered all Japanese expatriates living in the Hankou concession to evacuate. The very next day, when the Chinese police drove into the concession area, they discovered that the doors and windows of all Japanese stores and residences had already been bolted shut—the concession was completely deserted. It wasn't until August 12, when the Japanese learned from their intelligence that the Chinese government's commitment to resistance was set in stone, that they ordered all Japanese living in Shandong province to evacuate to the coastal city of Qingdao and Japanese citizens in Suzhou to immediately withdraw to Shanghai.

The Nationalist government's authority responsible for orchestrating the warfare planned to seal off the Yangtze River before the beginning of all-out war. They hoped that the Japanese battleships patroling the Yangtze would end up trapped like turtles in a jar. Unfortunately, because traitors working in high government positions had leaked information about the time of the river blockade to the Japanese, those Japanese warships, which had literally been in the palm of the Nationalists' hands, escaped unscathed by slipping right past the blockaded Chinese battery. Filled with indignation, the people of Nanjing watched *The Marco Polo Bridge Incident*, which was fresh out of rehearsals. Little did the audience know that at that very moment, crack troops from the Central Army had already disguised themselves in plain clothes and secretly set out for Shanghai. Although Shanghai was Chinese territory, according to the Unequal Treaties signed by the Qing court, Chinese troops were not permitted to be stationed in the city or its surrounding areas. The Generalissimo's impetus for choosing the region around Shanghai as the battleground for this Second Sino-Japanese War came from his belief that the profusion of river bends and branching streams in the area would aid in holding off the well-equipped Japanese offensive forces. The Chinese army would be able to receive the best possible reinforcements because Shanghai wasn't far from the Chinese air force base. Fighting in Shanghai would mean that the Chinese air force, who by all accounts were clearly the underdogs, would have a chance to fight on more equal footing with the Japanese, who had to fly the long journey over the East China Sea to get there. Since this conflict with Japan was destined to be a full-scale war of resistance involving all of China, Chiang Kai-shek decided to dispatch his loyal army units as the first wave of troops before forcing local warlords and other military leaders in. A virtually unending supply of backup troops could be called in from Guangzhou, Guangxi, Sichuan, and Hunan—these local brigades were especially suited to do battle in the Jiangnan region around Shanghai. Shanghai was an international metropolis, and the Chinese army's brave resistance there was certain to have repercussions in the international community.

The battle near Shanghai aroused yet another climactic wave of anti-Japanese fervor in the capital of Nanjing. Everyone fought to get their hands on the latest newspapers and extra editions; people ran all over the place spreading the latest news from Shanghai. The army headquarters where Yuyuan worked was pure chaos as tensions rose and the headquarters entered into a state of war. All different kinds of military meetings followed one after another. As a confidential secretary, Yuyuan was over her head in work, preparing different types of materials for each meeting. So often war makes personal concerns seem trivial; yet whenever Yuyuan had a moment of rest from her incessant work, she couldn't help but wonder whether Ding Wenyu had found Yu Kerun. It was clear that there had been some delays with the mail—Ding Wenyu's letters usually arrived every day like clockwork, but it had already been three days since Yuyuan had received any news from him. Yuyuan couldn't help but imagine all kinds of scenarios that might have happened; she thought that perhaps Ding never even went looking for Yu, or maybe after Ding tracked Yu down, Yu flat out refused to see her. The first shots of war had already been fired; heaven only knew where Yu Kerun could be—perhaps he had already been sent out to the front lines and wasn't even in Nanjing.

The day after the Japanese air force carried out its first air strike on Nanjing, Yu Kerun rushed down to the army headquarters to see Yuyuan. At the time the headquarters was in the middle of a meeting and although Yuyuan knew that Yu Kerun was outside waiting for her, she had no choice but to wait until the meeting was finished before going out to talk with him. Because several high-ranking army commanders couldn't agree on some of the issues, the meeting went on for what seemed like forever; each of them stuck to his guns, refusing to budge even an inch. By the time the meeting finally ended it was already dark outside, and Yu Kerun was so tired of waiting that he let Yuyuan have it the moment he laid eyes on her. He flatly told her that he didn't have much time and would only be able to talk for a few minutes. At first Yuyuan had covered up her anger out of guilt for having made him wait outside so long, but instantly any shadow of remorse disappeared and a look of unhappiness came over her face.

Yu Kerun intentionally avoided eye contact with Yuyuan; it seemed as if he didn't care in the least about her despondent expression. Then, as if he had some kind of important decision he was about to announce, he said, "I only have a few words I want to say."

As Yuyuan waited to hear these words, she gently bit her lip and glared straight at Yu. As if intending to keep Yuyuan in suspense, Yu Kerun refused to go on. He felt that Yuyuan should be able to figure out what he wanted to say without him actually spelling it out. The two of them hadn't even begun to really talk and already they found themselves in a deadlock. Since Yu Kerun was only prepared to say a few brief words, it was obvious that he wasn't planning to explain what exactly was going on between him and Qu Manli. Just thinking that they hadn't even been married a year and already Yu was openly living with another woman was enough to make Yuyuan's heart break. She felt that she had been done a terrible injustice, without the slightest reason. But what made her most furious was the fact that even at this point, Yu Kerun still had that selfish, smug attitude, as if he were the only person in the world who mattered.

After each refused to put an end to the silence, Yu Kerun finally gave in with a minor declaration of self-mockery: "Actually, maybe it's better if I just keep my mouth shut."

Yuyuan wanted to get in a few biting remarks but couldn't think of any slanderous words to taunt him with. Yu Kerun was the last person to do anything that would make him lose face—if he hadn't had something he wanted to say to Yuyuan, there was no way he would have waited all that time for her. The reason Yu Kerun had come looking for Yuyuan that day was to tell her that his request to be sent to the front lines had been approved. The next day he was to report to the Jianqiao Airfield in Zhejiang to carry out his duties in air combat. Regarding their breakup, it seemed they had come to the stage where they would have to start making some arrangements. Qu Manli had already taken care of this for him. She had found Yu a lawyer to draw up the divorce papers; since neither of them had any real valuables to fight over, all that was really needed was a pair of signatures. Yu Kerun knew how proud Yuyuan was and was convinced that she wouldn't drag her feet when it came to signing on the dotted line. Unlike Qu Manli, Yuyuan would never nag and pester Yu; nor did she have that nasty habit of saying one thing and meaning another. Although Qu Manli kept repeating that she had no intention of marrying Yu Kerun, her secret scheme to become the next Mrs. Yu had already been set in motion. The unique quality about women like Qu Manli is that no matter what they might say or do, they always act as if they're in the right. Qu Manli dove wholeheartedly into her job of bringing an end to Yuyuan and Yu Kerun's marriage—her enthusiasm for this mission made it clear that what was at stake went far beyond the "unselfish reasons" that she professed. But all along Qu Manli still held to her position that she was only trying to save Yu Kerun from a loveless marriage.

Yu Kerun wanted to tell Yuyuan that it was not entirely his fault that their marriage had fallen apart like this. He wanted to explain that he wasn't leaving her because he didn't love her, but rather because he had finally realized that he wasn't ready to be any woman's husband. As far as Yu Kerun was concerned, marriage would probably always be a mistake. Already he was starting to have the feeling that his relationship with Qu Manli would end up even worse—he knew better than to tell Yuyuan this. Yu Kerun was actually terribly annoyed by the situation he found himself in; he felt as if his hands were tied. Yu was never much of a romantic and he felt utterly drained by this snare of love he had gotten caught in. Rushing into marriage with Yuyuan had obviously been a mistake, but it now seemed as if rushing into a divorce might be an even bigger mistake.

Their conversation didn't seem to be going anywhere; although Yu Kerun had spent some time preparing what he wanted to say, he still couldn't express himself clearly. He couldn't really latch on to the right words. They had been strolling along near the army headquarters and without even realizing it, they wound up beside a small lotus pond. Gazing southeast, they caught sight of the moon hanging in the night sky beyond the eaves of the tall buildings in the distance. The war had already begun and, being on active military duty, both of them were up to their ears in work; yet here they were, standing in the moonlight awkwardly discussing the crisis in their marriage—this in itself was a rather preposterous scene. Yuyuan was terribly confused; she didn't want Yu Kerun to think that she couldn't go on without him, but at the same time she couldn't take listening to him stammer on like that. Deep down, she already knew that she could never forgive him. Because of this, when Yu Kerun mentioned that he was about to be sent to the front lines, Yuyuan reacted strongly, immediately asking him when he wanted to have her sign the divorce papers. She put up a indifferent front while trying to hide the tears creeping out of the corners of her eyes.

During the battle going on near Shanghai, the Nationalist army relied upon favorable climatic, geographic, and human conditions, and in the beginning things went fairly smoothly. Three Chinese crack divisions planned to eliminate the Japanese marine brigade stationed in the Japanese concession before reinforcements from the Japanese mainland had a chance to arrive. The ensuing battle went on with an unprecedented intensity as the Chinese army commanders led their men in a fierce charge. On the first day of fighting the Chinese had already lost one of their brigade commanders. The Japanese army put up a strong resistance, and although the Chinese forces had successfully taken the peripheral regions around the enemy—at one point they even came close to taking the Japanese's most important stronghold, the port at Huishan—the Chinese effort ended in failure due to insufficient firepower. Every day the newspapers rushed to be the first to get their extra editions out to the newsstands. They always ran positive articles and failed to report any bad news, running headlines like BATTERED ENEMIES APPEAR TO BE LOSING GROUND or A GRAND VICTORY FOR CHINA AWAITS. News of an impending victory kept pouring into Nanjing and public morale was high. Even though the Japanese had begun air strikes against the capital on August 15, the citizens of Nanjing didn't seem the least bit scared. They seemed to know that the bombardments were coming and to be sufficiently prepared—some even started to grow weary waiting for these anticipated attacks. When Japanese fighter planes first visited the Nanjing skies, hordes of soldiers rushed out to the streets in a futile effort to shoot the planes down with their pistols and rifles. In the end Chiang Kai-shek was forced to issue strict orders that only troops from the air defense division were permitted to attack enemy planes.

In the ten years since the Nationalist government had established their capital in Nanjing, this ancient, dilapidated city had been completely transformed. New boulevards lined with large trees mercilessly cut through the tattered old section of the city; these wide, shady streets lined with thick vegetation became the city's best protection. All the recent architecture in Nanjing had been designed with air defense in mind; of all the cities in China, Nanjing was the only one that had taken appropriate measures to deal with air raids. Years earlier, the streets were already full of instructional posters and public service announcements about air defense. A few public squares even erected model bombs made from steel wire filled with cement, to educate the public about those damn things. To greet the coming war, the capital Nanjing had the most advanced antiaircraft guns, the most skilled artillerymen, and the most powerful searchlights. When an all-out air raid broke out, sharply dressed police and sentries and the well-trained emergency unit would all know exactly what to do. After the initial Japanese air attack on Nanjing on August 15, the air raid shelters, which had been ready for some time, were finally put to use. It only took minutes after the sirens sounded for personnel to be dispatched, citizens to scramble into the air raid shelters, and cars and trucks to pull over beneath the shady cover of the boulevard trees. Everything proceeded with perfect order; although the war had begun, things didn't really seem too bad at this early stage. Nanjing implemented martial law, strictly prohibiting the spreading of rumors and immediately investigating and trying all suspected traitors and collaborators.

Endless battalions of Chinese troops moved toward Shanghai as morale soared. Large numbers of citizens spontaneously rushed down to the train station to show support for those soldiers passing through on their way to the front lines. Jubilant soldiers beamed with happiness; there wasn't even a hint of fear on their faces. It had been years since the city of Nanjing had witnessed such excitement. Yu Kerun felt that flying to the sky to do battle with the enemy was the best way to escape the troubles he was facing in his personal life. Ding Wenyu had provided him with an opportunity to blow off some steam, but Yu felt even worse off than before. He had given Ding Wenyu quite a beating, but it didn't take long for him to realize that pushing around a bookworm like Ding, who was obviously too feeble even to truss a chicken, was by no means any kind of heroic deed. Yu Kerun imagined how much Yuyuan must hate him for this. Yu never really took Ding Wenyu's pursuit of his wife to heart—how could a woman who'd fallen for Yu Kerun possibly see anything in a pedant like Ding Wenyu? Yu Kerun firmly believed that Ding's crush would never turn into anything—Yuyuan would never in a million years fall for this ridiculously dressed, cane-bearing clown.

Yu Kerun and Yuyuan's conversation came to naught. Because of the strict wartime blackout, the entire city of Nanjing was pitch dark. The neon lights in the busy parts of the city were all turned off and the pair of calabash-shaped signs on the roof of the Bank of China in the downtown Xinjiekou district lost their brilliant splendor. Yu Kerun hadn't driven his jeep that day; instead he'd borrowed a friend's bicycle, and after he said good-bye to Yuyuan he rode through the main boulevards of the busy downtown area. Air-conditioned theaters went on showing films, and whenever they had the opportunity, the well-to-do rushed to the movie houses to escape Nanjing's searing August heat. Yu Kerun couldn't help but be surprised that people were still able to go to the movies during the enforced blackout. After the movie, people from the audience smoothly filed into the streets, disappearing into the darkness of the night. Just like always, high officials drove their cars down the main streets, their headlights cutting into the darkness like blades of light. Yu Kerun knew that if enemy planes were to appear, sirens would sound throughout the entire city and these cars would be forced to turn off their lights and pull over under the foliage of the trees lining the streets.

The war had just begun, and it seemed as if the well-ordered people of Nanjing still hadn't realized what the end result might be. The optimistic tone of the newspapers left people blind and credulous. Huge numbers held on to the silly belief that driving the Japanese out of Shanghai would mean full victory for the Nationalist army, and the Chinese would never again have to suffer humiliation at the hands of the Japanese. At the same time, there were still a lot of people who thought that if they turned out to be no match for the Japanese, they could always seek peace through the signing of more Unequal Treaties. They felt that since China had already signed so many other, similar treaties, ceding more land and paying more indemnities was no big deal. Yu Kerun knew that neither of these possibilities was ever going to happen. First off, there was no way they would be able to drive the Japanese back to the sea. The Chinese army was still a long way from any kind of all-conquering force, and Yu knew that as soon as Japanese reinforcements arrived the Chinese army, which was currently on the offensive, would have no choice but to switch to the defensive. Second, now that the war machine was already in full motion, bringing it to a sudden stop was easier said than done. With the fate of the country hanging in the balance, every man had a responsibility to his nation; as an enlisted man in active military service, Yu Kerun felt his sole course of action was to plunge into the battlefield. An army is trained for a thousand days, all for a moment of battle; Yu Kerun knew that this was the time to give full play to his air-borne skills.

Virtually overnight, Yu Kerun's name was all over the newspapers; once again he became the target of Nanjing reporters and a virtual celebrity in the hearts of the people. Although as a whole the Chinese air force couldn't hold a candle to the Japanese air force, because their base was nearby and they strategically waited for the enemy to exhaust themselves, during the first stages of the battle of Shanghai, the Chinese forces not only held their own but at times performed exceptionally well. The first time the well-trained Yu Kerun took to the air in battle, he became the first Chinese pilot to shoot down an enemy plane. After that he was able to take down enemy fighters virtually every time he flew; his superior skills quickly made him an almost legendary figure, even winning him the nickname, "Hunter of the Blue Heavens." For a time, stories about the outstanding achievements of the Chinese air force circulated throughout the city; from the main streets to the small alleys, everyone was talking about their country's heroes in the sky. Yuyuan's girlfriends still didn't know that her marriage with Yu Kerun was on the rocks and came over one after another to congratulate her, their words filled with admiration. Yuyuan had a million things on her mind and was in utter despair; mistaking her sadness for jealousy, Yuyuan's friends teased her for being so serious.

II

It was in September that Yu Kerun sacrificed himself for his country. The Chinese air force was hopelessly outnumbered and, as the fighting became more intense, quickly became the underdogs. The unit that Yu Kerun led had fought nonstop for days on end, taking to the sky several times each day. As Yu Kerun's popularity increased, the Japanese began keeping an eye on him. During each air battle there were always a few enemy planes on his tail that he could barely shake loose. Although the Chinese air force had delivered a strong blow to the Japanese, its losses were also quite severe. Yu Kerun's fighter had been hit several times and was lined with small bullet holes; fortunately, the enemy never managed to hit any crucial parts of the plane and it was still able to fly. However, red lights soon came on in the Chinese camp—if things kept progressing as they had, it wouldn't be long before the Chinese air force would be finished. By the time Yu Kerun heroically gave his life, there were only two fighters remaining in the once-large unit he had been responsible for leading.

The truth about the fighting around Shanghai couldn't have been further from the rampant optimism presented in the newspapers. The situation was developing exactly in the manner the Chinese feared most. After Yu Kerun was killed, the branch of the air force responsible for arranging his funeral was extremely hesitant about carrying it out. Because Yu Kerun was so popular among the people, he had enormous influence—his death would not be taken lightly. Yu Kerun had already been virtually deified by the press, and his death implied the destruction of a myth. China had to be extremely careful to avoid any action that might damage morale among the soldiers. However, since Yu Kerun had been lost in battle, there was no way to keep it a secret, as had sometimes been the custom when an emperor died. Reporters from small newspapers rushed to get the story out, paying no heed to the order that all wartime news reports were to keep with the official line. The first newspaper to run the story printed a short article the size of a piece of dried tofu; this put the air force in an awkward situation, leaving them with no choice but to organize a grand, stately funeral for Yu Kerun.

During the days leading up to the funeral, Yuyuan was terribly depressed. Although their marriage had had some serious problems and they had already decided to split up, they still hadn't signed the divorce papers. Yuyuan thought back to when she had first met Yu Kerun; at the time Yu, wearing that leather pilot jacket, drew the attention of virtually every girl who laid eyes on him. Yuyuan couldn't help but admit that she too was immediately carried away by his elegant demeanor. Complete strangers to each other, they fluttered in dance like a pair of celestial fairies. Song after song, they waltzed long into the night, until the ball ended. Everyone in the room gazed at them with envy; the zestful duo indeed made quite a scene that night. Their wedding was also quite an affair, and their seemingly perfect marriage made more than a few people jealous. When news of Yu Kerun's death first reached her ears, Yuyuan's mind went blank and she stood there utterly stunned and expressionless for what seemed like an eternity. The person who brought Yuyuan the news was afraid that she wouldn't be able to take the shock and motioned for her to sit down on the stone bench beside them as he awkwardly tried to find the right words to console her.

"I knew something like this would happen," Yuyuan quietly stammered.

Sacrifice is inevitable in times of war. As the spouse of an air force pilot and as an enlisted woman herself, Yuyuan had sensed that things would end like this. Even when Yu Kerun had rushed over to bid farewell to her before heading off to the front lines, Yuyuan had been struck with an ominous feeling. Yu Kerun had appeared very depressed when he came to army headquarters that day, but naturally this sadness had nothing to do with fear of going into battle. Yu Kerun never once displayed even a hint of fear when it came to war. He was obviously going through quite an ordeal with that relationship he was caught in; Yuyuan realized how much of a handful the woman he was living with must have been. This woman really knew how to deal with men; she must have had Yu Kerun's back against the wall and forced him to leave Yuyuan and sign his name to those divorce papers. Any woman who could force a man as irresponsible as Yu Kerun into moving in together is indeed far from a run-of-the-mill college girl. Yuyuan almost immediately forgave Yu Kerun for everything he had done to her. She felt that what had happened wasn't entirely his fault. She thought of Yu Kerun as nothing but an arrogant, overly self-confident man who refused to grow up. However, after she attended his funeral all of this changed; not only did thoughts of her deceased husband fail to induce sorrow but, from that point on, whenever he crossed Yuyuan's mind, a strange, almost indescribable feeling of resentment immediately welled up inside her.

Yu Kerun's funeral was a glorious affair attended by a wide array of famous military and government officials. As the Secretary General of the Aviation Committee, the first lady, Soong May-ling, chaired the funeral and said a few words during the ceremony. There were quite a few citizens, most notably a large crowd of teenage girls, who rushed over of their own accord to express their condolences. Because of frequent Japanese air raids, the public memorial ceremony for Yu Kerun had to be scaled down and was held in the Air Force Assembly Hall. Those army and government big shots all scurried in to make a quick appearance before dashing off. At the last minute, several sentry officers were called in to maintain order. According to China's air defense regulations, there was to be a strict ban on all public gatherings during times of martial law, yet one after another, an endless stream of people arrived. They all lined up quietly on the field outside the assembly hall, waiting to enter for the viewing. In order to ensure that all the important officials were able to expeditiously leave the hall, the slow line had to be stopped occasionally so that famous political figures could exit. Only after they had left could the line of mourners start moving again. With tears running down her face, Soong May-ling left a deep impression on everyone there. The atmosphere throughout the ceremony was extremely solemn. People hung their heads in sorrow, quietly sobbing as they stopped in front of Yu Kerun's photograph, unwilling to move on.

Yu Kerun's plane exploded in mid-air just as he had been approaching the runway. It was clear that his plane had already taken a heavy hit, but being overconfident in his flying skills, Yu Kerun tried landing instead of bailing out and abandoning his fighter. Planes were simply too precious to the Chinese air force; Yu Kerun was reluctant to let one go so easily. After he'd circled halfway around the airfield runway, something suddenly went wrong and, realizing his situation wasn't good, Yu Kerun decided at the last minute to bail out. Just as he ejected himself from the cockpit, the plane exploded into flames. Under the eyes of everyone down on the runway, Yu Kerun's body was blown apart and burned like charcoal. Pieces of his remains fell to the ground in two distinct places. When the mourners viewed Yu Kerun's body, all that was actually there under that white sheet were a few pieces of charred flesh and bones along with a few small remnants of his plane. It was because of this that when Yuyuan requested to see her husband one last time, the guard beside his casket adamantly refused to let her pull back that white cloth.

As his wife, Yuyuan entered the mourning hall an hour before the ceremony officially began. But when she went in, she was taken completely off guard by the presence of two people who shouldn't have even been there, yet had somehow gotten there first. The first person was Qu Manli, who was dressed in full mourning clothes; the second was Ding Wenyu, whose face was still black and blue from that last beating he'd taken. The two of them sat there in the utmost seriousness. Openly presenting herself as the deceased's widow, Qu Manli sat beside Yu Kerun's casket, wiping the tears from her face in a most affected way. From the looks of it she had some ulterior motive for sitting there; because most of Yu Kerun's friends and relatives already knew about her relationship with Yu, she decided it was better for her to play all her cards rather than sneak around as if she was nobody. By sitting there in deep sorrow with tears running down her face, Qu Manli not only changed her status from Yu's illegal live-in mistress but also gave everyone the impression that Yuyuan was nothing but the abandoned wife. Once the ceremony began everyone would simply think of Yuyuan as a woman who'd been on the verge of getting divorced from Yu, and their sympathy for her would disappear into thin air. Qu Manli was indeed one sharp lady; she made sure to get everyone she knew to come out and support her, from her senile old uncle and her middle-aged aunt to a whole bunch of close and distant friends and relatives. As for Yuyuan, besides her parents and her third sister Yujiao, the only other people there on her side were a few of her girlfriends from work. Compared with Qu Manli's virtual army of supporters, Yuyuan couldn't have appeared more alone.

Once the memorial ceremony began, Qu Manli proved insatiable in her appetite for attention. Because her status indeed had yet to be formally recognized, Qu had no choice but to take the seat reserved for Yu Kerun's closest friend, which was behind Yuyuan in a clearly inferior position. However, it didn't take long at all for Qu Manli to turn things around for herself. She understood that having people point and stare behind her back wasn't nearly as good as simply taking the stage and showing herself off. The funeral lasted for quite a while, with small climaxes coming with the arrival of each famous official. People standing in the back couldn't help but get up on their tiptoes for a better look at these political celebrities. After bowing before Yu Kerun's casket, the big shot officials proceeded to go over and express their sympathies to his family. Teary-eyed Qu Manli knew practically every one of these bigwigs and affectedly addressed them by their official titles and shook their hands, thanking each of them on behalf of the deceased. She expressed her gratitude that they were able to come and say a final farewell to Yu Kerun. Qu Manli's nauseating performance went way overboard, dragging Yuyuan's spirits even lower. She wished she could walk over and give Qu Manli a couple of good slaps across the face. Her friends were all surprised by Yuyuan's tolerance; they couldn't understand how Yuyuan, who was usually so proud, could put up with this shameless woman's unbridled behavior during this solemn ceremony.

Yuyuan's third sister Yujiao bit her lip in anger, saying: "Yu Kerun must have been blind! How could he possibly have fallen for a woman like *her*?" She couldn't stand watching Qu Manli's wretched act and quickly saw her elderly parents, Mr. and Mrs. Ren Bojin, out. Just as she was leaving, however, she threw down her gauntlet and walked over to Qu Manli. Pretending that she had no idea who Qu was, Yujiao asked sharply just who she was and what she was doing there. After hearing Qu Manli's response, she announced with surprise, "Oh, so you're that little bitch my brother-in-law has been sleeping with!" Qu Manli's face instantly turned red as she bit down on her lip, pretending not to hear Yujiao's comment. It wasn't appropriate to get into a fight on such a solemn occasion; anyway, Qu Manli wasn't the kind of woman who would let insults get to her—she always knew how to keep cool when the heat was on. Fifteen minutes later when some new big shots arrived, Qu Manli instantly returned to her old self—it was as if nothing ever happened.

What made Yuyuan and her friends most furious was, as Soong May-ling came over to shake hands with Yu Kerun's family members before leaving, Qu Manli had the nerve to embrace the first lady and break down in her arms. Everyone knew that the only reason the Chinese pilots were able to become the "pride of Heaven" was the first lady's partiality to them. Soong May-ling was always more than happy to take part in all of the air force's major events. And if the air force ran into problems, they were often able to resolve them with unimaginable speed by going through her good offices. In 1934, when the Aviation Association was first established, the Chinese air force didn't have even a handful of planes capable of air combat, but by the time the Second Sino-Japanese War broke out in 1937, the Chinese air force's rapid development and outstanding performance caused quite a stir both in China and abroad. Behind the scenes, however, no one could deny that Soong May-ling deserved a lot of the credit for this. As the Secretary General of the Aviation Association, she had had quite a bit of contact with Yu Kerun. On several occasions Yu had even flown the first lady in his plane. She always had a good impression of this celebrity pilot. Yu Kerun's heroic death and all the terrible losses the Chinese air force had suffered after just one short month of air battle, along with the barrage of bad news that kept coming in, all tore at Soong May-ling's heart. When Qu Manli tearfully dove into her arms, it actually provided the first lady with an opportunity to release all of the sadness that had been building up within her.

Almost everyone was touched and, for a while, the entire mourning hall filled with the sounds of weeping. If Yu Kerun's spirit in heaven had been able to witness this scene, he undoubtedly would have praised Qu Manli's move as a stroke of brilliance. Because Soong May-ling was an idol to countless girl students, everyone was immediately filled with envy, and all eyes focused on Qu Manli. Yuyuan's closest friends who had accompanied her to the funeral looked at Qu Manli with disgust. People exchanged whispered comments, trying to find out just who this amazing woman was and why she was so close to the first lady. At the same time, people's gazes also fell on Yuyuan and in their evasive eyes, she could sense the misgivings and resentment they held for her. This was undoubtedly the most awkward moment in Yuyuan's life, and under everyone's stare she found herself at a complete loss as to how to react. Qu Manli's actions and behavior seriously inhibited her normal thinking process. All Yuyuan could do was try her best to control herself in order to avoid doing something stupid.

Ding Wenyu's presence also occasionally distracted Yuyuan's attention. She wondered just where Ding had gotten news of the funeral. The whole time he was among a group of his friends and relatives, secretly watching Yuyuan's every move like a silent shadow. Yuyuan tried as hard as she could to pretend that Ding Wenyu wasn't there; however, the harder she tried, the more she found herself thinking about him. Ding Wenyu spent the first portion of the memorial service standing with Yu Kexia and his wife. His intentions were quite simple: this way he could show everyone that he had attended the funeral as a friend of Yu Kerun's brother. At least he had enough sense not to go out of his way and immediately rush over to Yuyuan. Actually, as soon as Yuyuan and her girlfriends walked into the mourning hall, one of her friends noticed him and said with surprise, "What in the world would possess *him* to come?" Another one of her girlfriends even asked Yuyuan if she wanted her to have Ding Wenyu leave.

The memorial ceremony lasted much longer than originally intended, partly because messages kept coming in reporting that several groups of mourners had been held up by Japanese air strikes on their way to the funeral. At one point, a few people even saw a Japanese fighter fly directly over the mourning hall. Several of the guests in attendance had left early. The first to leave were Yuyuan's parents and sister Yujiao, followed soon after by Mr. and Mrs. Yu Kexia. Although Qu Manli's aunt and uncle came late, they didn't waste much time before leaving either. Several people had encouraged Yuyuan to leave early, but she clearly didn't want to go before Qu Manli. Gradually, Qu Manli had no choice but to give in and leave first. Everyone Qu had brought with her to the funeral was either a member or an admirer of high society, and their reason for attending this funeral wasn't just to see the dead, it was to see the living—or rather, to *be seen* by the living. Their main goal was to get a dose of public attention; the last thing they were willing to do was waste their entire day at this mourning hall.

Ding Wenyu quietly made his way over to Yuyuan and, after bowing to the deceased, stood next to her like a statue as if he were her patron saint. His appearance was a bit ridiculous. Because Yuyuan didn't offer the slightest reaction, it was her girlfriends who ended up getting frustrated. They felt that unless they put a stop to him, this bookworm Ding Wenyu would certainly push his luck and end up doing something out of line. Ding Wenyu's behavior also caught Qu Manli's attention—women all seem to have an uncanny instinct when it comes to these things. Almost instantly Qu Manli was able to tell from the look in Yuyuan's girlfriends' eyes that this guy, whom Yu Kerun had given quite a beating not too long before, was actually pursuing Yuyuan. Qu Manli suddenly realized that only a person being tortured by jealousy would resort to violence against his romantic rival. The boldness of this Ding Wenyu, however, surprised even Qu Manli.

Trying to test the waters, Ding Wenyu stood beside Yuyuan for a while before lowering his head and softly whispering in her ear, "I know you'll be able to pull through this."

Yuyuan nodded her head with a pensive look; she realized that the eyes of almost everyone in the room were on her. There were already very few familiar faces left in the mourning hall, but among those relatives and acquaintances, virtually all of them had long ago gotten wind of Ding Wenyu's pursuit of Yuyuan. Not caring what other people might think, Ding leaned back over to her ear and said with concern, "He's gone now and can't come back. You need to take care of yourself."

Although Ding Wenyu tried to be tactful, Yu Kerun's body was, after all, still warm, and in other people's eyes Ding was clearly way out of line. Through her obvious tolerance of Ding Wenyu's actions, Yuyuan was in a way intentionally bringing him into the spotlight. Realizing that there was no point in staying any longer, Qu Manli hesitated a moment before preparing to leave. Yuyuan, who had been paying constant attention to Qu Manli's moves, suddenly decided that there was no way she was going to let that tramp get the last laugh by leaving first. Once Qu Manli left, Yuyuan would have no reason to stay behind. Since Yuyuan was going to have to leave sooner or later, why shouldn't she leave *before* Qu Manli? The sentries who had been keeping vigil beside the coffin cleared a path through the crowded hall as Qu Manli shook hands and said good-bye to the people around her. Yuyuan suddenly tugged Ding Wenyu's arm, motioning for him to see her out. A surprised, flattered look immediately appeared on Ding's face as he took a step forward, doing his best to protect Yuyuan on their way out. Ding was practically hugging Yuyuan around the waist as they made their bold, eye-catching exit. Yuyuan knew that this would incite a lot of talk among people she knew, but she couldn't care less about what they might say. She was terribly upset, and it seemed as though this radical move was the only way for her to get her frustration out of her system. Deep down she had the strange feeling that everything had all somehow been planned by Yu Kerun.

III

Yuyuan almost immediately parted company with Ding Wenyu. Just after they left the hall and got away from the crowds, before Ding Wenyu even had a chance to realize what had happened, Yuyuan forcefully pushed his hand off her waist and said with disgust that she hoped he would get the hell away from her. She told him that she wished she'd never see him again. She suddenly became extremely agitated and in the heat of the moment said all kinds of hurtful things. Ding Wenyu didn't understand why she was so angry. Almost losing control of herself, she screamed at him, warning Ding not to get any crazy ideas and think that just because Yu Kerun was dead now it was time for his lucky number to come up. Yuyuan was in a much worse mood than could be imagined; she was more upset than anyone ever expected. She told Ding Wenyu that although she already had no love left for her dead, heroic husband, she was even more fed up with Ding Wenyu and his utter impudence. A flood of tears began to pour down her face; there had been several times at the mourning hall when Yuyuan wanted to cry, but the tears wouldn't come. Now she finally had an opportunity to break down and let everything out. She buried her face in her hands and let go of herself, wailing aloud like a child.

Yuyuan's girlfriends, who were following close behind them, all knew that Yuyuan was just using Ding to let off some steam—they would have done the same thing if they were in her shoes. Poor Ding Wenyu was just a punching bag. Yuyuan's friends, however, felt that he deserved it—Ding Wenyu was finally getting what he had coming to him. A few people were watching them, but they were standing too far away to hear what Ding and Yuyuan were saying. In any case, under the circumstances it was completely natural for Yuyuan to be upset and make a scene. A jeep drove over to take Yuyuan and her girlfriends home, and she climbed in with the help of her friends. Ding Wenyu stood off to one side like a stray cur, not knowing what to do as he watched the jeep drive off into the distance. One of Yuyuan's friends couldn't help but burst out laughing when she looked out the window and saw Ding pathetically standing there. Ding Wenyu wasn't in the least bit troubled by the fact that Yuyuan had lost her temper at him; what made him upset was seeing how terribly sad she was. Yuyuan's tortured appearance made Ding Wenyu feel as if he were guilty of some unforgivable sin.

Ding Wenyu stood there blankly after they left, frozen for what seemed like an eternity. Qu Manli got into a car not far from where Ding was standing but, just before she climbed in, she turned her head and looked over at him in confusion. She couldn't understand why Ding didn't leave with Yuyuan. Mourners coming to pay their final respects were still rushing over in dribs and drabs, but there were very few students; most of these latecomers were military staff workers, and Ding could feel her pain gnawing at his heart. Owing to periodic Japanese air raids, the streets were virtually devoid of pedestrians and most of the shops were closed. Ding Wenyu finally found a small restaurant that was still open and went in to order a bowl of fried eel noodles. The restaurant owner was so happy to have a customer with the spare time to come and enjoy a good meal that he prepared the dish himself. First he killed a live finless ricefield eel; then he lightly pan-fried it, prepared the noodles, brought the dish over, and watched with a serious look of concern as Ding Wenyu ate. He had hoped to win a few words of praise, but all Ding Wenyu could think of was Yuyuan—he wasn't in any way prepared to comment on that bowl of delicious noodles. The noodle stall owner started to get fidgety and told Ding, "I guarantee you won't be able to find a better bowl of fried eel noodles in all of Nanjing!"

Ding Wenyu looked over at the stall owner but refused to comment. His lack of enthusiasm made the owner feel a bit confused and disappointed. If Ding Wenyu had said a few nice words, that stall owner probably could have gone on forever blowing his trumpet and bragging about his cooking. But Ding Wenyu didn't make a sound, and the owner started to get antsy about not being able to deliver his standard speech; instead, all he could do was stand off to one side staring at Ding Wenyu. Ding was a bit uncomfortable with that and finally nodded his head in an attempt to ease the situation. The shop owner jumped on this opportunity and immediately asked Ding whether or not he had noticed the special flavor in the soup. Before Ding Wenyu had a chance to respond, the noodle man was already explaining the reason his noodle soup had such a unique taste. Only after he had explained how the soup broth had been slow cooked with ricefield eel bones did Ding indeed start to notice how delicious it really was. It was at that moment that air raid sirens suddenly started to sound. Ding Wenyu and the noodle shop owner both looked outside, but neither of them bothered to actually get up. Someone ran down the street past the storefront as a woman anxiously cried out her child's name. The noodle shop owner muttered nonchalantly, "I'm not going to any air raid shelter. I'd like to see those damn Japs just try to drop a bomb on my shop!" Ding Wenyu never imagined that a petty owner of a little hole-in-the-wall noodle shop could remain so calm at such a critical juncture; his was indeed the kind of commendable attitude you don't see every day. Ding Wenyu leisurely slurped down his noodles as he complimented the owner on his cooking. In the end, that noodle shop owner finally heard what he had been waiting for. Wave after wave of air raid sirens sounded, but they might as well have fallen on deaf ears as the noodle man smiled ear to ear, relishing Ding's compliments.

As soon as Ding Wenyu left the restaurant and walked onto the street, he saw a pair of planes fly past. The air defense team on the ground continually fired their antiaircraft guns, but Ding Wenyu had no idea whether these were Chinese fighter planes or enemy bombers. A police officer standing inside a crude air raid shelter called out something to Ding Wenyu. With the air raid sirens blaring, Ding Wenyu could see the officer frantically waving his arms but had no idea what he was saying. He guessed that the officer was trying to tell him to hurry up and find some shelter, but looking for a place to hide was the last thing on Ding Wenyu's mind. The people of Nanjing had started to get fed up with the incessant air bombings and there were quite a few who simply ignored the sirens and went right on with their everyday affairs. Ding Wenyu was walking all alone along the main streets. When he came to an open square he saw a few more planes flying toward him; they looked as if they were preparing to dive bomb. By the time the air raid sirens ended, Ding Wenyu had already worked out a mental draft of what he was going to write to Yuyuan in his next letter. He felt terrible for making her so angry that day. If he had known that things would turn out the way that they did, he never even would have gone. However, after putting himself through the grinder of guilt, Ding Wenyu couldn't help but start to stick up for himself; he no doubt had done something wrong, but he didn't understand just *what*.

What Ding Wenyu didn't know was that after she left the funeral, Yuyuan almost immediately began to regret how she had treated him. Ding had no idea that when Yuyuan blindly poured her anger all over him like a bucket of dirty water, she actually didn't have an ounce of true hatred for him. Just the opposite, Yuyuan got so angry and lost herself precisely because she *couldn't* bring herself to hate him. Ding Wenyu wasn't the only one confused about what he had done wrong; Yuyuan herself didn't even know. Actually, she didn't really hate either Ding Wenyu or Yu Kerun; if there was anyone she should direct her hatred toward it was the Japanese—and, of course, Qu Manli. Even if he had made a thousand mistakes or told a million lies, in the end Yu Kerun made the ultimate sacrifice for his country, and Yuyuan couldn't bring herself to blame him for what he had done to her. As for Ding Wenyu, she couldn't help but admit that her impression of him kept getting better; Yuyuan slowly began to feel a kind of affection unlike any she had ever known. On her way home from the mourning hall Yuyuan not only forgave Ding Wenyu for his uncalled-for appearance at her husband's funeral but even began to feel sorry for treating him so harshly. Ding Wenyu hadn't really done anything wrong, and the last thing he deserved was to be treated so unfairly.

Because the city was in a state of war, it wasn't until Yuyuan got home from her husband's funeral that she received Ding Wenyu's last few letters. Postal service had been irregular since the air raids had begun and a bunch of letters that Ding had sent off on different days all arrived at the same time. Yuyuan had to read through them several times before she finally figured out the order in which they originally had been written. In the first letter Ding Wenyu casually mentioned that he had read in the newspapers about how outstanding Yu Kerun had been doing on the battlefield; the last letter was an expression of his condolences after hearing of Yu Kerun's heroic passing. Like his previous letters, these were filled with emotion, especially the last one. Ding Wenyu wrote with elegance and feeling; in the end, however, a letter that was meant to console her left Yuyuan in tears. Ding started off this long letter with an admission that he couldn't help but feel a certain amount of guilt-ridden happiness when he heard of Yu's misfortune. Although these thoughts were completely immoral, it was in a way only natural for him to feel this way; the war seemed to have given Ding Wenyu a new window of opportunity. In his letter Ding berated himself for being contemptible and shameless, cursing himself for even thinking about trying to take advantage of another's tragedy.

Halfway through the letter, Ding Wenyu's tone suddenly changed and he started singing Yu's praises, saying how much he admired Yu Kerun for being able to make the ultimate sacrifice for his nation. Ding Wenyu admitted that he would never be able to win over Yuyuan precisely because he was not the kind of man who would be willing to spill his blood on the battlefield. Yu Kerun's death gave Ding Wenyu an opportunity to reexamine himself. He realized that his love for Yuyuan was not as absolute, not as pure as it should be; during such unusual times Ding felt his foremost concern should be for Yuyuan's pain over the loss of her husband. Although Yu Kerun's sacrifice was indeed noble, Ding Wenyu firmly believed that in the process Yu had committed a small mistake: making one of the most wonderful women in the world suffer for his actions. Ding Wenyu's letter went in circles as he wracked his brain to find the best words to help relieve some of Yuyuan's pain. He was very careful to control the pace of his language, and by the time Yuyuan read the last climactic sentence she could no longer hold back her tears. Yuyuan could almost imagine Ding Wenyu shouting himself hoarse as he screamed out the final passage: "When I think of how your heart must be breaking, my heart breaks first. I wish I could do something to make all of your hurt go away!"

Holding Ding's pile of slow-coming letters in her hands, Yuyuan read them over and over. She wanted to write him back immediately, but her pride got in the way. After all, it had only been a few hours since she had snapped at him. Since the news of Yu Kerun's death had gotten out, virtually everyone Yuyuan knew went out of their way to avoid the issue. Yuyuan's close friends who knew about the problems in her marriage felt extremely awkward about even mentioning Yu Kerun to her. Naturally, Yuyuan felt even more awkward. The last thing she wanted was for people to feel sorry for her. Yu Kerun cheating on her and dying for his country had nothing to do with each other—somehow, however, these two incidents were intertwined in Yuyuan's mind. After returning from the funeral, Yuyuan thought back to Qu Manli's exaggerated performance and began to feel her resentment toward Yu Kerun welling up again. Ding Wenyu's condolence letter provided exactly what she needed to hear.

The war was becoming increasingly intense, and both sides entered into a deadlock; the situation was changing by the day. Two days later Yuyuan received another moving letter from Ding. The letter was brimming with a feeling of desperation; Ding Wenyu said that when he heard Yuyuan's parting remarks to him after the funeral, he felt as if he had just been handed his death sentence. He said that he had no reason not to respect Yuyuan's decision and dejectedly declared that this would be his last letter to her. Since he was such an annoyance to Yuyuan he decided that he shouldn't continue pestering her. He admitted that he would continue writing her, but he promised that he would never let these letters defile Yuyuan's noble eyes. In his mind, Yuyuan was eternally fair, and Ding Wenyu said that he should be content simply holding his love for her deep in his heart. He felt that by now he should know contentment; she had already given him more than enough happy memories to look back on.

Yuyuan realized that Ding Wenyu never would have written such a desperate letter if she hadn't hurt him so badly two days earlier. The letter was filled with an endless array of heartbroken self-condemnations, but there was not a single complaint directed at Yuyuan. Yuyuan immediately thought back to something her big sister Yuchan had once said about Ding Wenyu: that when it came to love Ding was an out-and-out lunatic. With her sister's words in mind, Yuyuan couldn't help but feel sorry for Ding. In all fairness, he hadn't really done anything wrong; he was a cutup, and that's just the kind of person he was. On a whim, Yuyuan decided not to worry about what other people would say and wrote a short letter to Ding Wenyu. It was barely a few sentences long; it was basically an apology for the things she had said the other day at the funeral. Yuyuan started to regret it as soon as the letter went out. After all, it wasn't appropriate for her to be writing another man when her husband had died just a few days earlier. She knew all too well that as soon as Ding Wenyu received it he would undoubtedly go even crazier and start trying to push things even further. Yuyuan had a handle on what Ding Wenyu was like and knew how stubborn he could be. Ding would never really lower his flag and stop writing letters just because of Yuyuan's little dressing-down. Without fully realizing it, by writing that apology letter Yuyuan was once again playing with fire.

The way things played out proved Yuyuan right. Before her apology letter even had a chance to arrive, Ding Wenyu had already broken his promise—the next day the mailman delivered Ding's most recent letter. A couple of days later when Yuyuan received yet another letter from Ding, his elation was practically dancing off the page as if he had just been granted a grand pardon. Just as she'd suspected, he not only failed to tone down his language from before but became much more unbridled. Imbued with a new confidence, he wrote at length, saying that according to convention he should probably give up on Yuyuan, but human action should not always be dictated by what one "should" or "shouldn't" do. Since Yu Kerun's presence wasn't enough to stop Ding Wenyu from falling madly in love with Yuyuan, it would be ridiculous to let Yu Kerun's death become a hurdle between them. Getting an inch and going for a mile like this was probably not the best way to handle things, it probably wasn't even a moral way to handle things, but Ding Wenyu was clearly set on doing things *his* way.

Ding Wenyu decided to strengthen his romantic offensive on Yuyuan. Due to the unreliable mail service, the first step in Ding's plan was to begin playing postman. During his years as a foreign student in Germany Ding Wenyu had learned how to ride a bicycle, and he finally had a chance to put his rusty riding skills to use. He bought an old-style Czech bicycle, the kind that braked by way of the pedals. If you pedaled backward while riding, the bike would instantly slam to a stop. To get from his apartment to where Yuyuan worked, Ding Wenyu had to go over several slopes in the road, and it was only after he fell a few times that his riding skills started to improve a bit. The War of Resistance that was roaring on seemed to have nothing to do with him; thoughts of love were the only thing on his mind. Each trip he would deliver his letters directly to the army headquarters mailroom. The sentries at the gate couldn't help but laugh whenever they saw Ding ride by; they had gotten to know him and knew that he was delivering a letter to one of the female confidential personnel workers on base. Ding would place the letter in Yuyuan's small mailbox, and it would be waiting for her later that day when she came to pick up the mail. At first she couldn't figure out how Ding's letters were getting to her so fast; often a letter written the night before would arrive the very next day, and sometimes he would even deliver his letters the same day they were written. The sentry working in the mailroom also made it a point to keep the method of delivery a secret from her. Yuyuan suspected that Ding Wenyu must have hired someone to personally deliver the letters for him, like he had before.

Yuyuan finally discovered Ding Wenyu's secret identity as her private postman. That day she had to go out to take care of something and saw Ding Wenyu in the distance, approaching on a bicycle. He had a serious expression on his face and looked kind of silly, but at the same time she couldn't help but admit that Ding Wenyu looked much younger without that cane he always carried around. She quickly ducked out of the way before Ding had a chance to see her. After discovering this little secret of his, she made it a point to slip out by the main gate and watch for Ding whenever she had any spare time on her hands. Ding Wenyu didn't seem to have a clue that she was there spying on him. This little game went on for about two weeks, until Ding Wenyu received a letter from Yuyuan. Ding Wenyu's university was relocating to inner China to avoid the coming crisis. However, since Yuyuan was still in Nanjing, Ding decided to stay behind. Yuyuan's letter was an objection to Ding Wenyu's decision. The situation in Shanghai couldn't have been more miserable; there was no longer any room for optimism. It looked as though Shanghai wouldn't be able to hold out for much longer and the Japanese were preparing to continue westward along the Shanghai-Nanjing Railway, fighting all the way to Nanjing. The Nationalist government had already made preparations to evacuate inland and, one after another, employees from the various ministries and governmental branches all began heading west toward Sichuan. Yuyuan was firmly opposed to Ding Wenyu staying behind on her account. She wrote to him saying that although she was moved by his kind intentions, she insisted that he leave the city with the rest of his colleagues. They were in the middle of a national calamity, and it was more important than anything else for Ding Wenyu to save himself. Yuyuan hoped that he wouldn't act like a stubborn child; after all, it wasn't as if they were married. Yuyuan never even considered marrying Ding; she told him that even if they had been engaged, that would be no reason for Ding Wenyu to stay behind waiting for death in a falling city. This was the first time Ding Wenyu had received such an emotional and caring letter from Yuyuan. He was so surprised that after reading through the letter a few times, he put it to his lips and kissed it madly. He was so ecstatic that he didn't know what to do with himself.

IV

On October 30, the Nationalist government officially decided to relocate the capital to Chongqing in Sichuan province. The next day the government issued an official proclamation on the decision and sent a series of wires to the troops on the front lines expressing the government's resolution to resist Japan to the very end. The Nationalist defeat at Shanghai was already a brutal reality. The Chinese army was no match for the superior power of the Japanese land forces and began falling back, eventually retreating. Commander Xie Jinyuan's battalion stubbornly held Zhabei for four days and four nights before abandoning their position at the Sihang Warehouse; with Commander Xie's retreat, the entire city of Shanghai was basically in Japanese hands. Backup soldiers for both sides continued pouring in, and the situation escalated until it was beyond anyone's control. Endless bad news funneled into the capital, and Nanjing was in utter chaos. Air raids were getting progressively worse as Japanese planes went from bombing primarily military targets to random sites. Countless citizens died, and hospitals were filled with the wounded. The jubilance and excitement of the early stages of the war completely disappeared as a looming cloud of impending defeat began to enshroud the people.

It was against this unusual backdrop that love between Ding Wenyu and Yuyuan began its untimely development. As one of the few big-name professors on campus who had decided to stay behind, Ding Wenyu was assigned the responsibility of aiding the Campus Committee in protecting campus property. This was actually a post in name only. Since he had no real commitments, Ding Wenyu simply poured all of his time and energy into love. Yuyuan firmly insisted that he leave Nanjing, but Ding was adamant about staying no matter what Yuyuan said. Somehow, however, while arguing about whether he should stay or go, the two of them became even closer. Ding Wenyu's decision to stay behind was already set in stone. Realizing that he was putting his own life in danger for her, Yuyuan was quite moved and decided that she had to be careful not to treat Ding so coldly anymore. She started to give in a bit, and Ding Wenyu jumped at the opportunity and started to press forward.

The insatiable Ding Wenyu finally got the chance he had been waiting for to advance his cause. Every day he pedaled over on that Czech bicycle of his to report to Yuyuan; rain or shine, wind or snow, nothing could stop Ding from making his daily visits. Before long Ding Wenyu wasn't simply delivering his letters; whenever the opportunity presented itself, he would sneak Yuyuan out for a short walk around army headquarters. Eastward, not far from the gate, was the famous Green Creek. It wasn't a very large body of water, just a gentle trickling stream that came down from Purple Mountain. Next to the creek was a tall weeping willow and a few scattered houses. The homes in the area were all made of greenish bricks and black tiles, with inconspicuous chrysanthemums growing beside the doors. As they strolled alongside Green Creek, Ding Wenyu and Yuyuan seemed to feel a mood no less special than when they had visited those famous scenic spots in Lushan. However, Yuyuan's main reason for bringing Ding Wenyu there for their walk wasn't the scenery, it was so her co-workers wouldn't see them. After all, it hadn't been that long since Yu Kerun passed away, and she didn't want to do anything that might cause people to have any ill-intentioned misunderstandings.

The entire city of Nanjing was steeped in am ominous, catastrophic feeling—on the verge of a major calamity. Yuyuan quickly noticed that virtually no one gave her relationship with Ding Wenyu a second thought.

All of her worries had been in vain. With the country on the brink of collapse, who could bother with petty personal affairs? People who could get out of Nanjing were by this time leaving in droves; the government appealed to the people to evacuate the city and seek refuge elsewhere. The splendor of days past was now just a memory. One after another, as all the high officials and party notables abandoned the city, small private automobiles, bodyguards in tow, became a rare sight on the broad Nanjing streets. Stores successively closed up shop, and all over the city were the bombed-out vestiges of the Japanese air raids. Most of the citizens who remained behind stayed inside unless they had some pressing business to take care of, leaving most of the streets utterly deserted. The city was like a ghost town; the only people in the streets were police, MPs, and newly enlisted soldiers about to set out for the front lines. As the combat battalions passed, accompanied by the rumbling sound of their war machines, the soldiers all seemed to have a peaceful expression as they prepared to look death in the face.

Before the Nationalist regime officially announced that the capital was to be moved west, arrangements had already been made for Old Ren Bojin to be taken to Hankou. After a brief stopover there to rest, this elder military statesman would go on to Chongqing. The day he left Nanjing, Ding Wenyu accompanied Yuyuan to the port to see him off. Traveling with Mr. and Mrs. Ren Bojin was their daughter Yujiao. They were indeed moving house, there was virtually no one left in their Nanjing estate; they dismissed all the servants they could get rid of and took the rest with them. Yuyuan was the only one in the Ren family left behind—as an enlisted woman she naturally had to listen to orders. They were all reluctant to leave her in the capital. Just thinking about her daughter all alone in this perilous city made Lady Miyako's eyes swell with tears; after raising Yuyuan for all those years, how could she just walk away from her like that? In the end it was Ren Bojin who talked his wife into going. He convinced her that there was no reason to get so upset; after all, this wasn't the last time they would see each other. Yujiao also tried to console her mother by adding, "Mom, don't worry. Yuyuan has Wenyu to look after her."

Yujiao was only trying to ease the mood; she never imagined that her playful comment would instantly make Yuyuan turn bright red. It was as if this one tongue-in-cheek sentence represented the Ren family's approval of Yuyuan's relationship with Ding Wenyu. An awkward expression also appeared on the faces of Mr. and Mrs. Ren; although they didn't outright reject the possibility of a real relationship between Ding and Yuyuan, it was clear that neither of them was ready to embrace the idea. The disparity in age was indeed too great. Besides, with Ding Wenyu's bookish appearance, he just didn't seem like the kind of man a woman could depend on for the rest of her life. During those times of chaos, people had enough trouble looking out for themselves, let alone others; and the Ren family had absolutely no real idea just what was actually going on between Yuyuan and Ding Wenyu.

Amid her embarrassment, Yuyuan forgot to defend herself. The result was that in the eyes of Yujiao and Lady Miyako, Yuyuan's blushing response seemed to indicate that she had indeed already taken her relationship with Ding Wenyu to the next level. Always with his head in the clouds, Ding Wenyu didn't seem to realize what was going on around him and continued chatting away with Ren Bojin. His nonchalant attitude, however, seemed to confirm the Rens' suspicions. It was a good thing that even in this hour of danger, Ren Bojin was able to maintain his noble bearing. Ding Wenyu made conversation, but before he could get more than a few sentences out, Ren Bojin started to get excited and began to give his opinion on the current state of affairs. What Old Ren said next he must have repeated a thousand times during the previous few days: "I still stick to the old view that 'mending the fence after the sheep have escaped is not necessarily too late to prevent it from happening again.' The decisive battle in the War of Resistance will not be fought in Shanghai. Our army committed an almost excessive amount of military power to Shanghai, but you should keep in mind the fact that the decisive battle will be played out along the Long-Hai line . . ."

Old Ren's impromptu speech was interrupted by the blaring sound of an air raid siren, which threw the entire port into disarray. The ship hands on deck called for all passengers to hurry up and get on board while urging all those seeing their friends and relatives off to leave the deck. It was better for the steamer to get moving than to remain docked there like a sitting duck. Time was of the essence, and the deck was transformed into a chaotic mess as people tried to get off the ship while others were boarding it. Ding Wenyu was so anxious that he didn't know what to do. It was Yuyuan who kept her cool; grabbing Ding Wenyu's hand, she made a quick break for the dock. The steamer started to pull away as soon as they made it off deck. The steam whistle heaved a long scream as the ship hastily left the port. Yuyuan waved to her family on board as her parents and sister waved back. Lady Miyako motioned for Yuyuan and Ding Wenyu to get going and find an air raid shelter. The ear-piercing air raid siren was still sounding as the Rens on both sides of the water worried about one another's safety. Yuyuan stood there on the pier unwilling to budge; not until the steamer slowly disappeared in the distance did she and Ding finally leave.

By that time, the port was virtually deserted. Those people who had-n't gotten to the nearest air raid shelter went somewhere else to take cover. It seems as though human nature shows its face at the most critical moments. Japanese planes dropped several bombs not far from the port, and after a wave of thunderous explosions all that one could see from far away was a slowly rising cloud of smoke. After the air raid sirens finally stopped sounding, Yuyuan and Ding Wenyu got back into the same car they had taken to see the Rens off. The driver asked where they wanted to go. Since Yuyuan had already taken the day off from work, she was reluctant to go immediately back to the army headquarters, so Ding Wenyu suggested they grab a bite to eat. Yuyuan wasn't terribly hungry but didn't think it was a bad idea. With a smirk she commented on how uncreative men are, as if the only way to a *woman's* heart was through her stomach—you would think that women were all nothing but a bunch of gluttonous insects. Ding Wenyu responded playfully, "What's wrong with being gluttonous? That just shows that you must have a good appetite. And a good appetite is a sure sign that you're healthy—I love a healthy woman!"

As they drove down the street there wasn't a single open restaurant in sight; not only were all the famous restaurants with the usually long lines closed, but even the second-rate no-name joints were too. Ding Wenyu wasn't about to give up, though. With animated gestures he came up with all kinds of crazy ideas where they should go. Although he didn't say anything, it was clear from the look on his face that the driver was getting more and more impatient. The car circled around the Temple of Confucius, which had been Nanjing's most flourishing district but was now just as dead as everywhere else. When they finally found a restaurant that looked open, they were already out of food. Ding Wenyu was suspicious, but the waiter inside explained that because of the recent Japanese bombings, all of the vegetable peddlers in the area only made their rounds when they thought it was safe—it had already been several days since anyone had seen a trace of them. The waiter felt terrible about turning them away, but he indeed didn't have a thing to offer them; instead he tried to let them down easy with some small talk. Losing his patience, the driver couldn't help but say, "Hey, if you're not open, just say so; but spare us your bullshit!"

Completely oblivious to the times, Ding Wenyu still insisted on finding a restaurant. Yuyuan apologetically told the driver, "How about this: head toward Pearl River Road, and if we don't pass a restaurant on the way, just let us out when we get there. We really appreciate your help."

The driver frowned and, with his hands clenching the wheel, resentfully muttered, "You think you can just push me around and I'll take you wherever the hell you want to go? Let me remind you, I'm not your private chauffeur."

Yuyuan kept saying nice things to the driver and his expression warmed right up; he was a real pushover—all it took was a few compliments to smooth him over. By the time they got to Pearl River Road the driver was like putty in Yuyuan's hands; he even offered to circle around once more. Yuyuan thanked him for his generosity but knew that driving around in circles wasn't going to get them anywhere. Thanking the driver profusely, Yuyuan and Ding Wenyu got out at Pearl River Road. Ding stood there watching the car drive off as he complained about not having found a restaurant. It was getting late, and they still didn't have the faintest idea where they should go. "It seems like all you can think about is food! You must be starving," said Yuyuan. Ding Wenyu was quick to earnestly explain that he was worried that Yuyuan was hungry. Yuyuan could tell from his expression that he was telling the truth and couldn't help but burst out laughing. Ding Wenyu misunderstood her laughter as a sign of disbelief and quickly swore that he was telling the truth—this made Yuyuan completely break down into hysterical laughter.

It seemed as though the two of them had returned to their days together in Lushan; although countless things had happened since then, both Ding Wenyu and Yuyuan were careful not to let them cross their minds. They were blindly strolling down Pearl River Road when another air raid siren started. The two of them were in another world. Ignoring the siren, they sauntered forward under the thick foliage and long shadows of the French parasol trees. The ear-splitting scream was stifling; the only thing Yuyuan and Ding could do was remain silent. Thunderous explosions roared nearby, but it was hard to tell whether they were caused by Japanese bombs or Chinese antiaircraft gunfire. A fire truck, also blasting its sirens, flew past them, quickly followed by another. Ding Wenyu made it a point to occasionally turn to Yuyuan and flash her a consoling smile, while in reality he was much more nervous than she was. Yuyuan noticed that his face was pale and his fists were tightly clenched. As they crossed the street, she nudged his fist to open up a bit so she could slip her own hand inside; only then did she discover that his palms were covered with sweat.

The sudden silence that accompanied the end of the air raid was like the strange feeling one gets after awakening in the middle of the night from a nightmare. The warning sirens ended, but the buzzing sound lingered in people's ears. It was especially strange for them to hear each other's voices against the dead silence of the empty streets. Seeing that Ding Wenyu didn't have any ideas about what to do or where to go, Yuyuan said jokingly, "Hey, now I'm really starting to get hungry. Anyway, we can't just go on walking aimlessly like this."

Ding Wenyu was really at a loss as to what to do. As it turned out, they weren't far from his apartment, and Ding suddenly thought, why not invite Yuyuan over to his place for lunch? Realizing that her relationship with Ding was moving further and further out of bounds, she was a bit hesitant, but in the end her curiosity got the best of her and she diffidently agreed. When they got to his university apartment, Ding Wenyu had his maid whip up something for them to eat. Since she was already there, Yuyuan figured she might as well take advantage of the opportunity to have a look around. Ding Wenyu's apartment was quite spacious, but because he lived alone it appeared a bit empty. Although he had a maid, it was obvious that because of Ding Wenyu's easygoing disposition, she had also taken to cutting corners where she could—except for the living room, the rest of the apartment was a mess. Yuyuan accidentally walked into Ding Wenyu's bedroom and noticed a small frame next to Ding's bed. Inside was a woman's photo, but Yuyuan couldn't quite make it out. She bent over to take a closer look, only to discover that it was a picture of her! She had no idea how Ding Wenyu had gotten his hands on it but was too embarrassed to ask. She couldn't help but blush. It didn't seem to bother thick-skinned Ding Wenyu that Yuyuan had discovered his little secret; he just patiently waited for her to ask about it. Yuyuan, however, not only avoided any mention of the picture but intentionally changed the subject of their conversation. All the while, Yuyuan's face grew redder and redder as she secretly began to regret ever going to Ding's apartment.

Dawdling about the kitchen, the maid finally managed to throw something together for lunch. By the time it was ready Yuyuan was starved—her mouth started to water as soon as her nose got a whiff of the delicious food. It was clear that Ding Wenyu wasn't a man who took food lightly. Although there were just the standard three dishes and soup, each had its own unique flavor. The maid prepared sliced pork and vegetables, sliced green loofah, stir-fried shrimp with peas, and a stew, all staple Chinese dishes. Although Yuyuan tried to show her manners, she was so hungry that they in effect went out the window; she couldn't help but laugh at herself as she wolfed down her food. Ding Wenyu barely paid attention to anything except what was on his plate. Taking big bites and huge gulps of soup, he ate like an animal, and by the time he was finished there were beads of sweat dripping from his nose. Looking at the time, who could blame them? It was already almost three o'clock.

Having nothing planned for after lunch, Ding Wenyu took Yuyuan for a walk around the campus. Because the school had already moved to the interior, the deserted campus was extremely quiet, and one could faintly smell the fragrance of the blooming osmanthus trees. Along the campus walkways a rainbow of chrysanthemums were in full bloom. Yuyuan walked over to the bed of chrysanthemums and bent over as if posing for a photo; she tried to be serious but couldn't help giving a playful giggle. Ding Wenyu was completely infatuated with her. He thought back to Lushan; it was truly a shame he didn't have a camera when they were there so they would have something to remember their trip by. Realizing that he was now missing out on another opportunity to take Yuyuan's photo, Ding made a mental note to go out and buy a camera as soon as he had a chance. He was also set on buying a book on photography so he would be able to take some nice pictures of Yuyuan.

The two of them strolled into an empty classroom and Yuyuan walked to the front row. Sitting down at one of the desks, she stared at the blackboard with a strange look in her eyes. Yuyuan always felt bad about never having gone to college, but now it was too late. She kind of regretted rushing into the military on a whim. Looking back, it had been kind of silly for Old Ren Bojin to encourage her to join the army. Other than her beauty, Yuyuan was just your average girl—she was never cut out to be a female warrior like the legendary Hua Mulan or Mu Guiying. Just the same, rushing into a marriage with Yu Kerun was a childish mistake. Having been born into a military family, Yuyuan thought that it was only natural for her to marry a military man. What's more, for a young woman in 1937 there couldn't have been a more popular choice for a husband than a promising young officer. Never in her wildest dreams could Yuyuan have anticipated that Yu Kerun would end up shacking up with another woman not long after their marriage. Perhaps Yu Kerun was right and a university student was indeed a much more attractive match for him than a confidential secretary. As she was lost in thought, Ding Wenyu took a few big steps over to the blackboard and, picking up a piece of chalk, wrote the day's date on the board. Yuyuan didn't understand why he would write something like that. Ding Wenyu told her with the utmost sincerity that this day was too important to him to forget.

Before it got dark, Ding Wenyu took Yuyuan back to the army headquarters; because he couldn't get a car, he had no choice but to ride her back on his bicycle. Ding Wenyu's cycling skills were only so-so, and halfway there Yuyuan couldn't take his clumsiness anymore and had him get off so *she* could ride *him*. Indeed, Yuyuan was much better behind the handlebars than Ding. She often used to practice riding around the headquarters when she had nothing to do; all the female soldiers on base were excellent bike riders. Ding Wenyu was a bit scared sitting on the back; he didn't dare hold on to Yuyuan's waist, so he held on to the rear frame to keep from swaying. By the time they finally arrived at their destination, Ding was so petrified that he was covered in sweat. As they were getting ready to say good-bye, Yuyuan thanked him for seeing her home. Ding Wenyu, however, was starting to get his courage up and said that he was hoping to get more from her lips than simply a good-bye.

Yuyuan responded playfully, "Don't you think we've already gone a little too far today as it is? What else do you want?"

It was starting to get dark, and Ding Wenyu looked around to make sure no one was around before boldly leaning over to kiss her. Yuyuan could feel her heart pounding and instinctively refused him, taking a big step away. Ding Wenyu was beginning to worry that he might have upset her. He never imagined that Yuyuan would call everything off by saying, "No, no. None of that."

V

The march of events took a turn for the worse. Following the loss of Shanghai, the Chinese army was forced to retreat, with the victorious Shanghai division of the Japanese army following in hot pursuit. At the same time, the Japanese suddenly advanced along the Wu-Fu and Zha-Jia lines; Suzhou and Jiaxing immediately declared a state of emergency. By November 19, the Nationalists lost their foothold along the Wu-Fu and Zha-Jia lines, throwing the capital of Nanjing into a tense state where combat could come at any moment. Posters reading DEFEND NANJING were plastered all over the streets and alleys as battalions from every corner of China speaking all kinds of strange dialects were called in under a state of emergency. These battalions were ordered to organize garrison defenses at different areas around the city; they piled up sandbags to blockade the major downtown intersections and arteries and set up antiaircraft guns on the rooftops of tall buildings. By the time Ding Wenyu attained a decisive advance in his love life, the capital of Nanjing had become one massive military fortress. Virtually everyone Ding saw remaining in this perilous city was a soldier. With stern faces, troops assigned to all different units passed through the city streets. Rubble and bombed-out debris from the air strikes could be seen everywhere. In order to get around incessant searches, Ding Wenyu made a trip to the Nanjing Garrison Command and, with the help of a certain senior staff officer by the name of Li, requested a special pass from the new garrison commander, Tang Shengzhi.

Ding Wenyu's cousin Ding Gongqia, who had been a student of military affairs, had at one point been Staff Officer Li's mentor. When Ding Wenyu was studying in Germany, Staff Officer Li was also there studying military affairs. After Li returned to China he started working under Tang Shengzhi, eventually becoming one of Tang's key aides. Tang Shengzhi had earned his reputation as a leading general during the

Northern Expedition and was a senior statesman of the party. Because he had opposed Chiang Kai-shek, he had been stripped of his military power after the Nationalists established their capital in Nanjing and had been pleading illness to buy himself time while remaining completely inactive in government. As Nanjing fell into a state of emergency, he argued that the capital, being the focal point of international attention as well as the final resting place of President Sun Yat-sen, needed to be protected, and he personally volunteered to undertake that awesome responsibility. Although Tang's offer seemed a bit *too* lofty, the Generalissimo did feel that failing to fight and simply handing Nanjing over on a silver platter to the Japanese would indeed be too much of a loss of face for the Chinese to accept. When Tang Shengzhi stood up and offered himself to the cause at this critical juncture, the Generalissimo deep down felt it was a true godsend. Chiang Kai-shek quickly bestowed on him the title of Commanding Officer and let him clean up the mess. Knowing all too well that the capital was doomed to fall, none of the other high-ranking generals dared to raise any objections.

As a career military man, Tang Shengzhi finally got the opportunity he had been waiting for to regain military power. He hadn't, however, given much thought to the consequences of his decision; he was only prepared to take things one step at a time. Tang was a romantic. Having grown accustomed to staying at home, once he was promoted to garrison commander he decided to simply move the newly established Garrison Command headquarters to his compound in Baizi Ting. Everyone serving under him also took advantage of the situation to get promoted a grade. Yuyuan's entire department, which dealt with confidential military information, was assigned to work with the Garrison Command and was ordered to relocate its facilities to Tang Shengzhi's compound. As it turned out, Yuyuan's direct supervisor for dealing with confidential wartime documents was this very same Staff Officer Li. The houses around the Tang compound were also taken over; provisional air raid shelters were dug, antiaircraft guns were set up in the area, and the Garrison Command was officially operational. Coincidentally, the very first time Ding Wenyu went to call on Staff Officer Li, he ran into Tang Shengzhi, who was just leaving on an inspection. Tang Shengzhi had also met Ding Wenyu on a few occasions and was even able to remember his name. Staff Officer Li explained the reason for Ding's visit and Tang

Shengzhi immediately agreed, promising to issue Ding a special pass as soon as possible.

A few days later when Tang Shengzhi needed a good interpreter for a press conference being held at the Sino-British Cultural Association, Staff Officer Li immediately thought of Ding Wenyu. Ding Wenyu was famous for his foreign language skills, and Li thought it would be really something to have him interpret for Tang Shengzhi. Commander Tang looked particularly handsome that day. Wearing his sharp garrison uniform, he took off his hat and handed it to one of his bodyguards before he began speaking. With a straight face, he turned to Ding Wenyu and told him, "Mr. Ding, I've heard that you can speak a lot of different foreign languages. That's good, you just translate what I say into whatever foreign languages you can speak. You tell those foreigners that I, Tang Shengzhi, am already firmly determined to stay here until the end and share the same fate as Nanjing!" As soon as he finished his statement, everyone around who understood Chinese was in shock. Although most people seemed to realize that Nanjing was bound to fall, at the time most were still unsure about what the official Nationalist position was concerning the future of the city. Ding Wenyu stood there panic-stricken as all the foreign reporters waited for his interpretation. Seeing that Ding still hadn't started translating, Tang Shengzhi asked calmly, "What's wrong, Mr. Ding? Don't tell me you don't believe what I said?"

Ding Wenyu translated Commander Tang's statement into English and then into German before questions were taken. Tang Shengzhi didn't have the patience to answer each and every question and instead pompously decided to give a short lecture. He took an extremely staunch position, and as he spoke saliva shot from his mouth like shooting stars. Ding Wenyu translated the gist of his impromptu speech, and the press conference was declared over. Tang Shengzhi was scheduled to go on an inspection tour of the city's defenses after the lecture, and Ding Wenyu asked if he could accompany the commander. Staff Officer Li was a bit reluctant and was quite surprised when Tang Shengzhi immediately agreed. Ding Wenyu ended up following right behind the commander in the same car with Staff Officer Li as they rode around the city in their stately procession. Those were indeed unusual times: just driving around Nanjing was quite an experience. The day before, after another wave of Japanese bombings, the Generalissimo and the first lady had driven around the entire city consoling the citizens of Nanjing. The newspapers all ran a special report about the event. As commander of the garrison headquarters, Tang Shengzhi couldn't resist the urge to jump on the bandwagon and go on his own citywide inspection tour. Standing in an open car putting on grand airs, Commander Tang appeared as if he already had the city under lock and key and the Japanese would never get in. As his car drove down the main streets, the splendor of the Nanjing of days past took on a tragically desolate air.

Staff Officer Li seemed to realize that holding on to Nanjing was already an impossibility. Since there was no one else in the car besides the two of them, Li told Ding Wenyu with a sigh, "With things in this state, Tang Shengzhi is virtually obsessed with shouting high-sounding slogans like 'Betray no fear in the hour of danger, stand tall in the face of disaster.' What else can the guy do?" All Ding Wenyu knew was that the Japanese army had almost reached the city gates, but he didn't have the slightest handle on what might happen next. Staff Officer Li provided Ding Wenyu with his analysis of the serious danger facing Nanjing. After he'd gone on and on, there still wasn't a hint of optimism in Li's words. It was a good thing that, as a military man, Li was calm and felt perfectly comfortable talking about the situation, even though his life was constantly at risk.

After talking about the war for a while, Staff Officer Li moved the topic to Ding's personal life. Li had already gotten wind of Ding's entanglement with Yuyuan; he was, after all, Ding Gongqia's student and also had a deep respect for Ren Bojin, whom he often called on. He felt that since Ren Bojin's youngest daughter was now working under him, he had every right to look out for her. His "looking out for her," however, actually meant making it easier for Ding Wenyu to pursue her. "Only a true hero can reveal his genuine face, a really unconventional man of culture remains forever romantic." Staff Officer Li truly admired Ding Wenyu for being able to risk his life for the woman he loved.

"True patriotism calls for you to love your country the same way you love the woman in your life—you've got to have a kind of crazy, passionate drive." Staff Officer Li brought Ding Wenyu back to his office for lunch and then decided, on the spur of the moment, to send someone to call Yuyuan in. Ding Wenyu was a bit surprised; he never imagined that things there were so relaxed. As the Garrison Command headquarters, the Tang compound didn't seem anything like the somber, heavily guarded military unit he had expected. Yuyuan had no idea what Li wanted her for and rushed back from the cafeteria where she had just finished eating. When she walked in and saw Ding Wenyu she was all at once both delighted and surprised. Staff Officer Li invited Yuyuan to eat with them, but since she had already eaten, he and Ding Wenyu proceeded to lunch without her. As Li ate, he kept making little jokes about Ding and Yuyuan. Yuyuan was completely embarrassed and turned a bright red. Eventually, she couldn't take it anymore and said that if there weren't anything else she was needed for, she would have to be going. Staff Officer Li laughingly replied, "As for whether or not there's anything you're needed for, you'll have to ask *him*! All I did was try to help out by delivering him to you!" Yuyuan was struck with a combination of anger and embarrassment as she turned and went out the door. Staff Officer Li broke into a fit of laughter.

Ding Wenyu unabashedly spent the next few days hanging around Staff Officer Li's office. The Garrison Command wasn't far from Ding's apartment; all he had to do was walk down two narrow lanes and he could be there in no time at all. Yuyuan hated the way Ding kept making a fool of himself, yet at the same time she had to admit that, with the city on the verge of being attacked, his decision to stay behind for her was no small thing. Whenever she had the opportunity, Yuyuan tried to convince Ding to get out of Nanjing while he still could. At first, all of Yuyuan's coworkers made Ding Wenyu the butt of their jokes, but it wasn't long before they were moved by his persistent spirit and couldn't bear to laugh at him anymore. Not everyone would be willing to go to such lengths in the name of love. Yuyuan's girlfriends started to feel a bit envious of her; not only were they no longer opposed to Ding Wenyu, but they even intentionally started to create all kinds of opportunities for them to be together. It seemed as if Ding Wenyu and Yuyuan's relationship had already won their approval. Yuyuan and her colleagues' office was in the east wing of the Tang compound. This had been the servants' quarters, so there was a small door that opened directly onto the main street. All the latest intelligence reports from the front lines came directly here where officials organized and classified them, drawing up all kinds of charts and diagrams before sending them off to Tang Shengzhi's office. Ding Wenyu made it a point to stop in every day at Staff Officer Li's office. He was able to see Yuyuan, but they didn't have much time to really be together.

Each day the situation grew tenser as, one by one, all the cities and strongholds around Nanjing fell to the Japanese and hope for the future became increasingly slim. As Garrison Commander, Tang Shengzhi had no choice but to continue fueling morale with an air of increasingly false optimism. Japanese fighters were now randomly bombing the city at virtually any time and any place. After a series of uninterrupted bombings, the municipal air defense system was but a phantom that existed in name only; the antiaircraft guns mounted around the Tang compound incessantly fired into the sky. People had long ago grown sick of the air raid sirens. Between the sirens, the thunderous sounds of the bombings, and the constant spray of firepower coming from the antiaircraft guns, workers were practically deaf. No one seemed even to have the patience to go inside those air raid shelters anymore. A tragic atmosphere spread throughout the Garrison Command. Since it was their job to defend the capital and stand side by side with Tang Shengzhi as he prepared to sacrifice himself with the city, as it got down to the wire, death seemed inevitable and everyone seemed to accept their fate.

Noticing that at a time like this, Ding still had nothing but Yuyuan on his mind, Staff Officer Li tried to make the best of the dire situation by doing whatever he could to bring about a union between Ding Wenyu and Yuyuan. One day the Japanese planes seemed to intentionally give the city a short reprieve and stopped their visits to the Nanjing skies for a full day. Staff Officer Li jumped at this opportunity and told Ding Wenyu with the utmost sincerity, "I suggest the two of you seize this chance and get your marriage over with. This is a great opportunity; don't pass it up. I'll even let Miss Ren take the day off."

Although Li's suggestion got Ding Wenyu's heart pumping, he quickly shook his head and naïvely explained that he was afraid that Yuyuan and he weren't yet at that stage. Being both a warm-hearted enthusiast and a notoriously impatient person, Staff Officer Li couldn't help but heave a deep sigh and say, "Don't you realize what's going on out there? What are you waiting for? Don't tell me you plan to wait to get married until the Japs enter the city and everyone is running for their lives?" With that, Li volunteered to go convince Yuyuan himself. He even promised that if it turned out he wasn't persuasive enough, he would mobilize the entire department to talk her into it. After countless days of living amid the explosive roars of bombing raids, it was a rarity to have a day of true peace and quiet. An opportunity for some fun suddenly presented itself, and everyone jumped at the chance to get away from their work and play matchmaker. Ding Wenyu felt everything was going too fast and was convinced that Yuyuan wouldn't agree; he actually started to get nervous that she would become upset over the whole affair. Yuyuan naturally refused to give in. She just blushed and refused to say anything. When she finally did start to talk, all she did was express her hope that her co-workers would help *her* persuade Ding Wenyu to leave Nanjing while there was still time.

"That's a piece of cake," said Staff Officer Li. "As long as you agree to marry him, we'll find a way to get him out of the city."

Yuyuan's face turned a bright crimson and she didn't reply.

Staff Officer Li continued, "If you don't speak up, that means that you agree." All of Yuyuan's co-workers, who were standing beside them, started to cheer, saying that because they were in a state of war, Yuyuan and Ding could be excused from all the social conventions that went with a matrimonial union. All the bride and groom needed to do was shake hands and kiss and they would be married! Staff Officer Li added, "Let's not cut too many corners now; we should at least run an announcement in the paper." With that, he immediately drafted a marriage announcement, which he planned to have one of his underlings take down to a nearby newspaper office and run on the front page. Being a long-time admirer of Chinese calligraphy, Staff Officer Li began the announcement by neatly writing out the names Ding Wenyu and Ren Yuyuan in standard *kaishu* script. The text, which was written in fluid running hand, or *xingshu* style, read: "On the seventh day of the twelfth month of the twenty-sixth year of the Republic we were joined in holy matrimony at the Tang Compound in Baizi Ting, Nanjing. As this was a time of national crisis, the ceremony was carried out in the simplest fashion, and we beg the forgiveness of those friends and relatives who were unable to attend." Once it was written, Yuyuan's co-workers passed it around, clapping aloud and laughing as they read it. The announcement went directly from Ding Wenyu's hand to Yuyuan's. Yuyuan was just starting to regain her composure when she laid eyes on the announcement and immediately turned red again. She read it twice before crumpling it up into a ball and tossing it into the garbage can. Turning to her co-workers, she said with the utmost sincerity, "Why do you have to run an ad? Even if I was planning on marrying him, there's no reason to be so ostentatious about it."

Everyone started to laugh and said, "If you don't want to make a big deal about it, that's fine with us! We'll carry out your wedding ceremony right here at the Garrison Command!"

"Stop fooling around," said Yuyuan. "I still haven't made the final decision."

The hubbub continued, with all her co-workers talking at the same time; voices cried out: "What do you mean?" "Who's fooling around?" "What do you mean by 'final decision' anyway? The Japanese are approaching; if you don't grab the opportunity now, when will you?"

Ding Wenyu naïvely tried to keep them from putting Yuyuan in a difficult position. That made everyone laugh even harder; now they really thought he was a bookworm. They couldn't believe that after spending all that time stubbornly chasing Yuyuan, Ding Wenyu would suddenly turn chickenhearted now that she was finally within his grasp. Ding Wenyu admitted he had been dreaming that such a moment would one day come, but even so he argued that that was still no cause to force Yuyuan to do something she wasn't ready to do. With this defense, Yuyuan's co-workers completely lost themselves in violent laughter; they jokingly told Ding that he could dream all he wanted, but now was the time for action!

Yuyuan was at her wit's end; she didn't know if she should laugh or cry. Finally, she flashed Ding a cold stare in hope of getting him to stop making such of fool of himself. Seeing the way they exchanged glances, Yuyuan's colleagues were now even less inclined to let them off. Just as they were all making a scene in the office, the air raid sirens began to go off. In no time, the entire situation underwent a massive change—no doubt for the worse. According to the latest intelligence reports, the Japanese army had succeeded in completely surrounding the city. The Japanese base camp had already officially sent down the order to "attack and occupy the enemy capital of Nanjing."

Nanjing was on the verge of a vicious military battle. In order to ensure that his men would defend the city to their death, Tang Shengzhi cut off all means of retreat by ordering all ships docked on the southern side of the Yangtze River to the northern side. Moreover, Tang informed the battalion stationed at the northern bank to summarily execute anyone found disobeying orders and trying to cross the river. The Garrison Command was thrown into utter chaos as everyone dove back into their work. There wasn't a single soul who didn't understand the implications of Tang Shengzhi's orders. The natural moat of the Yangtze was the Chinese army's only possible means of escape; it was clear that Tang Shengzhi was trying to erase the idea of retreating from everyone's mind. Filled with frustration, Staff Officer Li was busy making call after call, continually cursing as he spoke. It took Li forever to get off the phone and when he did, he turned to Ding Wenyu and said, "The two of you don't need to wait until the air raid sirens end before you can leave the compound. You've both been pretty lucky so far; I'm sure you'll be fine. Get going while it's still light outside. I'm giving Miss Ren a day off. If you want to get married, get married; if not, do whatever you please. I just want to make one thing clear: she has to be back here in twenty-four hours. You've already seen how damn busy we are, so make sure you bring her back on time."

Ding Wenyu and Yuyuan were both taken a bit off guard by Staff Officer Li's sudden decision. It seemed as if, even at this final juncture, Staff Officer Li was still set on helping bring them together. Yuyuan immediately realized that since Ding Wenyu wasn't in the army, it would be dangerous for him to remain at the Garrison Command any longer. If it was too late for him to get out of the city, he should at least find a safe place to hide. Since they only had one day, Yuyuan didn't have time to worry about what the implications would be, nor could she bother with what other people might think. She decided to take advantage of this reprieve to persuade Ding Wenyu not to be so stubborn and consider his own safety. Yuyuan knew that the cost of the impending battle to defend Nanjing would be too high to calculate. In the past it had always been Ding Wenyu who looked out for her; now it was Yuyuan's turn to start thinking about what was best for him.

Staff Officer Li had a motorcycle drive them back to Ding Wenyu's apartment. Air raid sirens sounded throughout the streets as Japanese planes dove low in their random bombing campaigns. Sitting in the sidecar of the motorcycle, Ding Wenyu and Yuyuan couldn't help but gaze upward at the enemy planes. The fighters were flying so low that they could even make out the Japanese national emblem on the underside of the planes' wings. For a while, it seemed as if one plane was following them. They pulled over under the shade of a tree while it circled low. Just as they started out again, that plane furiously dove forward after them. The orderly driving the motorcycle was a reckless kid who seemed to think he was invincible; revving the engine, he hit the gas and flew down the main street. Although he had long passed Ding Wenyu's apartment, he kept burning down the road as if he was set on finding out just who was faster, his motorcycle or that Japanese fighter. All of Ding and Yuyuan's attention was focused on the plane above them, and by the time they realized they had passed Ding's apartment they were already far, far away.

Once they got to Ding's apartment, the orderly could barely wait for them to climb out of the sidecar before revving his engine again and driving off into the distance. Standing on the front steps, Ding and Yuyuan were both struck with a strange, hard to describe feeling—they weren't nervous, nor were they relaxed, they felt as if they had just been abandoned on an isolated desert island. The air raid sirens stopped shortly after the enemy planes left the sky. Ding and Yuyuan were in a trancelike state, having just broken free from the outside world of terrifying, ear-piercing screeches—it was as if they had entered a realm of silent nothingness. There was not a soul in sight, and Ding Wenyu couldn't believe that what was before his eyes was real. He turned around to gaze at Yuyuan as he fished around his pocket for his keys. In a dazed tone he asked, "I must be dreaming?"

Yuyuan also felt like she was in a dream, but Ding Wenyu's charmingly naïve mannerisms and ridiculous look of disbelief somehow saved her from her awkward feeling of bashfulness. Yuyuan started to feel much more relaxed once she saw that silly expression on Ding's face. The way everything had unfolded seemed simply too strange to believe. Although people always say that timing is everything, neither of them had been really prepared for things to happen the way they did. Ding Wenyu had no idea where his maid had run off to, but the front door to his apartment was bolted shut. He kept searching for his keys but still couldn't seem to find them. It was apparent that Ding really did think he was dreaming; he even mumbled his earlier suspicion back to himself. Still a bit hesitant, Yuyuan blushed as she told him: "You *are* dreaming!" She actually meant the opposite but was hoping her answer would snap Ding Wenyu out of his daze of disbelief. Ding Wenyu finally got himself together and found his keys; unlocking the door, he pulled Yuyuan inside. They walked into the living room and Ding asked Yuyuan to have a seat, after which he started to get antsy again about what he should do next. Yuyuan couldn't help but laugh when she saw how edgy he was and decided to made herself at home and spread out on the sofa.

Ding Wenyu couldn't understand why Yuyuan would laugh and stared at her with a confused look, unable to get a word out of his nervous lips. Although she was right there before his eyes, everything seemed too good to be true. Noticing how happy Ding Wenyu was, Yuyuan couldn't help but blush and laughingly tease him, "Wenyu, do you have any idea what kind of a bargain you got?" Ding Wenyu didn't understand what she meant and looked at her with his big, puppy dog eyes. Yuyuan went on, "The only reason you were able to get such a bargain is that someone was too naïve. This 'someone' isn't you; if anyone was naïve, it was *me!*"

"What do you mean?" asked Ding. "You're not at all naïve."

"Oh, I'm naïve all right," answered Yuyuan.

Ding Wenyu still didn't understand.

"Don't tell me I'm not," said Yuyuan. "I walked right into this trap."

All of a sudden the two of them changed the way they addressed each other—no longer did they call each other Miss Ren and Mr. Ding. The extreme happiness weighing down on Ding Wenyu made him feel like he couldn't catch his breath. He carefully sat down on the sofa next to her and, still testing the waters, slowly worked his hand into hers. Then, in a voice that didn't seem his own, he whispered something to her in a soft, almost affected tone. Although Yuyuan thought that the two of them probably needed more time, at that moment nothing they could possibly say seemed to matter. There was no reason to ask any questions or give any explanations. Under the circumstances, talk became cheap, language lost its power, and time and space ceased to exist. Although the war was just around the corner, it couldn't have seemed farther away. Dusk was approaching and, as the sun descended into the western sky, its last fading rays shone through the window, projecting shadows of the patterned latticework onto their ankles and the floor at their feet. Yuyuan felt the best thing for her to do was simply close her eyes. Her heart was pounding as she felt Ding Wenyu caressing her hand. Tenaciously holding and fondling her hand, Ding's grip seemed to get stronger and stronger. She resisted him for a fleeting moment before finally letting herself go.

VI

It wasn't until the approach of dawn that Ding Wenyu and Yuyuan regained a sense of time. They suddenly realized that the time they had together was limited to these precious twenty-four hours. The lamp beside the bed had long since run out of oil, and the seemingly never-ending strain of destructive bombings had completely paralyzed the now inoperable power plant. Slowly, they used up all the candles Ding had stored as the pleasures of the night sneaked away. Except for getting up in the middle of the night to get something to eat, they spent the entire evening playfully wrapped up in bed. On this moonless night, Ding Wenyu seemed to be under a spell, utterly enchanted by Yuyuan. He repeatedly stroked and caressed her, feeling every inch of her body. Like an old collector who loses himself riding his treasured hobbyhorse, he looked at Yuyuan like a precious antique. He was like a pious believer carrying out some kind of holy ritual, endlessly repeating those same simple movements; it seemed he would never tire of caressing her, kissing her. It was as if he were kneading every last drop of his love into the very pores of her skin. Under normal circumstances, Yuyuan would have been humiliated just thinking about such a scene; however, as she lay there naked before him, her embarrassment slowly disappeared. At first she thought that the peculiar way Ding Wenyu tenderly caressed her was a bit strange, not to mention a bit excessive; however, she soon realized that this was probably exactly what she had needed. The way Ding Wenyu passionately lost himself in Yuyuan's body was just as impervious to reason as his love for her had always been. Images of Yu Kerun couldn't help but cross Yuyuan's mind and she thought back to their wedding night; she knew that it was wrong to think of Yu, but she couldn't help it. She thought of what Yu Kerun had said to her about "white tigers" and an indescribable feeling rushed into her heart.

The Japanese began their bombing again at dawn, but the interruption of enemy planes had no effect on them. The incessant screaming whistle of air raid sirens made its way inside as thunderous explosions of bombs being dropped raged through the city. They continued doing what they were doing, all the while playfully uttering all kinds of words that didn't seem to fit together.

Yuyuan wanted Ding Wenyu to promise her to start immediately looking for a way to get out of the city. Stunned, Ding Wenyu answered with silence. Yuyuan told him that it was too dangerous for him to stay. She explained that as an enlisted woman she couldn't desert, but there should be nothing keeping Ding Wenyu from leaving. It was clear that the Japanese would sooner or later breach the Nanjing city gates—it was only a matter of time. If Ding didn't take her advice, all of Yuyuan's efforts to convince him to leave would be in vain.

Ding Wenyu stubbornly replied, "As long as you're in this city, I'll be in this city! There's no way I'll leave you behind!"

"Don't be stupid," argued Yuyuan. "I'm in the army, you're not!"

Ding Wenyu didn't say anything, but it was clear from his expression that he wasn't planning to take Yuyuan up on her suggestion. She continued her futile effort to convince him, but Ding Wenyu just shook his head like a naughty child. Yuyuan said, "I'm already yours, how come you still won't listen to me?"

Ding Wenyu answered by saying, "I'll listen to whatever you tell me to do—but I won't leave your side." Ding Wenyu stood by his belief that he was Yuyuan's guardian angel; if something should happen to her, he would have no reason to continue living. Without Yuyuan, life had no meaning.

Yuyuan was suddenly moved by Ding Wenyu's words and felt herself choking up as she asked, "What's so great about me to make you willing to give up so much?"

"You're the only one I've ever wanted," Ding Wenyu responded. "Right now I'm the happiest man alive. Now that you're mine, what more could I ever ask for? There is a saying people use to describe a pair of lovers. They say, 'Envy not the celestial immortals in heaven, envy only the affectionate couple in love'—right now, that's exactly how I feel."

Yuyuan felt a sadness suddenly come over her as tears began to fall from her eyes, but at the same time she also felt a happiness unlike any she had ever known. For the first time, love felt so tangible, so real. Ding Wenyu asked her what was wrong and Yuyuan said that if she had known how much he loved her she never would have made him wait so long.

Ding Wenyu explained that true happiness only comes after waiting. The two of them were lost in deep affection; they went back and forth baring their hearts to each other. It wasn't until all of their talking started to make them hungry that they crawled out of bed to make breakfast. Actually, the night before they had searched the kitchen by candlelight for food, but besides a few pieces of candy there was really nothing to eat. By morning their stomachs were growling. Yuyuan finally found a package of dried noodles and volunteered to cook them. Ding Wenyu tried to fire up the stove by imitating the way his maid used to do it, but all he ended up with was a soot-blackened face, a pair of teary eyes, and one cold stove. Finally Yuyuan stopped what she was doing to go over and help him. Having had people wait on them since they were children, neither Ding nor Yuyuan had ever done housework. It took them almost a full hour to get that naughty stove started, just so they could cook their little pot of sodden noodles, which they hastily gobbled down to fill their empty bellies. "Look at how terrible I am, I can't even cook a bowl of noodles," Yuyuan said apologetically. "Are you sure you won't regret it if you marry me?"

"Don't be silly!" Ding Wenyu replied. "I'd never let you do this kind of work once we got married."

After they ate, the two of them went back into the bedroom and snuggled up under the covers talking. Suddenly, a clamor of voices sounded outside Ding's door. It was Mr. Gu from the Campus Committee. With a group of foreigners wearing red armbands in tow, Mr. Gu started rudely knocking on Ding Wenyu's door. Ding Wenyu threw on some clothes and opened the door, only to hear Mr. Gu apologetically inform him that his apartment building had been designated as part of the newly established Refugee Zone. There was already a group of refugees designated to be moved into Ding's apartment. Those foreigners with the red armbands were all members of the Nanjing International Safety Zone Committee; Ding Wenyu was actually on quite close terms with two of them and immediately struck up a conversation with them. Not much later, a huge group of refugees were led in; Ding's quiet, empty apartment was immediately transformed into a noisy, crowded camp for men, women, children, and the elderly who had been uprooted by the war. Except for the bedroom, which still belonged to Ding Wenyu and Yuyuan, the rest of the apartment was made a virtual public space. The refugees knew that it was Ding's apartment and were very polite to him; Ding and Yuyuan, however, were left with no choice but to stay holed up in their bedroom.

They could see a few of the refugee children playing in the field outside the apartment from the bedroom window. One kid noticed Ding Wenyu and Yuyuan looking at him and stared back at them with a tilted head. Ding Wenyu made a face at the kid, who in turn stuck his tongue out at Ding. Yuyuan couldn't help but laugh at the two of them. It wasn't long before the eyes of all the children outside were directed at the couple in the window. Both parties kept staring at each other until the two adults started to lose their patience and Ding Wenyu closed the window. Fearing that the kids would sneak over and try to steal a glance through the window, Ding also closed the blinds. Yuyuan said, "Okay, you stay here and play refugee." Ding Wenyu could tell from her tone that Yuyuan was getting ready to leave. He glanced at his watch on the nightstand and saw that it was already past noon; Yuyuan's short-lived vacation was almost up. Ding didn't know what to say and he looked back at his watch.

"How do I get back to the Garrison Command from here?" asked Yuyuan.

"I'll take you back," answered Ding Wenyu without hesitation.

"Maybe they'll send a car to pick me up," Yuyuan said, without any real hope that a car would actually come.

Another hour went by, and it was really time for Yuyuan to get going. They had a final playful frolic before emerging from the bedroom to see the entire apartment in complete and utter disarray. There were makeshift beds all over the floor and bundles of clothes and belongings in every corner. Now that they had moved in, the refugees suddenly weren't as polite as before—they didn't even bother giving Ding Wenyu and Yuyuan a second glance as they made their way to the door. Ding Wenyu held Yuyuan's hand as they squeezed their way past the refugees and headed off toward the Garrison Command. At first they didn't understand why the streets were suddenly filled with people, but in a moment they realized that these were all refugees. The situation was changing by the minute, and both Ding Wenyu and Yuyuan felt a bit down. Neither of them wanted to talk about anything serious like the war, but no matter what they said, they couldn't seem to escape the gloomy shadow of the times. They passed an antiaircraft gun that was being hauled away by a regiment of artillerymen. As it turned out, according to regulations dictated by the International Safety Committee, all military installations within the Refugee Zone were to be removed and the zone was to be stripped of all fortifications.

The scene at the Tang compound was also one of pure chaos. Staff Officer Li was standing outside directing a large number of soldiers who were moving everything in the office into a line of large military trucks parked outside. Afraid that people would crack jokes about her "day off," Yuyuan left Ding Wenyu outside while she headed to her office. Staff Officer Li couldn't help but be surprised when he saw Yuyuan run past him. Turning around, Li saw Ding Wenyu and shook his head in disbelief; he never imagined that Ding would actually bring Yuyuan back. Ding Wenyu thought that Staff Officer Li was just pulling his leg and said that he naturally wanted to keep her all to himself, but Yuyuan wasn't cut out to be a deserter so he had no choice but to risk his life and see her back. Staff Officer Li suddenly grew serious: "You're really an idiot! I'm telling you now, don't you ever show up here again. It seems that the Japanese have already discovered that this is the Garrison Command, and we are preparing to leave right away." It took a moment for Officer Li's words to sink in, but when they finally did Ding naïvely asked whether Yuyuan would have to leave with them. Seeing how completely out of touch Ding was, Staff Officer Li heaved a sigh and said, "How could you possibly be so stupid?"

If they had arrived just a few minutes later, Yuyuan wouldn't have had to immediately set out with the rest of the people from her department. But since she showed up, she had no choice but to go with them. Reluctant to leave Ding Wenyu behind, she turned red as she told him, "Take care of yourself! We'll see each other soon." She was on the verge of tears as she spoke and, regardless of the fact that people were bound to laugh at him, Ding Wenyu reached out and grabbed Yuyuan's hand, refusing to let her go. Yuyuan couldn't free her hand and had no choice but to forcefully pull it away. Yuyuan resolutely climbed into the waiting truck amid the jeers of her co-workers. She waved to Ding as tears started pouring down her cheeks. Ding Wenyu stood there like a wooden statue with his hand suspended in the air, a gesture meant to be a wave good-bye. He never thought that they would have to part so hastily, and never in his wildest dreams would he have imagined that this sudden good-bye would be their eternal farewell.

Only a certain portion of the army headquarters personnel were being relocated. With Tang Shengzhi's stubborn disposition, he flatly refused to move to a new location on account of a few Japanese air raids; he would rather brave death than cravenly try to run off and save his skin. His insistence on staying while ordering other personnel to leave ended up creating two sites out of the Garrison Command. Except for Tang Shengzhi, the deputy commander, and a handful of staff officers, aides-de-camp, and sentries, all personnel relocated to the Ministry of Railways, which was located in the northern section of the city. Closing in on the city gates, the Japanese army began viciously attacking Nanjing's outer defense line. The explosive roar of cannon fire rocked the city like thunder. On December 9, Japanese planes carried out their most violent wave of bombing to date as the Japanese commander in chief, General Matsui Iwane, delivered the Chinese their ultimatum.

Ding Wenyu couldn't stop worrying about Yuyuan, especially when he picked up one of those flyers about the Japanese ultimatum blowing down the street. He couldn't even go back to his own apartment, which had already been transformed into a mini-refugee camp. One after another, crowds of panic-stricken refugees were pouring into the Refugee Zone. All of the apartments and houses in the zone were already filled beyond capacity. Refugees who had arrived earlier bickered endlessly with those who had come later about the most trivial affairs. Rumors that the Japanese had already entered the city proper were circulating widely. Ding Wenyu had tried several times to get into the Ministry of Railways in hope of seeing Yuyuan, but each time he was turned away by the impatient sentries at the gate. Unlike the Tang compound, the Ministry of Railways was heavily guarded by a group of cold, stone-faced sentries. There was no Staff Officer Li to help him out, nor was there any secret servants' door through which he could slip in and out to see Yuyuan.

Ding Wenyu would never see Yuyuan again. All over the city, regiments of Chinese soldiers built blockades and fortifications at all the major intersections in preparation for the coming street warfare. Because Ding Wenyu carried a special pass issued by the Garrison Command, although he was continually stopped and questioned, he was always allowed to go on his way. He could freely roam the streets, but, no matter how hard he tried, he just couldn't get himself into the new Garrison

Command. The situation was changing by the minute, and provincial soldiers speaking all kinds of different accents seemed a bit apathetic about the impending battle. They acted according to the string of ever-changing orders, continually transferred around to relieve various garrisons. It seemed that fighting on the front lines was already quite intense, as regiment after regiment of soldiers were dispatched to where they were needed most. The first inkling of the chaos that would follow was already apparent. On more than one occasion, lost soldiers stopped Ding Wenyu on his bicycle to ask for directions. Certain Japanese detachments actually charged into the city but were quickly driven out. They launched a second charge but were again forced back by the Chinese defense. With all of this, the battle to defend Nanjing entered a phase of unprecedented brutality.

Japanese troops finally broke through the line of defense along the southern portion of the city wall, and swarms of soldiers began to rush in. Suddenly, what had been a case of periphery positional warfare turned into an intense, close-quartered bout of vicious street fighting. Nanjing, which had been a virtual fortress besieged, had now fallen; all over the city, flames lit up the sky as gunshots and explosions rang out like a string of endless firecrackers. By the afternoon of December 12, Ding Wenyu realized that the situation was taking a turn for the worse. He decided to risk everything by rushing down to the Tang compound in Baizi Ting, only to discover a few sentry officers dousing the place in gasoline, preparing to commit the entire compound to flames. Ding Wenyu learned from a guard he was somewhat close to that the Garrison Command headquarters had already sent down an order for all officers under their command to break out of the Japanese encirclement. They were supposed to be assembling at Xiaguan Port at that very moment. Ding Wenyu immediately set out for the port as if he had been bitten by a rabid dog. On the way there he saw units literately crawling all over the streets; some were retreating from the first defensive line, while others were on their way to the first line to provide support. The streets were a chaotic flood of troops coming and going, and all main streets leading to the port were blocked by the sea of soldiers. Amid the chaos, a soldier took Ding Wenyu's bicycle, so there was nothing he could do but proceed on foot, following the crowd of retreating soldiers toward the port.

When he arrived at Yijiang Gate, Ding Wenyu saw machine guns set up at the entrance and atop the adjacent city walls. Barbed wire was spread out all around with only a narrow opening in the middle; the soldiers stationed there announced that according to the Commander's orders, units retreating from the front lines were not permitted to escape through the port. In accordance with the plan for breaking out of the enemy encirclement, all units from the front lines were to charge straight out of the encirclement; only officers from the Garrison Command were permitted to cross the river via the port. The retreating troops were already out of control; stubbornly arguing that they never even heard of any "plan for breaking out of the enemy encirclement," they insisted on being let through. The sentries at the gate refused to let anyone by. The arguing went back and forth until both sides opened fire.

Several soldiers in the crowd were killed; the others started cursing out of indignation, but they still couldn't get any closer to the port. Military orders were, after all, set in stone. The Nanjing Yangtze River port was the sole means of escape, and the sentry unit stationed at Yijiang Gate knew that if they didn't stop the retreating troops from entering the port, they would risk endangering the sole means of escape for those officials from the Garrison Command, who were already boarding their ship. Because Tang Shengzhi had previously taken measures to cut off all means of escape to deter desertion, there was but a small handful of boats at the dock. The consequences of tens of thousands of soldiers rushing all at once into the narrow port area would be utterly nightmarish. The face-off at the gate was becoming increasingly tense as more and more routed troops arrived. Some of the soldiers realized that passage was impossible and began looking for a new way to break out of the encirclement. Others obstinately insisted on getting through and began to curse the sentry officers operating the machine guns. Ding Wenyu spent several hours being squeezed back and forth among the retreating soldiers. Then he suddenly heard someone calling his name and saw a soldier pushing his way through the crowd toward him. Ding Wenyu thought that the soldier looked familiar, but amid the chaos he couldn't seem to attach a name to the face.

"Mr. Ding, don't you realize what's going on? What are you still doing here?" As he spoke the soldier removed his cap to expose his shaven head.

Ding Wenyu finally realized who this was standing before him. It was Monk—the very man who had shaken the entire city of Nanjing and been sentenced to death for his case of murder and necrophilia. Ding Wenyu didn't understand how Monk could have ended up in the army. Monk did not have enough time to fully explain the situation, but he told Ding that just as the city wall was about to be breached, all strong young prisoners in the jail were given an opportunity to atone for their crimes through meritorious service. Monk and his fellow inmates were organized into a kamikaze corps and sent to fight to defend Nanjing. They were dispatched wherever conditions were worst and did well, but eventually the entire front collapsed; his unit was pulled apart and he was left to fend for himself.

"I'm trying to get to the port," said Ding Wenyu. "Where are you going?"

"Who *doesn't* want to get across the Yangtze?" Monk replied. "But they're not letting anyone through."

At that moment, an officer wearing a yellow woolen uniform approached, followed by a group of soldiers that looked like a unit of orderlies. Ding Wenyu saw the officer walk over to the gate and flash his credentials to the sentries. They let him through. Ding Wenyu suddenly thought of his own special pass and dashed toward the sentries. Seeing him take off, Monk ran after him in confusion. The sentries pointed their guns at him as Ding Wenyu quickly handed them his permit. The sentry examined the permit for a second before waving him through. He stopped Monk, however. Monk argued that they were together, but the sentry didn't seem to believe him. Only after Ding Wenyu turned around and nodded to the guard was Monk allowed through. Monk's face was filled with a look of happy astonishment as he ran up to Ding Wenyu and said, "Mr. Ding, you're amazing!" Monk continued flattering Ding as a means of showing his thanks, but all Ding Wenyu wanted to do was find Yuyuan; he didn't have time to deal with Monk.

The tumultuous scene at the port left Ding Wenyu completely beside himself. Everyone was fending for themselves, fruitlessly waiting by the riverbank for the next boat. There was only one boat on the river, which seemed to be hesitant about approaching the port. There were simply too many people waiting, and the captain was afraid that everyone would rush on at once, capsizing the ship. Every so often Japanese planes would swoop down, dropping bombs and spraying lines of bullets into the crowd; panic-stricken soldiers ran around the port in disarray like a swarm of headless flies. Finally someone couldn't help but jump into the river and start swimming toward that boat. The swimmer started a chain reaction: all of a sudden, people were diving into the river one after another and swimming to the boat. They climbed up the side of the ship and pulled themselves aboard; it wasn't long before the ship was filled to capacity and set off away from the port. Those who hadn't reacted quickly enough to jump in the water and those who had but weren't fast enough to get to the ship before it left could do nothing but curse themselves. Ding Wenyu went all over the dock asking people if they had seen anyone from the Garrison Command, but no one had the patience to even answer his question. Monk had no idea who Ding Wenyu was looking for, but nevertheless stuck close to him. Ding ran back and forth along the riverbank trying to find someone to help him; he came upon an old soldier who had had one of his legs blown off sitting on the sandy bank.

"What the hell are you looking for the Garrison Command for?" the old soldier asked in an expressionless tone. "Those fucking officials high-tailed it out of here a long time ago!"

Ding Wenyu saw several female soldiers standing on the shore in tears. These women soldiers who had fallen behind their units were at the end of their rope; just looking at them was enough to break one's heart. There were no other ships in sight and people started jumping into the raging water of the Yangtze, clinging to door planks, wooden basins, or other pieces of wood they were able to get their hands on. A skinny female soldier was clinging to a small raft some other soldiers had thrown together for her. A few soldiers pushed her off into the water, but before she could paddle very far the raft was capsized by the rough waves—that female soldier disappeared into the river. At that moment all kinds of contradictory feelings were going through Ding Wenyu's mind. He still wished that by some stroke of luck he would be able to find Yuyuan amid the frantic crowd of soldiers; at the same time he hoped that she had already safely crossed the river with the rest of the Garrison Command.

By the time the sun began to set behind the mountain, Ding Wenyu was sure that he wouldn't find Yuyuan. Everyone at the port and on the riverbank was as desperate as he was; they all wanted to get across the river, but none of them could—all they could do was wait. Finally a boat appeared on the horizon. It was a massive ship. Only as it gradually approached did everyone finally realize that it was a Japanese warship. Under the crimson glow of the setting sun, the Japanese flag, which looked like an oversized medicinal patch, fluttered in the river wind as bullets from a line of machine guns raced toward the shore. One after another, rows of people standing on the shore fell to the ground in an orgy of bloodshed. A line of bullets pierced Ding Wenyu's chest as he collapsed on the sandy riverbank; he would never get up again. Monk bent over to help him as a single bullet split his head open.

Nanjing 1937 is a time and a place that one cannot bear to look back upon. For the people of that city, there could be no more brutal historical moment than the Rape of Nanjing. According to historical records, more than 350,000 perished and approximately 20,000 rapes occurred during that tragedy. This novel ends precisely at the moment when the massacre was about to commence and countless women were about to meet with misfortune.

That I would write such a novel was something I never expected. I had originally planned to write a novel that chronicled the actual events of that year, an annalistic record of the ancient capital Nanjing in 1937. The result, however, came as quite a surprise. As I was writing this novel, I often heard the voice of Tsai Ch'in singing the serpentine and moving melody to "On the Banks of the Qinhuai":

> Tonight we have wine, tonight we shall become intoxicated,
> Intoxicated tonight on the banks of the Qinhuai,
> The reflection of the moon rippling on the water,

The lanterns shining on the embankment,
Beautiful as a flower, leaning against the rail.
Singing girls sing, dancing girls dance,
Words of lovesick yearning, to whom may I speak?
Steps of loving affection, with whom may I take?
Sweet and tender feelings, with whom may I share?
With whom may I share?
The song of the song, the dance of the dance,
Petals of cherry lipstick, for whom do I wear?
Layers of rouge, for whom do I apply?
The subtle look in my eye, who understands?

This is clearly the song of a fallen nation. "The sing-song girls know not the country's sorrow; across the river they still sing *Jade Flowers in the Rear Court*."* I do not know what the melody to the song *Jade Flowers in the Rear Court* sounded like, but it must have been quite a song to have had the power to bring a nation to its knees. Novelists sometimes cannot help but put the cart before the horse; I planned to write a novel about war but ended up writing a rather unorthodox love story. It is embarrassing just to mention it. Piled up on my desk and surrounding my chair is a huge stack of historical books and documents. The only other occasion when I devoted so much time to research was when I was in graduate school writing my master's thesis; never before had I gone to such lengths for a work of fiction. Time after time, I made trips to the library to go through old books and trudge through old newspapers and magazines. Those old books and magazines can leave you with the misconception that you are entering a history long past. This kind of misconception is essential for a novelist. As I read the Japanese writer Horiba Kazuo's *A Historical Guidebook to Japan's War with China* alongside *A Military History of the Nationalist Revolution*, which was edited by General Jiang Weiguo—two thick the-

---

*This is a quote from the Tang poem "Mooring on the Qinhuai" by Du Mu (803–952). The complete poem reads, "Smoke envelops the cold water, the moon enshrouds the sand. / An evening moor on the Qinhuai, close to the wine shops. / The sing-song girls know not the country's sorrow; across the river they still sing *Jade Flowers in the Rear Court*." *Jade Flowers in the Rear Court* refers to a famous erotic song that Emperor Chen Houzhu (583–587) had his courtiers compose. The song later became symbolic of Chen's neglect of state affairs in favor of licentious pleasure, which eventually led to the collapse of his court.

oretical books—I could not help but imagine how much more interesting life would be if I had been a career soldier instead of a novelist. An outstanding soldier is also an artist, but the art of war is a dirty art—an art destined to be cursed.

It seems ridiculous to even think about wartime love; against the backdrop of war, falling in love always appears comically outlandish. But if in people's hearts there existed true love, perhaps there would never be such a thing as war. There are destined to be many more love stories that take place in the ancient capital of Nanjing in 1937—what I have written is perhaps the worst of the lot. By the same token, there are all too many epic and moving stories that occurred that year, enough to make one dizzy, but for some reason my attention has lingered in a place it never should have. It was as if I had somehow escaped from the sea of books and documents that were surrounding me. The reality of the whole thing made me uncomfortable. Not only did I fail to write about what I should have, but my pen ended up going in a direction that I never intended. The one element of self-deception that I thought could save me from embarrassment was the thought that others are bound to tell all those stories about Nanjing 1937 that I missed. And at least for the present, no one else has tried to write a story like this one.

It was three hundred years ago that Kong Shangren composed his play *The Peach Blossom Fan.*[*] In the first scene, "The Storyteller," Kong wrote, "On Grieve-Not Lake beside the Poet's Tower, / The weeping willows burgeon once again." During a visit to the former residence of Li Xiangjun, the heroine of *The Peach Blossom Fan*, the modern poet Wu Mei wrote a new poem, the final couplet of which reads: "Beside the Wuding Bridge, / Standing in silence until the last rays of sunlight fade." Today when we read these famous lines that have been passed down to us, much of the original meaning and the subtle nuances seem to have been lost. Times change, and there are few places left in Nanjing where there is room for new weeping willows. Beside the Wuding Bridge, there are nothing but high-rise buildings. The stinking Qinhuai River indeed leaves one longing for the splendor of an era long past. In the modern

---

[*]The Peach Blossom Fan is a grand historical *kunqu* drama written in the 1690s. Set in Nanjing, the play juxtaposes the epic fall of the Ming dynasty with the love story between the promising young scholar Hou Fangyu and the beautiful courtesan Li Xiangjun.

metropolis, all are helpless to stop development—melancholy sentimentality is a luxury. The unforgettable year of 1937 has long passed, and those children born to the flames of war are now sixty-year-old men and women. I wrote this novel without any regard for what the consequences might be; heaven only knows if anyone will read it.

Y. Z. Y.
May 20, 1996

Bai Chongxi (1893–1966) A powerful warlord who helped form the Guangxi clique. He joined forces with the Nationalist army in 1926. The following year he took part in the Northern Expedition, and he later served in several important roles in the Nationalist government, including Minister of Defense from 1946 to 1948.

Cai E (1882–1916) After studying in Japan, Cai returned to China in 1904 to take part in revolutionary activities, especially in Yunnan, where he played a key role. He was placed under house arrest by Yuan Shikai in 1913; he escaped in late 1915. In the last year of his life, Cai proclaimed Yunnan's independence and led a major campaign to resist Yuan Shikai. He died of a throat illness in Japan in 1916.

Chen Bijun (1891–1959) Wife and political adviser to Wang Jingwei. She first met Wang in 1908 and accompanied him to Japan, where she joined the Revolutionary Alliance, an anti-Manchu organization founded in Tokyo in 1905 by Sun Yat-sen that eventually helped overthrow the Qing dynasty. After marrying Wang in 1912, she held a number of titular positions. In 1938 she played a key role in the puppet government. She was sentenced as a traitor to her country in 1946 and died in prison in 1959.

Chen Bulei (1890–1948) Early on Chen made a name for himself as a columnist for *Shangbao*, where he published scathing criticisms of warlords in support of the Northern Expedition. In 1927 he began working for the Nationalist regime and became Chiang Kai-shek's principal speech writer. He committed suicide in Nanjing in 1948.

Chen Guofu (1892–1951) An influential figure in the Nationalist government who, along with his brother, Chen Lifu, led the right-wing faction of the party. Over the course of his political career he held many high posts, including Chair of the Organization Department, head of the Control Yuan, Governor of Jiangsu Province, and Chair of the Government Personnel Office.

Chen Yi (1901–1972) A distinguished field commander during the 1930s and '40s who had studied in France as a young man. Chen participated in the Northern Expedition and the Autumn Harvest Uprising, following which he joined Mao Zedong. He led the New Fourth Army during the Chinese Civil War and after 1948 served as Mayor of Shanghai and Minister of Foreign Affairs.

Chiang Kai-shek (Jiang Jieshi) (1888–1975) The successor of Sun Yat-sen and the political and military leader of the Nationalist regime. He received military training in Russia and Japan and was appointed head of the Whampoa Military Academy upon his return. He led the Northern Expedition, which was aimed at freeing China from warlord rule, and set up a revamped Nationalist government in 1928. He held on to power throughout the War of Resistance, only to be ousted by the Communists in 1949. He remained President of the Nationalist Party in Taiwan until his death in 1975.

Chu Minyi (1884–1946) Joined the Revolutionary Alliance in Japan in 1909 and took part in the Revolution of 1911. After spending the years 1912 to 1924 in Europe, Chu returned to China to hold a series of academic and governmental posts, including Secretary General of the Legislative Yuan. He held several high positions in the puppet government under Wang Jingwei and was sentenced to death in 1946 for crimes against his country.

Dai Chuanxian (Dai Jitao) (1891–1949) An editor and scholar as well as an active political player in the Nationalist revolution. Dai studied in Japan between 1905 and 1909 and was an early member of the Revolutionary Alliance and a close associate of Sun Yat-sen. He was editor-in-chief of the influential magazine *Weekly Commentary* (*Xingqi pinglun*) during the May Fourth Movement. After 1927, Dai strongly opposed Nationalist cooperation with the CCP and lent his support to Chiang Kai-shek. Dai served a long stint as Director of Governmental Examinations before committing suicide in 1949, on the eve of the Communist victory.

Dai Li (1895–1946) Graduate of the Whampao Military Academy and a close adviser to Chiang Kai-shek. Renowned for his uncompromising tactics, Dai worked his way up through the Nationalist intelligence community, eventually becoming the government's chief intelligence officer and winning a seat on the Central Executive Committee in 1945.

Deng Xiaoping (1904–1997) Deng spent the years from 1920 to 1925 in Paris, during which time he joined the French branch of the Chinese Communist Party. After the CCP succeeded in driving the Nationalists out of power in 1949, Deng held many key governmental posts. He survived a series of political purges to reemerge in 1978 as the reformist purveyor of market economic policies.

Duan Qirui (1865–1936) Early in his career, Duan served as one of Yuan Shikai's top military aides. After the establishment of the Republic, he held several high posts, such as Minister of War, Premier, and Provisional President.

Feng Yuxiang (1882–1948) One of the most powerful and high-profile warlords of northern China. Feng won a broad power base in the 1920s; throughout the decade, he implemented widespread social reforms. He received aid from the Soviet Union and eventually joined forces with the Nationalists on the Northern Expedition in 1929, where he fought against other warlords.

Gu Zhutong (1893–1987) Career military man who joined the Revolutionary Army after the outbreak of the Revolution of 1911 and later graduated from the Baoding Military Academy. Gu later served the Nationalist Party as a general and commander during the War of Resistance and the Chinese Civil War.

Guan Songseng (1892–1960) Architect who, after foreign study in America, took part in several major projects in the 1920s, such as the design of the famed Peking Union Medical College. Guan also served as a committee member of the Nanjing Capital Construction Committee. After refusing to serve under the Manchurian puppet government, Guan was temporarily imprisoned in 1931. His architectural firm carried out projects throughout China until 1949, when Guan followed the Nationalists to Taiwan, where he designed a series of important structures in Taiwan and Hong Kong.

He Jian (1887–1956) After graduating from the Baoding Military Academy in 1916, He served under Cheng Qian and Tang Shengzhi. In 1926 he took part in the Northern Expedition, and his allegiance shifted many times in the ensuing years. He was appointed chair of the Hunan provincial government in 1929 and was transferred to serve as Minister of the Interior with the start of the War of Resistance. Due to illness, he largely retired from public life after the war in 1945.

He Yingqin (1890–1987) One of Chiang Kai-shek's closest and most reliable officers. He served as Minister of War from 1930 to 1944, Chief of Staff from 1938 to 1944, and Commander in Chief of the Chinese Army from 1944 to 1946. After 1949, he continued to serve the Nationalist Party in Taiwan.

Hu Shi (1891–1962) Educated at Cornell and Columbia (where he studied under John Dewey), Hu Shi was a writer, poet, literary critic, and philosopher and one of the foremost men of letters of the Republican era. He played a key role in the May Fourth Movement of 1919 and later served as Chinese ambassador to the United States from 1938 to 1942. In 1958 he assumed the role of president of the influential research institution, Academia Sinica, which he held until his death four years later.

Hua Mulan A legendary figure who lived during the Sui dynasty (581–618). Mulan was a woman warrior who disguised herself as a man to fight the Huns in place of her father. Her story has served as inspiration for countless tales, plays, poems, and paintings.

Huang Yifan (1896–1957) Huang was an oil painter and art teacher who divided her time between Shanghai, Paris, and London. She was also the mother of Eileen Chang (Zhang Ailing) (1920–1995), the noted author of such novels as *The Rouge of the North* and *The Rice-Sprout Song*.

Jia Baoyu The tragic hero of the fictional masterpiece *Dream of the Red Chamber* (c. 1760), which was written by Cao Xueqin during the Qianlong period of the Qing dynasty.

H. H. K'ung (Kong Xiangxi) (1881–1967) Educated at Oberlin and Yale, K'ung was a financier and industrialist who married into the influential Soong family. He served as Minister of Industry and Commerce from 1928 to 1933, and then as Minister of Finance until 1944, when he retired from public life.

Lan Ping (Jiang Qing) (1914–1991) A popular actress of the 1930s who was very active in the Shanghai film and stage community. After meeting Mao Zedong in Yan'an she became his third wife and largely retreated from public life. During the Cultural Revolution (1966–1976), she reemerged as a powerful cultural proponent and played a key role in setting artistic standards and promoting the "eight model operas." Purged with the Gang of Four after Mao's death, Jiang Qing took her own life in prison in 1991.

Lin Sen (1867–1943) An early member of the Revolutionary Alliance, Lin was an active political and diplomatic figure throughout the early Republican period. During the 1930s he served as Chairman of the Legislative Yuan and Chairman of the Nationalist Government. He died in Chongqing in 1943 from complications of injuries resulting from a car accident earlier that year.

Liu Jiwen (1889–1957) Studied abroad in Japan, where he joined the Revolutionary Alliance, and then in England at Cambridge. He served in several key political positions under the Nationalist regime, including two terms as Mayor of Nanjing and Mayor of Canton.

Liu Xiang (1889–1938) An influential Sichuan-based military man and warlord. He advocated autonomous rule for Sichuan and became the single most powerful warlord in the province after defeating Liu Huicheng in 1933. The same year, he led attacks against the Communists. He lent his support to Zhang Xueliang (1898–2001) during the Xi'an Incident and joined the Nationalists in their fight against the Japanese during the War of Resistance.

Long Yun (1884–1962) Yunnan warlord who early in his career served under Tang Jiyao, before forcing Tang out of power in 1927. He served in a number of military capacities under the Nationalist regime and held several political and defense titles in the PRC after 1949, including Vice-Chair of the National Defense Committee.

Lu Rongting (1859–1928) A powerful warlord based in southwest China. Lu joined the military during the Sino-French War and later served as a general under Yuan Shikai. He took over Guangdong province after Yuan's death in 1916. Lu was eventually driven out of power in 1924.

Matsui Iwane (1878–1948) A career military man of the Japanese Imperial Army who held many key titles. He was considered one of Japan's "China experts" and, after time in China as a military attaché, he served in Taiwan from 1933 to 1937. He returned to China after the Marco Polo Bridge Incident and was appointed commander of the Japanese forces in Shanghai before leading Japanese forces in Nanjing, where a major massacre ensued. Matsui was executed in 1948 after being sentenced by the Military Tribunal for the Far East.

Mayor Ma (Ma Chaojun) (1886–1977) Early in his military career, he served as a commander during the Wuchang Uprising, before being trained as a fighter pilot by order of Sun Yat-sen. Ma continued to fight and organize strikes during the 1920s, before being appointed Mayor of Nanjing and Minister of Farmers and Workers. He followed Chiang Kai-shek to Taiwan in 1949, where he served as a presidential adviser.

Mei Lanfang (1894–1961) One of the most beloved and popular stars of the Chinese stage. Mei was famous for his roles in such Beijing operas as *Farewell My Concubine*, *Hua Mulan*, and *Yang Guifei Intoxicated on Wine*. He moved to Shanghai in 1931 and performed in a series of patriotic productions like *Resisting the Golden Army*. He refused to perform during the eight years of Japanese occupation and returned to the stage in 1945. After 1949 Mei remained active in cultural and political circles; he continued performing intermittently until 1959.

Mu Guiying A fictional folk heroine from the classical novel *Yangjiafu shidai zhongyong tongsu yanyi*. Mu has been hailed as a symbol of patriotism, loyalty, and courage for her daring in challenging feudal traditions and morality.

Nie Er (1912–1935) Modern composer who worked in the Shanghai film industry and is known as the composer of more than thirty classic works, including "Anthem of the Great Road" and "March of the Volunteer Army," which was later officially made the Chinese national anthem. Nie was also active in politics and joined the Communist Youth Group in 1927 and the CCP in 1933. He drowned in Japan in 1935 while en route to Russia to escape Nationalist suppression.

Aisin-Gioro Pu Yi (1905–1967) The last emperor of the Qing dynasty. The Xuantong emperor, Pu Yi ruled as a child emperor from 1908 to 1912 before he was forced to abdicate at the age of six. He later was reinstalled as the puppet leader of the Japanese regime Manchukuo from 1932 to 1945.

Song Zheyuan (1885–1940) Career military man who served under Feng Yuxiang from 1913 to 1930. In 1937, after the Marco Polo Bridge Incident, Song served as a Nationalist military commander during the War of Resistance.

Soong May-ling (Song Meiling) (1897–) A 1917 graduate of Wellesley College and daughter of the influential banker Charlie Soong, May-ling was the youngest of the Soong sisters (her sisters Song Ailing and Song Qingling married H. H. K'ung and Sun Yat-sen, respectively). She was the wife of Chiang Kai-shek and played an active and highly visible role during the 1930s and '40s, especially when it came to rousing support for China among western powers. After her husband's death in 1975, she largely retreated from public life and immigrated to the United States.

Sun Chuanfang (1885–1935) Joined the Revolutionary Alliance while a student in Japan. Sun played an important role in the Beiyang Northern Warlord government. He unsuccessfully resisted the Northern Expedition's entrance into Jiangxi in 1926. After suffering a second major loss near Nanjing in 1927, Sun moved to Tianjin and took up Buddhism. He was assassinated in 1935.

Sun Yat-sen (Sun Zhongshan) (1866–1925) Regarded as the father of modern China, Sun inspired the Republican revolution and founded the Revolutionary Alliance and the Nationalist Party. A medical doctor by training, Sun became involved in revolutionary activities in his twenties, which culminated in his overthrow of the Qing dynasty. After the success of the revolution, he ceded power to the warlord Yuan Shikai, who became the first President of the Republic. After Sun's death in 1925, work was begun on the Sun Yat-sen Mausoleum in Nanjing, which was completed in 1929.

T. V. Soong (Song Ziwen) (1866–1925) Educated at Harvard, T. V. Soong was a crucial figure in the development of the financial and banking systems of Republican China. As brother-in-law to Chiang Kai-shek, Soong helped finance the Northern Expedition and held several key roles, such as Governor of the Central Bank of China, Minister of Foreign Affairs, and Minister of Finance.

Tang Jiyao (1883–1927) Joined the Revolutionary Alliance while a student in Japan and took part in the Revolution of 1911 in Yunnan. He supported Yuan Shikai in 1913 but later joined with Cai E in proclaiming Yunnan's independence in 1915. He subsequently threw his support to Sun Yat-sen in his endeavor to uphold the constitution against the Northern Warlords.

Tang Shengzhi (1889–1970) After graduating from the Baoding Military Academy in 1914, Tang served in Hunan before joining the Northern Expedition as Corps Commander of the Eighth Army and Commander in Chief on the front line. He was forced out of power after suffering military defeat in 1927. With the support of Chiang Kai-shek, Tang returned to power in 1929; however, in December of that year he went against Chiang and was stripped of power a second time. He held a number of titular posts in the Nanjing government before volunteering to serve as Garrison Commander on the eve of the Japanese invasion of the capital.

Tang Youren (1894–1935) Career politician who held several high posts in the Ministry of Foreign Affairs and the Ministry of Transportation. Tang was assassinated in 1935.

Tian Han (1898–1968) A dramatist and playwright, Tian went to Japan for study in 1917 and co-founded the Creation Society upon his return to China in 1921. He was active in political and artistic circles and joined the Leftist Writers' Association in 1930 and the CCP in 1932. In 1934 he co-composed the future PRC national anthem, "March of the Volunteer Army," with Nie Er. After 1935, Tian wrote and directed a string of popular stage dramas, such as *Melody of Returning Spring* and *The Marco Polo Bridge Incident*. He continued to play an important role in state cultural affairs after 1949, until his imprisonment by the Jiang Qing clique during the Cultural Revolution. He died in prison in 1968.

Wang Chonghui (1881–1958) Earned a D.C.L. from Yale in 1904 and passed the bar exam in England, where he joined the Revolutionary Alliance. After returning to China in 1911, Wang held a series of posts including Minister of Justice and Chief Justice of the Supreme Court, and served as a judge on the Permanent Court of International Justice in The Hague. From 1930 to 1935 he served as Minister of Foreign Affairs, and from 1937 to 1941 he was Secretary-General of the National Supreme Defense Council. In 1945 and 1946, Wang alternately took part in the meetings that produced both the United Nations Charter and the Constitution of the Republic of China.

Wang Jingwei (1883–1944) An early colleague of Sun Yat-sen who worked with Sun to establish the Revolutionary Alliance. He held several top posts in the Nationalist government and was elected to the Central Executive Committee in 1924. Wang traveled abroad several times in the 1920s and '30s during a series of power struggles, and after a failed attempt on his life in 1935. In 1938 he began to collaborate with the Japanese and was installed as the titular head of the Nanjing puppet regime in 1940. He died of illness in Japan.

Robert Wilson (1904–?) Born in Nanjing to a family of Methodist missionaries, Wilson was a medical doctor educated at Princeton and Harvard. He returned to Nanjing in 1935 to practice medicine at the Nanjing University Hospital and teach at the Ginling College Medical School. Dr. Wilson stayed in Nanjing during the 1937 massacre and played a key role in the International Committee for the Nanjing Safty Zone.

Wu Peifu (1874–1939) The most powerful warlord active in the Hubei and Hunan regions of China in the 1920s. He was responsible for a violent suppression of a railway strike in 1923. Wu was ousted from power in 1926, as a consequence of the Northern Expedition.

Wu Zhihui (Wu Jingheng) (1865–1953) Achieved the traditional degree of *juren* in 1891 and studied in France, where he joined the Revolutionary Alliance in 1905. He occupied a number of posts in Chiang Kai-shek's Nationalist regime and was an elected member of the Nationalist Central Supervisory Committee. Wu was also a recognized philosopher, scholar, and language reformer who directed the task of creating a Chinese national language.

Xie Jinyuan (1905–1941) A 1926 graduate of the Whampoa Military Academy, Xie later took part in the Northern Expedition. After the Marco Polo Bridge Incident, Xie and his battalion of troops were sent to defend Shanghai, where they fought a series of legendary battles with the Japanese. After repeatedly refusing to serve under the Japanese puppet government, Xie was assassinated in 1941.

Xu Beihong (Ju Pion) (1895–1953) A renowned painter and art educator. Xu studied at the National School of Fine Arts, Paris from 1919 to 1923 and served alternately as professor, dean, and president of several colleges and institutes, including National Central University (1927–1929), Peking University Art Institute (1929–1946), and Beijing Arts College (1946–1949). He was the author of several influential fine art books and recognized as one of the most important Chinese painters of the twentieth century.

Yan Xishan (1883–1960) Yan was a warlord who controlled major portions of Shaanxi province from 1912 to 1949. In the 1930s he aligned himself with the Nationalist Party and was successively appointed to a number of important posts, including vice-president of the Military Affairs Commission.

Yang Hucheng (1893–1949) Took part in the Revolution of 1911 and the Northern Expedition in 1927, during which time he served as commander of the Tenth Revolutionary Army. In 1936, Yang, alongside Zhang Xueliang, conspired to kidnap Chiang Kai-shek as a means to force him to cease the Chinese Civil War and form a united front against Japan. After the Xi'an Incident, Yang remained under house arrest for twelve years until he was murdered in 1949.

Yang Tingbao (1901–1982) Well-known architect and educator. Yang earned a degree in architecture in the United States in 1925. He returned to China in 1927 and is credited with designing some of the most recognizable structures in modern China, including the Beijing Peace Hotel, the Monument to the Peoples' Heroes, and Chairman Mao's Mausoleum.

Ye Jianying (1897–1986) Served as a deputy director at the Whampoa Military Academy before being appointed Chief of Staff of the First Army during the Northern Expedition. In 1927 he joined the Communist Party, and he held a number of prestigious military posts under Mao's regime.

Yu Hanmou (1896–1981) Graduate of the Baoding Military Academy who later served as General of the Fourth Revolutionary Army. Yu played a prominent military role in Guangdong during the Republican era. After 1949 he served as a strategic advisor to the Nationalist government in Taiwan.

Yu Youren (1879–1964) Government official, newspaper editor, and poet, Yu joined the Revolutionary Alliance in Japan in 1906 and edited several newspapers in Shanghai to propagate revolutionary sentiments. He later held a number of high governmental positions, including President of the Control Yuan, and was a member of the Standing Committee and the Nationalist Central Executive Committee.

Yuan Shikai (1859–1916) Yuan was the leader of the powerful Beiyang army, which, once loyal to the Qing dynasty, played a key role in hastening the decline of the court. Owing to his massive military influence, Yuan emerged from the Republican revolution as the first President of the Republic of China in 1911. He abused his power and was planning to install himself as a new emperor when he died in 1916.

Zeng Zhongming (1896–1939) Scholar and official who early on joined the Revolutionary Alliance and formed close ties with Republican revolution leaders, especially Wang Jingwei. Zeng served as an administrator in several different governmental capacities before he was killed in Hanoi in 1939 when an attempt was made to assassinate Wang Jingwei.

Zhang Daofan (1897–1968) Nationalist official, educator, painter, and playwright. Zhang was a 1924 graduate of the Slade School, University College in London and studied art in Paris until 1926. In addition to holding a number of high-profile academic and governmental positions, Zhang was the author of several well-known plays and the founder of the National Academy of Drama.

Zhang Xun (1854–1923) Qing general who remained loyal to the court even after its fall. He unsuccessfully defended Nanjing during the Revolution of 1911. After the death of Yuan Shikai he initiated a coup in 1917 aimed at restoring the child emperor Aisin-Gioro Pu Yi to power. His restoration attempt was suppressed by Duan Qirui, effectively ending Zhang's military career.

Zhang Zhidong (1837–1909) Qing official who served as governor of several provinces. Zhang was a strong advocate of Chinese self-strengthening efforts and worked to establish arsenals, build the first modern mint, and encourage railway building and industrial development.

Zhang Zhijiang (1882–1969) Career military man who served under Feng Yuxiang and the Nationalist government. A master of traditional Chinese martial arts, Zhang was the founder and President of the School of Martial Arts and Physical Education and the author of several books on martial arts.

Zhang Zhizhong (1891–1969) A 1916 graduate of the Baoding Military Academy who later studied social science and languages at Shanghai University. Zhang served as an instructor at the Whampoa Military Academy and as a senior officer during the Northern Expedition. In 1937 he was appointed Commander of the Ninth Bloc of the Nanjing-Shanghai Garrison Command, and he took part in the August 13 battle in Shanghai. Zhang served as chief representative for the Nationalists in peace talks with the CCP during the Civil War and remained in Beijing after 1949, serving under the Communist government.

Zhang Zuolin (1875–1928) A powerful warlord who rose to power during Yuan Shikai's presidency. He consistently worked to wipe out the Communists while consolidating his strength in northern China, major portions of which were under his complete control. His forces were defeated by the Nationalists in 1928, and Zhang was killed during an attempted escape by the Japanese.

Zhou Enlai (1899–1976) Zhou studied in France between 1917 and 1919 before returning to China to take part in the May Fourth Movement. A Marxist since his days in France, Zhou played a key role in the early development of the Chinese Communist Party and the organization of labor unions in Shanghai. He helped arrange the release of Chiang Kai-shek during the Xi'an Incident and was the Communist liaison officer to the Nationalists during the 1930s. After 1949, Zhou was appointed Premier and became regarded as one of the most popular and admired leaders of the Communist government.

Zhou Zhirou (1899–1986) A 1922 graduate of the Baoding Military Academy, Zhou later became an instructor at the Whampoa Military Academy. He took part in the Northern Expedition in 1926. In 1934 Zhou was appointed President of the Central Aviation Academy and Chairman of the Aviation Committee.

Zhu De (1886–1976) After serving in the local Sichuan military, Zhu De went to study in Germany in 1922. There Zhu joined the Chinese Communist Party and took part in several student demonstrations, which got him expelled from the country in 1926. Upon returning to China, Zhu played an increasingly visible role in the Communist military and became Mao's chief military adviser. During the War of Resistance, he served as Commander in Chief of the Eighth Route Army. After the Communist victory, Zhu was appointed Commander in Chief of the People's Liberation Army and was made a permanent member of the Politburo.

Zhu Kezhen (1890–1974) Meteorologist, geographer, editor, and educator. Zhu was educated at the University of Illinois and Harvard, where he earned his Ph.D. in 1918. He alternately held positions at Wuchang Teachers College, Nanjing Teachers College, South East University, and Nankai University and worked as an editor at the Commercial Press. After 1945, Zhu advocated a pacifist resolution to the Chinese Civil War through democracy.

Zhuge Liang (181–234) Legendary statesman and strategist of the Three Kingdoms period, who later became associated with wisdom and resourcefulness in Chinese literature and folklore.